PRAISE FO

"[Hawker] is a master of her craft, a storyteller of supreme talent."
—Julianne MacLean, *USA Today* bestselling author

"A deeply moving novel that is so beautifully crafted you can't help but feel the sun beat down on your back or the snow bite into your skin. The evocative setting and well-researched history combined with nuanced characters make this novel one not to miss."
—*Historical Novels Review*

"Enchanting . . . A skillful storyteller, Hawker serves up seemingly endless pages with vivid Wyoming descriptions."
—Authorlink

"An absorbing read from first page to last, and highly recommended."
—Midwest Book Review

OCTOBER

IN THE

EARTH

ALSO BY OLIVIA HAWKER

OCTOBER

IN THE

EARTH

A NOVEL

OLIVIA HAWKER

Published by Lake Union Publishing, Seattle

www.apub.com

Amazon, the Amazon logo, and Lake Union Publishing are trademarks of Amazon.com, Inc., or its affiliates.

ISBN-13: 9781662511080 (hardcover)
ISBN-13: 9781662511097 (paperback)
ISBN-13: 9781662511103 (digital)

Cover design by Mumtaz Mustafa
Cover image: © Smith Collection/Gado / Getty; © Heritage Image Partnership Ltd / Alamy

Printed in the United States of America
First edition

For Dan.

1

Love is a thing that's given, not taken. This is something I know far deep inside, in the quietest part of my soul where loneliness can't reach, where even fear can't touch me. I guess I've always known, but it's easy to forget when all your life you've heard the same voices shouting that love is obedience, love is a debt unpaid.

Long before I ever took to the rails, I'd already made a habit of slipping away from those voices—though of course, I didn't realize at the time that I was skittering off to find a little truth in the silence. I thought I just liked a good long walk. You see, there was this dirt road, pretty near five miles long, and it led from the middle of town up into the sloping shadows of hill country, all the way to the front step of the house where I'd grown up. Whenever I felt the urge to wander, I took that road and made no haste. The road carried me like the slow drift of a crick in summertime, and together we parted the shadows of the forest, that road and me; we climbed above the valley with its fur of yellow haze, up into the breeze and the birdsongs where I could hear the faintest whisper of my heart.

Now, going off to listen to my own thoughts wasn't the excuse I gave my husband for those long afternoon excursions into the hills. Truth to tell, I had yet to admit the real reason to myself. No, I was just paying a visit to my folks. I was their youngest, you see, and since I'd gone and married Irving Wensley eight years before, I felt a little guilty about leaving them alone. Anything would do for a reason to call on Mom and Pop. That day, it was the loaf of peanut butter bread I'd baked—studded with bits of chocolate, which had appeared unexpectedly in Woods's general store, and which I'd snapped up for the outrageous price of twelve cents a bar.

Oh, yes, I recall every detail about that day, even now, years after. It was the 5th of May 1931—a day no one from Harlan County is like to forget.

That afternoon, I came up the last shaded rise of the old road with that loaf of bread tucked under my arm, and I rounded the bend, and there before me was home—the only place that had ever felt like home to me, even after I'd settled with my eminent husband in the finest house in the whole danged valley. My parents' place could scarcely be called a house at all. It was a shack, by rights—slat siding sun-faded to gray, an uneven roof from which the tar paper sagged over the eaves. But there was the old front porch, its pillars nothing more than peeled pine logs, where I used to sit, dangling my skinny legs over the edge while I watched my brothers shoot marbles or wrestle in the dusty yard. And there was Mom's kitchen jutting from the side of the house—nothing more than a raised platform with no walls, a flat roof of corrugated tin, a butcher block, a few pails for washing, and the big round belly of the iron stove.

Mom was in her kitchen stirring the laundry kettle. She looked up as I came around the bend, as if she'd been expecting me.

"Adella," she called. "What a nice surprise, honey."

Considering I made that walk at least once a week, I could hardly have surprised her. But I grinned and picked up my pace, and as she came down the steps from her kitchen platform, I held up the loaf of bread, which I'd wrapped in a good linen towel.

"What did you make this time, girl?" Mom took the bundle and folded back its wrapping.

"Just some peanut butter bread."

"Is that chocolate you've put all in it? Land sakes, honey, you do spoil us."

"You deserve to be spoiled, Mom." I noted her shoulders, stooped from a lifetime of hard living, and the deep wrinkles scored into her cheeks. She was no more than sixty that year, but her hands were tendinous, gnarled as the branches of some ancient tree. "I only wish I could do more for you," I said. "Let me help you with the wash."

"I'd like to see you try," she said in that tone I remembered well from childhood. She wouldn't hear another word about it, and there was no point in arguing—not if I didn't want a tanned hide. "You set yourself down on the porch and I'll go slice up this bread." Then, "Daniel," she shouted in the direction of the woodshed, "Adella's come up from town."

In a few minutes, I was perched on the old pine bench under the tar-paper eaves, watching the barn swallows glide into the shelter of the porch and out again while my pop came hobbling up the steps to set beside me. He looked still older than Mom did, for he'd worked down in the mines since he was knee-high to a grasshopper, and the bend in his back was permanent even when I was a child. The walk from the shed to the porch had made him wheeze. He sank onto the pine bench slowly, humoring his stiff knees, and wiped his brow with a much-mended hankie. The backs of his hands and forearms bore permanent marks from the coal mines—old cuts into which the black dust had settled, crisscrossing his skin in lines of blurred inky blue.

I kissed his cheek and listened while he told me all about the letter he'd received from Pearl, my oldest sister, who'd just had her fourth baby. Another boy. I tried not to look too worried over Pop's rattling lungs, which sounded a little worse every time I saw him, and tried harder still not to fret over the sharp contrast between Pearl's life and my own.

Mom stepped out onto the porch, carrying a small platter heaped with slices of my bread. We passed the platter back and forth, availing ourselves of the alluring sweetness. Since the Great Crash nearly two years earlier, chocolate seldom made its way into the heart of coal country.

"How much did you spend on this stuff?" Mom asked, closing her eyes in bliss. "No, don't answer. It's rude to ask."

"It doesn't matter, anyway," I said. "Irving will never notice. He doesn't keep tabs on my spending." My own comment struck me as immodest, too casual a dismissal of my own good fortune. I added hastily, "Not that I go overboard. I stay frugal, like you taught me, Mom. A few Hershey's bars now and again won't drive us into the poorhouse."

"I just guess not," Pop said with evident pride. "You've done right well for yourself, Del-my-dearest. That fine house of yours down in the valley, and Irving the most popular preacher in all of Harlan County. Well!"

"Wouldn't you like to live in the valley, too?" I said. "Isn't it time? Life's a little easier down there, and I'd sleep easier at night, knowing you were both close by."

Mom said softly, "Land sakes, Del, if we've told you once, we've told you a hundred times."

"This is our home," Pop said. "I built this place with my own two hands as soon as your mother agreed to be my wife, and I don't intend to leave it, not on any account. You kids will have to bury me where I drop."

Though I took great comfort in my own righteous obedience—in those days, anyway—I couldn't resist pressing him a little. "And what if you drop before you're dead? That's what worries me. If you can't get around, Pop . . . if you fall, or—"

"The Lord's will shall be done," he answered solemnly.

I looked to my mother for support, but she nodded solemnly and reached out to pat Pop on his knee. Mom always did take his side. She was a Bible-believing Christian, right to her core, and no doubt her favorite scripture was *Wives, submit to your husbands as to the Lord.*

"Did Pop tell you the latest news?" Mom asked, helping herself to another slice of my bread. "Pearl's new baby has come."

"A boy," I said rather weakly. "Isn't that something?"

"And how about you?" Mom asked. "Any news to tell?"

She was only interested in one kind of news from me—the same announcement my sister had made four times already. My brothers, too, were all fathers by then. Even Benjamin, second-youngest next to me, had already achieved fatherhood twice.

As I made no answer, Mom's face fell into a frown. I couldn't decide whether she looked more sympathetic or disappointed. "Oh, Adella. You've been married eight years!"

"Well, it ain't my fault," I snapped. "I don't think, anyway. It's just as much Irving's doing as mine."

"And are you?" Mom said.

"Am I what?"

"Doing?"

"Jiminy Christmas, Mom!"

Pop gave a wordless cry of protest, throwing up his hands between us.

"Oh, don't bust your britches, Daniel," Mom said dryly. "You're a father six times over. You know how it works."

Six kids. By the age of thirty—my own age—Mom had already birthed every one of her children. And there I was, still deprived of the blessings of motherhood despite my otherwise admirable life: married to the biggest preacher in eastern Kentucky, mistress of the finest home for a hundred miles in any direction. It wasn't that I was especially eager to experience the pains and inconveniences of pregnancy, the danger of birthing, the long drudgery of nursing and diapering and trying to keep house in the whirlwind path of some feral toddler. But as each year passed and I remained without a child of my own, a dreadful feeling settled more firmly within me, a certainty that despite my meekness and faithfulness to Irving, despite how tirelessly I organized and ministered to the women of the county—as any preacher's wife ought to do—still I was failing at the one task that truly mattered.

As if she could read my grim thoughts, my mother dug in. I loved her—God knows I did—but the woman was relentless as winter. "And what does Irving have to say about all this?"

"He's bothered by it, of course," I answered with a sigh. "He keeps saying it'll happen in the Lord's time, but the Lord has had eight years now and still nothing."

"Don't you blaspheme, Adella Wensley."

"Sorry, Mom."

"You ought to go and call on Anne-Celeste Skaggs," my mother said. "Don't know how many times I've told you so. Maybe one of these days, you'll listen."

"The granny woman?" I said. "Isn't all that herb medicine a lot of backwoods bunkum? Gosh, Mom, it's the twentieth century! There are modern ways of doing things now, even out here in Harlan County."

Mom arched her faded brows. "Well, after you came along and I decided six was enough, I never had another baby again. That's all thanks to Anne-Celeste and her 'bunkum.' So you tell me, Adella."

Before I could cook up a snappy reply, my father leaned forward on the bench. "You hear that? Truck's a-coming up the road, and it sounds like Benjamin's."

Mom and I fell silent. Below the spring-drunk chittering of sparrows, a deep metallic rumble sounded through the forest. I had only a moment to think that Pop's hearing was still sharp as ever, even if the rest of him was going downhill, when the rusty nose of my brother's Brockway pickup came chugging up the slope.

Even from the porch, I could see that Benjamin was pale, and he gripped the steering wheel with white-knuckled fists. Something had shaken him, and badly, too.

I was down the steps in a blink, flying across the yard to Benjamin's truck, my head spinning with every imaginable disaster. Had one of his children taken a fever . . . or fallen into the well? Had something dreadful happened to his wife?

He cut the engine and jumped from his truck, came striding toward me shaking his head. He was dressed more neatly than I ever saw him—clean white shirt, bib overalls of unstained denim—for he'd been out of work since the middle of February, when the mine owners had cut wages by 10 percent and dang near the whole valley'd gone on strike in protest.

"What is it, Ben?" I demanded. "You look like you've seen a ghost."

"Oh, it's bad, Del. It's real bad. I flew up here soon as I could, just to tell Pop. He'll want to know—every mining man in all Kentucky will want to know, even the old-timers."

Pop appeared at my side, having scurried down the porch faster than he ever moved. "Out with it, son. What's happened?"

"Me and all the boys were down at the Eatle digs, standing across the mouth of the shaft—you know, to keep those damn scabs from getting inside. A couple of fellas pulled up in a truck that was all painted with the sign of the Evarts company."

I nodded impatiently. The town of Evarts lay some twenty miles to the southwest. It, too, had been drawn into the strike.

"They jumped out of the cab," Benjamin went on, "hollering and wringing their hands about a full-on war. Something's gone bad down in Evarts. There's men killed—gunfire. And we don't know yet whether it's miners or scabs."

Pop took my arm. For one dizzy moment I wondered why. Then I understood. He was clinging to me for support, trying to hold himself up. I could feel his hand trembling.

"If the mine owners are gunning down our men," Pop said, "then this won't end pretty."

That was an understatement, if ever I'd heard one. Life in the county had been hard enough before the Great Crash of 1929, and since then it had only gotten worse—hunger propagating throughout the valley at a pace that was both steady and cruel, poverty deepening so relentlessly it seemed almost deliberate. Was God testing our faith the way He'd tested poor old Job? Even Irving and I had begun to feel the pinch, now and then.

When the mine owners had slashed wages earlier that year, there'd been no reasonable way for any man to respond, except to join the strike. Most in Harlan County were already suffering so badly, it didn't make a terrible lot of difference whether a man had an income or not.

But if the bankers and businessmen who owned the mines were ready to open fire on the workers—if they were ready to shed blood— then life in the valley would grow bleaker still, and ten times harder to bear.

"I've got to get back home," I said. "Irving needs to know. He'll want to minister to the folks who've lost someone in the fight. And he'll want to brace the whole valley for what's coming. I need to be there to help him. He relies on me."

"Get in the truck," my brother said. "I'll drive you back to town."

2

The sun was glaring low on the pink horizon by the time Benjamin pulled to the edge of the road outside my house. I thanked my brother and exited the cab of his truck as fast as was seemly. I didn't want to appear in too much haste, but that evening, the sight of my new-built brick colonial home left me feeling twisted up with guilt. It was my family's tradition to gather for Christmas Eve supper at the home of Benjamin and his vivacious wife, Nadine. My sister-in-law was a smart homemaker, and clever enough to turn a soup bone and a few frostbitten vegetables from the garden into a feast fit for any holiday. But their house a few miles down the valley was little better than my parents' shack up in the hills—and today, with the weight of the miners' strike bearing down on both of us, the stark difference in how we lived struck me as something next door to sin.

Benjamin slid back the pane of his window. "I got to be off, sis. Got to spread the word."

"You be careful, you hear? Goodness knows what else the owners might get up to. Anyone who strikes might be in danger. Say hello to Nadine for me, will you?"

Benjamin raised a hand in farewell. The Brockway chugged off to the west, kicking up a thin cloud of dust. The setting sun hung itself up among the spinning motes and glowed there.

When I turned back toward the house, Irving was just stepping outside. He nodded when he saw me and waited on the stoop between the two white pillars.

"Did you hear what's gone down in Evarts?" I called to him as I hurried up the footpath.

"I heard, all right," Irving said. "It's a dad-gummed shame. I've been telling the boys to have patience and trust in the Lord. Been reminding them every day to be meek and endure like Jesus."

"Who was it? And how many's shot—does anyone know?"

Irving held the door open. I stepped into the serene coolness of our home. Placid evening shadows lay along the elegant, papered walls, dimming the corners of the parlor, taming the colors of the Turkish rug, which Irving had brought all the way up from Charlotte.

"Four men dead," he said quietly. "None of them miners, and I guess that's something. But it's still four men dead. God rest their souls."

After the expected reverent pause, I asked, "Were they scabs? Not that it makes a difference. I only want to know."

"None of the dead men were strike-breakers—no." Irving sank onto the green-velvet settee and pressed his hands against his eyes for a moment as if he could shut out the images inside his head. "They were deliverymen in the employ of the mine owners. Bringing supplies in to the strike-breakers who were down in the mineshaft. They were riding a couple of Kalamazoos—you know, those little carts that run along the train tracks; the kind you power with your arms."

"I know the kind," I said. "Pump trolleys."

"I guess a pack of our boys got tired of the scabs crossing the picket line. They laid in wait along the tracks, thinking to ambush the next wave of scabs, but along came these hapless deliverymen instead. It's a dad-gummed shame," Irving said again, driving a fist into his palm. "That's what it is—a crying devil of a shame."

"Ben drove up to my folks' place and gave us the news. My pop thinks there's worse to come."

Irving nodded. He was staring past me, out through the parlor window to the railroad berm that ran along the opposite side of the street. Or maybe he stared beyond our town, into the green body of the hillside, as if he could see through the clay flesh of the earth, through its bones of ancient shale, into its coal-black heart. "Worse to come. I'd bet on that. You mark my words, Adella—this whole county's a powder keg and the fuse is lit. There's no putting out the fire now."

"But surely there's got to be something we can do, Irving. Why, nothing's beyond the Lord's power, and you're the minister of these parts, after all."

He looked at me then, a quick flick of his eyes and a brief smile that was almost sad. "Such faith—such belief. Like a child."

Now, I don't mind telling you, that comment didn't set well with me at all. I'd spent every Sunday of my life in my family's pew at the Church of God with Signs Following. Hadn't I had it drilled into my head—hadn't everyone in the whole damned valley had it pounded right into their brains—that no feat, no miracle was beyond the strength of the Almighty? But I had also received a lifetime's worth of lecturing on the sin of saucing back to either your husband or the preacher. And when your husband *was* the preacher—well! I lowered my eyes and kept my mouth shut, no matter how Irving's dismissiveness rankled me.

"Might be you're right, after all, Adella. We might *could* cool folks off a little, if we went about it the right way." Irving rose from the settee and began to pace across the parlor, turning on his heel at my piano and striding back again. His hands were clasped behind his back. I could see that his shirt had darkened under his arms and around his collar where sweat had soaked through. "Bring a little happiness back to the valley, lighten spirits some, before every man in the Cumberland takes up his gun and goes looking for satisfaction. What we need is a distraction—a celebration."

"What," I said, with no small amount of irony, "a picnic?"

Irving stopped at the parlor window and spun to face me. The evening light lit him from behind, so I could scarcely make out his face, but the gleeful pitch of his voice told me everything I needed to know. "That's it exactly. We'll have a picnic."

"Oh, Irving, I was only kidding! No one wants a picnic at a time like this."

"The heck they don't, Adella. Why, it'll set the whole valley to buzzing. An excuse for fun and games and coming together? It's just what we need right now."

Despite my strict training in womanly meekness, I couldn't help scoffing at the idea. "Be serious, now. Four men are dead in their graves, and for all we know, the mine owners might come looking for revenge. If you get up a picnic at a time like this, Irving Wensley, the whole valley will think you're nothing but a fool. And they'll think I'm a fool, too, for going along with it."

"That sounds very much like pride, honey pie."

"It ain't pride, it's common sense. At times like these, nobody feels like gallivanting around with a basket on their arm. And it's too damn hot already, and only the first week of May. If you wanted a picnic, you should have done it weeks ago, when the sun wasn't fixing to kill anyone who steps outside. Why, folks'll be too busy to come to your party, anyhow. Trying to get their gardens to give something worth eating before summer sets in and all the plants dry up to nothing."

Irving clapped his hands and rubbed his palms together—a gesture he only made when he was cooking up a scheme he expected to be especially fruitful. "Oh, they'll come. I'll see to it. I'll put up the tent; we'll have ourselves an old-fashioned revival. You just see if they don't come running, honey pie."

I shrugged. There was no sense arguing further, and I'd already pushed the boundaries of righteous behavior more than was prudent. Besides, I knew that if Irving put up his revival tent, the thing would be packed full from dawn to dusk. Everyone in the valley knew Irving

Wensley put on the best show in the Cumberland. He never met a snake he wouldn't take hold of and raise up above his head, and whenever he did, his great band of followers would throw their hands up to Heaven and shout praises to the Lord. They'd get to stamping their feet and shaking till they fell down from the force of the Spirit, and the women would sing and the men would come crawling up to Irving's pulpit and he would cast out their devils with a touch, and just then, at the right moment, when his service reached a fever pitch, he would send his collection plate around the crowd so everyone could drop in their nickels and dimes.

"You do as you like," I said. "I guess it can't hurt any—though I still say too many folks will think it's a foolish waste."

"Can I count on you to help organize it?"

I stifled the sigh that was filling my chest. Of course I would help organize the picnic. In fact, I knew already that I'd be doing damn near all the work. What else was a preacher's wife for, if not to be a helpmeet, to make affairs run smoothly where the congregation was concerned? The preacher might get all the glory, but it was always his wife who rubbed a little grease on the axle of the church and kept the wheels turning.

"I'll go make some coffee," I said, "and then you can tell me what you want for this big hullaballoo of a picnic. I'll do what I can to make it happen."

As I left the parlor, something caught my eye in the hall—an envelope lying on the floor, just under the mail slot. Neither Irving nor I had noticed it when we'd come inside. Too preoccupied with the news out of Evarts, I guess.

When I retrieved the envelope and read its return address, a prickle of caution ran through me.

"Irving?" I called. "There's a letter for you. Says it's from Senator Logan."

He took the envelope with an expression that said he was every bit as mystified as I was. There was no point in my hanging around while he read the letter; the demands of the picnic were already weighing on me. Planning a party for the whole congregation was work enough. Now I needed to get up a celebration that would cool tempers and stop the men from shooting one another all up and down the valley.

"Don't worry, Del," I muttered as I cranked the coffee grinder and filled the percolator's basket. "All you have to do is save a few hundred lives with a little old picnic. Easy as pie."

As I set the perc atop my stove and turned the range's electric dial, Irving burst into the kitchen so suddenly I jumped, biting back a shriek.

"Listen to this, Adella." He waved the senator's letter above his head, then cleared his throat and read it aloud in his best preacher's voice.

"'Dear Mr. Wensley. I have taken much interest in your tireless work on behalf of the spiritual well-being of the good people of Kentucky. Your service to the Christian souls of our state is notable. I shall watch your career closely as it continues to develop.' And it's signed, 'Senator M. M. Logan.'"

"My goodness, Irving. A letter from the new senator himself? What does it mean?"

"I don't know, but I suppose it can only be good. He called me notable. Notable!"

Irving caught me by the waist and swung me around the kitchen.

"I tell you, Adella, this picnic of ours is going to be a great success. The Lord is smiling on all my endeavors. What do you say to a little splash of whiskey in the coffee tonight? This is reason enough to celebrate, I'd say."

Grinning, Irving flicked the letter. It made a crisp popping sound. "Notable!"

That sounds very much like pride, I didn't say. I was a good girl back then, and still thought it best to keep to my place.

~

Four days later, on a Saturday glaring with yellow heat, I brought Irving's plans to fruition. I found a few strong boys to drag the great canvas rolls of the old revival tent out of the barn behind the meetinghouse. In the crisp, dewy chill of dawn, the boys set the poles and raised the tent in the big field between the riverbank and the Church of God with Signs Following, and before the day's heat set in, I had the tables arranged in the shade below the tulip trees. I laid brightly colored cloths on the tables myself, smoothing the creases with my hands.

The women of the church arrived first, spreading cheerful quilts across the dry grass. From their baskets they produced the simple things women could bake on tight rations—egg bread and chocolate wacky cake made without milk or butter, spice loaves flavored with simmered lard, and water pie so sweet it would make you drool from ten feet away. The children came shouting from town. They ran over the bridge that spanned the Cumberland River and tumbled across the picnic field, and long before the men arrived from their fretful watch over the picket lines, there was joy in the valley—singing and laughter, and paper kites bobbing in the sky, and Mr. Knott playing his fiddle under the biggest tulip tree, which set its branches to swaying so dapples of sunlight moved across the grass as if the day itself were dancing.

Once I'd finished the worst of the work and the strain left me, I began to think Irving had been right after all—the picnic was a splendid idea, and just what the doctor ordered to lighten the dead weight of our spirits. If the men were leaner and quieter than ever before, if the women's cheeks were hollow, if the children were bony as underfed pups, what did it matter that day? We were smiling, all of us, and singing along to the fiddle, and for one afternoon, all souls in the valley put the anger and despair of the strikes behind them.

Irving had spent the morning down in Evarts, engaged in another meeting with the company owners. He'd sat down with the owners twice already in a bid to find common ground. As the noon hour passed, Irving's black Gardner appeared at the vanishing point of the road, nearly a mile off and spitting up a banner of dust. I made my excuses to the women at the party and walked down to the meeting-house so I'd be first to greet my husband. I was eager to tell him how great a success the picnic already was.

As I approached the church, two furtive shadows broke from the tree line and slipped around the corner of the building. The sight of them caught me up short. Instinctively, I knew they must be strangers. Anyone who called the valley home would have no cause to hide from the preacher's wife. For a hair of a second, I wondered if they might be agents of the mine owners. Had the companies sent men to spy on the folks who'd taken a stand against their injustice? Were they simply looking for a chance to avenge the men who'd already been shot? If so, the whole con-gregation might be sitting ducks. I thought back to the Ludlow Massacre. I'd never forgotten the terrible story—no daughter of a coal miner could. On that terrible day in 1914, in far-off Colorado, the National Guard had attacked a whole camp full of striking miners . . . and their families. At least twenty people had been killed, women and children included. Were the mine owners setting us up for another massacre? Had Irving and I led the entire congregation into danger?

All those grim thoughts flashed through my mind in the blink of an eye. But as the two strangers dodged out of sight, my better sense caught up with my wild panic. Those men wore ragged clothes—far too shabby for any company fellow—and each had a flour-sack bindle slung over his shoulder. They were only hobos. The strangers must have ridden into town on one of the coal trains that rolled through the valley three or four times a day—for even now, in the midst of the strike, the trains continued to run. The nation's appetite for coal only seemed to grow, even while the workers of America tightened their belts and hunkered down under the relentless blows of deprivation.

"Hello," I called. "I see you, friends. You don't need to fret. Come on out; I don't bite."

There was a pause. Birds and crickets sang in the lazy heat. The distinctive rumble of Irving's motorcar swelled a little in the stillness. Then one of the strangers leaned around the corner of the church, his flat cap pulled away, his dark hair standing up in a wild mess. Through the grime of travel and poverty, I could see that he was young, somewhere in his early twenties. His eyes were sharp and wary.

"We're having a picnic," I said. "Can I get you a bite?"

The young man edged back around the corner of the church, slouching a little, as if ashamed of his dirty appearance. He was thin as a scarecrow and twice as ratty, his shirt long since grayed by the grime of the road, his britches more composed of patches than the original worsted wool. A moment later, his friend came out of hiding, too. The other was short and stocky, yet no less ill-used despite his robust build. The shorter one seemed to be a few years older, with a florid Irish complexion and carrot-red hair.

"We ain't looking for charity, ma'am," the taller one said. "We're looking for work."

"That's right," his friend added. "If you got any chores that needs doing, we'll be handy, and glad for any pay you might give. A few coins or a bit of bread, or a pair of socks if you've got some to spare—"

The tires of Irving's car spit gravel as he pulled to the front of the church. The engine coughed into silence. Then the car door slammed, causing both drifters to flinch.

Irving came out swinging, hollering at the top of his voice. "Gol dang it, you no-good bums better get out of here, if you know what's good for you."

"Irving," I protested, "they're only looking for work."

"Like hell they are."

The hobos cringed toward the corner of the meetinghouse, but Irving was in no mood to suffer their hanging around.

"I said get away!" He made a shooing gesture with his hands. "The last thing we need just now is more trouble."

"Can't we give them something to do?"

"Damn it, Adella, they don't want to work. Look at them! Never worked a day in their lives—you can bet on that."

One glance at the strangers was enough to convince me that Irving was dead wrong, for both men had taken on such an instant and aggrieved air that I knew they'd reacted honestly to my husband's words. This was no put-on meant to coax a soft-hearted woman into parting with her money. They'd truly come in search of work, and Irving had insulted them with his accusation. Even a hobo had his dignity—and why not? Weren't they men like any others?

A wave of embarrassment ran through me, followed by a rebellious urge to rejoin with scripture. Maybe *Inasmuch as ye have done it unto one of the least of these* . . . But no. The mere idea of criticizing my husband, particularly where other men could see, embarrassed me even more. What would those strangers think of a woman who calls her husband to account right in front of other men? I didn't quite know what to say or do in the face of such turmoil—Irving's rudeness, my own unfeminine drive to fling scripture into his face—so I did what I usually did during my tenure as a proper woman. I kept my mouth shut.

The red-haired man turned pointedly away from Irving, giving me a gracious nod. "We thank you for your kindness, ma'am, but we'll be going. We don't want trouble, either, no more than anyone else does."

Without another glance at Irving, the strangers set off along the side of the meetinghouse, making for the road and the tracks beyond.

"No-good rats," Irving muttered, just loud enough for the men to hear. "Living off of honest people's work."

Tears stung my eyes. I rounded on Irving as the hobos continued down the drive. "Really, you could have shown a little Christian charity."

He laughed in that way he had, one short bark that managed to convey a whole text and verse of condescension without a single word. "I think I've got a pretty good handle on what's Christian and what's not, little lady. Now forget those bums and let's get back to the picnic. I think I made some progress today with the mine owners. I let them know that Senator Logan has taken note of me—implied the senator will take my side if I bring his attention to what's going on here in Harlan County. The strike's far from over yet, but they might just come around to our side of things and give the miners their full wages. *And back pay, if I can pull it off.*"

Word swiftly made its way around the party that Irving had returned from Evarts and had gained some ground in the negotiation. He was soon the hero of the day, waltzing from one family to another, all grins and a glad hand as he basked in the praise. I busied myself with the tables, serving pie and biscuits and opening fresh crocks of butter, and chatting with the women of the valley as they stopped to fan themselves in the shade.

But though I mingled as readily as any preacher's wife ought to do, I couldn't get those hungry strangers out of my head. How far had the hobos walked by now? Could I still find them if I followed the train tracks? The sun on the field was brighter than it should have been, bouncing from the ground with a vigor it usually reserved for August. Through the glare, I couldn't make out much more of the railroad than a thin black line running to the west through the mobile, clamoring light.

Soon I lost track of Irving; he'd vanished among the milling circles of the congregation, the packs of children who ran shouting from one quilt to another with biscuits or toys in their hands. While Jeanetta Greenup chattered on about how fast her little ones were growing and the bedspread she was making from her dad's old shirts, I wondered at Irving's whereabouts and watched the gathering for any sign of him. But I could find no more knots of men shaking hands, no band of enthralled sheep tagging after their shepherd. It seemed to me that Irving had slipped away—gone back to the meetinghouse, maybe, to pick up one of his old Bibles, for he seldom liked to be seen in public without the Good Book tucked cozily under his arm.

Now's my chance. The thought occurred to me before I really knew what I intended doing. The moment I began stuffing biscuits into the pockets of my skirt, however, I understood exactly what I was up to.

Turning to Jeanetta with a ready, practiced smile, I asked her to mind the tables while I excused myself. "I need to run back to the house. Call of nature—you understand. Won't be more than twenty minutes, I hope."

"Was it May's potato salad?" Jeanetta asked. "It hits everyone that way, sooner or later. Go on; I'll keep an eye on things till you're back."

Crossing the field once more, and making for the meetinghouse, I was beset by a prickling fear, dead certain Irving would pop out of the church just in time to catch me and ask what I was up to. Or worse, some well-meaning busybody would follow me from the picnic and witness my act of rebellion. Then wouldn't the gossip circles just about have a heyday. But the church remained still, and if anyone had noticed me slipping away from the party, no one thought enough about it to shout after me and ask what I was up to.

From the drive of the meetinghouse, I could make out the railroad more clearly. Slightly raised on an old earthen berm and fringed with weeds, the tracks cut straight through the heart of our small town to bend around the foot of a hill some half mile to the west. At the far end of town, I could just make out two figures, small black silhouettes, standing idly beside the tracks.

About ten minutes later, I'd hustled to shouting distance from those two poor strangers. My breath came ragged in the stifling heat and my head began to pound—and that's to say nothing of the sweat that ran slick down my back. But I'd drawn even with the strangers, and despite the caution that nagged at me, my heart lifted a little as I crossed the road, scrambled up the berm through stickers and thistles, and planted myself on one of the black wooden ties of the rail line.

"Hey!" I waved both hands wildly above my head.

The hobos pretty near jumped out of their skins, but when they saw that it was only me, they relaxed. Something warm and powerful uncurled inside me, like a big critter waking from a long winter's sleep. The feeling was so foreign that I didn't quite trust it, and didn't know what to call it—that secret expanding strength. I just stood there grinning like a fool, even as I wondered whether I was committing some kind of sin. But I didn't feel bad like a sinner ought to feel. I felt as dandy as I'd been for years. Only when the strangers came close enough that I could have laid my hand on their heads did I find a name for that exotic sensation. Triumph. When I pulled the biscuits from my pockets and held them out for those boys to take, my elation grew all the more.

"You sure are generous, ma'am," the dark-haired one said. "We haven't had a bite to eat since yesterday noon."

"I only wish I could give you more." I meant it, too, and realizing how much I meant it, my throat went tight with gratitude. "I'm sorry for the way my husband spoke to y'all back there. It wasn't right—just two honest boys looking for a day's work. Life's hard enough for everyone now; there's no cause to go making it worse by being cruel to one another."

The tall one gave a sheepish laugh. He lifted his cap.

The other said, "Amen to that, ma'am, but Jim and me—we talked about it and we're getting out on the next train. This part of the country seems pretty bad off—worse than other towns we've seen. Even if we could find an honest day's work, we'd only be taking money or food or something else from folks who need it more."

Such a judgment from the mouth of an indigent took me aback. Of course the strike had stretched everyone thin, on top of the way the Crash had done for everyone, all across the nation. Did Harlan County really look so desperate through an outsider's eyes?

Before I could reply, a coal train's whistle blared at the other edge of town. The engine came crawling toward us, lifting a black flag of smoke.

"That'll be our ride, ma'am," said the red-haired hobo. "Thanks again for your charity."

Skittish of the approaching train, I descended the berm and retreated to the far side of the road. The two strangers packed the biscuits I'd given them into their flour-sack bindles and readied themselves to catch their ride. I hid my hands in the pockets of my skirt, where I crushed biscuit crumbs methodically between finger and thumb till the crumbs were only dust. Those two gentle-hearted strangers crouched among the weeds while the engine went growling and shuddering past. Then they rose and with the ease of long practice, stepped up to the creeping train and caught hold of the ladders that ran down the sides of the gondolas. Each climbed his ladder and disappeared into the open-topped coal cars. Their train had rounded the bend, vanishing behind the hillside.

They made it look so easy, to hop a train. Like anyone could do it.

I turned my pockets inside out, letting the powdered crumbs fall onto the dirt road. Soon the little birds would come down to peck and scratch till everything was gone and only the dust of the earth remained.

The birds of the air sow not, neither do they reap, I mused, *yet the Father feeds them.*

3

In the enclosing heat of afternoon, I walked back to the field behind our church, sunk deep in my thoughts. The stranger's words had troubled me, though I couldn't put my finger on why. Who in this country wasn't feeling the pinch of the Great Crash—who in all the world? Oh, I knew the barons of industry couldn't possibly feel any deprivation—those Rockefellers and Carnegies, the Fords and Astors and Vanderbilts with their fingers in every business and every factory from coast to coast. But the rest of us, the ordinary folks, we couldn't escape it. Even Irving and I were obliged to tighten our belts and lead more moderate lives. No more trips to Knoxville or Lexington to dine in fancy restaurants or take in a talkie at the jewel-bright cinemas. But surely, even with the miners' strike hanging over the valley, we didn't have it any worse than Americans elsewhere. The fact that hobos, of all men, had thought the people of Harlan County pitiable struck me as a caution. That day of the picnic, we were at our best—the women dressed in their faded finest, the children running and playing—but a pair of drifters, used to hard living and lean times, had taken one look at our community and had deemed us in need of more charity than any hobo on the rails.

I'd always thought our community rough and countryish, but never pitiable. The Cumberland was a place where the sturdy and the sensible thrived. And my own house of red brick with its Greek pillars flanking the stoop proved that the Cumberland wasn't entirely tar-paper shacks like my parents' home. Surely our valley wasn't in the dire straits those hobos had assumed. And once the strike was settled and men could earn a decent wage again, things would get better. There would be enough food to go around once more. The children would fatten up, the women would lose the lost and frightened shadows that now veiled their expressions. It was only the strike—and the strike, like the ripples of the Great Crash that still rocked our community, couldn't go on forever.

I paced down Main Street, frowning at the road, then frowning at the houses that lined the road. Plywood walls covered in tar paper, tin roofs rusted to red and patched with old scraps of discarded signs, with siding cut from the walls of boxcars. They were the homes I'd seen all my life, growing up a coal-miner's daughter in this deep green valley, the only home, the only world I'd ever known.

It's not as if we're the shabbiest people in all Creation, I told myself. *We get by all right. We don't need more than what we have—not much more, anyway.*

The hem of my skirt swung above my kid-leather shoes. In my best blouse and that skirt of fine twill, I thought I looked pretty sharp. No one had much cause to pity me. I'd even worn my best summer hat for the occasion—a straw picture-style number with an asymmetrical brim, as was the rage back then. I had a real fondness for hats in those days and had picked that one up the last time Irving and I had jaunted off to Lexington. We'd made that trip a few days before news of the Crash reached us in the Cumberland. Rarely had we visited any city since that memorable day.

When I returned to the picnic, I drifted among the groups of women, dodging their attempts to pull me into their gossip. Jeanetta had found someone else to mind the tables—old Anne-Celeste Skaggs, the valley's granny woman—and I was content to leave Anne-Celeste to the work, for she seemed to appreciate the shade. No matter how I tried to show the placid, womanly hospitality Irving expected of me, I couldn't find my way into any conversation. My thoughts were still back there along the tracks, hung up on the sharp hook of that hobo's words. *We'd only be taking from folks who need it more.*

As I stood shoulder to shoulder with a pack of other ladies near my own age, staring blindly into the middle distance, an elbow bumped my arm. I pulled myself out of the endless circuit of my own musing and saw—for the first time, really—the other girls looking at me with expectation.

"Sorry," I said. "Guess my mind went a-wandering."

Deborah Carter said, "I asked where Mr. Wensley got off to. No one has seen him for nigh on an hour, and we hoped to pull the raffle tickets soon. We ought to have the preacher pull the tickets, don't you think? After all, this whole picnic was his doing."

"No one's seen him for an hour?" I looked around the field, and sure enough, there was no sign of Irving. "I don't think he's gone back to the house. I was just up that way."

"Maybe he ran off into the bushes," Deborah said. "May Jenkins's potato salad."

The other girls laughed. I didn't. The subtle worm of anxiety, which had pestered me since I'd seen those strangers off, gave a sudden twist in my gut. It wasn't like Irving to be gone so long. He never missed an opportunity to put himself smack in the center of the action.

With a promise to the girls that I'd find their preacher, I set off to scour the church and the edges of the field. All the while, that tiny fear fed upon my heart and grew. Before long, the sense that something was terribly wrong wrapped around me, cold and strong as the coils of a serpent.

The church was still as a tomb. The edge of the picnic grounds yielded no sign of Irving. Finally, I set off into the woods along the river. Maybe Irving really was puking in the undergrowth and needed my help. Or maybe he'd finally taken a long, hard look at his flock, as I had. Maybe he'd removed himself to pray down blessings of mercy upon the meek and the struggling.

When I found my husband at last, there was no sort of holiness on his mind.

I came upon Irving in a stand of yellowwoods. There among the hanging clusters of white blossoms, he stood with his arms around the waist of Ruthie Bell. Ruthie was eighteen that year, fresher than any daisy, and Irving had buried his face in the girl's neck. Her head was flung back, eyes closed, as if she couldn't decide whether to be ecstatic or disgusted by what was being done to her. The front of her dress was open, the bright calico sliding across her skin, exposing one small breast.

I guess I must have made some sound, for Ruthie's eyes snapped open. When she saw me, the girl screamed and shoved Irving away.

"Damn it, Adella!" He rounded on me, red-faced. "What in holy hell are you doing here?"

I said nothing. Well—what could I have said, in any case? The only clear thought that occurred to me was that Irving never cussed.

Ruthie scrambled to cover herself. Tears ran down her cheeks. "Mrs. Wensley, I didn't mean it, I didn't even know what he was going to do—"

I paid no mind to Ruthie. Girls will do what they must to survive, but a grown man ought to be above such sinning, and any man who purports to speak on God's behalf sure as hell ought to act like he has the moral authority to do so.

Did I say any of that to my husband? If you think I did, you don't know the world I came from. The brash, independent New Woman had blazed her way across society in the years leading up to the Crash, but there were no New Women in the Cumberland. In my world, the fact that women had finally won the right to vote was still lamented, more than a decade later, as one of the greatest evils to ever befall America. As I watched Irving button his collar and straighten his tie with an air of stiff offense, every instinct of my heart cried out at the injustice—at the sheer, low-down, dirty *insult* my husband had thrown into my face.

But I was a good girl, a righteous woman of the church. Shame had been bred into my bones, obedience schooled into me from the cradle.

One thought rose up to overshadow my shock and my pain: not only was Irving my husband, but he was the spiritual leader of the entire valley. He couldn't have done something unrighteous; it was simply an impossibility, as mad an idea as the sun rising at midnight or the river reversing its course. I had misunderstood what I'd seen. Or I hadn't seen what I'd thought. Or . . . or it was my fault somehow. My doing.

It's the baby. My thoughts tripped over one another, tangling themselves. *No baby. I haven't given him a family. No wonder he's losing interest. No wonder he wants another woman, a younger woman, one who can make him a father. What kind of man can respect himself if he isn't a father? It's my fault. My doing. I've driven him to sin.*

Once he was properly dressed again, Irving said, "Really, Adella. You ought to mind your own damn business."

He stalked past me with an air of blunt outrage, as if I'd been the one who'd wronged him—as if he was deigning to forgive me for the intrusion. Ruthie Bell had already disappeared into the woods.

"I'm sorry," I said to Irving's retreating back.

He didn't answer, didn't even look my way, and I was left alone in the yellowwood grove, with my heart thundering in my ears and the candy smell of the flowers hanging all around me.

4

Would you believe me if I told you that wasn't the end of things? It seems impossible to me now, that I didn't up and leave Irving the moment I caught him in the arms of another woman. But I was so well trained by family and faith that I blamed myself more than I ever blamed him.

The weeks after the picnic passed in a dark fog. I went about my duties at home and in the church with a mindless automation, a placid smile fixed to my face. The smile was only a mask, of course. However it may have fooled Irving or anyone else, my expression of meek contentment couldn't convince me that all was well. As I went about each day with eyes downcast, never raising my voice to confront my husband with the evidence of his sins, I was beset by a constant agony. One moment, I would heap blame upon myself for Irving's infidelity. The next, I would berate myself for clinging so tightly to anger. Shouldn't a good woman forgive those who trespass against her? To be sure, all have sinned and come short of the glory of God. Irving made damn sure I didn't forget that point of scripture. Not only did he preach it privately to me in the stifling confines of our home, but he proclaimed it from his pulpit, too, for two Sundays after the picnic. It didn't matter a jot how I set my mind to forgive my husband. I just couldn't bring myself to do it, and the knowledge that I possessed a mean, cold heart only doubled the burden of my guilt.

Hoping to ease the weight of my shame, I threw myself into my duties. The tension of the strike hadn't eased, and Irving was busier than ever as he struggled to keep the miners of our valley on the righteous path. He feared that without a constant reminder of the Lord's commandments, the men of Harlan County might rise up in true armed revolt, and we'd be faced with another Ludlow Massacre, with miners' wives and innocent children gunned down in a storm of violence. With such danger hanging over all our heads, my pain seemed insignificant by comparison. I dedicated myself to Irving's cause and prayed each night that my loyalty would be rewarded with peace and understanding—or at least with the will to forgive.

The revival tent stood in the field behind our church all through the month of May, and Irving got up a proper meeting damn near every night. The tent was always full, and Irving preached with a passion that exceeded even his typical fire.

I found I couldn't stomach the inside of the tent once folks got to clapping their hands and shouting. The zeal burned around me like a fever, and the way the congregation turned to Irving with worshipful trust only heightened my awareness of my own failings. I alone, in all the valley, looked upon our preacher with misgiving. Despite my private admonitions to be perfect in faith, to listen to the wise counsel of my husband, I couldn't help but ask myself whether Irving's exceptional fire had more to do with the dangers of the strike or his need to soothe his own conscience, to plead a little more absolution from God. I could as well tolerate standing in that revival tent as being locked inside a trunk. The moment I'd made my expected appearance—welcoming one and all, smiling and waving in a display of warmth—I disappeared again into the relative quiet of the field, where the evening light lingered in a rosy flush and the cooling air raised a luminous mist from the forest.

One evening near the end of May, as I slipped from the revival into the solitude of the empty field, I discovered that someone had left an old three-legged campstool standing near the tent's entry. A wave of exhaustion swept over me at the sight of that unexpected object, as if all the sorrows I'd felt those past weeks were bearing down upon my heart in cruel and deliberate concert. The only clear thought in my head was that I would dearly like to rest my bones for a spell, as far from the tent as possible. I scooped up the campstool without a thought for its owner and carried it through the gathering dusk to the edge of the field. The cries of "Hallelujah!" and the whine of the fiddle dwindled behind me. At the shoulder of the long dirt road, I sank upon the stool with a weary sigh.

Irving's tent felt very small and distant now. The chorus of crickets was almost as loud as the noise of the revival. After so many days of relentless bustle, to sit still and watch the pale stars emerge one by one seemed the grandest blessing the Lord had ever bestowed. In that solitude, with the great colorful arch of the evening sky above, I thought if I prayed earnestly enough, God would grant an answer to all the questions—the demands—that clamored inside me.

I tipped my face up to the cool, vivid sky and closed my eyes, and asked in my heart just what I should do.

To my surprise, it was my mother's voice that answered, the faint echo of a memory. *You ought to go and call on Anne-Celeste Skaggs. Don't know how many times I've told you so.*

Now, this was the first clear thought I'd had in days—the only thought I could recall in weeks of stumbling through a fog of shame. Its very sharpness struck me with significance. Surely the Lord was speaking to me, and I had better listen.

Well, as soon as I made up my mind that I was receiving instruction from On High, everything spun into a dizzy kind of order. Of course it was my fault Irving had strayed, for I'd failed to make him a father. Little wonder he'd taken to lusting after other women. All I needed to do was that one precious task—which any wife ought to manage—and all my troubles would vanish. Never again would my husband be tempted by forbidden fruits, and with a child for atonement, I would be freed from anger and discontentment. I would see my husband in a new light—in the radiance of a father's love—and then, at last, I could forgive him. I made up my mind right then and there that I'd call on Anne-Celeste the very next day. She would repair everything that had broken in my marriage, my life.

Wasn't I a fool in those days? You don't know the half of it.

Flooded by a warmth of certainty, I rose from the campstool and opened my eyes—and pretty near jumped out of my skin, for there on the road before me stood three people so gaunt and gray they might have been specters.

"Land sakes," I nearly hollered. "Where did you all come from?"

The tallest among them swept off his hat—the broad-brimmed sort most often worn by farmers. "Beggin' your pardon, miss. Me and my wife and my son here have come looking for work—that's all."

The jolt of shock dissipated. Despite the rapidly fading light, I could see now that the other two figures were a woman and a child of about ten years, both as thin as needles with a sharp desperation in their eyes.

"We come from the other side of the tracks," the woman said. "Crossed over just now. Didn't mean to give you a fright."

I blinked through the dusk at the railway, raised some six feet above the valley floor on its berm. "You all rode the rails into town?"

"Been here since this morning," the man answered. "All of us has been out beating the bushes for work since then, up and down this valley, but haven't had a bit of luck. We thought we'd try that town over across the tracks but it seems nobody's home."

"Guess no one is at home tonight," I said. "Everyone's at revival."

I paused, and those three tattered souls looked at me with such hope and longing that my heart burned—and withered in regret, for I had no choice but to dash their fragile hopes.

"I'm awful sorry to be the one to tell you this." My eyes slid away from the woman's thin face, the boy's trembling lips. "There's just no work in this whole valley—hasn't been for months. These are all mining towns, you see, up and down this river. The men have gone on strike. I don't know when work will pick up again, but it won't be for weeks at the soonest."

My words were met with a stricken silence. In the gray half light I could read the fear in their eyes. I wondered where these wretched souls had come from, how far they'd traveled in search of sustenance, and how they'd come to lose the life they'd known before. Their clothing was drab from road dust, a patchwork of mending. Even the boy had a distance and a suffering in his eyes. It plucked at my heart to see what a yoke of worries that child bore on his shoulders.

"Guess we might as well be on our way," the man finally said. He turned to his wife with a brittle smile, reached out to ruffle the hair of his solemn boy. "There's bound to be work elsewhere. We just got to keep on moving."

"There won't be another train coming through till late next morning," I said. "Why don't you all spend the night inside the church? There's a pump in the yard with good well water, and an outhouse, and I know my . . . that is, I know the preacher keeps a couple of cots and an old washtub in that barn out back. It ain't much, but it's better than sleeping on the ground. I'll bring you all something to eat. How does that sound?"

I set off for the meetinghouse. The displaced family strode along beside me.

"You're sure we won't be causing any trouble?" the woman asked. "We don't want to trespass none."

"Nonsense," I said. "Only . . . maybe you all should keep out of sight once the revival finishes up. Just till the folks have cleared out and the preacher has gone back home. My name's Adella, by the way. Adella Wensley."

The strangers introduced themselves as we made our way from the road to the lane, and up the long lane to the meetinghouse with its white walls standing out sure as scripture against the night. John Baker, his wife Margaret, and their boy Vernon had come all the way from Dunlow, West Virginia, in search of work.

"Never thought I'd leave the old farm," John said. "But my dad mortgaged it before he handed it down to me, and—well—the bank hasn't been too happy with the prices we've got for our crops the last few seasons. They called the mortgage in, and that was that. Out on the road like a pack of bums."

"What was John supposed to do about it?" Margaret said bitterly. "As if one man can control the rain! It's robbery—that's what it is."

John laid a hand on his wife's shoulder. "Now, dear, don't get yourself worked up. We'll make do, like we always have."

We reached the door of the church, and I pulled my key ring from the pocket of my skirt. The revival tent stood some two or three acres across the field, but the kerosene lamps within lit the entire construction with a forceful yellow glow, and from the corner of my eye the tent seemed to loom over me, near enough that at any moment Irving might reach out and seize me by the arm. The sound of his preaching seemed to come from everywhere at once—from the night sky, from the vast eternity beyond the stars—and I fumbled in the darkness, trying to find the right key for the church door, trying to fit it into the lock.

Repent! My husband's voice split the night like thunder. *Repent, for the End of Days have come—how can you doubt it, how can you fail to see the signs of the Lord when all these false constructions of Man are crumbling to dust around you? Fall on your knees, you believers, and confess your sins before the Lord! The hour grows late, and Judgment is at hand!*

Finally, the key slid into the lock and I pushed the door open. The Bakers followed me inside.

"Irving fitted the place out with electric lights," I said, "but you'd best keep them shut off all night. Don't want to draw attention."

I could just make out Margaret's uneasy expression as she looked from her husband to me and back again. "We don't like to cause trouble, Miss Adella."

"You aren't a speck of trouble. And what's the Lord's house for, if not to shelter the weary? Only I don't want anyone to misunderstand, you see? So lay low and keep quiet till that field out there is good and empty."

John accompanied me to the barn behind the church, where another bout of fussing with keys and locks ensued. But soon we'd located the two folding cots Irving had stowed in a dusty corner and the tin washtub. "The pews in the back of the church have cushions," I said as we carried our loot through the darkness. "The Ladies' Aid Society sewed them a few years back so the old folks could set easier during meeting. You can pile the cushions into a bed for your boy."

"You've done us a real kindness tonight," John answered softly. "I'm grateful. We're all grateful. It's been a shock, you know—losing the farm so fast, and being cast out on the road. We've had to depend on the charity of strangers for weeks now. That sort of thing isn't easy for a man like me to take."

"You seem like a real good fellow, Mr. Baker. I know you'll find a new place to settle, by and by. I'm just sorry Harlan County has so little to give, these days."

I helped the Bakers situate themselves in the pitch-black shadows among the pews. Then I slipped from the church and closed its door firmly, and there I remained for a good long while, leaning against the whitewashed timbers, trying in vain to slow my racing heart.

What in the blessed Savior's name do you think you're doing, anyway, Del Wensley?

I knew full well my husband would disapprove; Irving was convinced that anyone who rode the rails was a bum, and therefore no good to anyone. No doubt, I was committing a grave act of disobedience. And I was already on thin ice with the Lord—for I'd decided, as you'll recall, that it was my own shortcomings as a woman that had driven my long-suffering husband to sin. I had endangered Irving's soul, and now I was pouring vinegar on the wound by sheltering indigents inside his church.

Of course, Irving knew best—or so I believed at the time. If he felt that hobos were of no account and were better driven away than succored, it must be true. After all, he understood the Word and the Truth better than anyone in the valley. Yet, though I felt awful antsy imagining how Irving might react when he learned of my rebellion, still I knew I could only do exactly as I'd done. My conscience wouldn't allow me to turn my back on folks in need. The Bakers weren't no-good drifters; they were a desperate family driven to the road, like a certain family that had fled to Egypt so long ago. Whatever misfortunes had befallen the Bakers, surely they weren't to blame. Everyone hung from a thread in those years, and the Bakers' thread had snapped. It could happen to anyone. Comfortable as our lives were, I could even imagine it happening to Irving and me. After all, the End of Days had come—as Irving so often preached. Who among us could withstand the scouring fire of calamity?

A low rumble came rolling through the night, more vibration than sound. It cut through the singing and shouting from the tent, shivering up through the soles of my shoes and into my chest. Everyone in the valley knew that sensation—a train would soon pass through the town. But the coal trains seldom moved at this hour and only made night runs on Sundays. Something unusual was cooking, no doubt, and the mystery of it drew me out of my anxious musing, down the lane to the edge of the road.

There I stood for a long while, with Irving's tent glowing and ruck-using behind my back and the stars arching above in their distant, untouchable majesty. Little by little, the rumble swelled to silence the crickets, then to dim the cries of "Hallelujah!" from far across the field.

The cold-iron shriek of the train's whistle rose from the crossroads, and a lone yellow eye blazed at me across the night.

Ordinarily, the trains passed right through town, for the nearest mine was some eight miles off. But this one appeared to be slowing. I wrapped my arms around myself, watching the engine creep toward me. By now I could see that this was no coal train. Indeed, it wasn't much of a train at all, for the engine drew only a single car, and it was unlike any I'd laid eyes on. The car was striped darkly, top and bottom, with a band of white running all down its length. Several windows were set into the white panel, and each window was aglow with electric light, framed by draperies of fine green velvet. This strange conveyance drew level with the church. The engine gave a great hiss of steam, then subsided into stillness. I've never been especially good at reading, but I puzzled out the letters painted along the top of the car—"PULL-MAN"—and the word on a fancy gold-leafed plaque below one of the windows: "LEXINGTON."

So this was a Pullman car—one of the famed hotels on wheels. I'd heard tell of such cars before—fitted with plush seats and beds of goose down, staffed with cooks and ushers to see to a body's every need. Pullmans even contained toilets and showers, so I'd heard. The luxurious carriages were the travel method of choice for folks who had money to burn. I couldn't have been more astonished if the Titanic had sailed into Harlan County and dropped anchor right in front of my nose.

As I stood there staring like a stunned goat, a handful of men rose from their seats and began moving down the length of the Pullman, past its glowing windows. The door at the car's rear end swung open. A gentleman in a fine dark suit descended the little metal steps fastened to the car's side. He was a sizable fellow, tall and broad with a round stomach and a fleshy face. His dark hair was swept neatly to the side, and his brows were very heavy, his eyes keen and imposing.

Two other men, younger and slimmer, followed him out of the car and looked around with an alert air, but the first man moved with such confidence, such authority that I knew at once he was their leader, and they mere servants to his will.

He caught sight of me, standing as I was like a scarecrow beside the road.

"Evening, ma'am," he called. "The name's Logan—M. M. Logan—Senator. I've come looking for Mr. Irving Wensley." He pointed to the revival tent. A grin split his ample face. "I guess that's where I can find him. Came just in time."

So this was the very man who'd written to Irving just to praise his work. Snapped out of my stupor, I hurried across the road to greet the senator as he came skidding down the slope of the berm with his two attendants scrambling in his wake.

"Pleased to meet you, Senator," I rattled. "Yes, sir, I know just where you can find Irving Wensley. I'm Mrs. Wensley, in fact—his wife. Yes, sir, he's there at the revival, and if you've come to hear him preach, why, I reckon you're just in time. He's got another twenty minutes at least, and it's a good sermon tonight."

At that moment, the whole tent sent up a collective cry of amazement. Irving had brought out the snakes, from the sound of things.

"Sounds like a good one, at that," Senator Logan said. "May I go on in?"

"Oh, certainly, sir. You go on ahead."

Hospitality demanded that I accompany the senator and his guests across the field and into the tent, but the worm of an idea had twisted its way past my bewilderment and had settled firmly in my mind. Once the revival let out, the whole congregation would be distracted by the spectacle of the senator and his fancy train car. It was all the cover I needed to slip a bit of food into the church so the Bakers wouldn't go hungry that night.

I waited till Senator Logan and his friends were well off across the field. Then I dashed over the berm, skirting the shining hulk of the Pullman car and hustling through town to my home. Quickly, I filled a basket with jars of home-canned soup, a loaf of bread, and the apricot cake I'd baked the day before. Irving and I had only eaten about a third of the cake; there was still plenty left over. Then I slipped, quiet as a thief, into the night. I returned to the church just as the final song of the revival was ending.

I dallied only a few minutes with the Bakers—long enough to clasp their hands and wish them well—and left the church again as the crowd began to disperse across the field. As I'd hoped, folks got up to whooping and pointing at the Pullman car. No one asked why I was out there alone under the naked stars. In fact, no one paid me any heed as I threaded my way through the crowd toward the emptying tent. It still glowed as brightly as ever, a shining beacon against the night-black hills.

I could hear Irving's voice before I reached the tent flap. "Well, of course, Senator, of course. I'm honored—downright honored."

I ducked inside. Irving had left his wooden stage at the far end and stood right beside the center pole, vigorously shaking the senator's hand under the watchful gaze of the senator's two men. No one else remained under the peaked roof. The trampled ground was littered with scraps of paper and the odds and ends that had fallen from people's pockets—thread bobbins, a child's doll. The smell of many bodies pressed close together still hung in the confining space.

Irving caught sight of me and called brightly, "Adella! Come on over and meet Senator Logan."

"We've already met," I admitted as I crossed the lamplit space. I offered the senator my best smile.

He took me in with a swift glance that passed from the crown of my head to my shoes. I couldn't help but feel as if Logan dismissed me with that brief assessing look, but he said to Irving, "Why, this gal of yours is even prettier now that I can see her face properly."

Logan turned to me again with a smile that looked as manufactured as the one I wore. "The pleasure's all mine, Mrs. Wensley. And my goodness, but can't your husband preach."

"He sure can, Senator," I answered.

"What do you think, Mrs. Wensley—I've just invited your husband to become my spiritual advisor. I think the folks of Kentucky want to see that their senator gets right with God and stays that way. And I can't think of a better man to keep me on the straight and narrow than Irving Wensley, the preacher who's set all of Harlan County a-burning with the spirit."

Later that night, after the congregation had finally stopped gawking at the Pullman car and wandered back to their homes—after Irving had shaken Logan's hand for the hundredth time and seen him back onto his fancy railcar—my husband and I walked side by side to our home. I was relieved, for all the while as Irving and Logan showered one another in praise and made outrageous promises, I'd itched with the temptation to glance over my shoulder at the church and see whether the Bakers were keeping well out of sight.

"The senator came all the way down here to ask me man-to-man if I'd be his advisor," Irving said, hands deep in his pockets. "He said I've got a real future in politics, if I want to shoot for it."

"Do you?"

"Well, sure! Why not? The senator said I've got the right kind of air about me. This is the first step, I tell you—only the first step. Today I'm the personal advisor to Senator M. M. Logan. Tomorrow—who knows? Maybe a congressman. Maybe I'll be a senator, too, one day. Imagine how we might come up in the world, then. There's no telling how far I can go. Maybe all the way to the White House, if God is good. Writing laws, shaping the future of Kentucky—maybe the future of the whole nation. What do you think about that?"

I thought Irving was a damn sight too giddy over money and power, to tell you the truth. Didn't the Savior say that it was easier for a camel to pass through the eye of a needle than for a rich man to enter the kingdom? But I told myself I had no room to criticize Irving. It was

I who'd driven him to sin, and I who'd defied his authority to shelter that family in his church.

That night, I did what I'd been accustomed to doing all the years of my marriage, all the days of my life. I kept my mouth shut, like a righteous woman should, and I smiled and turned my eyes meekly down to the road.

5

The morning after Logan's visit, I walked through town and across the tracks, following Collier's Crick deep into the holler where blue shadows fell gently across my trail. Wake robins bloomed amid the roots of oak and hickory, carpeting the steep slopes in snow white and blood red, but I paid little mind to the display. My thoughts were all hung up on Senator Logan—on Irving and his brand-new passion for politics. If my husband meant to aim for a political career, then he'd need to present himself as the sort of man anyone could respect. That meant Irving had best become a father, and right quick, too. The sooner I could give him a baby, the sooner he'd repent his wicked doings and return to the path of righteousness—a path he'd sorely need to walk if he hoped to win votes someday.

The crick took a sharp turn. I followed it around an outcropping of shale and there, at the end of the holler, stood a one-room cabin of old pine logs. The house was surrounded by an extensive garden—vegetables and herbs of every kind flourished in green rows, even in clay pots and old rubber tires stacked one atop another. The garden was so large that it ran from the cabin's front door clear to the bank of the crick. Trellises built from willow twigs were overrun with vines, and tepees of bean plants dwarfed the small chicken coop that stood in their midst. The air was sharp with the medicinal scent of dozens of plants, and the droning of bees came to me over the whisper of the crick. I'd never called on

Anne-Celeste Skaggs, but nevertheless I knew her home at first sight. Who but a granny woman would devote so much of herself to a garden?

"Been wondering when you'd pay me a visit."

I pretty near jumped out of my skin at the sound of that voice. I whirled to face the granny woman herself. She'd come up the trail behind me, though I hadn't heard her footsteps. Anne-Celeste beamed at me while I pressed a hand to my heart and tried to gather my wits. She was somewhere in her upper fifties, with the well-browned, deeply lined face of one long accustomed to working out-of-doors. I'd met Anne-Celeste plenty in town, of course, but she'd always worn a dress on those excursions—faded but well mended, with a serviceable apron tied at her waist. That day she wore old dungarees of some coarse brown cloth, the knees patched with bright-red cotton, and she sported a man's shirt, the sleeves rolled up past her elbows. A gathering basket swung from one arm, its flat belly spilling over with the plants she'd collected somewhere along the crick. Long silver hair lay in a braid over her shoulder. In the seclusion of her own holler, Anne-Celeste seemed more a spirit of the forest than a woman of flesh and blood.

"Come on in," she said, striding past me, "and we'll have a talk. Guess it's been overdue for some time now."

I followed Anne-Celeste through her garden, into the cabin. Though the granny woman's home was small and humble, it was also an inviting place. A bed with a carved headboard stood near the river-stone hearth, and a fine quilt of Carolina lilies was spread neatly across the mattress. An old horsehair rocker with a high back dominated the other end of the hearth, the knitting basket beside it bursting with the folds of a sweater, almost complete. Across the room, a round table stood in the friendly light of a window, crowned by a pitcher of Vaseline glass— its lime-green vibrancy made a pleasing contrast to the bouquet of red flowers it held. A cat lay curled upon the table, sleeping in the warmth of the sunny pane.

"Set yourself down at the table, there," Anne-Celeste said. "I'll put these herbs away and then we'll have a nice cup of coffee, and you can tell me whatever you come to say."

Accordingly, I sat, stroking the cat's tabby fur while Anne-Celeste puttered about her cabin, opening the various cupboards that lined the walls, closing them again, murmuring over her work. She set a tin percolator in the coals of her fire, and a few minutes later she was striding across the small room with a chipped enamel cup in each hand. Her smile had something soft in it, something that spoke of sympathy—even pity.

"I guess you know why I've come," I said, face burning with shame.

Anne-Celeste passed me a cup, then shooed the cat away. She sank into her chair, never taking her eyes from my face. No doubt about it, there was a gravity to her expression. "I never assume the cause for any woman's visit. You'll have to come right out and tell me, Mrs. Wensley—that's the best way to go about it."

"Well . . ." I sipped my coffee to stall for time. Never in my life had I spoken of my predicament to anyone, save my mother. "As you know, I haven't managed to have a baby yet."

"Of course. It has been several years since you and the preacher married."

"Irving has always said it'll happen in the Lord's time, but . . . but the Lord has had plenty of time already, and I'm not getting any younger. I guess there's no harm in helping the Lord along."

Anne-Celeste chuckled. "No, there's no harm that I can see. Been doing just that all my life, more or less. And I reckon after so many years of happy marriage, you're just about busting to have a little one to hold."

Some shadow must have passed across my face at those words—*happy marriage*.

Anne-Celeste paused. "You are eager for a baby, aren't you, Mrs. Wensley? I mean to say . . . this is what *you* want, isn't it?"

"Well, of course I do. What kind of woman doesn't want to be a mother?"

Maybe I sounded too forceful. The granny woman tilted her head to one side and waited for me to go on. But I've always been a stubborn cuss when I want to be. Sensing I'd given too much away, I held my tongue and lifted my chin. Anne-Celeste could make whatever she pleased of my words.

"You know, my dear, a baby won't fix a marriage that's hurting. In fact, babies are a powerful lot of work. They tend to make everything tougher."

"Our marriage isn't hurting," I said, much too quickly.

The corner of her mouth tightened. It wasn't much, but it was enough to tell me she'd seen right through my ruse.

"I do so much for Irving already," I said. "Helping with the church and his revivals, staying in touch with all the women of the valley, keeping house for him. But this one thing—this one thing all women are supposed to do—it's the one thing I can't."

"And if you could only make him a father," Anne-Celeste said gently, "then he might love you again. Is that it?"

My throat tightened so suddenly that I set my cup down with a little more force than I'd intended. Coffee splashed over the rim. "I'm sorry," I croaked.

She rose smoothly and fetched a linen towel from one of her cupboards. She handed the towel to me, and I wiped up the spill first, then dabbed at my burning eyes.

Anne-Celeste laid a hand on my shoulder. "You surely have given Irving all a woman can give."

"Not all."

"Enough that any man ought to be grateful. Let me ask you a hard question, my dear, and take your time in answering. Do you suppose your husband loves you?"

"Well, of course Irving loves me," I said at once.

Anne-Celeste tutted softly and resumed her seat. She sipped her coffee with that warm, motherly smile, allowing me plenty of time to think the matter over.

I didn't want to think it over. The answer was staring me straight in the face. I could see the dreadful answer still, in the form of Ruthie Bell with her dress unbuttoned and her eyes tightly closed, wreathed all about by the sweet blossoms of the yellowwoods. That damnable vision hadn't left me a moment's peace since the day of the picnic.

"Let me tell you something," Anne-Celeste said. "It's the one bit of wisdom I've learned in all my years. Folks that take from you without ever giving . . . they don't love you none, no matter what they say. You're a preacher's wife; you know the Good Book better than most. Now which Gospel is it that says, 'By their fruits you shall know them'? I can't keep the Gospels straight, myself."

"Matthew," I said, automatically, miserably.

"Ah, yes, that's the one. 'By their fruits you shall know them.' I always found that a useful bit of advice—maybe the only advice I've really needed to find my way through this life."

"Irving doesn't just take from me," I said. "He's been awful good to me. We have a fine, lovely home—the best in the valley, I'd wager."

"But is that enough? Is a fine home what you really want from this life?"

She sipped her coffee again, the picture of patience, allowing me to wrestle with this new and startling quandary. I'd never asked myself whether the brick house and the Turkish rugs were things I'd truly wanted. The telephone, the indoor toilet, the electric lights and stove—they were all great luxuries, and truth to tell, I had reveled in my good fortune plenty. But did I have what I wanted? The memory of Ruthie came to me again—Ruthie in my husband's arms—and I recoiled from the truth as from a lick of flame.

"I think you have a powerful lot of love to give," the granny woman went on quietly. "But if the giving doesn't feel like enough, if the giving doesn't bless you as much as any blessing from the Lord ever could, then maybe you're giving to the wrong person. And giving even more—that won't solve the problem. It'll only burn you out, in the end, and leave you empty of everything."

Dazed and sickened by the power of her truth, I shook my head. "I don't follow."

"Let me put it all nice and blunt, then. Do you really want to give a child to a man who has given so little to you? You work and work for Irving's ends, but does he appreciate it, Adella? Or does he only expect more, and better, while he lets his own soul go sliding down into sin?"

I looked up suddenly, held the woman's eye. "What do you know, Anne-Celeste?"

For a long moment, she said nothing. The light seemed to tremble among the flowers in the pitcher, breathless and fragile.

Finally, the granny woman exhaled. "I don't want to break your heart. But I think it's only right that you should know."

"What is it? Tell me. Please."

She reached across the table, laying her callused hand atop my own. "You know I sometimes help women who find themselves in trouble."

I nodded. No need to expound on her meaning; a granny woman could end a pregnancy as easily as she could help bring it about. Maybe more easily, come to that.

"Over the last few years, my dear . . ." Anne-Celeste trailed off. She squeezed my hand, and I couldn't have said whether she hoped to impart strength into my spirit, or find a little will of her own. "I've helped several women of this valley get out of trouble that was caused by your own husband."

The cabin seemed to come apart around me. Table, floor, each individual log of its walls—all felt as if they were drifting up into the vast, airless sky, and I was rising helplessly with them.

"Are you sure?" I stammered.

"I only know what they told me," Anne-Celeste said. "Ordinarily, I wouldn't breathe a word about this to anyone. But it has weighed on me, all these years, to know that the preacher of this town—the most respected preacher in the whole county—has been carrying on like a perfect devil. I've hoped for a chance to tell you the truth. You needed to know, my dear. You needed to know."

A great black weight of grief pulled me back to the earth. I could feel the world reassembling itself; the cabin came together before my burning eyes, the log walls fitting themselves into place, the floor definite below my feet, the bouquet in its green vase filling the air with a cloying sweetness. And the granny woman kept her hand on mine, holding me tightly, lending me her strength.

As I sat dumbfounded in the little pinewood chair, I was beset by the sensation of waking from a dream. There was no going back to the world I'd known before. I could tell that much by the swollen heat in my chest, the way that fire burned hotter by the moment. Blinking and gasping, I asked myself what that feeling was—the roaring blaze that had taken the place of my former shame, burned all my meekness away.

It was anger, I realized with a thrill of wonder. It was outrage. And it made me feel more righteous and mighty than I'd felt in all my life before.

"What do I do now?" I asked, startled at my own calmness.

"Think," the granny woman answered. "Give yourself plenty of time to think over all we've talked about. When the time comes to act, you'll know just what to do, and just how to do it. You'll feel it in your heart."

6

I guess I don't need to tell you that I thought of nothing else in the days that followed my visit with Anne-Celeste. Whenever I closed my eyes, or paused in the housework into which I'd thrown myself with a focus I'd never possessed before, the yellowwood grove would reveal itself again, the branches with their bowers of white blossom lowering into view with a cruelly deliberate slowness. The smell of the flowers would choke me, and I couldn't quite make myself look at Irving directly. The shape of him blurred, or turned transparent as smoke, or darkened into a silhouette, featureless and black.

But the woman in his arms—she was someone new every time. Jeanetta Greenup, with her full bust and her laughing eyes. Or Lindy Wood, whose sleek dark hair had always made me think of the sealskin pelt my grandpop had traded for when he was a boy. May and Amanda, Jenny and Rue—their faces and figures displayed themselves in my mind. Endlessly I questioned which of them had done it, who Irving had pursued. What did they have that I didn't, I asked myself in a rush of agony. I asked, and I found plenty of answers. The curves of their bodies, the lushness of their mouths, the music of their voices. They were more than me, more beautiful, more pleasing to any man. Irving was only a man, after all. Only a man. And they were mothers, most of them, which—as I told myself in those rotten days—made them more woman than I was, too.

How I managed to keep my head around Irving is a mystery I'll never understand. Maybe you can chalk it up to training. In the days that followed my trek to the granny woman's cabin, while I wrestled with the images in my head and did my best to take Anne-Celeste's advice, I gave every impression that nothing was amiss. When Irving entered the house and called out hello, I managed to greet him without any malice. I fixed his supper as ever, ate with him at the table, made all the small, polite noises of approval and support he expected. When he touched me, I managed to stop myself from recoiling. And all the while, I asked myself—asked him, in the silence of my mind—how he could carry on just as he had, preaching to his flock of purity and sin while all the time *(For years, Irving, for years!)* he'd been carrying on like the Devil himself in rut.

As I scrubbed the floors and beat the Turkish rug and dusted the fine linen valances above the windows, I wondered again and again whether any of those girls had done what they'd done with my husband of their own free will, or whether he'd . . . well, not forced them, not exactly. Low-down, no-good, hellfire-bound scoundrel that he was, I knew he wasn't the type to get mean.

But Irving had been the spiritual leader of the whole valley for years. He was the right hand of the Savior, interpreter of God's word. What could any obedient woman really do if the Lord's own mouthpiece took her aside and whispered, *Thou shalt?*

Oh, I thought, and thought, just as Anne-Celeste recommended, and I thought a little more till I wished I could shut my head off like the light switch. *Blink!* Done as quick as that. For with all this thinking, the dark cloud of shame had blown back into my heart, and it battled there with my outrage till the war between the two set a constant queasiness to brewing in my stomach. More than once, I found myself running to the scrap pail in the kitchen, where I spewed up what little was inside me. Wasn't I a miserable mess? You know, it's funny to me now, what a fuss I made over losing Irving. He was never worth the suffering.

On the last Saturday of May, I was scrubbing soot from the bricks of the fireplace with a stiff brush and a bucket of lye water. Another placid supper was behind us, during which I'd scarcely managed to worry a little pork and collards into my churning guts, and Irving had taken himself off to the library room where he liked to compose his sermons. He'd been quieter than usual at supper, almost tense, and for one brief moment I'd allowed myself to wonder if maybe he was feeling guilty for the way he'd done me dirty, for the whole sordid life of lies he dragged around like his own shadow. But no, I wasn't fool enough by then to truly believe Irving had much of a conscience. I finally decided he was probably suffering from a bout of indigestion.

I'd turned myself to scrubbing the fireplace with a zeal that might as well have been intended to scour the helplessness from my heart, and after a while my arms grew weary and the water in my bucket was greasy and black, and the warm flush of pink in the sunset sky looked inviting enough to stand under for a few minutes. Maybe fresh air would help me *think* the way the granny woman had admonished.

I straightened from the hearth, surprised at the pains in my back and my knees. How long had I been down there, after all? Taking up the little tin pail of lye water, I walked through the kitchen to the back door. In one motion, I pushed the door open and flung the contents of my pail. Only after I'd let the water fly did the slender figure in a dress of pale cotton leap into my awareness. I shouted—whether in surprise or remorse for my hastily thrown water, I couldn't say—but thank the Lord, Ruthie Bell dodged aside, and my missile sailed past.

She turned to me on the instant, though, her stricken eyes welling with fresh tears—and they'd already been puffy and red to begin with. The poor creature must have been weeping pretty near the whole month of May.

"I guess you have every right," Ruthie choked out. "I guess I had it coming. I should have held still and let that water hit me."

"No, Ruthie, I didn't mean it. I didn't know you were there at all."

Quickly, I glanced back through the kitchen. Irving was still seques-tered in his library on the west side of the house. I slipped out onto the back stoop and pulled the door shut behind me, watching Ruthie in a stiff, clumsy silence.

She dabbed her eyes with a hankie. "Mrs. Wensley, I came to speak to you tonight. I owe you an apology. I don't have any right to ask your forgiveness, but . . . but I hope I might get it someday. When feelings aren't so hard."

Don't mistake me; it's not that I was happy to see that girl material-ize like a spook in my backyard. But somehow, the sight of Ruthie—so young and yet so brave—set order to my thoughts. I recalled her words on the afternoon of the picnic, as she'd tried to cover her shame. *I didn't even know what he was going to do.* My darkest fears had proven true, then. Irving really had bullied all those women into sin. And this girl was as much a victim of the preacher's lust as I was.

I stretched out my arms and went to her, catching sight of her amazed expression as I pulled her into a tight hug. "You poor girl," I said. "I know what he did. I know everything. Of course I forgive you, Ruthie. It wasn't your fault. I know that now."

She sobbed against my shoulder. "Oh, Mrs. Wensley, if you only knew how bad I've felt about it."

"Hush, dear, hush. I know."

"I wanted to come to you ages ago, but I was dreading it something awful. I was so frightened just to knock on your door. Because what if *he* opened it, you see?"

I clucked and cooed over Ruthie, and held her close till her weeping had ended. Then we sat together on the garden bench, watching the hawk moths dart among the tobacco flowers in the soft blue dusk.

"He's inside, you know," I told her. "But if he comes out and says boo, I'll snap his head right off, don't you worry."

She laughed weakly. "I've been thinking about what I should do."

"Do?" A fresh, new fear unfolded in my gut. "You aren't in the family way, are you?"

Ruthie shook her head. "It never got as far as that, thank the Lord. But it's funny, Mrs. Wensley, how your feelings change. When it first . . . I mean, when you saw . . ."

Gesturing, I urged her on. No need to put words to the thing neither of us wanted to relive.

"I felt so ashamed," Ruthie said. "I pretty near could have died from shame—that's how bad I felt. I thought I'd rather take it to the grave than let anyone know what a harlot I'd been."

"Ruthie—"

She silenced me with a pleading look. "But now," the girl went on, "I think I want folks to know. I mean to say . . . the folks of this church, they deserve to know what kind of a man they've been taking their preaching from. And maybe it'll keep him from going after more girls. Maybe it'll keep the rest of the girls safe."

Ruthie's courage brought tears to my eyes, and a wave of grief to my heart. "Oh," I said quietly, "you do have a very fine spirit. I wish I could agree with you—that it'll keep anyone safe, that anyone will believe you."

She'd been twisting her hankie in her lap. Now she looked up with a tragic face. "But it's true!"

"I know it is. But Irving's the preacher. There isn't a bigger authority in all the valley, unless you count the mine owners, and no one likes them much now. Irving has power, honey. Every man and woman in this valley looks at him and sees truth with a capital *T*. It won't take anything more than a single denial from Irving and they'll turn on you."

"Not if you stick up for me, Mrs. Wensley. If you say you saw it all, they'll believe you."

Swallowing hard, I stared across my dry, struggling garden to the dark line of the woods beyond town. The girl was right. The congregation would believe me if I spoke in her defense, for what woman would admit she'd lost her husband to another girl if it weren't the plain, honest truth?

One idea shone before my inner eye with a serene, moonlike clarity. *I can bring Irving down. End it all for him—his career, his chances with Senator Logan, even his legacy. It's all in my hands. I can make him pay for wronging me. And turnabout is fair play.*

Something long-seeded and rooted deep within my soul recoiled at the thought of crossing Irving's will. A righteous woman would never strike at her husband with such devastating force. Shame billowed inside me, casting its shadow and dimming the fire. But through the density of my guilt, a small voice whispered. *Be as brave as Ruthie. Just this once, Del. Prove to yourself that you can.*

I slung my arm around the girl's shoulders. "Ruthie, I've given you the wisest counsel I know how to give. It's your decision to make, and I hope you'll think it over with care—for I truly believe it won't go kindly for you, if you take on Irving and all his power. But if you decide to speak up, I'll stand with you. You've got my word on that."

We parted ways as the stars emerged in a velvet sky, above the arched backs of the hills. I kept my gaze fixed to Ruthie, who strode, upright and strong, through the night. The moonlit wisp of her figure disappeared up the road, and I thought about endings—how they always came, sooner or later, to every imaginable thing. Irving had always loved to preach about the End of Days. Maybe there was some truth in what he said, for everything was falling to pieces—the mines, the weather, the banks, the tidy order all our lives once had. And maybe something even bigger was breaking apart inside me, dwindling away in a cool, black distance.

∼

I don't mind confessing that I was a perfect tangle of nerves the next morning when Sunday meeting began. I sat, as ever, in my family's pew right up near the front, and though Mom chattered happily beside me and Pop bounced Benjamin's little girl on his knee, I couldn't muster much beyond an occasional weak smile. The church was filling—the crowd pressing at my back, voices rising, the air growing close with the presence of so many people, and all of them eager for Irving to take his place at the pulpit.

I hadn't the least idea when Ruthie Bell would make her declaration—her accusation against my husband. Surely the girl had more sense than to stand up during Sunday meeting and point her finger at the preacher. But though I expected no fireworks that morning, still my thoughts returned unceasingly to the conversation Ruthie and I had shared the evening before. My stomach was knotted on Ruthie's behalf. As the whole community gathered in the chapel, I felt more certain than ever that our congregation would take Irving's part. It would be my testimony—mine alone—that would bring justice for Ruthie and the other women who'd found themselves in Irving's hands.

If Ruthie chose to speak—*when* she spoke—would the congregation turn on me, too? These kindly neighbors and lifelong friends were the sum total of my world. When I assured them that Irving Wensley was an irredeemable scoundrel, they might believe me. But would they forgive me for shining a light on the ugly rot at the heart of our community?

The crowd hushed and settled onto their benches as Irving entered the meetinghouse. I kept my eyes fixed to the back of the pew in front of me, but I could tell from the sound of his clipped, purposeful stride that Irving was in a high dudgeon. We were in for a real fire-and-brimstone sermon that morning, no doubt.

Irving mounted the steps at the front of the chapel. He gripped the sides of his pulpit, his knuckles white with pressure. His stern gaze traveled around the congregation till absolute silence fell. Not even a rustle of movement sounded from the expectant gathering. Irving waited till the silence was absolute, and when he finally spoke, his voice was so calm and precise it sent a chill through my blood.

"My friends, it saddens me—after all the work we've done together to build a righteous kingdom unto the Lord, it breaks my heart to know that there is still a spirit of wickedness that persists in this church. Yes, this very congregation. There are sinners who walk among you, who live among you—yes, even as ravening wolves wearing the clothing of mild-mannered sheep. I tell you, my friends, the Devil is here among us, and he has his claws in some of you."

For one wild moment I was tempted to shout, *Who knows the Devil better than you, Irving Wensley?* As soon as the impulse arose in me, the same old dark fear of judgment hushed it up again.

"You'd be surprised," Irving went on, "who's got the Devil in them and who doesn't. Some of the most innocent-looking lambs of the fold are wolves under the fleece. For I know—the Lord has given me to know—that certain young women of this church have been tempting men and leading them astray. And I know that certain young women have been thinking of spreading stories—lies!—about certain men. Now, I don't know what kind of wickedness leads a girl to seek the destruction of any man, but I know the Devil's work when I see it!"

"Amen," someone cried.

My heart pounded in my ears. Somehow, Irving had learned of Ruthie's plan. Frantically I wondered if he might have eavesdropped on our conversation the night before—but no. The garden bench on which Ruthie and I had sat wasn't close enough to any window. Irving couldn't have listened.

Ruthie must have told someone else. Someone she thought she could trust. My stomach went sick with pity. Whoever Ruthie had turned to—a beloved friend, a sister, maybe even her own mother—had run straight to Irving with the tale.

"And you out there, you girls who might be thinking of setting a lot of gossip running around this church just for the sake of a thrill.

You girls out there who lead men into sin with your wanton ways, you ought to remember the fate of Jezebel. The Bible tells us that Jezebel was an arrogant, scheming woman of loose morals. She thought she could manipulate the powerful men of her father's land. She thought she could make those men dance for her like puppets on a string. She thought she could take what belonged to the great men of the city by rights, but in her arrogance and her lust she reached too far. The Lord did not permit the good men of Tyre to fall into Jezebel's trap—oh no. For the Lord sends his wrath on all the wicked, be they great or small, weak or mighty, man or woman!

"How did Jezebel meet her fate, my friends? Thrown from a palace window—from the very place where she believed herself to be untouchable. And her body was eaten by dogs!"

A sudden commotion at the back of the church drew every eye. I turned on my pew and there was Ruthie, fighting her way past the knees of her benchmates, stumbling over their feet. She broke into the aisle, and for one dizzy moment I thought she would stand strong, throwing her truth into Irving's face. Time seemed to dilate, every beat of my heart hanging like an eternity as I watched Ruthie right herself in the aisle. She tugged her dress straight and faced the preacher with a cold, accusatory stare.

Do it, I urged silently, ready to play my part no matter what the cost.

But Ruthie never said a word. She spun on her heel and fled the church, leaving the congregation to murmur in her wake.

～

How did I ever manage to sit through the rest of Irving's mad spectacle? After Ruthie left, the congregation buzzed with speculation, even as Irving preached on. A smug note of victory rang in his voice and vibrated down my nerves with every word.

I was so full of rancor I could have spit nails, yet what good would it have done now that Ruthie had left? The only clear thought in my head was that I must leave, too. My conscience wouldn't suffer me to remain at Irving's side now that I knew him to be a liar, a cheat, and ten times more a devil than anyone he accused of wickedness.

Through the remainder of the sermon, my toes tapped anxiously, and I wiped my sweating palms on the skirt of my dress. When Irving finally gave the closing prayer, I was on my feet the moment he said "Amen." Not for one more second could I tolerate sitting obediently in my family's pew.

Pacing along the outside of the church, I waited for my parents to finish shaking hands and swapping stories with the friends they saw only when Sundays drew them down from the hills. The moment my mother appeared in the church door, still calling goodbyes over her shoulder, I hooked my arm through hers and tugged her around the corner of the building.

"Land sakes, Adella, what's gotten into you?" she said.

"I need to talk to you, Mom. It's important."

We stood alone in the blue shade on the lee side of the meetinghouse. She blinked at me, shaking her head. "I should guess it's pretty important, for you to haul me around like a sack of potatoes."

"Listen, Mom. That sermon Irving gave today—"

"It was something, wasn't it? All that talk of Jezebel and wicked women."

"Irving isn't the man you think he is."

My mother goggled at me. "What on earth are you saying?"

"He's been cheating on me. Running around with other women—"

"Adella!"

"—and that damn fool sermon of his was just his attempt to place the blame on anyone but himself."

Mom stepped back as if my words had burned her. "Well, I never."

From her reaction, I hadn't the least idea whether she was outraged on my behalf or offended that I would dare to speak ill of the preacher.

Finally she asked in a cautious whisper, "What do you intend to do about it?"

My answer came without hesitation. "I'm going to leave him. Divorce. I'm splitting with that rotten man, and let everyone make of it whatever they will."

I don't know what kind of reaction I'd expected, but I certainly hadn't banked on the one I got. Mom's eyes filled with tears. She covered her mouth with both hands. When she'd more or less composed herself, she said in a trembling voice, "I never thought I'd hear such words from my own daughter. You can't be serious."

"Mom! He's done me wrong."

"The proper thing for a woman to do is to bear up and get through it with prayer."

"How can anyone bear up under such an insult—"

"Divorce, Adella! Why, it's more shameful than any cheating your husband might get up to. I won't hear of it. If you cast off your husband over something as small as this—"

"Small!"

"—then you needn't bother to come around our place any longer. You ought to heed your husband's preaching about Jezebel and the sins of a wayward woman."

With that stinging slap, my mother stormed past, around the corner of the church. As I watched her walk away, I wondered miserably if she was striding out of my life for good.

7

That night over supper, Irving was quiet, but not from any displeasure. On the contrary, his silence carried a distinct flavor of self-satisfaction. While I made the same small talk we were both accustomed to—chattering away about the new baby that needed blessing over at the Estills' place, and how I hoped to put up a few quarts of green beans before the weather got too hot and dry—Irving smiled catlike into the middle distance. He was congratulating himself on the success of his sermon; I could tell that much from the look on his face. However he'd learned of Ruthie's intentions, it was plain as day that he thought himself well clear of harm now. Irving had won that fight before Ruthie could even swing her fist.

Once I understood the reason for his contented smile, I kept my gaze fixed to my soup bowl, even while I talked on in my smoothest, most ladylike tone. I knew by then that I couldn't remain with that man for one hour longer, but the last thing I needed was for Irving to see the going in my eyes. If he discovered my plan before I was halfway out the door, he would find some way of stopping me, just as he'd done to Ruthie.

My mother had made it perfectly clear that if I left Irving, I might as well leave the whole family behind, and the knowledge set on me with a suffocating weight. But the compass of my heart had been pointing in one direction since my visit with Anne-Celeste, and Irving's vicious sermon had only planted my feet more firmly on the path. By and by,

I would find some way of making peace with Mom and Pop. Though it might take many years of patient argument—and a capacity for forgiveness that I doubted even Heaven itself possessed—I was determined to prove to my parents that I was better off a divorcée than married to a low-down snake of Irving's brand. Mom's disapproval wouldn't keep me tethered to the Devil. On that point, I was determined and settled.

That night, as I'd fixed the last supper I would eat in my home, I'd arranged my plans with a calm and meticulous care. We finished our meal. I began clearing the dishes away, feeling the moment of departure drawing steadily nearer. I prayed Irving wouldn't notice how my hands shook and my eyes darted. I wondered whether my cheeks were bright with a flush of excitement—they certainly felt like embers to me. But Irving was still wrapped in the mantle of his victory. He retreated to his library and closed the door, and with a quick sigh of relief, I went up to our room.

I paused only a moment to look around the bedroom. The carved furniture and plush wool rug had once been the special pride of my home. Now I saw nothing to admire in those trappings of wealth. The comfort in which I'd spent the last eight years struck me suddenly as a kind of profanity—for where had Irving's money come from, if not from the pockets of poor miners?

Those two hobos who'd passed through town on the day of the picnic—they'd seen the poverty of our people clearly enough, but Irving's collection plate hadn't slowed its circulation since the Great Crash. Nor had he given the congregation any respite since the strikes began. If anything, he'd leaned harder into his apocalyptic fervor, banging his fist on the pulpit and shouting, *See how the fields are barren and dry! The land itself cries out for relief! See how suffering and degradation have touched every man, every household. How can you deny that the End of Days has come? How much time do you have left to get on the right side of the Lord?*

Blind fool that I was, I'd gone along willingly with Irving's wicked scheme. I had profited from the suffering of my own people—from the fear my husband instilled in them every Sunday of their lives. He didn't thump his Bible and raise serpents in the air for the salvation of anyone's soul. He did it to make them all afraid—to keep the collection coming, even when their money would have been better spent feeding and clothing their children.

At my bedroom window, I pulled back the velveteen curtain and gazed across town to the blue hills. The sky above the forested ridge was gentle and sleepy with dusk. As a child, I'd often set at the edge of the porch with my head on my mother's shoulder, watching the same soft twilight pour down into the valley below.

Desperate and grieving, I sent my heartbroken thoughts toward my parents' home with all the sincerity of a prayer winging up to Heaven. *I can't stay with him, Mom. You'll just have to understand. It isn't only the women—though all that's bad enough. But if I stay with this man one minute longer, it'll damn my soul for good.*

The curtain fell from my hand. The time had come to find my salvation.

I reached behind my back and fumbled loose the buttons of my dress. When it fell around my ankles, I shimmied out of my slip and rolled down my stockings, then put everything neatly away in the carved-oak chifforobe. Stockings and ladylike attire wouldn't do a bit of good where I was going.

In Irving's wardrobe I found an old pair of his trousers, a linen shirt with a turned-down collar, and his spare set of suspenders, the leather almost black with a patina of age. Quickly, I yanked a set of sturdy wool socks onto my feet and stuffed them into my gardening boots. In minutes, I was dressed for travel.

Irving had been a great camper and mountaineer in his younger days; he kept his old gear stowed in the back of our bedroom closet. Fearful of making the smallest sound, I eased the closet door open, then sank to my knees to paw through forgotten relics of our eight years together. Looking back, I'm surprised at how dispassionately I cast aside the memories of a marriage—the album of photographs, the little gifts Irving and I had given one another, the cards and letters our friends had written to us on our anniversaries and at Christmastime. I don't recall the least twinge of regret as I dug through the contents of that closet. Maybe some instinct in me knew that memories would have locked around me like shackles if I'd allowed them to touch my heart.

My groping hand closed on the strap of a canvas rucksack. I eased it out of the closet and, when I saw Irving's army bivouac tightly rolled and strapped to the bottom of the pack, I took it as an encouraging sign from On High.

Into the rucksack went a change of clothing, the rags and belt I used for my monthly indisposition, and all the small objects of value I could round up on a circuit of our bedroom: the pearl earrings Irving had given me for my twenty-third birthday; a silver bracelet and a gold chain; my mother's wedding ring, too small to fit onto any of my fingers. Mom had given me the old ring a few years before, when her hands had grown too puffy to wear it any longer. I intended to keep that ring with me forever, not to sell it, but the rest of the jewelry I would gladly sacrifice—even my own wedding band, which I slipped from my finger without a pang of remorse.

Last, I went on my toes to the highboy that stood beside our bedroom door. Irving kept his cache of emergency money in the top drawer, behind his collection of neckties. I opened the drawer slowly, fearful that it would let out a squeal. He'd rolled the sheaf of bills just like his neckties—a coil of cash standing on its side, loosely bound with a piece of twine.

Now that I'd come to see my situation with agonizing clarity, I knew the money wasn't mine to take, any more than it'd been Irving's to keep. It belonged to the congregation. I stared for a good, long while at that roll of cash, wondering whether I could forgive myself for the theft.

But I would need something to sustain me till I could find a new place to alight, a new life to lead, and if I left the money in Irving's drawer, it would never make its way back to the congregation, anyhow.

"Sweet Jesus, forgive me," I muttered, slipping the cash from its hiding place.

I counted the money twice: fifteen dollars, all in single bills. Into the rucksack it went, nestling deep in an inner pocket, and all the while I prayed that I hadn't gone and made myself into as big a sinner as Irving was.

Once I'd safely stowed the money, however, a warm sense of satisfaction came over me. No doubt, Irving had squirreled away many such reserves, all around the house. After all, he'd never told me about this money in his necktie drawer; I'd stumbled across it one day while doing the housework. If he had one secret hoard of money, why not others? And maybe it makes me wicked, but I confess I got a real tickle out of picturing Irving's dismay when he reached into that drawer only to find that his fifteen dollars had up and vanished.

Surely the residual thrill of that image inspired me to commit another act of petty theft. As I adjusted the pack on my shoulders and breathed deep, ready to step outside the room and into my new life, my eyes landed on Irving's tweed cap, which he wore out hunting. I snatched it from the top of his dresser and crammed it onto my head with a triumphant laugh—though not a very loud one, to be sure. Only then did I discover Irving's bone-handled hunting knife—the one that folded its blade neatly into the handle. The knife had been hidden under the cap. Well, I took the blade, too, and dropped it in my pocket. A gal could never tell when such a tool might come in handy, and I aimed to be prepared for anything.

Just then, the night was pierced by the familiar high-pitched whine of a coal train's wheels rolling slow along the track. Owing to the strike, two trains had run through town every Sunday, causing Irving to cuss under his breath at the disrespect to the Sabbath. No more trains would pass through the valley till late the following morning. My time had come.

I descended the stairs with an exaggerated tread.

Irving stuck his head out of his study, just as I'd expected—as I'd meant for him to do. He was scowling, ready to tell me off for stomping like a buffalo while he was trying to read and pray. But when he saw me in a man's getup, the rebuke died on his tongue.

I took the last few steps with my eyes locked on his, holding his attention with a ruthless mettle.

"Just what do you think you're doing?" he finally said.

"Going." My hand was already on the door.

"Where?"

I shrugged. I didn't know the answer to that question, anyway.

Irving recovered a little from his shock. He started toward me. "You can't leave the house looking like that, Adella. It's scandalous."

"Just try and stop me."

I stepped out onto the porch. Summer had arrived, and the light lingered, deep and blue, along the dells. The coal-rich hills that stood sentinel over our valley were already grading into the falling night, and the first white stars looked down to see what I would do. There was a cool, bright scent to the air—a breeze off the Cumberland River, heady with the promise of a broader world out there along the tracks. Through this easy stillness, the coal train moved slow and steady, the rattle of its cars and the rhythm of its wheels calling to me, calling.

"What is this?" Irving asked, urgent and low, fearful of drawing attention from the neighboring houses.

I looked back at him, tempted to laugh at his helpless expression. "Why, I'm surprised you don't know. This is the End of Days, Irving, just like you've always said. And here comes your judgment."

I set off for the rails. What little effort it cost me to turn my back on my husband. All my life I'd lived in fear of these men of God, and yet when the moment came, when I felt a greater power summon me, I didn't even have to say the words *Get thee behind me*. I marveled at my own ease, the steadiness of my legs, as I walked away. I thought, *No one ever tells you how easy it is to up and go*.

His hand came down on the rucksack, snapping me to a halt.

I spun on him, quick as a dog fit to bite. "Get your hands off me, you no-good cheat!"

"Adella, really—"

"I should have done this the day I caught you at the picnic with Ruthie Bell. Just be glad I didn't cut you dead in front of everyone then—or today at meeting. Why, you two-timing son of a—"

"Adella! Your language! And why are you still dwelling on the past? I told you, the Lord forgives—"

"Good for Him. I don't. Now, if you want the whole town to witness a scene, keep it up, and I'll go hollering up and down about what you've done. But if you want to keep your dignity intact, you'll take your hands off me and let me leave without a fuss."

There was a pause while he considered my threat. His throat worked. I had him where I wanted him, and we both knew it. The wheels were singing high-pitched and sweet on the rails—*Come on*, they crooned. *Do it now, while you know you can.*

"You can't just go." He sounded urgent now—desperate. "A woman can't look after herself in this world."

"Oh, the world has already ended," I rejoined. "Didn't you hear the news? The old ways are scorched in the fire of God's wrath. I'm going out there to make a new world, without you. I don't need anybody but myself."

The train made a rhythmic *thunk* as its last few cars began to bump and jar along the tracks.

I stepped away from Irving. The hand that had restrained me fell to his side. He cast one final, helpless look at me. "Del," he said quietly, "please reconsider."

But of course, that was just the trouble. I hadn't reconsidered anything till recent days, and now I couldn't help but see this life I'd led—this marriage to which I'd submitted—in the stark light of God's honest truth.

I walked away from Irving Wensley and strode into the twilight. He wouldn't follow me, I knew, nor would he shout. The last thing he wanted was to draw the attention of the whole damn valley. There were only a few steps between our garden gate and the road, and only a few steps more to cross that road and climb the berm with its knee-high weeds trembling from the vibration of the train. The train cars rolled past, docile dragons moving in a tame file, like creatures in a dream, trailing the smell of coal and a bright, watery, cold sense of rusted steel.

Through narrow eyes and the dim colors of dusk, I watched for one of those ladders at the ends of the passing gondolas, like the ladders I'd seen the two hobos climb on their exodus from the valley. Most of the cars were open-topped coal carriers, but I spotted a regular boxcar, four-sided with a proper roof, though its rolling door was gone—removed or fallen away. My attention fixed on the wide-open mouth of that boxcar. I put out my hand and my chosen mount seemed to come to me eagerly, obedient. It was the simplest thing in the world, to place my palms flat against its floor, kick my feet off the earth, and roll inside. The car lifted me from the bosom of my valley. It carried me into the night.

The inside of the car was black as pitch. It smelled faintly of rot with a sweetish overtone, and of drying hay and river water, of a wide-open world, of movement, of a wise and sacred lonesomeness.

The pack fell from my shoulders. I crawled back to the car's open mouth and crouched there, watching the town grow smaller and dimmer as I rode farther along the track. Irving was a small, pale shape at the edge of our yard, and then he was a dot, and then he was nothing, consumed by the vast hills and sky, by the darkness that made both mountains and sky into one.

No one ever tells you how easy it is to up and go. Just like that, I was free.

8

Once distance had swallowed my hometown, exhaustion struck me, sudden and powerful as the onset of some feverish illness. Hollowed out and shivering, I pushed my rucksack against the wall of the car and huddled beside it, facing out where the forest and the river and the lonesome shacks of bent-bodied miners had vanished into the same vast body of the evening.

The black sky, the world, the state of things were all so much bigger than I'd understood them to be, than I'd even thought possible. I'd lived all my life in a dream where one only needed to call upon the Great Name if one wished to take hold of the world and master it. Proclaim the power over sickness and misfortune, and they would meekly vanish. Tell the Devil to get out, and the Devil would go running. But we'd prayed against the poverty, all of us in the valley, and it had only sunk its talons deeper into the body of our church. We'd proclaimed ourselves untouched by suffering, by drought, by hunger and want, yet there wasn't one of us who didn't suffer—save for Irving and me, and now I understood that we had multiplied the pain of our followers by taking what we didn't need.

The train picked up its speed. Night expanded around me, the dim, half-seen landscape flying past. A new world revealed itself, the velvet folds of forested hills so numerous they rivaled the stars in the sky, and the silver track of the river scribing itself into darkness. The water, with its dim adornment of reflected stars, drew shyly toward the tracks and receded again and hid itself among shadows, and as I watched those arcs of river reach for me and withdraw to a mysterious expanse and purpose, I was beset by a helpless fear, certain I was looking upon the very face of God, or one of His faces, and seeing Him clearly for the first time in my small and wayward life.

How tiny it all had been—our church, even the county Irving ruled like a king. These insignificant particles of dust, these specks among the immensity of Creation—how quickly the valley that had once been the sum total of my world was lost to sight. Once, I'd thought my life important and whole. The realization that I had only ever been small and broken set my head to spinning. And it sickened me, how easy it had been to leave everything behind. Irving's hand had stalled me, but only long enough for me to proclaim my strength and send that devil packing.

And oh, the bile that rose in my throat when I realized I could have left any time I pleased. It was pretty near enough to choke me, for now I saw my own unhappiness, not through a glass darkly but with relentless clarity. I looked unflinching into the past, and though the cup of my years was bitter, I drank of it, and swallowed the truth.

I'd never been happy as Irving's wife—not truly, not for long. Whatever moments of peace or pleasure I'd gained from my marriage had been brittle as ice, and quickly buried under the weight of a stifling, ever-present shame.

Now, I don't mean the shame that had come on me lately—the realization that Irving and I had been sucking our poor flock dry. I mean a deeper degradation, the kind I believe all the women of my church carried somewhere in their hearts, even if they didn't wear it on their sleeves. I'm a daughter of a Cumberland miner; my roots were sunk in Appalachian soil since the time before my birth, and the only word I'd ever received was handed down to me from the pulpit of the Church of God with Signs Following. Never mind that Irving couldn't have tied his own shoes without me there to help him. He couldn't have fed himself a proper supper, or pressed the wrinkles from his own shirts, or kept the congregation following in line behind him without my aid—my unseen, thankless work among the women of the valley. Hell, Irving couldn't even organize a picnic without me. But what did God have to say to the women of His church? Repent, you sinners—you ingresses of evil, you wellsprings of lust and disgrace. Be meek, be silent, and let Man guide you, guard you, tell you how to think, tell you how to speak, tell you how to live.

That first night on the train—my first night of freedom—the days of my youth crowded around me like moaning specters, and I pulled the rucksack onto my lap and pressed my face against the familiar substance of canvas and the things I'd packed inside, but nothing could shut out the vision of my wasted, stolen years.

The first ghost that cried over my trembling shoulder was the memory of Irving's courtship. I was twenty when he first took an interest in me—a tall, slender girl with a serious demeanor. But I knew when to laugh, and I was never last to enter the grange hall when someone cooked up an excuse for a dance.

That was where Irving first made his intentions known—the harvest dance of my twentieth year, a few months after he'd won the coveted nomination to the ministry at our church.

You see, Irving had just replaced old Mr. Leslie, who'd been preacher all through my childhood and who died peacefully in his sleep at the end of August. Leslie had been white-haired and wrinkled for as long as I'd known him, so didn't I think it was fine and exciting to see a young, handsome minister taking the pulpit every Sunday. And Irving's sermons had been full of fire, right from the start. He pulled the snake trick on his first day, raising a twisting rattler in his strong, young fist, shouting that the Devil had no place in our valley. We were sold, all of us, by his display of righteous power. I guess I was more sold on Irving Wensley than anybody else was.

The new preacher was the most thrilling development to hit Harlan County in decades, and when he asked me to accompany him for a song at the harvest dance, I gladly accepted. Before our reel was half-finished, he leaned close and murmured in my ear, "Miss Adella, the Lord is moving me to ask your daddy if I might have his blessing to court you properly. What do you say about that?"

Well, what would any Kentucky girl say to being courted by the preacher? And a minister of Irving's stature, drawing bigger crowds every Sunday and getting up revivals that had the whole valley talking for weeks afterward—well! I was so delighted by the prospect that I left the dance before it had finished and begged a ride up the long dirt road to my home in the hills, and I threw my arms around my daddy's neck and told him breathlessly that the new preacher wanted me to be his wife.

There's precious little to say about the courtship itself. I can't recall much of those months; the whole affair blurred right past. I know I went walking with Irving, always with some cousin or aunt along as chaperone, and cooked him supper in my mother's outdoor kitchen so I could impress him with my housekeeping. If Irving and I ever spoke of our plans for the future—our ideas about love and eternity, our thoughts about the small and temporal but lovely things—I can't recall a word of it now.

I do remember this: Irving's all-valley meetings, the old-fashioned tent revivals, were growing in popularity. Each month when he raised the canvas tent in the field behind our church, the crowds would flock from all points along the valley. Some two or three hundred miners and millers and their families would get to singing and stomping and shouting "Hallelujah!" while Irving strutted on a stage built from old crates and plank wood. Revivals were the only fun to be had sometimes in the hard gray lives of mining families—and when he got the crowd good and whipped up, the collection plate made its rounds. Irving trusted me to count up the collection when the revivals were finished, and as the coins slipped through my fingers, I thought God had blessed me for sure, to drop me in the lap of such a capable provider.

Another ghost, more haggard and harrowing, leaned across my other shoulder to cry into my ear.

Irving and I were married after a year and a half of courting. I moved right into his fine brick house, which he had built almost the moment I accepted his proposal. Within the year, as his revivals continued to flourish, he equipped our home with electric lights and running water—luxuries few in the valley enjoyed. I settled into my duties happily enough. If Irving bossed me a little, I didn't mind—not for long—because that was the order of things. The husband was supposed to be the head of the wife, like the Good Book said, and I had no reason to feel discontent with such an arrangement. Wasn't my life immeasurably better than it had been before our marriage? Didn't I have more than any country girl could dream of?

But as the months passed and my body refused to do what the Lord had created it to do, Irving took to praying over me each night, begging God to bless this marriage with abundance and righteous issue, and the seed of failure and misery was planted in my heart.

Irving's discontent grew over the years. By and by, the character of his nightly prayers changed. They were no longer beseechings to a merciful God but rebukes toward the Adversary, toward whatever foul spirit had bedeviled my womb and left it stubbornly empty. Many a time I was tempted to pipe up midprayer and suggest he pray over his own self, for it took two to make a baby. But such impertinence was beyond me then. All I could do was hold my tongue and keep my eyes turned down and bear with patience my husband's rebukes, and criticisms, and sly insinuations, and the way I'd catch his eyes wandering to younger, fresher girls.

I bore it more often than I'd realized. I'd put up with more than any woman should bear in silence, till the whole facade of our marriage had fallen in like a collapsing mine shaft, in a great cloud of choking dust and a rush of scouring fire.

Collapsed. Ended.

The ghosts crowded against my shuddering body, leaning over my bent head to cry and wail. I had cared for the women of the valley and given them kindness, but I had also led them like a bellwether into my husband's tent. Every good thing I'd done was undone by the sin of my willful blindness, my complacency in Irving's devilish work. The life of service I'd lived so gladly revealed itself among that crowd of specters as a cold body unanimated by any least spark of the divine.

As if the dissolution of my past weren't enough, I now understood that everything was falling apart at once—the strikes at the mines, men killing men, the countless families suffering—all across the land, not only in Harlan County. Good people, kind people who trusted in God yet hadn't two pennies to rub together. Nor would the God in whom those good souls believed send a drop of rain to fall on their fields.

The End of Days had come, just like Irving had always said they would, but where was our sweet return? Where was the Savior who would lift up the righteous and allay the suffering of His people?

God didn't seem much bothered by the fact that everything had come crashing to its bitter end while He had failed to provide the relief the Good Book promised. And as the vibration of the train shuddered through me, as the rocking of my car and the rumble of the wheels seemed to disperse the very substance of my soul into the cool, blue night, I asked myself what we were all careening toward—all of us who made up this ended, unmade world. Before the world ripped apart for good and scattered its own ashes to the wind, could I find the purpose and divinity that had eluded me all these years?

The dreadful cold in my gut told me such a hope was futile. But my heart was still beating, and the tears on my cheeks were warm, so I knew I hadn't been ripped apart and scattered yet. There was still time to live a life of good works. And I would do it on my own terms.

I prayed. What else does one do in these situations?

"Oh God."

But I couldn't think of anything else to say.

I went on saying it. "Oh God, oh God," and little by little the ghosts that surrounded me quieted, and stood up straight, and drifted out through the boxcar's open door, where they joined the pale mist gathering above the black density of the forest. "Oh God, oh God," I muttered, till I could no longer say if I was afraid or rejoicing, till I no longer felt as if I were praying at all.

I thought, *Maybe there isn't much difference between fear and rejoicing. Maybe it's all the same wellspring of awe. Maybe we decide whether the water tastes of joy or despair once it's in our mouths and we're already swallowing it down.*

Panic left me then. I uncurled myself, crawled on hands and knees to the open mouth of my boxcar. Outside, the long sweep of night sky dipped into the cleft of the valley, into the mist that held all my ghosts, and the greatness of the sleeping earth filled me with a peace no prayer had ever granted. The world was boundless. Nothing out here would constrain me. I sat cross-legged in the door, and by the stars' borrowed light, I watched the land ripple and move and echo itself in shades of deepest blue. Nearer to the tracks, suggestions of life froze between clumps of brush—owls lifting from the ground, the slinking bodies of coyotes suspended midtrot, isolated images in a blur of movement.

I watched the ended, endless world till my eyelids grew heavy and my neck ached with weariness. Then I crept back to my rucksack and propped myself against it, and despite the chill of the night wind, I slipped into a rough, shallow sleep. My dreams were all of movement, of wide-open spaces, of all the hands that held me opening and falling away.

9

The day I met Louisa Trout, it was June in the sky but October in the earth.

At dawn I'd woken from my very inadequate sleep with a crick in my neck and a gnawing hunger almost powerful enough to overwhelm my sense of sheer amazement. I'd actually left the Cumberland—my church, my husband. It was all behind me now. The lonesomeness and fear of that first night was behind me, too. Day had come in bright jubilation; the land flew past the door of my boxcar, enticing and new. I'd rolled right out of the valley and into another life.

I sat myself down at the edge of my car, dangling my legs in a wind of motion, watching the last blue whisper of Harlan County's flat-topped hills sink into the haze. Under cover of night, while I'd slept against my rucksack, the train had traversed from coal country to farm country. Farmland proved to be a damn sight emptier and grimmer than I'd imagined. I felt certain that the countryside should have been green in early summer, but the low hills and broad fields were bare and brown, dry as the heart of autumn.

Anyway, I was set right there at the edge of my boxcar because I hadn't a lick of sense that first day and didn't yet understand the danger. I can laugh now at the purblind callowness of that woman in stolen trousers and suspenders, her legs hanging off the side of a freighter. The truth is, I'm lucky to be alive and laughing. Only God knows how many never made it through those years between the two great wars. Only God can say how many more were left permanently hollowed out and bleak, every good thing that had once been inside them withered down to dust, like those fruitless fields. But there I was, entertaining myself with the mere fact that, because of my boxcar's doorless state, I could sit deep inside and watch the world move past like an endless talkie on a theater screen or I could perch right at the edge of my conveyance, and out on the edge I felt like I was a part of the film, the star of the show.

I couldn't tell you exactly where my train was that morning. You get out into farm country and it's all the same flatness, an identical array of barns and fields and farmhouses, a washed-out gray in a long, glaring distance, and any little town you find clinging to the edge of the tracks is exactly like all the others. But the engine blared ahead of a crossing, and I pulled my legs back inside fast, which was all that saved me, I'm sure.

A deep, metallic boom repeated down the line of the cars, growing louder the nearer it came, till with a burst of thunder the reduced momentum took my car and tumbled me right over into the back of the conveyance. The wall of the boxcar smacked cold into my face. I was dazed by the noise and the violence, and for a moment I felt as if I were suspended in some unsettling dream or in a substance thick as honey. I could detect the graininess of corrosion and grime against my cheek—elemental particles of boxcar. The metallic shudder ran right through my body, and the moment my bones quit shaking, I snapped back into reality. I crouched on the floor, ready to spring up and dart in any direction, but where could I run to? One after another, the cars crashed and lurched and rocked on their wheels, slowing with the engine.

The train was crawling, or so it seemed to me after hours of smooth gliding through anonymous farmland. The train rolled through a stand of chinquapins whose leaves had given up their gloss to the dust. Beyond the oaks, a park spread along one block—pagoda, stone benches—and it would have been pretty if spring hadn't been so dry that year. The town itself came into view, not much more than a handful of white-washed houses, a few brick shops along Main Street, and barefoot children following a skinny dog along the sun-struck curb.

The town was gone in a blink, but the inevitable railyard followed, where during harvest season—and assuming the drought didn't hold—the cars would fill with grain and roll off along the tracks to feed a hungry nation. That morning the yard held only a few freight cars, rust red with an air of patient waiting, or of abandoned hope; I couldn't decide which.

"Hey!"

It was a woman's voice shouting from somewhere in the yard. I scuttled to the edge of my car and peeked out, and there she was, running alongside, dressed in trousers and a man's shirt, like I was. She was red-faced from the effort, and her eyes held an unmistakable strain of desperation. A man sprinted behind her, too—her mate, I thought. I didn't have time to take in more than his general shape, which was big and broad. He loped like a wolf on the woman's heels.

The woman stretched out a hand. By instinct, I reached for her and caught hold and heaved myself backward into the car. She came up after, legs still kicking, and sprawled atop me. She rolled away at once.

I picked myself up, crouched and cautious, for the crossroads were behind us now and the train would soon increase its speed. The man's big slab of a hand caught onto the edge of our car where the door ought to be. I took hold of his wrist, just as the woman cried, "No!"

It was already too late. The man had jumped as I'd pulled, and all at once he was in the car with us. Maybe it was the triumphant way he rose to his feet and stood there, black against the square of sunlight, or maybe it was the way the woman pressed herself in fear against the forward wall of the boxcar. One way or another, I knew on the instant that I'd made a dire mistake.

The man looked down at me with a slow grin. His face was dark with grime, his beard bristling like the ruff of a hunting animal. But he was no beast of forest or field. His eyes shone with an all-too-human hunger for violence.

"Got any money?" he said.

Somehow, I restrained myself from glancing at my rucksack, stowed in a corner of the car. The fifteen dollars I'd taken from Irving's dresser were hidden in that pack, along with the jewelry I'd brought. I could feel the bone-handled hunting knife in my trouser pocket, pressing against my hip, and I asked myself frantically whether it was smarter to stand up and face him—draw my knife to defend myself—or remain cowering on the floor.

The man took a step toward me. "I said, got any money?"

"No."

"Let's see if you do or not."

Between one beat of my heart and the next, he held a knife of his own; it flashed in the morning light as it leaped into his hand. My eyes fixed on the blade's edge. A yellow bead of sunglow moved there, slow as a drop of honey. The hand that held the knife was perfectly steady. I knew he would gut me like a fish and never think twice about it.

Before I could so much as scream, the woman hurled herself across the car and seized our tormentor by his forearm. She was shorter than I and thinner, but she bore that great snarling bear of a man toward the doorless opening with astonishing energy.

Just like that, he was gone, shoved out into the mobile landscape, and I found myself on my feet with one arm around the woman's waist to stop her going out after him.

I didn't look to see what became of him. I didn't want to know. I just stood there holding on to the woman while she cussed and spat into the open air. Then the train screamed again, and the cars took up the familiar banging, and both of us crouched on the floor, side by side, while the boxcar shuddered around us.

She introduced herself once the town was far behind and there was nothing to see but more of the same dry farmland. She'd caught her breath by then. We both sat against the rear of the car, heads leaning back to rattle against steel, legs stretched out before us in near-identical tweed.

"I'm Louisa Trout," she said, "from Seattle, or close enough to it."

Now that the immediate danger had passed, I looked her over closely. She looked younger than I, twenty-two or twenty-three at most, though long exposure to the sun had browned her skin deeply and lines of laughter or worry had already begun forming around her eyes. She had wind-tousled hair the deep auburn of aged copper, cut in the cheekbone bob women of our age favored back then.

"You seem awfully cool," I observed, "for a gal who just threw a man from a moving train."

Louisa rolled her ankles comfortably and yawned. "He deserved it. Anyway, you can't get all worked up about things like that, or you'll never make it from one day to the next."

That philosophy seemed sensible enough. Yet as she watched the landscape rolling past, I observed her closely, albeit from the corner of my eye; I didn't want to give offense by staring. Louisa was young, but she wasn't youthful. She had an air of thoughtful sobriety, as if she were used to weighing and calculating every scene, every moment—alert for any small opportunity that life might cast in her path and ready to seize it, to make the most of the slightest advantage—which might, after all, spell the difference between disaster and survival. Merely by sitting close to her, I imagined I could feel the pressure of some tender and beloved burden, the weight she carried upon her heart. Well, who didn't carry a burden, those years? We all felt it—the dissolution, the knowledge that the old world had slipped irretrievably from our hands.

She said, "I sure do appreciate you pulling me aboard back there."

"I wish I hadn't pulled that man up," I said. "I thought he was with you—thought he was only running to catch the train."

"He was running to catch me. I don't have any money—just sent what little I could spare back home. But he would have chicken-hawked me for sure."

"Chicken-hawked?"

Louisa turned her head and looked at me, expressionless, except for the grim line of her mouth. I took the meaning from her ominous silence.

"This train showed up just in time to save me," she said. "Any other hobos on board?"

"*Other* hobos? I'm not."

She glanced at me sharply, and one corner of her mouth tightened in a saucy smile. "Oh, aren't you?" Before I could defend myself, she added, "What's your name, anyway?"

I hesitated. For the first time it dawned on me that I was never going back to Harlan County, not even if I brought Mom and Pop around to my way of thinking. A preacher's wife who'd walked away from her marriage would never be welcomed back into the fold. She'd be cast to the fringes of the flock, left to live on the edge of society, the object of every suspicion and the subject of every crass rumor that slinked its way along the valley floor.

And I hadn't merely walked away. I'd jumped a freight train like a perfect hoyden. Like a Jezebel, in fact.

There didn't seem to be much danger that this wiry little she-hobo would recognize my husband's famous name. Her accent was all Yankee, and if a gal like Louisa had ever set foot in Harlan County, I would have heard about it. The women of the valley would have buzzed over that story like bees after a bear busts open a hive. Still, caution restrained me.

"Del," I answered.

"Just Del? Nothing more than that?"

I shook my head.

She said, "Where do you come from?"

"Oh, some dusty little town in Kentucky. Not worth mentioning."

"Not too far from home. You fresh out here? A greenhorn?"

"First day." I laughed at myself, aware of my unawareness. "Afraid I don't know the first thing about riding trains. I just knew I had to go, so when I saw my chance, I took it."

"That's the way for most of us." She closed her eyes, leaning her head back again. The deep shadows of the boxcar fell gently on her face and her hard, thoughtful expression softened and lifted away. For a moment she was cast in a gentle, girlish peace. "One day, you realize you've got to move on, or you'll wither up and die where you are. I wish somebody told me sooner there's better money on the rails than in any town—or, I guess, any city. Not that the money's *good*, mind you—nobody's getting rich. But if you're willing to hop a train and go wherever it takes you, at least you can get by."

The next moment, she opened her eyes and looked at me with a cajoling, almost mischievous expression. I couldn't help smiling; she already seemed so much a friend, even though we'd only just met, and not in the best of circumstances. "Well," she said, "what's your story, Del? How did you end up on the rails?"

I decided it couldn't hurt if she knew one small part of the truth. "I left my husband. He hasn't been treating me right, so I walked out on the lousy bum and took off to make my own way."

Louisa laughed. "That's how you do it. I find myself without my husband, too, but you won't catch me crying over him—not anymore. He was a real shit. Took me long enough to figure that out."

"Took me long enough to figure out the same," I said quietly. "Eight years."

Louisa whistled. "That's a long time. Too long, if you ask me. But you're clear of him now; that's all that matters. Where you headed, anyway?"

I'd spent the whole morning asking myself that question—first with the edge of panic pressed against my throat, and then, once I'd wrestled my anxiety back into silence, in a stoutly practical way. But I hadn't come up with a good answer. I didn't even know which direction my train was headed in. How could I decide where I was going?

I turned the question around on Louisa.

"Just now," she said, "it appears I'm headed south. Damn it, anyway. I need to get out west. I intend to be in Wenatchee by September."

"Where the heck's Wenatchee?"

"It's in Washington," she said, "this side of the mountains."

Struggling to recall the map of the States that had hung on the schoolhouse wall, I rustled up a vague recollection that Washington was far across the continent, butted up somewhere against the ocean.

"That's awful far away," I said.

Louisa sighed comfortably, folding her arms. I wondered if she was settling in for a nap. She said, "Washington is worth getting back to, I can tell you that, and Wenatchee is as close to Eden as anyone's got since the days of Adam and Eve. Fruit trees as far as the eye can see, covering the golden hills."

"That's . . . good," I offered.

She eyed me for a long moment, her expression wry, almost mocking.

"Fruit-picking pays better than anything else," she said. "Apple pickers can make almost a dollar a day, and there are weeks' worth of apples to harvest. You'd know that, if you weren't such a greenhorn."

For all I'd mused that morning on the questions of where I was going and what I'd do when I got there, I still had no good answer, and my brush with the chicken hawk had driven home the grim reality that I hadn't the least idea how to survive on the rails. I didn't even know how to get off the train—and nature was calling with an increasing urgency, which served to underscore my helpless state with especial emphasis. As Louisa and I conversed, I found myself taken by her confidence, her independent spirit—to say nothing of her ready knowledge of the rails, the destinations that lay along them, the best ways a hobo might earn her pay. It occurred to me that Louisa would make an ideal teacher, and she was the perfect pattern for my future, a woman self-assured, determining and building her own future, her own fate. In short, she was exactly the sort of girl I wanted to be.

"Guess I've got a lot to learn," I conceded, "but it's only my first day. I pick things up quick. You'll teach me what I need to know, won't you?"

"You'll have to pick things up from someone else. It's nothing personal, Del, but I don't have the leisure to play nursemaid to a wet-behind-the-ears hobo. I've been riding the rails more than a year now, and I aim to make this my last season. If I can get to Wenatchee in time for the apple harvest, I should be able to earn enough dough that I can go back home for good."

"I won't hold you up," I said. "Swear on all that's holy."

"You will. I'm sorry, but I've got to move on faster than you'll be able to travel. Three months will go by fast—thank God—and there's nothing in the world that can keep me from that apple harvest. I'll make it to Wenatchee by September or die trying. It's one or the other, this time."

"Then I'll go to Wenatchee, too. I've got no other plans."

"Hard as I'm going to push it, you'll never make it to Washington, Del. Not new as you are. You need some time and experience to toughen up. A hobo's like a shoe: it takes plenty of miles and plenty of work to make him useful. He's too stiff and clumsy to be much good to anyone till he's broken in properly. The best I can do for you is get you to a good jungle."

"Jungle?"

"A camp of sorts," Louisa said, "full of hobos. Jungles are inside cities, or right at their edges. See, there's always plenty of work in a city, and you can break yourself in that way—get used to the routine of walking around town, asking for a job. Figure out how to spot the best kinds of folks, the kinds who're likely to take pity on a hobo—and the kinds who're likely to chase you off just because you look a little grubby. The kinds who'll call the cops the minute they see you."

"Call the cops," I said, "just for the way you look?"

She laughed. "Damn, Miss Del, you are as fresh as they come, aren't you? But you see, that's just why we aren't made to be traveling companions. I'm on a tight schedule, and you'll hold me back. But cheer up; you'll find plenty of help in the jungle, and before you know it, you'll be ripe and ready to strike out again on the rails. By the time winter sets in, you'll be almost as experienced as I am. You'll be able to take yourself anywhere. You hungry?"

I was starved. As I'd laid my plans the previous evening, I tried to imagine some way to fill my rucksack with food. But I hadn't found a way to do it without raising Irving's suspicion. He would have caught me out too early if I'd gone down to the kitchen to rummage in the pantry. So I'd brought nothing to eat, and my stomach had been growling and aching for hours.

Louisa shifted herself around till she could reach into a pocket of her voluminous trousers. She pulled out a bundle of old gingham cloth tied with a bit of twine. In a minute she picked the knot open and folded back the corners of the cotton to reveal several strips of jerked meat and some dried apple slices.

"This was my pay for the last job I worked," she said, "hoeing weeds for a widowed mother a few miles outside that town where you picked me up. I don't know if the meat is venison or jackrabbit or what, but it goes down easy enough. Help yourself."

I did, praying I didn't dig in with such haste that I seemed rude. The meat was stringy and tough, but it had been preserved in a delicious combination of smoke and spices. I chewed every bite slowly, lingering over the flavor and the frank and instinctive pleasure of filling my empty stomach.

While I devoted myself to that humble meal, Louisa told me how she came to be in that unknown town somewhere in the north of Georgia, which was where she estimated we were by that time.

"You sure know the rail lines," I said.

"It's the land that tells you where you are. The shape of the hills, the kinds of trees, the way the rivers bend or don't bend—they're like signs you can read. They'll point you to wherever you're going."

"I've only ever seen one type of hill, and the trees that grew in my valley, and the Cumberland River. Well, and the country between where I live and Lexington. That wasn't much different, though. Is one river really so unlike another?"

She chuckled, sizing me up with a look that made me feel weighed, measured, and branded a hopeless neophyte all in a single heartbeat. "Shoot, kid. You've never seen the Mississippi, for sure."

She told me she'd been following the crops and seasons across America. "I work the farms, mostly—I like outdoor work best. But I'll take any job that comes my way. Everything I earn, I send on back to my family."

"Couldn't you find work in a factory or a store?" Ladies seldom worked in Harlan County—that just wasn't our way—but these were modern times, and even in the heart of the Cumberland, we'd heard tell of gals taking up the yoke when they'd been widowed or left by no-good men, or when they simply wanted to provide for themselves.

"Lord, no," Louisa said. "Haven't you seen how bad things are these days? Anyone who stays put is likelier to lose his job than keep it. That's assuming there's any work to be found in the first place. The cities are bad, just now—fifteen, twenty unemployed men for every job that opens up. They walk around the streets with signs pinned to their chests—"Good Man, Father of Three, Looking for Any Work." It's worse for the ladies. Most businesses won't hire women, and if they do, they pay us half of what they pay the men. Or less."

"I didn't know. It's been years since I've been to the city. Back in '29, Irv—my husband—took me up to Lexington; he was there on business. We went to the talkies and had supper in a restaurant, and it was real fine, but that was before the Crash. Ever since I came back from Lexington, I thought our town was behind the times, but at least every man in the Cumberland has a job." Thinking of the strikes, which seemed endless now, eternal, I added, "Though, he might wish for better pay."

"That's why the hobos have it better than anyone else. Except for the big fellows on top of the heap, of course—I doubt any one of those fat cats has even noticed that the world has fallen apart. Oh, I've seen them when I've worked in the cities; the rich don't get anything but richer, no matter how bad things may be for those of us on the bottom. But if you can get out on the road, or on the rails"—she thumped the floor of our boxcar appreciatively—"you can hire yourself out as a farmhand for steady work, even if you're a woman. The pay is just about worth the effort, too."

Louisa told me how she'd left her home in Washington the spring before last, tempted by the rumor that a girl could earn better wages in field work than she could in any factory.

"I was bound for Oregon first," she said. "Worked onions there, then planted cabbages and carrots. Spent the summer in the northern states, harvesting lettuce and peas. I got back to Oregon last fall for the wine grapes. That was fine work, and good pay, too. I don't think I've ever had so much fun as I did that fall, stomping grapes with a bunch of other gals. It's a better diversion than dancing, though a shame you get to be such a mess doing it. My legs were stained purple to the knees for two weeks after."

"What did you do for the winter?" I asked, starting in on a leathery apple. It was sweet as honey, so good I almost cried from it. "Did you head back home to your family?"

"No, I went to Sacramento. Caught the last of the potato harvest, then rode to the San Joaquin Valley to help prepare the cotton fields for the next planting. California's a good place to be in wintertime. If you get down south far enough, the nights are so warm you can sleep under the stars."

"You make it sound almost romantic," I said, "this . . . what do you call it, anyway?"

"Hoboing." A matter-of-fact answer.

"We saw hobos come through our town," I said. "Guess they go everywhere the rails run. But the hobos I met were always men. I can't seem to wrap my head around it, that a gal could be a hobo."

Louisa laughed quietly. "Well, what are you, Miss Del? You look like a hobo to me."

"I never meant to be one. I only meant to get away from my husband, and the train was the fastest way to do it. But if I'm a hobo after all, then so be it. Anyway, I'll have to do something to earn my keep, cause I'm damn sure I won't be going home again. I might as well work the fields, if the pay's as good as you say it is."

We both stared out through the gap in our boxcar. Whenever the smooth roll of hillside and forest receded from the tracks to reveal a flat stretch of valley or a patchwork of cultivated fields, the scene looked too bare, too dusty, and I was beset by a small and curious dread, a suspicion that I looked upon too much of nothing, and the emptiness was fit to spread itself across the land till it reached every horizon. Then the Georgia hills closed in again and the gentle forest concealed the rack and ruin of human endeavor, and I breathed out, relieved I could pretend I hadn't seen what was really there before me.

"The trouble is," Louisa said quietly, "the drought has hit the wheat and barley farmers hard, and rice will be a lost cause down in the Delta. You won't find much work in this part of the country. You'll have to go north—damn my luck, anyway, sticking me on a southbound train. I'll turn myself around as soon as this old horse stops in another railyard, get back up to the Midwest, work my way from there to Wenatchee."

Louisa was so self-assured, such a wealth of all the knowledge I needed, that I could never get on my own. I had to try again.

"Please let me come along. I know I won't be trouble, Louisa. In fact, I'll be a real useful gal to have on hand, I know it."

She answered kindly, but with a resolve that I knew I'd never overcome with mere pleading. "I can't let you weigh me down, Del. Green as you are, you'd be no use to me. What have you got to offer, anyway? Can you hunt? Can you smooth talk a fellow into giving you work when he thinks he's got nothing for you? Hell, I bet you couldn't even get off this train if you wanted to, could you, now?"

There was no arguing with her; she was dead right, all the way through. The best skill I had to offer back then was keeping house and convincing a lot of women to continue taking their men to the meetinghouse every Sunday. It was plain to see I'd find no utility for those talents out on the rails.

But I couldn't let a teacher like Louisa slip through my hands without one last attempt. "I could be a friend to you. A companion. I could look out for you, and keep you company, and . . . I might not know as much as you, just yet, but I can lend a hand when you need one. Everybody needs a hand sometimes."

Louisa shrugged. "I don't. I've got this far on my own, and soon I'll have got myself back home again, all without anyone to coddle me or mind me. But I'm not cruel, Del; I'll get you to a good jungle, like I promised, and see that you land on your feet."

A blue melancholy came over me then; there was such finality in her refusal. I guess I must have felt pretty down for a good long while after that conversation, but I look back now and I don't remember anything but the pleasure of sitting side by side with Louisa, watching the forest blur, green and black, past our boxcar, and breathing in the sharp, sweet smell of the pines.

It might seem funny, to think anyone could feel so chipper about riding the rails. But nobody called it the Great Depression that summer.

No one had even dreamed of such a name. That June, we saw our circumstances as a temporary hardship, Louisa and I, and to this day I still consider the summer of 1931 to be the freest, the loveliest season I've ever known.

Maybe the reckless innocence, the sheer damn-fooledness of my first hoboing days never quite wore off. Or maybe, after all, it's not the view that's beautiful or ugly. Maybe what counts is the way you look at it.

10

The coal freighter swung west and made its way across northern Alabama, up into a corner of Tennessee. Louisa and I dozed as best we could in the afternoon heat. It's no easy task, to sleep sitting up in the belly of a rattling train, nothing but hard steel to rest your bones on, and many a time I wavered up from a groggy sleep to watch the country shifting and changing in the sun-struck glare beyond our boxcar. Fields of stunted cotton gave way to a roll of hills with forests shadowing their gullies and marching up their sides. By the time the light was mellow and golden, I could see the tentative peaks of mountains nosing up into a hazy distance.

Louisa had risen and stretched, shaken the cramps from her legs, and now she stood at the mouth of the boxcar, holding on to its side, tipping her face in the afternoon light so the wind of motion could wash the sleep away.

"Those will be the Ozarks," she said, gazing out into the world. "We must be in Arkansas by now. I haven't been down this way in a long time. It'll probably cost a week or two to make my way back north."

"I'm sorry," I said, though it sure wasn't my fault she'd ended up on this train. Still, I felt somehow responsible, or at least I felt myself to be a burden then, and I didn't like that I should make her life any harder than it was.

She looked at me over her shoulder. The breeze caught her hair and lifted it, and sunlight flared through the wild reddish mess, surrounding her face with a halo of fire. "Couldn't be helped. Anyway, it was a good thing this ride came along when it did. That bastard who was chasing me—you can guess what he would have done if he'd caught me."

It was on the tip of my tongue to insist, *You see, that's just why you need me; we girls have to look out for one another,* but Louisa had already turned back to watch the mountains arrive in slow and ancient procession, and I would get nowhere by belaboring the point. I hadn't been long in Louisa's company, but already I understood that she was stubborn as a mule, not the type of person who could be coaxed or argued out of her position.

Evening found us deep in Arkansas, and when the train cried its warning and the cars began to buck and jar, Louisa declared we would soon pull in for the night.

Our train came to rest with a hiss and a groan in a railyard halfway between Memphis and Springfield. The heat still bore down on us, but as twilight advanced, the air began to shed its oppressive quality. An immense blue stillness crept like a fog between the rounded shoulders of the foothills as we climbed down from the good old car that had carried us all through the day. The linemen working in the railyard gave us no grief. One even lifted his cap and said, "Good luck to you, ladies." The night's first whip-poor-will raised a song from the crown of a cherry tree not far from the tracks.

We managed to squeeze inside the town's general store just before the owner closed up, and I bought a few necessities with a precious dollar or two from Irving's stash. As the shopkeep locked his door behind us, Louisa and I stepped into the summer night, breathing deep, savoring the feel of solid ground beneath our feet and the wildish green spice of the air, the smell of forest and shadow and leafy things that hadn't yet succumbed to the dryness of the year.

Shortly before our train had pulled into the yard, Louisa spotted the unmistakable high, narrow roof of a mill peeking above the treetops. "Maybe a mile back," she told me now, gesturing into the gathering darkness. "It'll do for a place to make our beds. It's always better to sleep with a roof overhead than without one. Even in these dry times, you never can tell when a storm might blow in to surprise you."

We walked the dirt road in affable silence while Louisa squinted through the trees, searching for the mill. Ahead, where the road vanished into shadow, the foothills sloped down to meet one another in a soft, purple V of cloudless sky. I could hear the rustle and steps of small creatures in the brush, little lives stirring to alertness now that the temperature was more forgiving.

My whole spirit was suffused with a satisfied glow, only slightly impinged by an occasional flash of guilt. The sheer, hard fact that I'd cut and run from my marriage kept lurching up before me so I walked smack into it, and whenever reality struck another blow, it left me blinking and smarting.

Two Dels seemed to war inside me—one wild and new, eager to learn what shape she would take in the world beyond the Cumberland. The other was the old Del—who, to my fury, still sought to be as meek and obedient as she'd been raised to be. No sooner would I think, *Irving will be fine without me, the heartless bastard, and even if he isn't fine, that's nothing to trouble me,* than the guilt-laden aspect of my spirit would cry out in despair that I might have every reason to disdain my husband, but a proper wife, a righteous wife, would never up and leave.

A distant rattle and bang distracted me from my thoughts. Two glowing yellow eyes appeared on the road ahead—an automobile coming around the bend.

Louisa and I left the road and walked among the nettles as the auto approached. The engine coughed and sputtered as it drew near. I blinked in the glare of the headlights, throwing up a hand to shield my eyes. Then the vehicle chugged past—old-fashioned, with a long rectangular hood, deflating tires on spoked wheels, rust spotting the door. There was nothing to cover the cab; it had been made open to the sky God-knew-how-many years before. A haggard couple was perched on the bench seat, the man gripping the steering wheel, the woman turning her desolate face to examine Louisa and me. Whatever had once made up the rear of that vehicle had been replaced by a collection of slats, a kind of handmade truck bed, and it was piled high with every sort of household thing you could imagine—iron bed frame, mattress springs, stove with a bent pipe, the legs of tables and chairs poking out haphazardly from the whole great mass, which was lashed together with a fraying net of rope.

We stared after that strange apparition, watching till the auto was swallowed by the dusk, till not even the glow of its headlights remained.

"What do you suppose?" I said.

"Tenants," Louisa answered.

No need to say more. Even in my sheltered town deep in the Kentucky hills—where there was no one for miles but coal miners and poor milling folk—even there, we'd all heard the sad story of the tenant farmers.

Some of them had worked their families' farms all their lives, born in the same old houses as their mas and pas, houses their grandpas had built from trees cut down with their own hands and worked into beams and planks with the tools their grandpas had used.

But the farms didn't belong to those families any longer. The last generation had been pressed by an unlucky combination of bad years—drought or flood or cold that lasted a little too long—and a mad crush of tractors and seeders and other motorized things, all owned and operated by the companies that had already fattened themselves so much that they could only swell to consume one another. Faced by such powerful and hungry devils, most of the farmers had little choice but to mortgage off their land one acre at a time. In the final extremity, they'd borrowed away the last acre on which their homes stood. Who can blame them for making such a dire choice? Bad times come—they always do—and what sort of man wouldn't borrow to feed his children rather than hold to his land and let his little ones starve?

Hard as life had been in coal country, especially since the miners had got to organizing and fighting their bloody wars against the owners, at least more than half of us lived beyond the company towns, up in the hills, where we'd been free to raise our own crops and animals, where no one could kick us out from under our roofs. For that's precisely what happened to the tenant farmers that year, and the year before. The banks that owned the land called in their debts. They said to the people who'd been born there, married there, who'd buried their dead in that soil: "This is our land now, not yours, and we can make better use of it if you aren't on it so kindly get lost and leave us to our business." Why, the Bakers—that family I'd sheltered for a night without Irving's knowledge—had almost certainly been tenants, too. Maybe it was my brief association with the Bakers that caused me, as I stared after the overburdened truck, to feel the injustice in my own guts. It might as well have been my story, my farm taken away by the holdings, rather than some other poor soul's—a thousand other poor souls forced onto the road or onto the rails.

"You think they'll find work in that town back there?" I asked Louisa.

"God knows," she said, and turned resolutely in the other direction.

We never found the old mill house, but when a fat, round moon came peeking up over the crest of a hill, Louisa stopped me with a hand on my arm and pointed to something ghostly and white that lifted above the forest and vanished again. I thought it was smoke from a campfire, but in the moonlight, it held a curious radiance, a transparent glow no smoke ever had.

"What is it?" I whispered.

"Something better than a mill, if I'm right. Come on and see."

She led me from the road into the forest, following a deer track that could scarcely be seen in the dark. The narrow trail cut between the trunks of trees, through dense thickets of crackling undergrowth. Twigs and thorny things caught at my shirt, scratching the backs of my hands as I struggled to keep pace with Louisa, who was a pale specter half-revealed and hidden again behind swags and bowers of redbud.

Deep among the oaks, the forest gave way to a sudden clearing. The dark crowns of the trees defined a near-perfect ring of sky, framing the golden, imperious moon. Below, a limestone pool sent gusts of steam into the canopy. The surface of the water bubbled and rippled in the silver light.

"A hot spring," I exclaimed.

Louisa crouched at the pool's edge, testing its temperature with a finger. Then her whole hand dipped into the water. "It's perfect. Not too hot to stand. Come on; let's take a dip."

I'd never stripped down to the ivory in front of any soul but my husband. The habits of a preacher's wife reasserted themselves with unexpected force, and I took a step back, my cheeks burning.

"Oh, Del," Louisa said, "there's no one to see except the hoot owls and raccoons, and they don't care."

She pulled her ample shirt over her head, not bothering with the buttons. Before I could avert my eyes, she'd loosed the hooks on a very grayed and shabby bandeau. The thin straps slipped down her shoulders and she cast it aside, baring small, flat breasts. A round object lay against her chest, glinting in the shine from above. I realized it was a gold locket, though it had no chain. Louisa had strung it on an ordinary piece of cotton twine. I hadn't noticed the strange necklace, all these hours since I'd met her, as we'd acquainted ourselves in the shade of our boxcar. She slipped the twine over her head and placed the locket carefully atop her shirt.

"What are you waiting for?" She faced me with fists on hips, entirely unashamed, and the sight of her—bare-skinned above and still clad below in the trousers of a man—filled me with a giddy panic I could neither stifle nor comprehend. "We're just two girls," Louisa said. "There's nothing wrong with it."

I did want to feel that spring water wash the sweat and dirt from my hide. But still the old church-born habit of modesty restrained me. Louisa pulled at her belt.

Quickly, I turned my back, muttering a prayer for the Lord's forgiveness. But I did it—I slipped my feet from my boots and dropped the rucksack beside them. The suspenders fell from my shoulders. I let my trousers drop, then the drawers underneath. My shirt hung down to cover my nakedness, but I knew already the shirt would come off, too. I'd committed myself to this shame; there was no going back. With a long breath and one last silent prayer, I stripped the shirt off, keeping my eyes resolutely on the dark forest. Last of all, I shed my brassiere and laid it on my pack.

When I worked up the courage to face my companion, I found Louisa busy at the pool's edge, not paying the least mind to my bare skin or my flustered state. She was half-submerged already, bending at the waist to hold on to a projecting ledge of limestone while her feet prodded the pool's floor with tentative care. The colors of her body struck me—the contrast—a sunbaked brown at her chest and the nape of her neck, and up her forearms to where she rolled her sleeves. The rest of her skin was so pale she might have been carved from marble.

"It's nice, Del. Get in quick."

There were only a few steps between where I stood and the lip of the pool. I crossed the space with the same floating daze in which one moves, or seems to move, in a dream. Moss cushioned my bare feet, and every step gave up a green and earthy fragrance.

I crouched beside the pool, then set my bottom right down on the moss and scooched forward to dip my feet in. The water felt so hot and good, it sent a honey sweetness flowing up my legs and into my spine, then up into my head, where I felt plumb dizzy with relief and wonder. I eased myself in, and the deeper I waded into the spring, the deeper the heat reached, loosening what was tense, soothing what pained me. The floor of the pool was soft with a velvety silt. My toes sank right in. The dirt released from my skin, drifting away in the gentle current of the spring's bubbling.

"What did I tell you?" Louisa was across the pool, opposite me, sunk down so only her face was visible. Clouds of steam drifted between us. She wrinkled her nose in a way I'd already come to recognize as silent laughter. "Worth it?"

For answer, I sighed and lowered myself till the water lapped at my chin.

"You were afraid," Louisa said.

"I wasn't afraid, exactly. But where I come from, ladies don't do this sort of thing."

"Swimming?"

"Not bare. Not if anyone can see."

"And you're a lady—is that it?"

She'd asked the question without any challenge or malice, but she'd hit so close to the heart of my guilty conscience that I couldn't crack a smile.

"I was raised to be a lady," I answered a little sadly. "Good church girl and all that. But what's it for, anyway? What's the point of living life on the straight and narrow if it only gets you—"

"What you got. A broken heart."

I couldn't look at her. Tears blurred my vision, anyway, worse than the steam was doing.

"I guess you can tell," I said, "just by looking at me. Can you read it in my face?"

"No one takes to the rails unless they've got a broken heart. If there's one thing every hobo has in common, it's that. A no-good husband did the job for one of us, a no-good wife for another. Or someone you love dies and leaves you all alone. You lose your job—your place in the world, your standing, your respect. That's why all of us are out here hitching on a train. The stories are different, but the hurt's the same, when you really get down to the heart of matters."

Below the surface, I'd wrapped my arms around my body, as if by main force I could keep myself together—as if my arms were a shield or a steel cage strong enough to protect my heart.

I said, "I guess it's the same hurt, and everyone's feeling it, not just the folks out here on the rails. The town I left . . . my town. When I took off, it was just awful, Louisa. Coal miners striking and hoping those strikes will make some difference, having to send their kids to bed crying with hunger. And miners shooting up the company men—killed a few, too. And look at the land, look at the farms—not a green thing growing. You know, the preacher at my church"—no need to confess that the preacher was my husband—"he says all this extra suffering piled on these last couple of years, it's because the End has come. The Last Days. He says we all better repent extra hard and get right with Jesus or else."

An unexpected fury came over me. I couldn't have named the source. Maybe that hot water loosened me up so good that it even set free all the most secretive thoughts I'd ever had, ideas so strange to me, so dangerous, I hadn't even realized I'd been thinking them.

I found I could meet Louisa's eye, after all. I held her with a challenging stare, and said, "You know what I think? I think if the Lord sees fit to punish folks who've already been suffering so much, then he isn't much of a Lord after all. And I think that preacher at my church is a damn fool. And a big dumb pig, into the bargain. And if God don't visit a judgment on *his* head before anyone else's, then it won't be much of a Second Coming. That's what I think."

While I'd been ranting away, Louisa's nose had taken on that characteristic wrinkle, and by the time I got to my windup, she was laughing openly, mouth wide and eyes bright with appreciation.

"Damn," she said. "Listen to you, spitting fire."

"I meant every word." But I will confess that I glanced up nervously at the moon, half-convinced the Lord was about to send down a lightning bolt as punishment for my blaspheming.

She said, "I never got much church stuff growing up, but I got enough to know it wasn't for me. I especially had no use for that 'End of Days' nonsense. What a bunch of hogwash."

That startled me so thoroughly that my arms fell loose from around my body and drifted out a little into the rippling spring. If there had been one consistent theme running through my whole life at the Church of God with Signs Following, it had been the imminent threat of the Lord's most fearful and dramatic wrath, due to descend upon the earth any day now—any moment, in fact. Everyone I'd ever known believed in Judgment Day so fervently that the mere suggestion that anyone could discard the notion, easy as flicking away the butt of a cigarette, pretty near stopped my heart.

Louisa noticed the way I gaped at her, like a catfish hauled up out of a river, and her white shoulders lifted in an eloquent shrug.

"But look around," I argued. "You can't deny how bad everything is. The Crash, the drought, the miners shooting at company men . . . and those tenants we saw not an hour ago, kicked out of their home. It's *bad*, Louisa—for everyone, everywhere. Life has never been so bad, not like this—not that anyone can remember. Even the oldest folks back home all agreed: these are the worst times the world has ever seen. What else would you call a disaster like this, if not the End of All Things?"

She smiled, and there was such peace in her expression that again I felt tears sting my eyes. I was grateful for the gusts of steam, for they hid my face from Louisa.

She said, "If the old world has ended, that just means we're free to make a new world. And we can make it after any pattern we choose."

A whip-poor-will called from somewhere close by, and an owl gave his lazy answer from far off in the woods.

Louisa's philosophy made an insidious kind of sense. But all my church training reared up and pushed against the idea. It couldn't be so easy to pick apart the whole thrust and purpose of the Good Book. The Eternal Word should hold up better to criticism or examination. Otherwise, it wasn't much of a guide by which to live a proper life.

"You can't make the world yourself," I said. "That's God's business."

She grinned. "Says who? I took off and made a new life for myself as a hobo, and I'm doing better than most folks I know back home."

"That's not the same as making a new world."

She lifted her shoulders again. "Have it your way. I won't argue with you if you want to go on believing what you believe. It's all one to me."

I was silent for a spell, trying to work out how to approach her line of reasoning, and trying harder still to figure out why it stung me so. A sly, little voice whispered that I ought to shrug like she'd done, and declare right back to her, *It's all one to me, too.* But something about her nonchalance clung to me like a burr. It chapped me.

I said, "God's the Great Judge, and He's planning to wipe the whole slate clean anyhow, so what's the point in trying to build something of your own?"

"He hasn't wiped any slates clean yet—not as far as I can tell. Things are bad now, sure. But we aren't goners yet, you and me. We're still here, and that means we still have time to make something good of our lives despite the Crash, and the hardship, and every-damn-thing else. And I don't know about you, but I'm not about to give up hope as long as I'm still living."

"Tell me what there is to hope for."

I'd meant that for a bitter challenge, but Louisa seemed to take my words for earnest. "I can only say what *I* hope for. It's a dear dream. You won't laugh, will you?"

I shook my head.

"Once I've made enough money to see myself back home—once I've put the hobo's life behind me for good—I'd like to be a real, proper lady."

I busted out with a laugh like somebody stepped on a goose. I couldn't help it. Louisa was about as far from a proper lady as anyone could get, but I liked her that way.

She scowled. "Double-crosser. You promised you wouldn't laugh."

"I'm sorry. It's just that . . . if you want to be a lady, you probably shouldn't strip down buck naked and go jumping into pools."

She dashed her hand on the surface of the water, splashing my face. "I mean it. I'm not playing. I've seen how the finer sort lives in the cities. I could get there someday, if I find the right man. If I could convince him to marry me."

"You told me not half a day back that your first husband was a real shit. And here you are, a girl who can take care of herself—who doesn't need any man to boss her—talking about tracking down another. What for?"

"The first wasn't worth spit," Louisa said, quiet and thoughtful, "I'll admit that. But there must be a good man out there somewhere. Some nice fellow who wants a gal to be sweet to, and a family—a good little family, with children to raise and love. And it would be nice, after all the hard work I've done, to tend one home, and wear pretty dresses, and—I don't know, have a friendly dog in the yard who wags its tail when it sees you."

A curious sickness settled in my stomach—a longing for a thing that never was, and never could be. I wanted that life as much as Louisa ever did. But the hurt was still too fresh in me for gentleness or mercy.

I said, "Being a lady isn't all you've cracked it up to be. I lived that life you've been wanting so badly—well, most of it, anyway; I never had any children. The whole thing left me cold. It left my heart on the floor for that damned man to walk on. The pretty house, the nice dresses, the motorcar. I had it all—the best of everything, the easy life, not a worry about a thing, not the way most folks worry. It doesn't make you happy, Louisa, living like a lady. It's just a different kind of misery."

She said nothing for a long, long time—only stared at me, her eyes expressionless save for a stunned disbelief, an unwillingness to accept or comprehend what was right there in front of her.

"What?" I demanded.

Slowly, that bright spark returned to Louisa's eyes, but she turned her face away, as if she couldn't stand to look at me. My heart kicked hard, and a fearful light-headedness flashed through me. The pool was much too hot; I needed to get out before a dizzy spell dropped me, senseless, in the water.

Louisa straightened to her full height. Water ran down over her thinness and her paleness. The gold reflection of the moon splintered and multiplied itself on the surface of the pool as Louisa waded toward me.

"You aren't just green," she said, "you're dumber than a bag of hammers. Giving up a perfectly good life to slum it like this?"

Before I could answer, her hard, little hand came down on the crown of my head. Fingers dug into my scalp. Louisa's grip was strong, constraining; I couldn't dodge away from her.

She pushed me hard, and I went down into the water. It closed over my head with a roar of heat.

When I came up, coughing and sputtering, Louisa was already on the mossy bank, skipping on one foot to pull on her trousers, and I was alone, waist-deep in the pool with the moon laughing down from above.

11

Now, it happened that Louisa, being a northern girl, wasn't suitably familiar with the routes of the South. As a consequence, we wandered a fair bit that June. We looked for work, true, but also for a train that would carry us up into the Midwest, where Louisa planned to ride a Union Pacific horse through the Rockies and back to her home state. The search resulted in a crisscross tour of the South, from Greensboro to Charlotte, across the Smokies to Chattanooga and clear down to the cliffs of Alabama, all white chalk and silted water. Along the way, Louisa taught me what she knew of the hobo life.

Or she tried to teach me, anyway. I'm afraid I wasn't as sharp a student as I'd thought myself to be.

In fairness to the gal I was back then, let me say this much: I'd perfected the art of being a preacher's wife and had worked my tail off for Irving's sake. But nothing in my previous life had fitted me for the demands of rail-riding. Truth is, the wife of a preacher as big as Irving was—I mean, a preacher who can fill his collection plate every Sunday and twice a month at revival—leads a pretty cushy life. She isn't obliged to hoe in the garden or break her back doing the washing and cooking for a passel of kids. Even if she has a passel, she can afford to hire a little help. The greatest physical strain I'd faced in my life before was walking for miles at a time, visiting the ladies of the flock. All this meant that

I wasn't nearly as strong or resilient as Louisa, with her sixteen months of hard-earned experience.

Despite my shortcomings, I managed to pick up the less taxing aspects of hobo life with relative ease.

Louisa taught me how to choose the best boxcars to ride in—the ones that carried fruit and other delicate items. Fruit cars always held plenty of packing materials, and we piled up the cardboard and wood shavings to make ourselves a good nest. There we caught a few hours' sleep amid the clamor and bang of the boxcars, surrounded by the sweet odor of apricots and honeydew nailed up in their crates.

She taught me how to hang on to the side of a moving train, and with her encouragement, I got so I could cling to the ladder of a boxcar for hours while it rolled through the glare of a summer afternoon.

When the sun lowered itself to the west and the train sped on into a land of long shadows, I learned how to give my tired limbs a rest by riding possum belly on the roof, splayed out on my stomach, one cheek pressed against the subtle curve of steel, which held a memory of the day's heat. Lying there with the wind riffling my hair, with the silent, dozing Louisa for company, I would watch a procession of hills and forest and a bright flash of river slide past, an endless revelation of the deep and wild places, the country I'd only thought I'd known from my enclave in Harlan County.

The night we slept in Greensboro, some six or seven days after leaving Arkansas, Louisa undertook to instruct me in the fine points of hobo code.

We'd made camp for ourselves at the edge of the railyard, well hidden in a grove of shade trees, with the stately redbrick turret of the train station peeking at us through the boughs. We'd just finished a supper of corn and baked beans, heated right in their cans among the coals of a tiny fire, and I'd stretched out along my army mat, heavy with contentment, for I'd already come to appreciate the rare luxury of a hot meal.

Louisa stirred the coals of our dying fire. "I guess I ought to teach you the ins and outs of the hobos' code."

I sat up, all interest. "There's a code?"

"Of course. How do you think we manage to keep on folks' good side? We've got to distinguish ourselves from the riffraff if we hope to find a day's work."

Hobos, you see, weren't common drifters, nor were we layabouts. We might have looked like scarecrows, but we were honest working men and women who moved from place to place because it was the only surefire way to find a job.

"Every hobo looks out for his fellows," Louisa said, "by minding his behavior in accordance with these rules. So pay attention, because if you break the code, you could muck things up for yourself and for every hobo who'll come through town after you. Once a town has been spoiled, and the folks no longer trust us, there's not much hope of finding work, or even a bit of charity."

"All right," I said, "I'm listening."

Louisa broke up the stick she'd been stirring the fire with, tossing pieces onto the coals while she spoke. "Most of it's just what any halfway decent person would do. We never steal—not anything—and we don't drink booze. At least, no hobo with his wits about him will drink where he might be seen."

"Drinking's illegal, anyhow," I pointed out.

"Exactly. That's the main thing to keep in mind: we break no laws and cause no trouble. Hobos are strictly forbidden to take advantage of any vulnerable person. That includes women and children."

"That chicken hawk—" I was referring, of course, to the vicious creature who'd followed Louisa onto the train the first day of our acquaintance.

"He was no hobo, you mark my words. He was one of the other kind—a no-good drifter, and I promise you, he wasn't bound by any code. You've got to keep a lookout for folks like him. They might seem

111

all right—might even have you convinced they're real hobos, men you can trust. But they can turn on you in a second, and if you find yourself alone with that sort, you'll wish you'd never got the idea of riding the rails into your damn fool head."

That sent a chill up my back. "How can you tell the difference between a real hobo and . . . that other sort?"

"Sometimes you can't." She spoke airily, and threw the last bit of stick into the dying fire. "You just have to trust your gut where that sort of thing's concerned. And you pray your gut doesn't steer you wrong."

No likely response suggested itself, so I drew my knees up to my chest, waiting for Louisa to go on. She eyed me over the red embers, and seemed satisfied that the gravity of her lesson had sunk in.

"Above all else," she said, "no hobo will ever interfere with the duties or the comfort of any worker on the trains or on the tracks. Trains are our best hope for getting from place to place—from one paying job to the next. If any of us sours the train workers, or earns a reputation for theft, the gig will be up for all of us. One bout of hell-raising can ruin an entire city for weeks or months at a stretch. If ever the linemen come to distrust a hobo, you'll find a long, weary road ahead of you, rebuilding that trust."

Her point wasn't lost on me. For folks on the rails, a town full of hostile people who won't feed you and linemen who'd as soon toss you in jail as look at you might be as bad as a death sentence. I said as much.

"It *is* a death sentence for some," Louisa answered. "Don't you forget it."

As we crossed and recrossed the South, we worked in true hobo fashion, earning our keep by any means—by whatever means presented themselves. Outside Dalton, we dug postholes for an ancient farmer. We harvested rhubarb somewhere in Tennessee. In Guntersville, I took work for three days in a gentleman's home overlooking the great sapphire plane of the lake, for his wife was laid up, recovering from surgery after her appendix had burst—and the man, for all his wealth, couldn't so much as boil an egg. The fellow was grateful for my housekeeping, and paid me handsomely. Louisa and I lived for days off the money.

We ran from the bulls—the hostile cops who patrolled the rail-yards. We made our camps in thickets and fields, on the banks of irrigation canals, never close enough to a farmhouse to rouse the suspicion of its occupants. Each night, I stretched my weary self along my old bivouac pad and pillowed my head on my hands, and blanketed only by the white band of stars that girded the sky, I would listen to Louisa sing a broken, unschooled melody. Her songs were all of gentle things—a mother's love, a sweetheart's kiss, the simple satisfaction of home. The words and the sound of her voice filled me with an ache of beauty I'd never felt back in my own home, not even when we'd raised our voices to sing praises on Sundays.

Despite the many ways I came along, there was one hoboing skill I couldn't master. No matter how many times I attempted to hop a moving train, I couldn't quite force myself to run fast enough, or to come close enough to the thunderous power of all that metal in motion that I could lay hold and pull myself aboard. We tried in Shreveport and Meridian, and outside Tuscaloosa—Louisa running beside me, shouting encouragement and instruction—but my fear of those wailing, pitiless wheels won out in the end, and I would fall back and drift farther from the tracks till the train went roaring beyond, and I would stand with hands braced against my knees, panting and sweating, while Louisa watched me in silence, the disappointment plain to read on her face.

One muggy afternoon at the edge of Jackson, Mississippi, we crossed paths with another hobo, a sunburned fellow with hair as coarse and pale as straw. He was young—maybe not even twenty—but he limped like a battered old man.

"Merciful Heaven," Louisa called out to him, "what on earth's happened to you?"

The boy spat into the road. "Bulls. They're awful bad in the yard today."

"We just came through the yard this morning," I said. "Didn't see a single bull. Nobody bothered us."

"Well," the boy said, "wherever they come from since, they're here, all right. Lots of 'em, too. Seven, eight—I don't know—but they got clubs and they ain't afraid to use 'em. They nabbed my friend Jonesy. Don't know when they'll let him out of the pen. Almost nabbed me, but I got away. Poor Jonesy—he's awful scared of jail."

"They beat you up pretty good?" Louisa asked.

He said nothing, clearly ashamed to confess to such a thing in front of two women.

"You should get to a jungle," she told the boy. "Might be somebody there who's got medicine for cuts and bruises."

He said, "I'm afraid there's no jungle in Jackson. Used to be a nice one, but the cops come through a few weeks ago and busted it all up, drove everybody away. Jackson has been pretty scarce on hobos since then."

Louisa cut a furtive glance at me. No doubt she'd been thinking she could unload me in a city of Jackson's size—pass me off to more experienced hobos and allow them to take over my care and training. I felt an absurd need to apologize, though it sure wasn't me who'd busted up the jungle.

The yellow-haired boy seemed so down on his luck that Louisa and I bought him a sandwich and a Coke and pointed him in the direction of the neighborhood where we'd found a few hours' employment. But as we parted ways with that fellow, Louisa muttered, "We can't risk the yard if the bulls are that vicious."

"Surely they won't go beating women," I said.

"Maybe not, but they'll throw us in jail without any qualms. You can count on that. I can't risk jail, Del. God knows how long they'd keep me there, and I—"

"Need to be in Wenatchee by September," I said. "I know."

"There's nothing for it but to catch the train as it rolls out of town. And that means you've got to hop it at a run."

My stomach went tight. "Are you sure there's no other way?"

She strode ahead, obliging me to scramble after. "No other way. The time has come, all right. You'll jump that train like a proper hobo or I'll leave you in the dust."

Needless to say, I was sick with worry as we staked out a hiding place in a stand of brush some half mile outside the city limits. Louisa was pensive, watching the curve of the tracks for the first signs of a departing freighter. I crouched in the dirt beside her and tried not to fidget.

We'd sat there almost an hour when she said, "Train coming. Now remember what I told you, all those times before. Keep your eyes straight ahead while you pick up speed. Don't get too close to the tracks till you're ready to make a grab for a ladder. And once you go in for the hop, stay strong. Don't baby out at the last minute."

"I'll try," I said faintly, wondering how I'd ever survive the afternoon.

By that time, I could feel the vibration of the approaching engine. It gave a harsh metallic moan, and then the shuddering black hulk came around the bend, all snub nose and gnashing wheels, its coal breath heaving out into the oppressive sky.

The engine thundered past. Louisa took off running, light and sure as a deer, and I lumbered after her with my rucksack bouncing against my back.

Boxcars slid past in a dazzle of color, hornet yellow and rusty red. I couldn't pick a single car out of the rest; I hadn't the presence of mind to sort the cars visually to find the few with ladders or other projections a hobo could grab on to. They all melded into the same violent rush of painted steel.

But I ran, just as I'd promised Louisa I would. My feet kicked hard against the ballast stones, and my breath was a fire in my throat. I kept my eyes on Louisa, determined to do exactly as she did, praying she wouldn't steer me wrong.

I saw her dart toward the train and thought, *This is it. Do or die.* I swerved, too, forcing myself closer to the flying cars, closer to the hellish rattle and bang of wheel and side-iron and couplings. Willing myself to concentrate, I tried to pick out a handhold from the dizzy blur of metal, but the sheer power of the train overwhelmed me, and my eyes filled with tears of the purest and coldest terror I'd felt in all my life.

"Come on," Louisa yelled over the cacophony. "Do it, Del!"

Just as she said my name, I tripped over something—probably my own damned feet. The ground came up to meet me with shocking force. Pain flared at the point of my chin, and a heartbeat later I realized I couldn't breathe. I don't know whether the fall knocked the wind from my lungs, or whether it was the sheer panic of being only feet away from the crushing wheels. As I rolled helplessly onto my side, clutching my throbbing face, my only clear thought was, *I hope Louisa made it onto the train.*

The caboose roared by. The freighter banged and rattled into the distance. A thick, hot silence descended over the tracks.

I managed to suck in a breath at last, just as Louisa's old, battered shoes stepped into my line of sight. She hadn't jumped on board, then. Blinking back tears, I looked up at her and gasped for words that wouldn't come.

Louisa loomed over me. "I swear to God, Del, you are the worst hobo I've ever seen."

Whatever I attempted to say came out as a pathetic croak.

"You bleeding?" she asked.

I pulled my palm away from my chin and looked at it. I might as well have dipped my hand in red paint, so thoroughly was it covered in blood.

With a heavy sigh, Louisa reached into her pocket and sank onto her heels. She pressed a square of soft cloth against my chin. "Hold that till it stops bleeding."

I wrangled my shocked and battered self up to sit on my bottom, right there on the sun-hot sleepers. Louisa sat beside me. "Why did you come back for me?" I managed to say. "Why didn't you hop that train?"

"Oh, it's likely I'd leave you here to fend for yourself, isn't it?" she answered scornfully. "Weak little kitten like you. How in hell did you manage to get on that first coal train, I wonder?"

"It wasn't going nearly as fast as these others. It was just crawling. I never had to run at all."

Louisa sighed and hugged her knees, staring off across the feed lots and the run-down houses clinging like creeper vines to the edge of the city.

"You should have got on the train," I said after a while.

"Shut up."

"What are we going to do now?"

"Lose time—that's what. We'll go back to town. Wait till dark. Hope and pray the bulls aren't in the yard by night. If we're lucky, we'll find some ride around midnight, and hide ourselves aboard. It'll leave in the morning."

"That'll be hours," I said. "Half a day."

"Yep."

Once my chin stopped pouring out blood, Louisa offered her hand and pulled me to my feet. We returned to the city in an awkward silence—Louisa tense with anger, me aching in every bone and crumpled up inside with humiliation.

However, that night luck was on our side. The bulls cleared out when darkness fell, just as Louisa had hoped, and we managed to spirit ourselves onto a freighter bound due north for Springfield, Illinois. Louisa's mood improved considerably once we'd hidden ourselves in a fruit car, for she would soon be in the northern climes again, well within range of the Union Pacific lines.

When our freighter pulled out of Jackson early the next morning, we vacated the fruit car and climbed its ladder to the roof, and there we sat side by side, watching the great blue brilliance of the Mississippi curve and fold upon itself among the lazy hills.

"There's a good jungle in Springfield," Louisa said. "That's where I'll leave you."

"Do we have to part, after all? Just think of how well I worked back in Guntersville. All that pay! Who else could have convinced a rich man to take her in and let her run his home for a few days?"

"You've been handy here and there," Louisa admitted. "I'm not saying you're entirely useless. But here it is, practically July already, and September will be on us before we know it. I can't afford to lollygag. A few more delays like the one we had back there, and my number could be up. It's a long way between Springfield and Wenatchee. It's nothing personal, Del, but if we stick together, you'll only hold me up worse than you have already."

Glumly, I made no answer, but clung to my rucksack, watching the river sparkle and flash in the exhausted, half-green earth.

"You'll be in good hands," Louisa promised. "I'll set you up with a proper gang of folks to look after you—teach you the rest of what you'll need to know."

What else *did* I need to know? I was beginning to realize, with a cold, sinking sensation, that I had no clear picture in my head of life after Irving. I couldn't live as a hobo forever, but my thoughts refused to proceed beyond that frank and stony realization. Only one thing was clear to me: I wanted to be like Louisa—laughing, self-assured, speeding fast as a barn swallow over the hills and the plains. She was unfettered by any man.

When we reached Springfield, Louisa made me wait in the too-sweet closeness of the fruit car. She peeked through the wooden slats, watching the yard for bulls. When she gave the signal, I followed her out of the car and across an expanse of empty tracks, into the fringes of the city.

It had been months since Louisa had passed through Springfield, but she remembered the way to the jungle. "A real nice one," she said as she guided me through narrow alleys and across paved roads. Motorcars swerved around us, leaving us to contend with clouds of choking exhaust. "It's almost in the heart of town, so you can walk anywhere easy as pie, and there's plenty of work to be had in this city—or there was last time I came through."

As we approached the stand of brick warehouses that marked the jungle's location, Louisa lost all her animation. A stillness came over her that worried me something terrible. When we traversed the final alley and came out into a courtyard between two large and silent buildings, I understood her distress.

A colony of hobos had surely once occupied the courtyard, for the remnants of makeshift canvas tents stood here and there, stirring forlornly in a breeze. A few lean-tos fashioned from scraps of wood rested against the warehouse walls. But the place was utterly silent. Nothing moved except the fat, gray pigeons pecking around a charred metal barrel that had once served as a cookfire.

We bedded down that night in one of the abandoned lean-tos, stacking all the cardboard we could find into a mattress of sorts. It wasn't comfortable, but it was better than sleeping on the cobblestones.

When we lay side by side, staring up at the black roof of our lean-to and the paltry threads of starlight that showed in its cracks, Louisa said quietly, "They've all left. Every hobo in the place has cleared out."

"What does it mean?"

"No work. All dried up. No money in Springfield—not even a handout anymore."

I lay as still as I could on that hard pallet, miserably sure that if I so much as shifted or kicked my feet, I'd remind Louisa what a damnable burden I was, and compound her misery.

"I don't know what to do," she said. "I don't know what to make of this. Springfield was always good for work. But if it's dried up as bad

119

as this . . . things are rougher than I thought, this year. Does this mean everything will keep getting worse?"

Surely I had no answer to that question. I didn't dare offer any comfort.

"There's nothing for it," Louisa said. "You'll have to go on with me till I find another place to leave you. Omaha, maybe, or Kansas City. I can't just leave you here, on your own—not with the place dried up worse than any desert."

"I'll make myself useful," I said, hoping I didn't sound too happy about this turn of events.

"Like hell," she muttered, rolling onto her side. "Useful—a damn pup like you."

I rose early the next morning. Between the hard bed and my guilty conscience, I'd scarcely slept a wink, and I was stiff and aching, my head groggy, the taste on my tongue sour. Louisa had decided the night before that we'd try our luck at the railyard, hoping for a westbound freighter. Rarely did trains leave their yards before sunrise, and dawn was almost an hour away.

That left plenty of time to wash—a rare luxury that we never passed up, for one could never say when the opportunity for a proper scrub would present itself again. The abandoned jungle had grown up around a hand-pumped water source behind one of the warehouses, and I found two old tin pails stacked beside the pump. I filled the pails and carried them back to our lean-to, where Louisa had just risen, stretching and yawning in the pale morning light.

Without a word, we set our respective pails in the space between our lean-to and the remains of another. In moments we'd both stripped down and piled our clothes neatly to the side, and with the spare scraps of cloth we each carried, we scrubbed ourselves from head to foot, shivering despite a thick, humid quality to the air. The morning might have felt brisk, but the day promised a furious heat.

When I finished washing, I tipped my pail with one foot and let the water run across the cobblestones. Turning my back to the empty courtyard, I wrestled with my clothes—stockings wrenched up over my damp legs, drawers and trousers wrangled into place, brassiere clinging to my skin as I grunted and cursed and fought to turn it from back to front.

I'd wrestled the shirt over my head when the slick laughter of a man cut through the morning. Jerking my shirt into place, I looked around with a frantic urgency. Louisa had just fastened the buttons of her trousers. She stood bare above, except for her silk bra. The locket on its cotton twine rested between her breasts. Her face had gone pale, and she was staring past me into the open courtyard.

When I spun to face whatever Louisa had seen, I found a tall, broad man in a red buffalo-check jacket stepping out from the mouth of an alley. He hadn't shaved in days. The dark hair along his jaw seemed to bristle like the hackles of a dog.

"Well, well, well," the man said, "what've we got here? A couple of girls on their own. Not even a fellow to pump water for them."

Those words sickened me, even as they sent a chill to my gut. He had watched us—watched me pumping the water. He'd seen us both naked. I could read that much in his arrogant grin, his predatory glee.

"Guess you girls like being bare, don't you? What else you like to do in the buff?"

To my left, I could hear Louisa fumbling with her shirt, cussing under her breath, trying to get the sleeves straightened out so she could cover herself. I stepped between her and that man, my hand tingling to reach for the knife in my pocket, though I didn't quite dare to pull it out.

"Get out of here," I said. "We don't want no trouble."

"Oh, I ain't gonna give you trouble. I was thinking I'd give you something else."

"We don't want that, either," I said, "so get on out of here."

Louisa stepped up beside me. She had dropped the shirt—no use trying to cover herself now—and had picked up a large plank of wood. She brandished the board, ready to strike, and I couldn't help but notice how steady her breathing was, how coolly she confronted our attacker. My hand rested at the edge of my pocket.

The man crept closer. "What say we all three have a nice time together?"

The makeshift shelters to our right and left surrounded us like the bars of a cage, and a few paces behind me was the cold brick wall of the warehouse. In another step or two, the man would block our only way out of that trap.

"What say you go to Hell?" Louisa spat at him. "One more step and I'll bash your head."

"Oh, I don't think you'll do any such thing." He reached behind his back. In one smooth motion he drew a bowie knife, big enough to gut an elk. "You want to see how good I can throw this thing, honey?"

Louisa dropped her plank. It fell against the cobbles with a crack that jarred along my nerves.

The moment the board fell, the man seemed to focus all his attention on Louisa. At first, I thought he was staring at her bosom, and I wanted to fly at him, take him apart with my bare hands, never mind his knife.

"That's gold," the man said.

Louisa's hand flew up to catch her locket, hiding it from that predator's eyes.

"All right, ladies," he said, "let's make a deal. You hand over that gold trinket and I'll go on back to town and leave you be."

"You're plumb stupid if you think we'll trust you," I said.

"Honest. Look, I'll make a peace offering." His arm snaked behind his back again. He re-sheathed his knife, then held up both hands—empty. "Hand over the gold and I'll leave you in peace. Or keep it, and I'll take everything I want anyways, the gold included."

Louisa pulled the cotton twine over her head and tossed the locket to the man. He snatched it from the air. Between finger and thumb, he held the pendant up to the lightening sky, admiring the filigree and the flash of precious metal.

"Pretty," he said, and slipped it into his pocket.

"Now get out of here," Louisa yelled. "We've done what you wanted."

The man backed toward the alley. "Like I said, I'm a man of my word. Good day to you both. I'll be on my way."

His oily laugh hung behind as he vanished into the shadows.

For a long while, both of us remained stock-still, listening to the thud of his footsteps retreating. When the courtyard was silent again, I turned to Louisa, ready to ask if she was all right, ready to comfort her.

An astonishing thing happened then—a most unsettling thing, and it unnerved me even more than that creature's sudden appearance had done, more than the sight of the bowie knife in his hand. Louisa crumpled before my eyes. All the strength went out of her body like air from a punctured tire. She sank onto the wet cobbles, curling in upon herself, hugging her knees tightly to her chest. There she rocked like a helpless child, senseless to the water soaking up into her clothing, senseless to me as I crouched at her side, patting, pulling at her, begging her to listen.

She didn't listen. I don't believe she was even aware of my presence. All she seemed capable of doing was crying—a gut-wrenching wail like her very soul had been lost, like all the light had gone from the world, like every last hope was dead and buried.

I clutched her against my body as if I could draw that terrible suffering into my own flesh and relieve her of the pain. But I was no good; she'd been right about that. My poor embrace held Louisa's sorrow at bay about as well as a wire fence holds back the wind.

"It's gone," she cried. "It's gone, it's gone forever, and what will I do now, oh God, what will I do?"

12

Louisa may not have known what she would do, but there was no doubt in my mind as to what I'd do. I didn't know what that locket meant to her, but Louisa's suffering sent an unendurable pain through my heart, hotter than the fire of the Holy Spirit.

"Listen, Louisa. Listen to me. I'm going into town."

She gave no indication that she'd heard, only went on rocking and keening.

"God willing," I said, "I'll be back soon. Don't you budge from this place; I'll come back for you. Understand?" I allowed myself to rest my hand on her damp hair, only for as long as I could stand. Then the pain redoubled in my heart, and I knew I must go. "I'll come back for you, Louisa, I swear I will."

I stuffed my feet into my boots and lit off across the courtyard, then dodged into the same alley the man in the red-checked jacket had taken. Dawn was rising, bright and rosy. Morning touched the smokestacks and the stair-stepped facades of high-rises with a carmine glow. I prayed the emerging day would give me enough light that I could find that vile man before he delved too deep into the city. But I was determined to hunt the bastard till I found him, even if I must scour every street, every alley—even if I must fight my way through the whole police force, the county sheriff, and every one of his deputies. Never before had such a fury overcome me. I was hungry for the man's blood, itching to make him pay for hurting my friend.

There's no doubt in my mind that if I'd caught him just beyond the jungle, I would have struck him down—and probably been hanged for a murderess. Such was the power of my rage. As it happened, our tormentor had beaten a hasty retreat to the heart of Springfield. I hustled up the main road that passed through the warehouse district, and I could just see a tiny speck of red far in the distance—his distinctive jacket cutting across a street as the city came to life. He was making for the northern edge of town.

I kept my eyes on the man till he vanished around the corner of a hotel, and then I watched the spot where he'd disappeared while I trekked across Fifth Street, paying no heed to the blaring of horns or the shouts of drivers as I scrambled through traffic. The warm colors of sunrise had almost faded by that time. The luminous blue of a new day hung over roofs and chimneys. Beyond the hotel where I'd lost sight of my prey, I hunted up and down the alleys and side streets, alert for any sign of him, for a flash of red and black or the rasp of his laughter.

By and by, I came to a street where women in colorful dresses were filing out of the three- and four-story buildings, flaunting their shoulders and lifting the hems of their skirts a little too high. They were already calling out to passersby. In those hard times, even the bawdy girls had to start their day at dawn's first light. We all worked ten times harder, back then, no matter what our mode of employment.

One of the gals called to me, waving her hand and twiddling her fingers in the air. "Yoo-hoo! Looking for a nice way to start your morning, Johnny?"

The woman beside her—years older, with a cynical mouth—said, "Jesus, Nadine, that's a woman. Can't you tell?"

"Doesn't matter to me," Nadine answered. "I'll swing either way, if she's paying."

"Shit, you're stupid," the older woman muttered. "She's a hobo. She's got no money. And if Mikey catches you going after hobos, he'll beat the snot out of you."

"Look for customers who've got some cash to spend," another woman added, this one a blonde in pale green. "Train rats don't have anything to give you but fleas and the clap."

"Speaking of Mikey . . ." Nadine jerked her head toward the end of the block. A man in a brown suit was strolling easily down the sidewalk. He carried himself with an undeniable confidence, which was no doubt justified by his size. The man was pretty near big as a barn with the shoulders of an ox.

"Look alive, ladies," said the girl in green.

I'd gathered everything I needed to know about this Mikey character from the way the women spoke of him and hustled about more smartly as he approached. My life in Harlan County may have been sheltered, but even there, we'd heard tell of such businesses . . . and such businessmen. My moral side recoiled at the thought of speaking to such a lowlife, but a greater need urged me on. I made my way toward Mikey at a brisk walk and called out a hello long before I'd reached the man.

"You seen a man in a checked coat," I asked, "red and black? He might have come this way some five minutes ago, maybe ten."

The pimp knit his brows together, looked me up and down as if he couldn't quite make sense of me—a woman in trousers and suspenders, questioning him with all the boldness of a cop.

At length, he seemed to decide I posed no threat. He shrugged. "Yeah, I saw a guy in red check. Went down that alley there, right beside Clawson's. That's where the roughs play dice."

I nodded my thanks and turned for the alley, resolute, my fist closing around the knife in my pocket.

Mikey called after me, "Say, you looking for work?"

"Not just now," I said over my shoulder.

To myself, I added, *Not ever.*

Even in the morning air, the alley was stifling, dense with shadows and reeking of old piss. My eyes took their time adjusting to the dimness, so I was obliged to step along more slowly than I liked. The alley bent around the corner of a building some twenty or thirty feet ahead. The terminus was entirely hidden from my view. I slowed my pace yet more as I approached the bend, my right hand ready to draw out the knife and flick it open. Only then did I think to ask myself just what in the Savior's name I'd do if the man in the red-checked coat wasn't alone—if his dicing friends had already gathered.

I'll take them all on, I decided, guts quivering.

Surely I could never win such a fight, but I might drag two or three of them down to Hell with me before they put my lights out for good.

When I rounded the corner, however, the alley ended abruptly against a tall board fence topped with wire. There was nothing to be seen but a pile of old shipping pallets—and my friend in the checked coat, with his back turned to me as he pulled from a hip flask. His wicked knife was clearly visible in its belt sheath. The blade was near as long as my forearm.

All the righteous rage that had propelled me from the jungle through the streets of Springfield into that reeking alley faltered. *What have you gone and done this time, Del?*

But in the next moment, as the villain tipped his flask again and drank with a greedy haste, the slenderest barb of an idea embedded itself in my mind. Those girls out there on the street had inspired me. It was a wild, crazy, desperate gamble, but if I worked quickly, I just might pull it off.

"Hey there, mister," I said.

The man whirled to face me, stuffing his flask back into his pocket. "What in hell?" Belatedly, he recognized me through the fog of booze. His eyes narrowed in suspicion. "What're you doing? Followed me all this way? What for? A deal's a deal—now get lost."

"That's what I come to talk about. Deals. You wanted something back there on the riverbank, and me and my friend—well, we need money."

He grunted, which was supposed to pass for a laugh. "Who doesn't need money?"

"We talked it over, and decided we'll give you what you want . . . if you can pay."

"Well, I can't," the man said, and punctuated his statement with a belch. "Why you think I was gonna take it? If I could pay, I'd be out there with the pretty girls in their nice dresses—wouldn't come sniffing after the likes of you, all duded up like a man."

I forced myself to move toward him, offering a smile. "Bet we could work out a good price—better than you'd get from any of those gals on the street, with their pimp hanging around, watching like a hawk. Come on; don't you want a little fun? I can be quick. Get you taken care of before the boys show up to play dice."

He eyed me, considering, then said, "Fifty cents."

It was an insulting price—even a preacher's wife knew that. But I nodded, forcing another smile. "All right. How should we do this? Up against the wall?"

"Hell if I know."

He loosed his belt, and as I'd hoped, the weight of that knife immediately pulled his trousers around his ankles. It was the chance I'd hoped for. While he cussed and fumbled to reach his downed pants, I whipped the bone-handled knife from my pocket and flicked out the blade. I was around back of that drunken fool before he even saw me move, seizing his hair in one fist. With the other, I pressed the point of my knife hard against his throat.

"Whoa, now," he shouted, "steady!"

"Steady, my ass," I hissed into his ear. "Now it's your turn to do exactly what I say, or I'll flood this piss-stained alley with your blood. You hear me?"

He tried to nod, but that only made my knife dig in deeper. He gave a desperate little yelp of fear or pain, and a hot trickle ran over my knuckles.

"Hold still and answer me if you don't want to bleed more," I said.

He kept himself still as you please, waiting for my instructions.

"Where's the locket?" I said.

"I don't know what you're talking about."

"The gold. The gold you took from my friend. Where is it?"

"My pocket," the man gasped. "My trousers."

I glanced down. His trousers were still around his ankles. No way either of us could reach the locket now—not unless I backed off with my knife, and that was the last thing I intended doing.

I planted my foot atop his trousers and said, "Walk."

"Walk? I can't—not like this."

"Do it. Get going."

He stumbled and whined and cussed, but eventually he worked his feet right out of his trouser legs, boots and all. With my left hand still clutching his hair and my right pressing the knife to his throat, I marched him down the alley, around its blind corner, and into the open street.

Hoots and catcalls greeted us. The working girls and their early customers had caught sight of the spectacle.

The noise died down a little, and I yelled, "This pig tried to gut me and my friend—helpless women, both of us. He's a danger to girls everywhere. Now where's Mikey? Do you want him, or should I haul him to the cops?"

The pimp's booming laugh filled the street. I glanced up over the shoulder of my captive and found Mikey strolling toward us.

"Would you look at this," the pimp said. "Little lady's got some bite to her."

"You know this trash?" I asked Mikey.

"Yes ma'am, I do. He's been hanging around my streets, worrying my girls—really gets going when he's drunk. I'll take him from here."

Mikey laid hold of my captive's arm. Only when I felt the chicken hawk shudder in surrender did I dare to let go of his hair. Slowly, I withdrew the knife from his throat.

The pimp laughed again. "Sure you don't want a job? I could pay you to chase all the riffraff off the streets. Keep my girls safer while they're doing their work."

"No, sir," I said at once. "I've got a train to catch. I'll let you take out the trash, if you don't mind."

With a final laugh, Mikey began hauling the man down the street. The chicken hawk's bare white legs kicked and scrabbled as his drawers slid down, exposing his crack. The girls looked on in amusement—maybe in relief—but I could only stand there shaking, stunned by my own boldness. Now that my mad gamble was over and done with, it seemed impossible that I'd actually pulled it off. I turned my back on the cheers of the street workers and scampered back into that alley, convinced the man's trousers would have somehow vanished, leaving all my effort wasted.

But there they were, exactly where I'd left them, in a tangled heap on the cobbles.

I wiped my knife's blade on the man's pants, folded it, and put it away. Then I plunged my hands into both of his pockets till my fingers closed on something round and cool.

I pulled my prize out into the light. It was Louisa's locket, all right, though the man had discarded the cotton twine.

In our struggle, the catch of the locket had sprung, and now it lay open on my palm. I don't know what I'd expected to find inside—portraits of Louisa's parents, maybe, or a beloved grandma. Maybe even the picture of a sweetheart. Instead, the locket revealed the face of a small child—no older than two or three years, its sweet, round cheeks and soft eyes so like Louisa's that I knew on the instant that this could only be her own child.

13

Nearly two hours after I'd left, I finally found my way back to the abandoned jungle. Springfield was a maze to me, and all the anger that had sped me through its streets earlier that morning had vanished, leaving me with nothing but a breathless disbelief in my own audacity. It was only by the grace of God that I'd come upon the man in the checked coat after he'd hit the flask. If he'd been in his right and sober mind, no doubt he would have speared me on that terrible knife.

Yet despite my frank astonishment—which overtook me a little more with each city block I crossed—I knew if the choice were mine to make again, I would have done nothing differently. The sight of Louisa crouched and rocking, the sound of her stricken cries, still hung like a black veil across my mind. I'd traveled with her for weeks, and in all that time, I'd known her to be unflappable. She had faced down dangerous men, braved the railyard bulls with their swinging clubs. She had soldiered on through hunger and thirst and the fury of the beating sun. She'd even taken on the great thundering trains themselves with the same implacable confidence. Each night since we'd first made our acquaintance, I'd prayed that God might make me a woman of Louisa's sort. To see her reduced in an instant to that frightened, hopeless state was more than I could bear.

The morning sky had deepened to a clear, true blue above the jungle warehouses. I gripped the locket so tightly it might have bruised my palm. Surely Louisa had left without me. The apple harvest wouldn't wait, as she'd told me countless times, and after the mess I'd made of the Jackson hop, I knew I was nothing but a burden. She'd gone to the railyard, I told myself, and boarded the westbound freighter. Or she'd wandered off into the city, distracted by her grief. But the small artifacts of our time together lay scattered about the jungle, exactly where we'd left them—the pails we'd washed in, Louisa's still standing upright; the small tin cook pot in which we'd heated our supper the night before. My rucksack leaned against the warehouse wall, beside the sloping structure of the lean-to where we'd slept—and yes, Louisa's boots were there beside my pack, one fallen on its side with its laces snaked out across the cobbles.

I hurried across the courtyard, calling her name, and ducked into the lean-to. There she lay, curled in a ball on my sleeping mat. Tentatively, I knelt on the mattress of cardboard and touched her shoulder. She lay so still that I thought she might be dead.

When she felt my hand, Louisa sat up at once, blinking through the gloom of the lean-to.

"Del. You came back."

"Didn't I say I would?"

"I thought you'd left me. I thought I was alone. And I didn't even have—"

I opened my hand in the space between us. Her eyes fastened on the small, golden circle in my palm. I don't believe Louisa so much as drew a breath till she took the locket with trembling fingers. Her face crumpled with fresh tears—but she wept in relief this time, and gratitude. Her slight frame sagged toward me, and I caught her in my arms, holding her close, rocking as she wept against my shoulder.

I don't know how long we stayed that way, the two of us one small and insignificant point of love from which everything seemed to spread—the city and its grid of streets, the bustle of people going about a hard and weary day, the long roll of land beyond Springfield, the web of tracks that ran from us to every imagined destination. Even the pure blue arch of the sky seemed to rise from us, and I would have stopped the world from turning, held back the aging of the day, but it wasn't in my power, and anyway, nothing ever lasts.

When Louisa no longer shook, when her breath was steady, I released her gently and sat on the mat beside her. I took her hand in mine. "Why didn't you tell me you have a child?"

"I couldn't." She sniffed, wiping her nose on the back of her hand. "I can't ever speak of him, though I think about him every minute. I dream of him at night—I hold him in my arms, then, and it's like we've never been parted. But I can't speak of him, you see, because I love him too much, and I despise myself too much for leaving him. But I had no choice. I had to go, Del; I *had* to do it, or he wouldn't have made it. He'd have starved, or been taken away and put in some orphanage, and I'd never see him again."

She was working herself into another fit of tears. I squeezed her hand. "All right, take it easy. I believe you. But suppose you tell me everything now. I want to know all about him, Louisa; he's your baby. Your little son. Tell me his name, at least."

She took a long, shuddering breath. "I met my husband at a grange-hall dance in my hometown—not much of a town to speak of, north of Seattle. His name's Howard—my husband, I mean—and I guess he's handsome, or I thought him so, back when I was young and stupid. I was seventeen that year."

"I was pretty stupid at that age, myself," I muttered.

Louisa gave a small, brittle laugh. "Howard and I danced to a few songs, and after a while we got to kissing out back behind the grange, and one thing led to another. As it does, I guess." She paused, gazing down at the locket. "Well, I found myself in trouble just after I turned eighteen. So I married Howard. What else was I to do?"

My heart was pounding unaccountably. "Did you love him?"

Louisa shrugged. "It wasn't a happy marriage, not from the start. But I was determined to stick it out and do the right thing by my baby. And when little Eddie was born, he more than made up for the other happiness I lacked."

With a warm, distant smile, she told me all the ways she had doted on her son, as much as the wife of a poor farmhand could dote. She sewed the prettiest clothes for him and sang to him in his cradle. She played with him whenever there was no pressing housework to distract her, and cuddled him while he slept, and in the evenings when Howard came home cold and angry from the fields, Louisa kept the baby quiet so Howard wouldn't turn his hatred on the child. When Eddie was big enough to eat real food, she made strawberry jam and fed it to him on crackers, and gave him sweet cream to drink, and the boy grew and thrived in the sunshine of his mother's love.

"At the best of times, there was nothing but cold courtesy between Howard and me," Louisa said, "but I didn't mind, because Eddie was growing up healthy and strong, happy as a bee in clover. That was all that mattered to me. And then . . . well, then it was 1929."

She didn't need to say more than that. I understood. The Great Crash exacted its toll from Louisa, same as it'd done to every person who wasn't already living high on the hog.

"Howard lost his job and couldn't find another—not till he went all the way out to Idaho, where he was hired on for the potato harvest. I thought it a great thing at first, because there was some hope that he might be kept after the harvest to work the oats and the sugar beets. I went out to be with him—that seemed proper to me then—but almost as soon as I got there, Howard pulled up stakes and moved again."

"He didn't," I said, astonished.

"Went back to Seattle, where his mother lived. He said he hoped his mom's connections might bring him steadier work with better pay."

"And what did you do?"

She sighed and clicked the locket open to look at the face of her child. Then she closed it again and slid it into her pocket. "I was left alone in a one-room shack at the dying end of an Idaho town. It was a small, gray place, and I was stuck there with a baby to care for. Didn't even have running water in the house or an indoor toilet. I scrimped and begged for months to afford a bus ticket. I even sold off the baby carriage, which wasn't worth much anyhow since I'd found it alongside a road and it was in sore need of repair—patched it up myself with scrap wood and wire. But I got that ticket, and I was determined to make it to Seattle and hunt down my husband, make him own up to his responsibilities and care for us properly. We were his family, after all."

"That must have been an awful long trip," I said.

"You don't know the half of it. I'd only been on that bus for a couple of hours when I became convinced I'd died in my sleep and woken up in Hell, and the bus was my eternity of damnation. It was hot and stinking and packed full of crabby people—Eddie not the least among them. Have you ever tried to keep a fussy baby quiet on a crowded bus for hours on end?"

"Can't say I have," I chuckled.

"Count your blessings. It might not have been so bad if I'd had anything to distract Eddie, but all I had to my name was my handbag and an old hatbox, which I'd stuffed with the few old rags that served as Eddie's clothing. I'd crammed a packet of oats in the hatbox, too, and a bowl and spoon so I could feed us both. Oh, it was torture, Del—that long ride all the way back to Seattle."

"What happened when you reached the city?" I asked.

"Not much, at first. I spent three days tracking my husband down. By night, I slept in a hotel room—it was awful, dim and dripping with leaks from the roof, and it was right next door to a brothel, so you can imagine the noise. By day, I scoured the city with Eddie in my arms, looking for some sign of Howard. Finally, I learned his whereabouts and knocked on the door of an old Queen Anne house with peeling paint and a broken windowpane, yet it was far finer than any home I'd stepped inside for years."

"I guess that was Howard's mother's place."

Louisa nodded. "My mother-in-law opened the door. I'd never met the woman before, but she looked so much like Howard, there was no mistaking her. She took one look at me with her grandson in my arms—we were both dirty and exhausted. The old hag said, 'I'll put you up for one night, seeing as how he's my grandchild and it's the charitable thing to do. But after that, you're out again. I won't keep a no-good girl like you. I won't even hear of it.'"

"Lord have mercy," I exclaimed. "Hasn't she got a heart?"

"I guess not. I found out that day where Howard got his disposition from. And before I could so much as spit on his mother's shoe, Howard himself came storming out, shouting till poor little Eddie was red-faced and crying with fright. He said, 'Get away, you damned bitch. Can't you see I don't want you? Not you or the kid! You're both just a lot of weight to drag around, and I don't need either one of you no more.'"

Louisa recounted those cruel words with perfect calm. I didn't see how she could relive such a memory without bursting into tears. But maybe she'd lived it over so many times, it no longer had the power to hurt her.

Yet I could scarcely imagine the scene without a pang of reflected suffering—a poor little mother and her innocent child, having come so far and sacrificed so much, only to be met with cold rejection like a brick wall to the face.

"I backed out into the street," Louisa went on, "with my husband barking at me, and then he seemed to realize he might have some use yet for his wife. He said, 'Have you got any money?' I told him I had nothing, but he tried to snatch the handbag right off my arm. I clutched it tighter and held on to Eddie tighter still. I said, 'There's nothing but a quarter in there!'"

She sighed. From across the jungle, a crow called, and a motorcar's horn honked, tinny and quiet across the distance. Finally Louisa continued. "He said, 'Domino smokes are only ten cents a pack. Hand it over. I can get two packs and they'll give me more pleasure than ever you did.'"

I stared at Louisa, making no attempt to hide my disgust. "If I ever meet that pig's ass of a man—"

She laughed. "Don't worry, I got him good for both of us. I didn't give him that quarter, but I gave him something else. I kicked him hard. I tried to take out his knee, but I missed it by a hair. Still, he was howling and hobbling and cursing my name by the time I was done with him."

"Wish you'd kicked even higher," I said. "God knows, he deserved it."

"Well, I didn't know what to do then, or where to go. My parents had both died of consumption a few months after Eddie was born, so I couldn't go back to their place—though I doubt they would have taken me in, anyhow. They were sore when I got myself into trouble with Howard. They never approved of the marriage. But I did recall that I had an old uncle in a dairy town called Carnation, some way beyond Seattle in the foothills. I used that last quarter to hire a man to drive Eddie and me as far along the highway as we could get, and then I walked the rest of the way to Carnation—ten more miles. I asked around till someone pointed the way to my uncle Burke's place."

"Was he still living?"

"Oh, yes. The one stroke of good luck I'd had in years."

"Thank God for that."

The warmth returned to her now. "I do thank God for sweet old Burke, every day. He's the dearest man you'd ever hope to know. He hadn't seen me or even heard from my parents since I was a little girl, but once he was satisfied that I was a Trout, he vowed on the spot that he'd take care of me and my baby. His house was old and drafty, more spiderweb and mildew than solid wood, and there wasn't any bed for us to sleep on—not even a sofa. I found some old carpet pads in a back room, and piled those pads up into a little pallet, and crawled atop them with my boy snuggled up against my heart, and fell into the first deep sleep I'd had in weeks or months of worry."

Uncle Burke was as tenderhearted as Jesus Himself, to hear Louisa tell it, but that tender heart troubled him, and his useful days as a worker had long since passed. Before Louisa showed up on his doorstep, Burke had been scraping by off of what he could raise in his garden. He had a shotgun and picked off squirrels and rabbits from his back porch—that served for his meat.

Louisa said, "I knew if Eddie was to have all the clothes and medicine and proper food a growing boy needs, it would fall on me to earn the money. I tried for months to find work close to home, but there was nothing steady. Once, on a temporary job at one of the dairy farms, I got to talking with some hobos who'd been hired on for the day, and by the time our work was finished, I was convinced the only way I could hope to support Eddie and Burke was to take to the rails. And it has worked out pretty well. I send money transfers by telegram whenever I'm in a big city, and I call the Carnation church to check up on Burke and Eddie—Burke doesn't have a telephone, you know, but the pastor keeps an eye on things and lets me know how they're both doing."

"You haven't laid eyes on your boy for—"

"Fifteen months, three weeks, and four days," Louisa said promptly, "but who's counting? He was two years old when I left him. I don't know if I'll recognize Eddie when I finally see him again; children grow so fast. I don't know if he'll recognize me."

In silence, I watched the sunlight flare through the cracks in our lean-to's roof. I couldn't imagine the pain of parting with a child, especially one so young and needy. If I'd been forced into such a terrible choice, my anger would have known no limits; I would have drowned in a flood of my own bitterness. And yet Louisa was ever the steady and optimistic one. Just then, I felt such admiration for her spirit that I couldn't speak a word. The light from the roof merged into a bright blur, and the tears burned in my eyes, and even that burning held a little of the beautiful in it.

"I guess it's too late to catch that westbound train," I said. "Do you think another will come along tomorrow?"

Louisa sniffed away the last of her tears. "Probably."

"You get on it and get out of town," I said. "Get yourself to the orchards and then back to Eddie. It's long past time."

"But you—"

"Don't worry about me. I met a man this morning. He said I could take a job looking after his girls, scaring off the riffraff—"

"His *girls*," Louisa erupted. "Del, don't be a fool."

I went on as if she hadn't spoken. "I don't know how serious he was—about the nature of the work, I mean. I don't even know if I could do it properly, looking after the . . . the working gals. But I could try. It's a hope for me. If he's an honorable man—"

"He's not!"

"—he might pay me enough that I can look after myself right here in Springfield. So I'll be all right. You can go on without me."

Louisa rounded on me with a scornful expression. "Did you just fall off the turnip truck, or what? That sort of man is dangerous, and he's only got one job in mind for you, I can promise you that. Listen, Del—it was wrong of me to say what I said to you. You aren't a burden, and you aren't a bother. You gave me back the only thing I have left to remember my boy. Keep on with me, won't you? I kind of like having you around."

Such a fire burned in my heart at those words, it was a wonder I didn't light up the inside of our lean-to. I said, "You sure I won't hold you back?"

"I believe we'll make it to Wenatchee on time. I must believe—lately, believing's all I have. Besides, I don't want to part with you. You're my friend. And you came back for me."

I put my arm around her shoulder, though it made me feel giddy and wild to do it. I said, "All right. We'll stick together, the whole way. Clear to the end of the road."

14

Sad to say, we did not find a westbound freighter the next day, and as afternoon closed in, Louisa decided it was wiser to keep moving than to remain stalled in Springfield, which after all was too precarious a city to support a jungle. Instead, we boarded a train headed back to the south. As we rode atop a boxcar, sharing a supper of bread and cold ham, we watched Springfield dwindle at the vanishing point of the long black rails. The great enduring sweep of the land spread in a wake behind us, and as the sun settled into a blazing horizon, I felt more contented than I'd been since the earliest days of my marriage.

That night, Louisa and I slept sitting up on the narrow platform at the back of the train's caboose, leaning against one another for warmth. By dawn we arrived in St. Louis, but we didn't linger in the city. We dodged the bulls in the railyard and slunk between waiting trains to one whose locomotive bore the red-striped badge of the Union Pacific line.

We managed to find a fruit car on that train—always the most pleasant of accommodations—and caught a proper rest in its umber, honey-sweet confines. That train bore us across the state of Missouri. It paused for the night in Kansas City, and we liked our car so well that we held still as mice while the bulls inspected the train. We spent the night there among the fragrant crates where I dreamed of apples, alluring as the fruit of Eden, filling my arms till I couldn't hold them all and they fell down around my feet and piled up to my knees.

At dawn, we pulled out of Kansas City, but a few hours later, the train jarred and shuddered, its whistle blaring in a sudden parody of panic. With a long, black hiss of smoke, the engine dragged its burden into the tiny yard of a nowhere town, somewhere between Kansas City and Topeka.

Louisa peered out through the slats of our car. "Shit," she muttered. "Engine's broken down. No telling how long it'll take to repair, in a town like this. Our only hope is to get out and walk."

I helped her push the rolling door open—a tricky task from inside a car—and in a pensive silence, hoisted my rucksack while Louisa took up her bindle of tied cloth. We jumped down from our car into the heat of the day, which was already punishing, though noon hadn't yet arrived. At least there were no bulls to trouble us. There seldom were, in the smaller towns.

We set off through the heart of the village, which took no more than a few minutes to cross. Soon the town was behind us with miles of struggling corn stretching out ahead, the plants brown and weary, the distant farmhouses ominously still. We walked an unpaved road—no great novelty to a gal like me, who'd spent all her life in the backwoods of Kentucky—but even so, I'd grown used to the sight of cement as Louisa and I had traveled from one sizable town to the next. The ceaseless blowing of dust made me blink and sneeze, and the air carried a dry smell, as of long-exposed stone or weathered wood, which seemed to work in a strange, oppressive harmony with the relentless churring of insects in the fields.

"Heaven have mercy," I said after a good hour of walking, "why didn't we stay back in that town?"

"There'll be another up ahead. Roads always lead to somewhere, even dirt roads. We can find work along the way. The important thing is to keep moving west till we hit another railyard—and then we'll ride. June is just about over now. We've got two months to reach Wenatchee. We can't waste a day sitting around waiting for another train."

That made little sense to me, for a train could carry us much farther in a single day than our legs ever could. But I didn't dare to say so. Louisa was restless, gripped by a need to keep moving, haunted by longing I could never understand.

When the sun and the dust and the noise of the crickets became too much to bear, we left the road and skidded down into one of the many small gulches that yawned among the fields and useless pastures. You could spot these small oases by the presence of trees—cottonwoods or willows, usually, offering kindly shade as well as water. We found a crick at the bottom of our chosen gulch—thin and much diminished, judging by the swath of bare sand through which it ran. But the water was running, and the willow shade was sweet, and we both lay on our stomachs and drank directly from the stream, plunging our faces into the cool, clean water.

We dozed through the heat of afternoon, then extracted ourselves reluctantly from the blessing of the shade and walked on with the evening sun in our eyes. As it sank toward a purple horizon, the unmistakable outline of another small town appeared before us like the enchanted castle of a fairy tale, its humble houses and grain silos wavering and shimmering around their edges in a ripple of heat mirage.

In another hour, we arrived at the town's edge, a dusty sprawl of homes with bare wood planks for siding, all of them faded to anemic silver by the prairie sun and each one surrounded by fences of paling, which did little to contain the flocks of scrawny hens that scratched and pecked down the rows of drought-racked gardens.

There was more commotion in one yard, however, than hens could account for. A stout, gray-haired woman bustled about, unfurling cloths across a hodgepodge of tables—most of them borrowed from her neighbors, I assumed—and clucking at the troop of younger ladies who followed in her wake. The younger women smoothed the tablecloths with their hands and set bowls of cut glass on each table. A dark-haired girl of perhaps sixteen years seemed to almost dance among the tables as she filled the bowls with the black-eyed Susans that grew in profusion along the sides of the dusty road. The matron wore a remarkably old-fashioned and severe style—black dress with long sleeves, high collar buttoned tightly at her throat. She must have been in misery, for even as the sun set, the day's heat still lingered with a ruinous strength—but she never showed it. In fact, the younger women in her cadre seemed to scramble and fret to keep up with her.

The whole lot of them chattered to one another in a language I couldn't understand.

"Spanish?" I asked Louisa.

"I think they're Italian," she said.

At that moment, the matron took notice of us. She paused in her flight around the yard, then gestured to the youngest of her followers—the girl with the flowers—speaking in that rapid, indecipherable tongue. The girl broke away and approached the fence, raising a hand in greeting.

"Are you looking for work?" she asked.

Louisa and I glanced at one another. I shrugged under the weight of my pack.

"We are," Louisa said. "What can we do for you?"

With a nod, the girl indicated the gray-haired woman. "My nonna there says she'll give you something nice if you help us set up for the wedding party."

"Has there been a wedding?" Louisa perked up at the news; she was positively grinning.

"My sister," the girl answered. "Just got hitched this afternoon at the church, and we're to host the supper party, but Nonna couldn't find enough tables in time, and now we're all scrambling something awful to make the place look nice before Bea gets here with her new husband. You'll lend a hand, won't you, girls? Nonna doesn't have much money, but she's an awful good cook and she makes . . . well . . . all kinds of nice things."

Of course we were willing to help. Even if no compensation had been on offer, I believe Louisa would have thrown herself into the work for free. The prospect of a party—even one to which she hadn't been invited—seemed to fill her with an energy and a joy I hadn't much seen in her, all the weeks of our acquaintance.

With her granddaughter close at hand to translate, the brusque old lady directed us in moving the tables this way and that around the bare yard till they were placed to the matron's satisfaction. She sent us running to neighbors' sheds and porches to gather benches, chairs, and stools for use by the happy couple and their teeming family. Finally, Louisa was told to go fetch a pail of water from the well, and with a long tin ladle, I filled the cut glass bowls so the flowers would stay fresh through the night. It was the most pleasurable work we'd done in ages. Who can help but be delighted by a wedding? And to find such a joyful gathering in the long, brown, beaten-down expanse of the prairie—it was like stubbing your toe on a stone, only to discover a vein of pure gold running through the offending rock.

Just as the girls were carrying platters of food and baskets of little white cookies out from their dear nonna's house, the quack of an old car's horn sounded from somewhere up the road. Louisa and I withdrew to a corner of the house, well away from the celebrating family, and watched as a Model T came rattling and banging through a glorious, red-gold glow—the setting sun casting its rays among a stray cloud of dust.

The motorcar shuddered and fell still at the gate. The groom jumped from the driver's seat, calling and waving to his new family, blond hair slicked back to Clark Gable perfection, boyish smile crowned by a natty little mustache. He loped around the front of his car and opened the door for his bride—a laughing young woman with a round, dimpled face, her hair every bit as dark as her little sister's, though it was bobbed and curled in flawless waves around her ears. A tiara of yellow flowers held back a lace veil.

The bride's dress wouldn't have set any girl's heart to pounding. It was rather plain—a dove-gray cotton, which was, I assumed, the closest any poor family could come to white silk or linen. But someone had tatted an intricate collar with evident love and care, and though the cut of the dress was more serviceable than fashionable, it showed off the young woman's alluring figure, and she wore her dress with as much pride as if it were the trimmed-and-trained finery of a queen.

We beamed at the happy scene, Louisa and I, while family and friends greeted the new couple with kisses and tears. An old man, bald-headed with a round belly, took up a small accordion and began to play. His singing voice was unexpectedly basso; the contrast of his deep, rich warble against the whine of his instrument set me to giggling.

Only when the music began did our young translator seem to recall the two lady hobos who'd been hired to lend a hand. She broke from the crowd of celebrants and busied herself at a table—the one that held the better part of Nonna's cooking. Then she came to us, grinning.

Before she made it halfway across the yard, I was staring at the items she carried—a knotted bundle of cloth and a long-necked bottle sealed with wax, full of some amber liquid.

"Thank you both for your help," the girl said. "We wouldn't have had the place ready in time without you. Here—I've got you some wedding cookies in the napkin, and this is Nonna's specialty. Don't tell a soul, will you?"

Louisa accepted the bottle and held it up to the dying light. She cast a curious look in my direction, half fretful but brimming with mischief.

That bottle contained alcohol of some kind, no doubt. I believe Louisa was on the point of refusing it, and maybe she would have been wise to do so, but something wild and rebellious rose up in me. I'd lived all my life obeying every kind of law—God's law and Irving's, and the tight, confining rules of society within my church, within my valley. Why had I departed from that life, if I didn't really intend to leave it all behind?

"Thanks," I said to the girl, even as I snatched the bottle from Louisa's hands. "We'll enjoy this. Our best wishes to the bride and groom."

I picked up my rucksack and hurried from the yard. Louisa scrambled a few steps behind. Twilight had fallen by then. Windows glowed across the small town, and on the water tower that gloated fat and round above the tracks, the yellow orb of an electric light popped on. As I made my way back up the road, I could hear the light's faint buzz over the sound of the celebration.

"Are you crazy?" Louisa said when she caught up to me. "You know that stuff's illegal, and anyway, drinking is against the code."

"Only if we do it in the open," I reminded her. "It's fair game if we keep it secret, where no one else can see."

"We? You don't think I'm dumb enough to risk jail, do you?"

"For heaven's sake, Louisa, live a little. There's no one around to find us out."

She followed me off the road and into the open prairie. I'd spotted the dusky outline of a shade tree and suspected we would find another gulch at its foot, complete with some convenient water source. We skidded down the steep side of the depression and found neither pond nor stream, only a private gully well hidden from the road. The music and happy shouts of the wedding party could still be plainly heard. We hadn't wandered so very far from the house—maybe forty or fifty yards. The gully would make an ideal campsite, I thought, and I dropped my rucksack with a sigh of contentment.

I sank onto my bottom and leaned against the pack, examining the bottle as best I could in the gray half light. Thick wax at the bottle's mouth held a cork in place. I picked at the seal experimentally while Louisa propped herself against the trunk of the willow.

"What do you suppose it is, anyway?" I asked.

"Hell if I know, and you're better off not finding out."

"Well, I'm going to find out anyway. Would you believe I never had a single sip of booze?"

"Neither have I," Louisa said, "and it hasn't hurt me any."

"But you're so much younger than I am. Why, I was nineteen when they outlawed hooch—old enough to have tried it. I would have, if I hadn't been so damn set on being a good girl."

"There's nothing wrong with being a good girl. If I'd been good, I wouldn't have gotten into trouble so young. I wouldn't have ended up with that horse's ass Howard. My life would have turned out a whole lot happier if I'd been good."

"But then you wouldn't have . . ." With a guilty glance at Louisa's face, I stopped myself. The last thing I wanted was to remind her of the baby she'd left behind. I said, "The Lord works in mysterious ways. Sometimes our greatest blessings proceed from the things we believe, at first, to be curses, or outright damnation."

Louisa snorted, a cynical little laugh. "Is that what they taught you in your good-girl Kentucky church?"

I withdrew the knife from my pocket, flicked out the blade, and dragged its tip through the wax, all the way around the neck of that bottle. "I learned a lot of things at church. Turns out most of them weren't true—or not true enough to satisfy me. Does that make me wicked, do you think? Am I a sinner because I up and went my own way?"

Louisa only watched while I pried at the cork with the tip of my knife, and finally worked it up to where I could grasp it with my fingers. When I pulled it from the bottle's mouth, the cork gave a loud and comical pop.

"Smell it—it's sweet." I held the bottle out so Louisa could take a whiff.

"Apples," she said, "or pears, maybe. I'd think an Italian grandma would make something more traditional—a grape wine."

"Maybe grapes have been scarce these past few years," I suggested. "Guess old Nonna back there used whatever fruit she could get her hands on. Well—bottom's up."

Louisa winced as I tipped back the bottle and took a tentative sip. The cider was crisp on my tongue, with a curious bite like the flavor of sourdough bread. It wasn't half-bad, I decided, and went in for a proper swig. The bottle chugged with bubbles as I swallowed down its generous offering.

"Sweet baby Jesus," Louisa cussed, "you better slow down. Here, hand it over."

I passed the bottle and wiped my mouth on my sleeve. Resigned, Louisa rolled her eyes, then tasted the cider. Her expression brightened.

"Good, isn't it?" I said.

"You're a real devil, you know that, Del?" She took a proper pull.

We remained hidden in that gully, just the two of us, passing the bottle back and forth while the stars came out to hang among the willow branches and the music went on at the nearby house—and laughter, and exclamations in which we could hear the love and the hope, even if we couldn't understand the words. Little by little, the cider worked its spell, suffusing me with a fuzzy warmth, weighing down my eyelids and my tongue. My thoughts were all very comfortable, easy to abide, even when I mused on Irving and the home I'd left behind, and my parents who would never welcome me again. I should have felt melancholy, but with that accordion singing away and the hands clapping and the voices calling in joyous discord, there was no room for sadness in my heart. There was only a calm and grateful acceptance of the here and now.

What if I was wicked? What if I had sinned? God and His angels hadn't come flying down to punish me. Maybe that was a thing the church had gotten wrong, too. Maybe there was no punishment coming—nothing worse than what I'd made for myself by taking off on that train. And even that had turned out all right, I thought, as I watched Louisa tip back the bottle. Her sun-browned throat tensed as she swallowed, and when she lowered the cider from her lips with a melting sigh, I could feel it in my own warm body—her breath, her exhalation, her surrender to the drink.

"You know what I'd like?" Louisa's words were a little slow, a little mushy. "Another shot."

"At what?" I found to my embarrassment that my tongue was every bit as clumsy as hers was.

She waved a hand in the general direction of the revelry. "Mar . . . marriage. Husband and wife. That whole . . . thing."

"Not me," I said decidedly. "Once was enough."

"But you got to be a real lady. You got to have a nice home and a respectable man—"

"That's a matter of opinion," I slurred.

"All I ever got was Howard. And a shack in a potato field. Damn it."

She tried to spit but only succeeded in running a line of slobber down her chin. She wiped it away with a bleary grin. Laughing, I reached my feet across the space that separated us and pressed the soles of my boots against hers.

"I wouldn't have left." Louisa's head fell back against the tree. She gazed up through its branches to the white, white stars. "I wouldn't have left at all if I had what you had, Del. I would have put up with damn near anything to have a nice, pretty life."

Her declaration sent dread into my tipsy heart. It seemed the worst kind of blasphemy, for a woman as brave and strong, as magnificent as my friend Louisa to put up with the least speck of nonsense from any man. And when I tried to imagine her meekly tolerating the outrage Irving had heaped upon me—well, my drunken spirit rose up in protest.

I kicked at her boot. "No, you wouldn't."

"I would."

"You would not, by God. Don't say it. Don't even think it. You're better than that, Louisa. You're . . . you're the best girl I ever knew."

And I wanted to tell her, then, what a miracle it was that I knew her at all, how improbable this all had been—our meeting by chance on a boxcar I'd only boarded in a fit of pique, miles and miles away from where either of us had originated. Still we'd come together, and that night, under the stars that sang along to the humming of the accordion, I understood that this was something rare and holy, this unlikely union. Our friendship was meant to be. It was bigger than us; it was something, really something. It was everything to me.

I tried to form the words to say, *God works in mysterious ways,* but all that came out was a slurred mess, and I started over again and failed, and tried once more till Louisa and I were both rocking with helpless laughter, tears running from our unfocused eyes.

A train cried in the distance. The long, mournful call caught at my heart and stilled me, and the sound and the distant vibration of its wheels passed through my addled self, and I felt as if every part and fragment of me would shudder to pieces and blow away on the wind, except for the bottoms of my feet, which were still pressed tight against Louisa's—the only bit of me that remained real and whole.

"What's that?" she whispered, sitting up straight.

"Train," I said.

"No, you dummy—listen."

My thoughts treaded water and turned in upon themselves, but by and by, over the rumble of the approaching train, I understood what had set Louisa on edge. The accordion had fallen silent. The sounds coming from the nearby house were no longer those of laughter and fun but of anger, distress. Together, Louisa and I scrabbled up the slope of our gully and peered over its edge, back toward the celebration.

We hadn't gone as far from the house as I'd originally thought. Now the yard seemed painfully near—close enough that even through my befuddlement I could see the uniformed police striding about, pointing their clubs at the Italians and ordering them to stand along the fence.

Louisa let fly a cuss worse than any I'd heard before. "They'll find the hooch. They'll come looking around the property, too. They'll find us, for sure, and in this state . . . damn it, Del, I told you it was a bad idea!"

The train pounded toward the sleeping village. Its lone yellow eye blurred and fuzzed in the darkness. It would slow as it reached the crossroads. I said as much to Louisa.

"You can't hop a moving train," she snapped. "We're sitting ducks!"

"Like hell I can't hop it."

I slid back to the floor of the gully, retrieved my pack. The danger had sobered me up a little—enough, anyway, that I could secure the rucksack on my shoulders and clamber back up the side of the gully without losing my balance.

"It's our only chance," I said. "We've got to run for it before the cops come searching for more booze."

"We'll draw their attention if we run."

"It won't matter, once we're on that train."

I took off across the field before Louisa could argue again. The ground seemed to lurch and wobble under my feet, giving me the dizzy impression that I was moving across the surface of some enormous aspic. But I kept my eyes on the locomotive and the string of cars behind it, just visible now in the night. I could hear Louisa scrambling and cussing under her breath as she followed me across the road. The terrible urgency of her subdued voice sped me on, driving back a little more of the alcohol's haze.

"Who's that?" I heard a man shout behind us. "Look—a couple of tramps! You there! Stop!"

"Run!" Louisa cried.

The engine thundered past as we left the road, sprinting for the raised berm on which the tracks ran. Long weeds whipped around my legs. The noise and coal stink, the shuddering of the passing cars shook the last of the drunkenness from my mind. I staggered as my feet found loose stones, but regained my balance in a flash and ran hard alongside the great black dragon of the freighter. Louisa was just ahead of me, her left arm flung out, ready to catch hold of a ladder and pull herself aboard.

As I raced after my friend, one thought remained clear in my fevered head, and it was this: every time I'd tried to catch a train at a run, I had failed. Oh, I'd pulled myself onto slow-rolling freighters as they'd crept through crossroads, trotting easily along to get up my speed, and I'd boarded more stopped trains than I could count, when there was nothing more to trouble me than the bulls lurking at the far end of a yard. But every time I'd had to really run—every time I had to force myself closer to the mindless, uncaring beast that flew so powerfully along its track—my courage and my strength had failed. And I was in no fit state now, to say the least.

Serves you right, a sly voice whispered in my head. *A wicked gal like you, a sinner right through to the heart of you.*

I hadn't run more than a few dozen yards but already my breath was like fire, and my legs had turned to jelly. Louisa seemed to sprint on, easy as a greyhound. I kept my eyes fixed to her back, pushing away my fear of the train—its crushing weight and relentless motion.

That insidious voice tried to whisper at me again. I shut its mouth. *You can't let her get on that train without you,* for, you see, it wasn't the cops I feared most. Rather, it was being separated from Louisa. The very thought that she might go on without me—that I might be left alone in this dry, mean world—flooded me with such despair that my legs seemed to pump of their own volition, and I ran with the mechanical power of the side-irons that flashed as they spun the locomotive's wheels.

Even as we ran, the cars moved steadily past—open-topped gondolas loaded with steel, the wooden slats of the fruit cars from which a vegetal stink trailed. Louisa veered closer to the train. Like some half-trained animal, I whined in terror, but I kept as close to my friend as I could manage, forcing myself nearer to the thundering beast, then nearer still.

For a moment, our pace fell into a smooth synchronicity with the train's speed. A boxcar drew level with our position and held there, rather than passing us by. Louisa caught hold of a narrow ladder riveted to the side of the car. She leaped and pulled in the same instant. Her feet found the lowest rung.

"Come on," she shouted down to me, then scrambled a little higher.

I'll never do it. I'll never—

I could feel myself flagging, my pace slowing; the car was edging ahead.

"Del!" Louisa screamed. "Run faster!"

I can't! I didn't even have the breath to speak those words, let alone yell them back at Louisa. My throat was raw with the effort, my chest stuffed with coals.

Then, for no reason I could name, a memory came back to me of the yellowwood grove. Irving's arms around that girl, the bodice of her dress fallen open, the paleness of her private flesh exposed.

You bastard, Irving. You low-down, no-good, lying son of a bitch.

That was the life Louisa aspired to—that good, unshaken, long-suffering woman wanted nothing more for herself than the comfortable lies Irving had fed to me. If I let that train roll on without me, not only would the cops nab me and toss me in the pen, but Louisa would go on and find the life she only thought she wanted. I wouldn't have the chance to convince my friend that she was so much greater than the small, complacent, useful thing that was all Irving had allowed me to be.

A final burst of strength hit me in a warm flood. I pushed harder, harder, drew level with the ladder on the boxcar.

It's easy, I reminded myself, and reached out a hand.

My fingers closed around steel. I leaped, lashing out with my other arm, caught the ladder, and lifted my flailing boots to snag on the lowermost rung.

Above the rattle and scream of the train, I heard Louisa's voice: "Follow me!"

I clung to that ladder like a flea on a dog, and as I crept upward, I kept my eyes trained on Louisa's bottom so I wouldn't see the ground rushing below. She had slipped her hand through the ties of her bindle; it hung from her wrist as she scurried up the rungs to the top of the car. In another moment, she vanished over the edge of the boxcar's roof.

When I too pulled myself onto the roof, every shred of strength left me. I could only crawl on hands and knees, my body racked by terrified sobs. Someplace far below—and much too close for comfort—the black ground hurtled by at a deadly speed.

"You did it, Del!"

Louisa had dropped the bindle at her feet and now she stood, fists braced on her hips, facing into the wind. Her white shirt snapped and fluttered around her wiry body, and the dark banner of the engine's smoke fattened and trailed above her head, smothering the stars. She lifted her hands in a gesture of wild exhilaration, howling at the sky, just as the train opened its throat again to sing its long and melancholy verse.

Slowly I sat up, blinking at the wide-open world. Even by starlight, I found a certain austere beauty in the Kansas plain—the long, ancient curves of land, their undulating blackness against a faint flush of purple light that still lingered, summer-low, at the horizon. The narrowness of the train and the sheer plunge from the top of the car to the ground sickened me, and the cider sloshing in my guts threatened to heave up and splash all over the roof at any second. But when I held still and kept meticulously to the center of our car, I felt safe enough, and the sickness receded. The fresh air blowing into my face even soothed me a little and cleared the last of the haze from my head.

I slid out of my pack carefully and took out my canteen. I'd filled it hours before in that little crick where Louisa and I had lain against the warm earth and watered ourselves like beasts of the field. A long drink steadied my nerves still more.

Louisa set down beside me. I passed her the canteen. We watched the town fly past, then the unlit mystery of the prairie lands, which rippled out from our vantage point like the gentle waves of a pond when a pebble is tossed into its heart.

"You're a real hobo now, Del." She leaned away from me, caught hold of her bindle and dragged it across the steel roof. "This calls for a celebration."

Louisa opened the bindle with expert speed. The cloth unfolded to reveal the remains of our food, which she'd brought from the jungle—half a loaf of bread, a wedge of hard cheese, and a small jelly jar a quarter full of molasses. She opened the jar with a flourish, as if she were uncorking another bottle of wine.

"Go on," she said, "rip off a good chunk of bread and dip it in. Tastes better than anything you've ever eaten before."

After my fear and exertion, the pure, decadent sweetness did soothe me a little. Louisa and I dipped our bread and ate, grinning, till the molasses was practically gone. Then we took turns wiping out the inside of the jar with our fingers, licking and grazing our own flesh with our teeth, and soon the sweetness was only a memory, and around us, the open country slept through the black and silver of night.

15

We slept possum belly that night, blanketed by the brisk wind, and in the rosy flush of morning we found the sun rising to our right hand.

"Turned north," Louisa said, "sometime in the night. We'll be in Omaha by evening, I guess. Good yard there; we'll find plenty of freighters headed west."

All day long, we rode atop that train. The climbing sun touched the land with a honey-colored light, casting the contours of dry crick beds and disused irrigation ditches in shades of ethereal violet. We passed whitewashed villages with all the hope beaten out of them—towns that, at a distance or in flashing proximity to the track, seemed huddled in upon themselves or emptied like the husks discarded after a harvest. Sometimes I would catch a glimpse of a tattered green curtain in a window or a yellow cat sitting on a roof, or a line of some small child's dresses hung out to dry in the unforgiving sun, and some great, invisible hand would take hold of my heart—and then the sight would fall behind, gone in a blink the way things always go, and I'd be left swallowing down that sudden ache, asking myself why the vision had affected me, why it still rang like an echo in my mind, miles down the track.

As the afternoon drew to its languid close, Louisa and I found ourselves clinging to the space between two cars on a slow approach to Omaha. The Union Pacific line ran across the Missouri River on a long trestle bridge, and under normal circumstances, we would have been someplace up top, riding the roof of a fruit car or sitting on a heap of coal under the open sky, enjoying the sight of the long brown river stretching from one horizon to the other. But that particular train had picked up hobos at every yard and crossing—we'd watched them run, as we'd done, to climb aboard the boxcars or, when the train had halted to couple with a few more cars, the hobos had come skittering out of the brush to fit themselves in among the steel beams of an undercarriage, where they would ride mere inches above the track. About an hour before we'd come within sight of the river, word had made its way from car to car that the Omaha yard was bristling with bulls, and they were as vicious as any that had been encountered along the whole great network of the rails.

Now, bulls—as I've mentioned before—were the cops who worked the railyard beat. Their sole purpose was to deter hobos, under the mistaken belief that our kind posed some danger to the folks who worked on the trains and in the yards, or, more likely, some danger to the cargo. You couldn't tell bulls one word about the hobos' sacred code. The cops were convinced that anyone who rode a freight train and looked a little shabby must be a thief and a murderer, come to town in single-minded pursuit of law-breaking and general mayhem.

I hadn't encountered many bulls while traveling with Louisa, and when we did spot cops in the railyards, we'd been able to keep a respectable distance between ourselves and them. But we'd mostly stuck to small towns in the middle of nowhere. Omaha was a thriving city—that is to say, it was thriving as much as any place was in 1931—and as we drew closer to its low red sprawl and its bristle of smokestacks, I understood with sinking dread that I'd soon have a brush with the law that I wasn't likely to forget.

Therefore, Louisa and I vacated the roof of the box we'd been riding and clambered down the handholds into the precarious space between the rushing cars. My feet were braced on the hand brake's gearbox and

Louisa's on the coupling rod, not even a yard above the tracks, and we hooked our arms through the rungs of the ladders. There we hung like a couple of shot pheasants, limp from the heat, battered by the noise and vibration of the train, trying to make up our minds what to do when we alighted in the yard and faced down the worst bulls any hobo had seen that summer. At least the air was cooler between the cars. The sun could no longer sap us the way it sapped the land, and when our freighter began creeping out onto the bridge over the Missouri, a merciful wind came up off the river to cool our heads.

"So what about these bulls?" I asked.

Louisa reached across the coupling to unhook the canteen from my pack. She managed to work its top open without dropping it on the tracks. Then she took a long swallow and exhaled in satisfaction.

"Nothing to do but run," she said.

I took a drink, too. The water had gone warm, and it tasted strongly of dirt. It didn't set easy in my stomach. The other hobos on that train had been properly anxious about the stop to come. Their fear had worked deep into my own nerves.

Some ten minutes later, the crawling train arrived in the biggest yard I'd seen on my travels so far. A dozen different tracks crossed a gray expanse of gravel. Spare sleepers, black with creosote, and even a few lengths of iron rail were piled to one side. A collection of cars stood here and there on various tracks, waiting to be coupled and hauled away. Along one edge of the yard, just past the unused ties, a low brick building seemed to watch our approach, its track-facing windows like small, suspicious eyes. I knew instinctively that the jail cells were in there—the pens where the bulls would toss any hobos they might snag.

The engine breathed out its steam. The cars nudged against one another, and the train came to rest.

I was on the point of asking Louisa again what we ought to do, but before I could open my mouth, she dropped from the edge of the car. Her feet hit the loose stones with a clatter. A moment later, her crouched figure went scurrying toward a trio of waiting cars at the far end of the yard. I cursed under my breath and jumped as she'd done, stumbling under the weight of my pack. But I caught myself quickly and strode after Louisa, too frightened even to look around for the bulls.

She crossed a couple of empty tracks and dodged behind one of the unused cars, a big yellow one. I stayed close on her heels, pressing myself against the painted steel. The car was warm, holding the day's brutal heat. Beyond the yard, the city of Omaha seemed one low mass of brick under a dome of pale sky. An early chorus of crickets called among dry weeds, where the yard gave way to roadside and vacant lots and the shabby gardens of the poorest houses. Louisa had no attention for Omaha, however. She was still half-crouched, cautiously watching the yard from the edge of the yellow car. I was taller than she, and after a moment, I grew brave enough to slide in close above her head, peering likewise into the yard.

The train we'd just left was astir with activity. Some fifteen or twenty cars ahead of ours, the engine still panted out smoke, and from the couplings between boxes, from the chassis below, the ragged men emerged. Their clothing was gray and torn. Some had faces and hands blackened by the thick dust of the coal carriages. Every one of them ran like the Devil himself was on his heels.

Into that flurry of dodging bodies, a handful of police officers strode, each carrying a short wooden club with a leather strap at one end. The bulls flailed at the running men, knocking some from their feet. Once the hobos were down, the police kicked at their ribs and legs. Most of the stricken men struggled back up and evaded the officers, but two were quickly handcuffed and made to sit on the sharp ballast while the officers gave chase to the others. The scene reminded me of nothing so much as a pack of dogs gleefully snapping at panicked hens.

"They're distracted by those poor saps they've caught," Louisa muttered. "Now's our chance."

She headed for a vacant lot. I followed anxiously, glancing back to make sure the bulls hadn't seen us. I watched the cops drag the two captured men to their feet; the hobos were so weak and weary that they gave no resistance, and only one officer was needed to frog-march both men toward the brick jail.

The yard seemed to stretch into eternity; there were always more tracks to cross, and the lot that offered its scant protection never seemed to come any nearer. Again I glanced over my shoulder, just in time to see one of the two remaining bulls point at us with his club. He shouted something to his partner, and both took off running in our direction.

I brayed Louisa's name.

She didn't need to look around to know what had frightened me. "Run, and don't stop for anything!"

We sprinted side by side for the tall grass at the yard's edge. Sharp stones clattered and sprayed from our feet; the breath came hot in my chest. I could hear the heavy tread of the bulls' boots gaining on us, and I strangled a scream. Then the yard was gone; waist-high grass as yellow as buckskin surrounded me. The crickets fell silent as we stampeded into their sanctuary.

"This way!" Louisa cried.

She darted to the right. I straggled after, and a heartbeat later she vanished. I had only a moment to wonder where she'd gone before the ground was no longer below me. I rolled down a steep embankment, hot earth pummeling the breath from my body, the world spinning in a confusion of dust and yellow grass. I fetched up against the trunk of a tree and lay there, aching and dazed, trying to decide whether I was alive or dead.

On her feet, Louisa skidded down the slope and hurried to my side.

"Good God almighty," she said, crouching on her heels. "Didn't you see the drop-off?"

I could only croak in reply.

"Anything broken?"

I shook my head. Every inch and surface of my body throbbed miserably, but nothing hurt bad enough for serious injury.

We heard men's voices somewhere at the top of the embankment.

Louisa whispered, "Lie still. They won't spot us through the branches of this tree."

She was right. In another moment, the bulls drifted back to the yard. The crickets resumed their singing.

I sat up slowly, easing the pack from my shoulders.

"It was your bag that did it, more than likely," Louisa said. "Unbalanced you."

I said, "We don't all have pockets as deep as yours."

Since I'd first met her, Louisa had been a great believer in carrying everything she needed in her pockets—or in the worst extremity, the simple bindle of cloth she sometimes tied around her possessions. She'd always thought my rucksack and camping mat a burdensome luxury.

The bank down which I'd tumbled was a steep spill of dry earth and pea gravel. It landed—as I had done—on a flat stretch of grass with a few trees that reached up toward higher ground. The river flowed swiftly past, some fifteen or twenty feet away. The location would have made an ideal place to rest our bones if not for the bulls, who were much too close for comfort. We shook our heads at one another in silent accord.

"There's a good jungle in the city," Louisa said. "I stayed there almost a year back."

"Can you still find it?"

She stood, offering a hand. "Let's see if I can. I hope you're up for walking a mile or two."

Louisa pulled me to my feet. Not one fiber of my body felt up to the walk, but I stifled my groans and picked up the burdensome luxury of my rucksack. I followed Louisa up the slope of the riverbank to the city beyond.

~

It took the better part of three hours to find the Omaha jungle. By the time we made it to that shantytown, I was limping and stiff, haunted by a fond recollection of the hot spring down in Arkansas. Afternoon deepened slowly, as it does in summertime, into a golden evening. We were still at the edge of Omaha, but two or three miles north of the railyard, in a district of great brick warehouses, most of which were clearly abandoned with windows smashed away and colonies of pigeons roosting on the rooftops, whitening the sidewalks with evidence of their long occupation.

"This is it," Louisa said, turning down a narrow alley between two empty buildings.

I couldn't see any difference between this alley and a hundred others we'd passed. "Are you sure?"

She pointed to a strange hieroglyphic scrawled in chalk on the brick wall: a large X with a line connecting its uppermost legs. From either side of the X's junction, a pair of eyes stared back at me.

"That's a surefire mark," Louisa said. "Hobo sign—the secret language of our kind. This is the place, no doubt—and it ought to be occupied, unlike the jungle back in Springfield."

She led the way down the marked alley. The walls seemed to press in from both sides. A strange, high wailing cut through the fading day; it sounded like the cry of a trapped animal or, God forbid, a woman in distress. After my brush with the bulls and that tumble down the hill, I was in a bad way, and the odd keening sound only heightened my distress. I felt certain I was limping into grave danger and wondered if the misery of my marriage might not be preferable, after all, to life on the rails.

The alley gave way to a wide courtyard paved in old cobbles which were still painted, here and there, in white stripes to indicate where trucks might be loaded. Frames made from discarded lumber formed rustic tents, their sides and roofs fashioned from canvas tarpaulins and shabby blankets. Lean-tos constructed from scrap wood, similar to the one we'd used in Springfield, lined the outer walls of the warehouse. As Louisa and I paused in the alley's mouth to take in the welcome sight, hobos began emerging from those shanties into the glow of evening.

The people made their way to a ring of simple benches arrayed around a steel barrel, which was much darkened and scorched, especially at its mouth. A lanky Black fellow presided over the barrel. Now and again, he reached down into its depths to stir something. A pale flame licked up from inside, and I realized the man was tending a kettle or pot suspended just below the rim above a blazing fire.

We'd arrived in time for supper. Hobos of every description assembled on the benches with tin plates in hand, awaiting a proper feed up. They were black and white, old and young—there was even another woman among them, middle-aged with a jolly smile, her hair bound in a silk scarf printed with yellow flowers. A man with a long, white beard sat a little apart from the others, close to the long-legged cook, playing a harmonica. It was this gentle sound that had so unnerved me only moments before.

The smell of supper reached me across the courtyard—rich onions, a medley of herbs, the familiar tang of celery and carrot. I sucked in the smell greedily. My stomach ached with anticipation.

The cook caught sight of Louisa and me as we entered the jungle. He dropped his ladle into a bucket of water at his feet, then swept toward us with a shout. "Louisa! By God, it's really you. Look, fellas; our ol' girl has come back through."

He wrapped my friend in such a tight embrace that he lifted her clean off her feet. Laughing, she kissed the man on both cheeks before he set her down again.

The others laid their tin plates aside and flocked to Louisa, greeting her with the same familiarity the cook had shown. I watched in dumbfounded silence; never had I imagined Louisa was so popular among the folk of the rail. The hobos pelted her with questions—how far she'd come, where she'd last worked, whether there was still any prospect for a job to the east or down south—and Louisa answered them all, grinning, entirely at ease.

When the general noise died away, she threw an arm around my shoulders. "This is Del, out of Kentucky. She's green, but she's been a good pal so far. You'll make her welcome, won't you?"

"Why, of course we will," the cook said. "Any friend of yours is a friend of ours."

He fetched a tin plate from the stack near his wash bucket, filled it with stew, and handed it to me. The stew consisted entirely of vegetables, yet even without meat, it was the most compelling sight I'd laid eyes on in many days of travel. How long had it been since I'd enjoyed a hot meal? My stomach growled again, and though I tried to keep my attention on the faces around me while Louisa introduced her friends, my eyes kept drifting back to the stew.

The cook—his name was Harney—chuckled and passed me a spoon. "Let this poor girl fill her belly. You can tell by that wild look in her eyes, she hasn't had a taste of stew in far too long."

Louisa and I were ushered to a bench; we took our place beside the white-bearded man with the harmonica. He was big as a bear and pretty near as broad, with a roundness you didn't find often among hobos. By his lean, corded hands and his flat cheeks, I surmised that his bulk had more to do with muscle than fat. He slipped the harmonica into the pocket of his shirt, giving me a nod that put me in mind of Santa Claus, if old St. Nick were to trade in his suit of furs for the patchwork trappings of a hobo.

"Welcome, Miss Del," the old man said. "The name's Skipjack."

There was no place to set my plate but on my knees. I did so, following Louisa's lead, and tried not to spoon up the meal with too much haste. I struck up a chat with Skipjack while I ate, asking about his origins and what work he'd done lately—that seemed to be the most usual topic among the hobos. He talked on as if we'd been friends for ages, though I confess I can't recall much of our conversation now. I was much too absorbed in my stew. The carrots and potatoes swam in a flavorful broth, and the miraculous feel of something warm in my belly filled me, moment by moment, with a contentment I'd scarcely known at any prior time in my life. If not for my aches and bruises, I could have lost myself entirely in the bliss of a hot meal.

Once they'd cleaned their own plates, the hobos began pulling items from their pockets or from the flour sacks they'd stowed under benches—a loaf of bread, a clay pot full of molasses, a shirt with red cloth patches at the elbows but freshly laundered, without a speck on it. Jenny, the woman with the flowery scarf, produced a small jar filled with brown sugar and a half-empty bottle of Pronto's grippe syrup from her trouser pockets. These, of course, were the wages with which the hobos had been paid that day. No one had any intention of keeping his pay to himself. Everything earned was to be shared with the whole. Each passed his contribution to Harney, who gathered the items on an upturned crate near the fire barrel.

The frank evidence of such care—of true community, brother looking after brother—raised a melancholic yearning in me. My throat went tight; I feared I might weep. I missed my home. Not Irving—he could go piss up a rope, as far as I cared—but my mother and my pop, my brothers and their families, the women of my prayer circle. Maybe it was only my aches and pains, which were formidable that night, but something set me to longing for everything I'd left behind. It was the first moment of real regret I'd had since taking my leave.

Oh, I'd been a fool to leave such goodness behind; Louisa was right about that. And as I watched those bedraggled specimens of humanity commit their earnings to the common good—as I watched the loaves of bread and the jars of medicine pass from hand to dirty hand—I understood how dire my circumstances were, how untenable. Till that moment, I'd looked upon hoboing as some sort of grand adventure. Now I saw it plainly for the desperate struggle it was—had always been, from the moment the chicken hawk had pulled his knife in my first boxcar. Louisa and I were never more than a couple of days away from starvation. Sure, we earned money as we bounced from town to town, but it was barely enough to keep our heads above water. The flood of hunger and weariness rose a little higher with each passing day. How much longer could we hope to tread water? How could we hope to beat back this brutal tide?

Swallowing my tears, I reminded myself that I still had most of the fifteen dollars I'd taken from Irving's dresser, and the jewelry to boot. It was some insurance against total ruination. I could get back to Harlan County on that money, sure enough—if I could reconcile myself to Irving's underhanded ways. But then there was the question of whether my family would welcome me home. I couldn't be sure they would.

"Weren't the best day we've had." Harney's sober voice snapped me out of my grim musing. "Two good loaves of bread, which is always welcome, and this nice bit of brown sugar will be swell in the morning porridge. But no coin, fellas—and we could have used a little. Coffee's running low."

Skipjack said, "I might have got paid in hard money if I'd got out to the farms at crack of dawn. By the time I arrived, they'd already hired a mess of kids to do the summer planting."

"Kids?" Louisa said. "Children out working in the fields? They ought to be in school."

"School's a fine thing," Skipjack said, "when a family ain't starving. I don't think many kids out here in farm country has seen the inside of a school since this emergency began."

This emergency. There was no need to give it a name, no sense in trying to encompass every fact and feature of the catastrophic end that had come upon us all. The heat, the desperation, the rains that existed only in memory, or in the unreality of a scarce-remembered dream. The dollars that were good for only half of what they'd bought the week before. This endless, permanent emergency. The frayed hem of our lives, a thread that only unraveled faster the more desperately we clung to it.

"The worst part is," said another man—I think his name was Porter, "those dang kids'll work cheaper than a grown man. You land in a town with a lot of desperate children, and you won't find much work for yourself."

"At least we're free to come and go as we please," Jenny said. "Most kids ain't so lucky. They're stuck wherever their ma and pa may be."

"Till they grow enough guts to get on a train," Louisa said.

"Or," Skipjack added, "till they find themselves without a ma and a pa."

"Well, those kids are what brung me here to the city," Porter said. "Needs must. Field work suits me better, but I'll take whatever's to be had in Omaha. I leave the fields to the little ones—poor hungry mites. I may be a good-for-nothing stiff, but I won't poach work from children who need it."

"If only the fellows in charge felt as you do," Louisa said.

Someone asked, "What fellows in charge?"

"Rich men," she answered. "The bosses of business. The steel tycoons, the railroad barons, the 'titans of industry,' as the papers call them. I stayed two weeks in Pittsburgh this April, working as a laundress, and I got to hear all about what goes on in the steel factories. It's enough to make you spit. Not one of those rich barons would balk at putting kids to work—or stealing right out of their pockets."

Porter nodded. "I've seen it myself. A fat cat sitting on the throne of his business is only too happy to hire a woman for factory work; she'll work cheaper than a man. And a child will work cheaper than any woman. That's all they care about—pinching pennies, and keeping everything they pinch for themselves."

Louisa flared up with a passion that startled me. In the weeks of our travel, I'd never known her to contain such fire. "God forbid they should pay a fair wage to the people who make their empires run. They'd be nothing without our labor, but do we come in for a share of what we've built? Do we, hell!"

Skipjack had been staring silently at the fire barrel while the rest of us grumbled around him. Now he spoke, and the distance in his eyes sent a chill all through me. The old man seemed to be staring into a bleak, inevitable future. "Someday it'll all be machines."

"Pardon?" Louisa said.

"Machines. Those fat cats, the barons—they'll build machines, one day, as'll do the work cheaper than any kid. And when they do, those children can go and rot in the slums, for all the wealthy may care."

A silence fell over the gathering. I believe every one of us in that jungle shared, for a moment, in Skipjack's dreadful vision. We all felt the truth of his prophecy.

He said, "I used to be a Christian, you know. Used to believe there was a spark of goodness in all men. That was before the emergency came, and I got uprooted. Now that I've seen how we make the little ones suffer, how those rich men chew them up like they're food to be swallowed . . . I can't believe it anymore. What goodness is there in a world like this, a world where this is how we do, even unto the least of these?"

A nagging pressure rose in my chest and fluttered in the general vicinity of my heart. That feeling—imperious yet warm—was almost a voice calling to me, commanding me, and yet I didn't hear it. I *felt* it, a compulsion I couldn't deny. Passing my plate to Louisa, I reached for the rucksack below my bench.

"What's this?" Louisa said quietly.

There was no point in explaining what I was doing; I didn't really know myself, and might have stopped if I'd put it into words—for the impulse to return to the life I'd left behind still pounded in me like a racing pulse, and I needed that money, I needed it for myself if I was to make it back to Harlan County.

But my hands moved as if enchanted by some divine power, untying the strings at the top of my rucksack. I reached deep inside, found the inner pocket where I'd hidden my money and jewels. A coin worked its way between my fingers. When I withdrew my hand, I found a silver half dollar in my palm.

"Here." I extended the coin to Harney. "For coffee."

He hesitated. "Miss Del, you've only just arrived. You haven't worked a day yet."

"Take it. I insist. I'll do my part, same as the rest of you."

After supper, Louisa and I pumped water from a spigot out back of a warehouse and helped with the washing up while Skipjack played his harmonica. The hobos sang around him in a careless, broken harmony. This was no tent revival with fiddles and guitars and the high fever of excitement. The peace of the night and the rough glee of the music caught at my heart and wrapped me in a warm contentment, and I swear I felt a greater sense of holiness in that hard, stinking jungle than I ever felt at one of Irving's meetings. How could I feel anything less, with Louisa walking beside me, helping my poor bruised self to bear the weight of the water. Her hand and mine gripped the bail of the same bucket, so close I could feel the warmth of her skin.

When night fell, we staked a claim on one of the lean-tos up against a warehouse wall. The dark grotto below its slanted roof smelled not unpleasantly of dry brick and old wood. Some sallow and feeble light— the spill of an electric lamppost or the dregs of a waning moon—seeped in through the cracks between the planks. I could just see Louisa's profile as she gathered cardboard into a bed. Her expression was sober, determined. She would go on doing this, living this fragment of a life, for as long as it took, as long as the breath remained in her body. What choice did she have, but to go on?

When she'd made a bed that satisfied her as much as a pile of cardboard could satisfy anyone, she rocked back onto her heels, smiling up at me. "We'll sleep properly tonight. I'm done in, and after that spill you took, I bet you are, too. It's early bed for me, but there'll be music and dancing at the fire—there always is, in a proper jungle. If you want to stay up and get to swapping stories with the rest, just be quiet when you come back in, will you?"

I laughed, which pretty near seared my bruised ribs. "I took the spill, but you're tuckered out?"

She straightened as much as the low roof would allow, kicked off her boots, and skinned down her trousers in that unthinking way she had, the efficiency of a long-experienced drifter. Then she eased onto our bed with a happy sigh.

I stood looking down at her in the fragile light. She was so small, so thin, and when she rolled onto her side and curled into a ball, she was no bigger than a child.

I said, "I ain't staying up tonight. Too tired and sore."

"Then shut your mouth and get into bed."

A cardboard mattress can scarcely be called comfortable, even if you're in the finest fettle. With my aches, I was about as far from peak condition as I'd ever been. Louisa seemed to find no trouble drifting off to sleep—the shack soon filled with the sound of her deep, even breath, which made an uncanny contrast to the singing and carrying-on at the fire.

I had a harder go. For hours, I lay awake, doing my best not to toss and turn for fear I'd wake Louisa. I watched the light around the tarpaulin roof fade into blackness as the moon sank behind the rooftops of Omaha, and in the blinding dark I wondered whether Irving was still smarting from my departure—or whether he'd moved on already, found himself a brand-new girl. The songs and laughter from the fireside dwindled to near-silence, till all that remained was the mournful melody of Skipjack's harmonica. I recalled with a deep stab of longing the way my dear sweet mother used to sing to me when I was a girl and sickness or nightmares had kept me from sleep.

My worn-out body did eventually surrender, despite the memories that plagued me. I slipped into a shallow, restless slumber, where all my dreams were a tangle of metal limbs with grasping hands, the angular joints of machinery, the wheels of freight trains rolling with pitiless speed. I dreamed of a hundred steel mouths that opened and shut and belched a thick, black smoke, and all the while inhuman hands shoveled children into those mouths, faster and faster while the gears and pistons worked and the jaws rent flesh from bone, and the automatic rhythm of industry was so loud around me, I couldn't even hear the little ones crying.

I woke upright in our bed, beset by a violent shaking. Louisa had her arms around me.

"Steady, Del." She stroked my hair, patted my cheeks as if to bring me out of a daze. "It was only a nightmare. You're all right."

But I wasn't all right. None of us were. I knew somehow that I had looked into the future, just as Skipjack had done. I had seen the new world we were building, right over the ashes of the world that had burned—and the ashes weren't even cold.

I held tightly to Louisa till my shaking subsided. Even then, I went on clutching her, just to have something warm and human to hang on to.

16

Next morning found me cramped and shivering on the hard ground, with only those paltry sheets of cardboard between my battered limbs and the cobbles. What an effort of slow unfurling was required to pick myself up and go about the hard work of living. Each tentative movement of each aching joint had to be coaxed and tested, and I groaned and cussed and asked myself why I hadn't thrown down the old army mat to sleep on. The bivouac pad was no feather bed, but it was a damn sight more comfortable than the torture rack I'd slept on that night.

When I finally clambered to my feet and hunched there, panting, I was treated to a sensation still more unpleasant: the telltale pain in my belly and the hot, panicky rush that meant my monthly visitor had arrived.

"Oh, hell's bells," I spat.

Only then did I notice that Louisa was gone—probably off to search for work. She'd left me to sleep in. No doubt she knew I needed the rest, banged up as I was.

In my rucksack, I located my belt and rags, and thanked God once again that I'd had the foresight to pack them. When I secured everything in place, I hobbled out from the lean-to into the morning sun.

The jungle was still, every hobo gone off into the city to hunt up a few hours' labor. A wisp of white smoke still rose from the cooking barrel, however, so I reasoned I hadn't slept too late. Louisa had pumped a fresh pail of water; it waited for me beside the canvas curtain that served as the door to our shanty. Despondently I stared down at the bucket, wondering whether it was worth the pain to crouch down and splash my face, rinse my sleep-furred mouth, maybe even indulge in a more thorough cleansing. My reflection looked up at me, but the morning sun was at my back and I could see nothing but the featureless silhouette of my head and shoulders. The Del-shaped void wavered as some stray vibration ran through the water. The edges of me fragmented, pushing themselves apart, coming together again. I went on breaking and breaking.

At the cook barrel, I found Harney's iron pot with the lid on tight. A handy bit of broken branch lay on the ground, and I used it to lift the lid and peek inside. There was just enough porridge left over for my breakfast, still tolerably warm.

After I'd eaten and bathed, I slumped on one of the benches near the fire. As long as I didn't move much, the pain was bearable. Motorcars hummed within the city, and the sound merged with the soft, foolish cooing of the pigeons. Distantly, I caught the sound of a window sash opening, then a woman's voice rising and falling—the tone, not the words, for she was too far off, and her voice was like white spikes of flower in a murmuring forest, a sudden brightness to punctuate a uniform flow of sound. A trumpet played from a rooftop—*Stardust*, which seemed a funny song to greet the morning.

As I dressed after my bath, I took the money and jewelry from my rucksack, transferring it all into the left pocket of my trousers for no reason I could name. I guess I was thinking of the life I'd left behind, still toying with the idea of going back. Maybe I wanted to keep those precious resources close. My hand rested atop the tweed, prodding the shape of that bundle of riches while I prodded my predicament with my thoughts.

This was crazy—all of it. I'd gone far enough, taught Irving his lesson—and even if he hadn't learned it, I had learned mine. Louisa had always been smarter than me; she said I was a dumb bunny for giving up my good, easy life, and she'd spoken no more than the truth. When she came back that evening to add her earnings to the kitty, I would tell her I'd made up my mind. I was going home, just like she'd told me to do. I was going back to Irving.

It didn't matter that my stomach sank and my heart went dead as a rock, just at the mere thought of returning to that man. At least I would sleep in a proper bed again. At least I'd have a roof above my head, and three square meals a day, and running water so I could wash whenever I pleased. Wasn't that enough? It seemed as if it ought to be enough, and I told myself very firmly that I would humble myself and go on home, and be grateful I still had a home to return to.

As I poked and fiddled at the bundle in my pocket, my forefinger slipped into the circle of my mother's wedding band. It rested just past my first knuckle. My hand went still, as did my mind, but after a moment I pulled the ring out and held it up to examine it—a simple band of gold, long tarnished, but its carving of delicate vines and flowers showed plainly through the dark patina.

What's the use in going back now? I asked myself, frank and sober. *You're the gal who ran from Irving Wensley's side. No one in the valley will let you forget it—not even Mom.*

That ring, then, would be all I had to remember my mother by.

Even determined as I was that day to run home with my tail between my legs, still I braced myself against the thought. Well could I imagine what waited for the prodigal wife when she came limping back to Irving. My husband would crow. He'd lord it over me all the rest of my days. The gossips of the valley would never stop wagging their tongues. And my family would be so mortified by my rebellious spirit that they'd scarcely acknowledge me. The choice was between one hard road and another, one brand of misery and its reflection. I would walk a grim path no matter which I chose.

I closed my hand around that ring and held it tight all through the morning, and returned it to my pocket only when sitting still began to hurt as much as moving did. Then I forced myself up to do what I could around the jungle, washing tin plates and sweeping ashes away, setting the disordered things in order.

The hobos trooped back to the jungle among the low red light and sideways shadows of evening. Louisa wasn't among them, but Harney assured me he'd seen my friend crossing to the hard goods store a couple blocks away. "She'll be back by suppertime, Miss Del—no doubt."

Louisa had surely stopped in at the store to make her usual telephone call to the pastor of her town and send the expected wire to her uncle's bank. I hadn't the least idea how long such an operation might take. As Harney dished up the nightly stew and the hobos began passing their contributions to the communal stockpile, I counseled myself to patience. All day I'd mused on the choice that lay before me, and now that I had made my decision, I itched to break the news to Louisa—tear the plaster off quickly and get on with feeling the sting.

The longer I waited for my friend to appear, the sicker I felt at heart. I kept anticipating the way her face would fall when I told her straight out that I was going back to Kentucky. No matter how she'd chided me for leaving in the first place, we'd both be left smarting when the bond between us broke. Each passing minute, I felt a little lower for the wound I was about to inflict on Louisa, and the turmoil in my chest grew thicker and blacker till I wanted to scream just to let it all out.

"By God, Dogbone, you know the code as well as anyone."

That had been Skipjack speaking, but I'd never heard such a note of authority in his voice before. It cut through my bleak distraction, snapping me back to attention.

The hobos had piled the evening's collection of goods and coins on the crate beside Harney's barrel, as on the night before. Again, there were loaves of bread and other edible things, and small tools, and jars of pickles or honey—the odds and ends of charity given by those generous souls who could have used a little help themselves. But in the middle of the pile, a fine gold watch chain lay like some magnificent and tempting serpent.

New though I was to the jungle, I understood at once. No one would have paid a hobo with such a valuable prize. Dogbone could only have stolen the chain.

Louisa slipped in among the benches and settled at my side, her mouth open as if to strike up a conversation. I stilled her with a warning look. She glanced from face to face, reading the grim mood of the jungle as cleverly as she did everything else. She gave a little gasp of pained understanding as Dogbone rose to defend himself.

"It don't hurt nobody. The man I lifted that chain from is so damn rich, he won't even notice it's gone."

"The code—" Skipjack began, but Dogbone rounded on him.

"To hell with the code! What good does it do any of us? We abide by the rules, we mind ourselves and never step out of line. We work ourselves into our graves, and for what? The rich keep getting richer while every day we walk farther and beg longer for a job, a damned job, just the right to work and earn a living like honest men!"

Harney laid a hand on Dogbone's shoulder. Such a dreadful sadness showed in Harney's eyes that I wanted to cry out from the ache. "No matter how hard it gets, my friend, we have to think of the ones who'll come after us. We can't spoil a city for our own folks."

With a violent wrench of his arm, Dogbone shook Harney off. "Fuck the ones who'll come after! My belly's empty now! My body's tired now! I'm a man, damn it, not an animal, and I'll do what I must to get by!"

No one stirred on the benches. Dogbone's last words rebounded thinly from the warehouse walls. Louisa's hand crept into my own, and her fingers were cold, trembling.

Finally Skipjack spoke in a hollow voice, an old voice that creaked with a terrible weight. "We got to send you on your way, Dogbone."

"On my way?"

"It's best if you leave the jungle. We can't have you hanging around here. Once word gets out that you've stolen, the cops will be on the lookout, and if they find you here, they'll break up the whole jungle. I'm sorry. I wish it could be otherwise."

Dogbone sniffed. He seemed to waver on his feet, as if he couldn't quite decide whether to remain upright or collapse back onto the bench. "Don't do this," he said. "Please."

But the whole jungle had made up its mind as one. Solemnly, Dogbone's friends set to work, gathering his few possessions from the shanty he'd occupied, tying up a bindle with enough provisions to keep him alive for a few days.

As the hobos went about their work, I clutched Louisa's hand. We too had broken the rules that wild night in Kansas—or at least, we'd skirted close enough to the code's edge as made little difference. If the jungle knew of our transgressions, would they exile us, too?

Harney passed the bindle to Dogbone and, to my surprise, pulled the man into a rough embrace. "May the Lord protect you," Harney muttered.

"Oh, fuck all of you," Dogbone answered.

He seized the watch chain, shook it at the gathered hobos. Irving used to handle snakes in just that way, raising them above his head in a pique of terrible triumph. "I'm taking this, you hear?" Dogbone cried. "It's mine. And it'll get me farther than any of you will go."

Those who'd been closest to Dogbone walked with him to the edge of the jungle, even as he continued to rant and cuss. Soon that small crowd disappeared into the alley.

"They'll go with him all the way to the railyard," Louisa said. "Poor fellow; it'll be a hard life out there alone."

We settled in for the night in a funereal mood. No one stayed up for singing or dancing, and under that density of sorrow I couldn't bring myself to tell Louisa of the decision I'd made. Sleep evaded me again that night. Somewhere in the city, firecrackers kept bursting and popping—it was the Fourth of July. Now and then a flash of color lit the edges of the shanty roof and brought Louisa's sleeping face briefly out of darkness. I lay awake on my army mat, arms folded tightly across my body as I stared up into the dark pitch of the roof, haunted by a memory of Irving strutting on his stage with a writhing serpent in his fist.

In my thoughts, I watched Irving pace that stage for at least an hour. Again and again, the memory replayed—the snake coiling its body around Irving's forearm, his shout of "Hallelujah," the eager roar of the congregation. Finally the memory became like a thorn in my flesh, a painful torment. Stifling a groan, I clambered to my feet. I had to get out of the lean-to. I needed to walk, to think.

"What's the matter?" Louisa whispered.

"Nothing. Just the call of nature. Go back to sleep."

When I stepped out into the courtyard, the jungle was as still as it had been that morning. A waning moon hung in the ink-blue night. By the moon's paltry light, I could make out a great, dark figure sitting alone beside the fire barrel, gazing up at the sky, where now and again the fireworks flared and sparkled and died away like the remnant of a dream.

I crossed the empty jungle in my stocking feet. Skipjack looked up at my approach. He smiled sadly, then nodded to the bench beside him. Without a word, I sat.

"I'm sorry you had to see all that tonight, Miss Del. Sorrier still that it had to be done. Dogbone's a good man. But it gets to you—the hardship, the need, the injustice of it all. It gets to the best of us. Sometimes I think the despair will get to all of us, sooner or later. I wonder if anyone's strong enough to keep out ahead of it."

"Y'all were so kind to him," I said, wondering. "Gave him food and other things. You gave him love."

"Who among us hasn't sinned? We're commanded by a greater power to love even those who trespass against us."

What a contrast Skipjack's philosophy made to all Irving's religion. I couldn't help recalling that terrible Sunday when Irving had preached about Jezebel—how Ruthie Bell had stared at him, stricken, before she'd run from the meetinghouse. I wondered if she was still in Harlan County. Surely she'd taken to the road by now. If the girl had any sense, she'd understood that day that she would find neither friendship nor succor in any town where Irving's power reached.

"You told me last night you weren't a Christian," I said.

"That's true." Skipjack rumbled with quiet laughter, slapping his own knee. "I ain't a Christian, these days. But listen, Miss Del"—soberly now—"that don't mean I don't hold to whatever's good and true and sacred. If this life has taught me anything—if this emergency has taught me anything, and I pray to God it has or else what's it all been for—it's convinced me that the fellows up in the pulpits don't have a bead on the good and the true and the sacred. They bluster and shout and do their best to impress their flocks with their own importance, but that was never the Savior's way. If you want to find what's really sacred, you got to get out into the places where the Savior dwelled. And He never hung around listening to no preacher; I remember that much from my Christian days."

Such a simple, unclouded doctrine stilled my heart. Another memory returned with sudden and relentless force—standing outside the meetinghouse, withering with embarrassment while Irving, cool as ever in his fine suit, leaned on the hood of his motorcar. *I think I've got a pretty good handle on what's Christian and what's not, little lady.*

All at once I knew I could as soon return to Harlan County as cut off my own leg. You don't turn your back on the sacred in favor of the profane.

The moment I made that decision, it settled in my spirit and filled me with warmth. This life on the rails was exacting, and I still suspected I wasn't half cut out for it. Hoboing might well be the death of me—I faced that possibility with sober understanding, there under the bursting lights of the fireworks. But the Savior had never hung around listening to any preacher. Skipjack was right about that. If I returned to Irving, I would lose my very soul—the treasure I'd only found once I'd left my former life behind.

I rose from the bench in a pensive silence.

"Miss Del?" Skipjack said. "You all right?"

"I am now," I told him, and bent to kiss his cheek.

17

Next morning, when Louisa said we must soon press on for Wenatchee, I readily agreed. For though the hobo's life had proven itself to be about as far as one could get from the Buster Keaton romanticism of the talkies, now I knew it to be my own, the life I had truly chosen. Besides, by that time most of my aches had subsided and the bruises were beginning to fade. I was pretty near fit to hop a train again, and the orchards were waiting.

Louisa and I dedicated that day to gathering a good stock of supplies for the journey ahead—mostly food that would keep on the rails, like jerky and dried fruit, tins of crackers and hard cheese. We parted ways in the morning light with a promise to meet that afternoon, sort through our goods, and plan the next day's hop on a westbound freighter.

Whistling, buoyant despite the twinges of pain that still flared up now and then, I trekked into Omaha with my rucksack and soon found a general store not far from the warehouse district—a place that didn't seem too hoity-toity to welcome an obvious hobo inside. The shopkeep was a white-haired fellow, thin as a piece of string with darting, suspicious eyes, but I gave him my list of wants and he went about collecting them without complaint. He assembled my goods on the counter: coffee, a jar of honey, a packet of salt and another of ground pepper. I added a small skein of gray yarn for darning up socks, for by then both my pairs of stockings were more holes than substance. I bought a couple of tin cups, too, and two deep plates and two forks, on the off chance that Louisa could scare up a better cooking pot than the one we already had—the prime object of her hunt that day.

While the shopkeep tallied the cost, my eyes lost their focus and I drifted into a fantasy of eating hot stew every night for supper, even far from any jungle. What a welcome change that would be, after the cold meals of bread and jerky we'd shared on our journey up to Omaha.

"Will that be all, Miss?"

The shopkeep's voice scarcely reached me. My eyes had fixed themselves on a rack of newspapers, and everything else receded into an insignificant, muffled distance—the general store with its tidy shelves, its smell of licorice and pine shavings; the presence of the man behind the counter; even all awareness of time and place, the feel of solid ground beneath my feet. For a moment I had no consciousness of anything except the face that stared back at me from the front page of the *Omaha World-Herald*. My face.

"Miss?" the shopkeep said again.

I came back to hard reality with a jolt like grabbing barbed wire. My face burned, my pulse raced in my throat, but I forced myself to look at the man calmly. I even managed a smile. Without looking at the paper rack, I grabbed a copy of the *World-Herald* and added it, facedown, to my other purchases. The man adjusted his tally with an unhurried air that made me want to yank my own hair out by the roots.

When he announced the total, I fished the sum from my pocket, laid out the bills and coins, and packed my supplies into the top of my rucksack as quickly as I could. When the shopkeep said, "You have a fine day, now," I showed my teeth in something resembling a smile. Then I clutched that treacherous paper under my arm and sped from the shop as if Hell itself had sent every demon on its payroll out to get me.

Outside the general store, I looked around wildly for someplace to sit, blinking back the tears I could no longer hold at bay. A convenient bench presented itself, just below the shop's window, partially hidden behind an ice chest emblazoned with the words *Drink Coca-Cola*. My knees buckled just as I made it to the bench. I unfolded the paper across my lap to read.

It wasn't a nightmare, nor a trick of the imagination. I really was looking into my own eyes. The softly smiling, dark-haired young woman on the front page almost looked happy; it was the portrait Irving had insisted on taking just before our wedding. Lord, but I was so young. Only twenty-two then, and dumb enough to believe everything would turn out all right, that Irving and I would make a happy life together. But though many years had elapsed since that portrait was made, there was no mistaking my face.

Just above the picture, the headline blared: Preacher's Wife on the Run!

"You rat," I muttered, as if Irving were close enough to hear—as if he might taste the bile I spat at him. "You no-good, two-timing weasel. What have you done?"

Reading was a slow process for me, but nevertheless I could do it. My heart pounded louder with every word as I puzzled out the story below my portrait.

> REWARD for information leading to the safe return of Mrs. Irving Wensley to her loving husband and family. Adella Wensley departed from her home in Harlan County, Kentucky, on the 31st of May. Her husband is the celebrated preacher Irving Wensley, advisor to Senator M. M. Logan of Kentucky. Mr. Wensley is most concerned for Adella's mental state and wishes to see his beloved wife home again to be held safely in his arms. Adella Wensley is 30 years old, stands 5'9" tall, has brown hair and brown eyes. Mr. Wensley offers a reward of $1,000.00 for her return. If you have

information on this woman's whereabouts, please
contact . . .

I crumpled the entire paper in my fists. That didn't prove satisfying enough, so I uncrumpled it, tore off the front page, and ripped that into ever-smaller pieces till the whole damn thing was obliterated. Then I dumped the paper, torn bits and all, into a nearby trash barrel.

Panic rose thick and hot in my chest as I made my way back to the jungle, scarcely restraining myself from running. *A thousand dollars.* It was an unthinkable fortune, and it put a bounty on my head few folks would be able to resist in those hard times. Any of the hobos back in the jungle would surely jump at the chance to earn a thousand bucks. Even Skipjack or Harney, kind as they were, might turn me in as soon as blink. A reward of that kind could change a hobo's life forever.

Would Louisa do it?

No answer came to me. I wanted to believe my friend knew and liked me too well; she would never sell me back into the hands of a man she knew I despised. But what if Louisa thought she'd be doing a kindness in returning me to my husband's keeping? She'd made her feelings clear: she thought I was a fool for abandoning the easy life. And a thousand dollars would set her up properly; she could skip the apple harvest, return to her son, care for him properly for years yet. How could my happiness weigh in that balance? What kind of mother wouldn't jump at the chance to hold her sweet child in her arms again?

It wasn't only my fellow hobos I needed to fear, either. Whoever I encountered—the sweet, old city ladies for whom I carried packages, the linemen in dusty, nowhere towns—anyone who'd read that notice might send off a telegram to Irving and rat me out for good. Only the Lord and Irving knew how many papers in how many cities carried the story. Wherever I went, wherever the rails carried me, I would be in danger.

A feeble light of hope flickered in my heart. If I could keep my companions ignorant of my true identity, I might hope to fool them—even if someone asked straight out whether I was Adella Wensley.

If anyone asks about Irving, I decided, *or Harlan County, or anything else that might give me away . . . I'll deny it. I'll run.*

But even then, I knew there was no place I could run to, no way to escape the desperate need that had consumed every soul in America. The best I could pray for was that I'd manage, somehow, to stay one jump ahead of my husband till he finally got tired of searching and admitted defeat.

It cost every ounce of my self-control not to run from the general store like Old Scratch himself was on my heels, but as I departed that street corner, I knew what my next move would be. I would find a telephone if it killed me, and I would give my husband a piece of my mind. He deserved that much, and more.

As I scoured the neighborhood for a telephone booth, I kept my cap pulled low and my face turned down to the sidewalk. There was no disguising the fact that I was tall, but I hoped if no one looked too closely, I might pass for a man—to a casual glance, anyhow. I didn't dare to lift my face, even when I was forced to cross the road and had to watch for oncoming cars. When folks offered benign greetings—the shoppers passing on the sidewalk or the hopeful salesmen leaning out from the doors of their shops—I responded with wordless grunts, pitching my voice low.

I must have beat around Omaha for an hour before I finally found a drugstore. I ducked inside, and there at the back of the store stood the expected telephone booth, wedged between a rack of comic books and a display of the colorful glassware that could be earned by turning in box tops or purchasing special items.

I slid the rucksack from my shoulders as I crossed the store, bracing all the while for one of the shopgirls or the soda jerk to call out my true name, to insist I wait right there while they dashed off a telegram to the celebrated preacher of Harlan County. No one paid me the least heed, however. Sometimes God is actually merciful.

I pressed myself into the small wooden booth, fished for a nickel in my pocket, and dropped it into the slot—all of this accomplished with my back turned to the store.

A blandly polite operator asked for the number. I gave it. The line crackled faintly while I waited, drumming my fingers on the little shelf below the telephone.

Finally: "I've connected you. Thank you."

The self-contained ringing sounded in my ear, far below the crash of my pulse. Between rings, the wire hissed quietly, and I realized only very gradually that my heart had been racing all this time, pounding so hard I could see stars at the edges of my vision, and the confines of the telephone booth seemed to lift and rotate around me. Forcing myself to stand still, I drew long, steady breaths. The world tamed itself some. At least, it spun at a slower pace.

The line went on ringing for an eternity, and finally I decided that Irving must not be at home. Maybe he'd gone out into the valley to tend to some business—ministering to his flock or wringing a little more money from those who looked to him for hope and guidance.

Or maybe he'd slunk off to the woods with another girl.

Just as I moved to hang up the receiver, his voice crackled on the line. "Wensley residence."

I'd heard that man preach at the congregation—and at me, in the privacy of our home—every day for the past eight years, but after these weeks free from Irving's rule, the sound caught me off guard. It was an echo rebounding from the walls of a life that was no longer mine. I opened my mouth, but nothing came out.

"Hello?" Irving said. Then he sighed. I could almost see him reaching to hang up the telephone. After, he would probably scratch himself and head back into his library. He'd settle on the sofa, all unconcerned, for a nice, cozy nap.

I forced out a response. "Irving. Hi."

"Adella?" I couldn't tell whether he sounded relieved or exasperated. "Where are you? Where have you been?"

I wasn't about to tell him where I'd been, and he certainly didn't need to know I'd made it all the way to Nebraska. "I went off for a while," I said, "to be on my own."

"But where?"

"Fat chance I'll say. You haven't got a right to know."

Irving laughed—smooth, unconcerned. The sound of his condescending glee sickened me. "You can come home whenever you've finished throwing this little tantrum of yours, honcy pie."

"Don't hold your breath. I've got more self-respect than to come back to a jerk like you. Catting around with other women. Of all the nerve!"

He didn't acknowledge my comment. "Your mother has been sick over this. How could you be so foolish, Adella? Why, you didn't even leave her a note, just abandoned her and your father, the same way you abandoned me."

"And what about you?" I asked pointedly.

Silence on the other line. Then, "What do you mean—what about me?"

He was a pig. He was an ass. He was a pig's ass, but at least I'd soon be done with him. "Weren't you concerned about me, too? Or did you have plenty of company to distract you from your worries?"

"Don't be boorish. Of course I've been concerned. Why, the whole valley has been in an uproar since you disappeared."

I rolled my eyes. I doubted Irving had told another soul, apart from my parents. Thank goodness no one in Harlan County went in much for reading papers; that was a thing only worldly folks did. Even if Irving *had* spilled the beans to a few souls—the *whole valley*? More likely, he'd made up some story to explain my absence, told the church I'd gone off to visit a sick cousin or to do charity work in some other part of the state. Irving would never admit his wife had up and left him; it would open the door for too many questions about *why* she'd done it.

I said, "You can tell 'the valley' I'm just fine. Tell them this, too: I've got no intention of coming back. I'm doing very well for myself on my own, and as far as I'm concerned—"

"Enough of this foolishness. Where *are* you, anyhow?"

"I'm safe," I said. "That's all you need to know."

"I've got a right to know more. I've got a right to know everything. Now cut this rebellious nonsense and answer my questions at once, Adella!"

"You've got no rights over me, you low-down scoundrel. Don't try to pretend you have."

"I'm your husband—"

"Some husband you are. I know you've been fooling around with more than just Ruthie, and I know it's been going on for years. How many girls have you kept on the side? That's what I'd like to know."

He gave a weary sigh. "I am but a man, made of flesh and blood—"

"Oh, that's some excuse. You're a preacher who's higher and mightier than everyone else when you need to tell the church a tale about the End of Days and keep the money coming in. But when I catch you with a half-naked woman, suddenly you're a plain old fallible man, prone to sin like all the rest."

"All have sinned and fallen short of the glory of God," Irving said.

"You've done more than your fair share of sinning, I'd say. I've seen your little article in the news, Irving. Where did you get a thousand dollars from? That's what I'd like to know. Did you finally take up an honest trade to earn your pay, or did you squeeze the poor sheep of your flock even harder than you've already done?"

"Preaching is my trade, Adella, and it's a perfectly respectable one. A man's entitled to pay in exchange for his work. I've got nothing to be ashamed of."

"Nothing—you sure about that? Think you can look the Savior in His eye and say the same thing on Judgment Day?"

"My sins are between me and God."

"Like hell they are."

"Adella! It's not like you to cuss."

"It is now," I said, "since I've had a little time and space to do some thinking. And here's what I think, Irving. For all the sermons you ever preached about sin and wrongdoing, the one text you should have taken to heart was the parable of the mote and the beam. All these years, we've lived high on the hog and where did that money come from? From the pockets of the poor miners who looked to you for hope in a mean, dark world. You've wrung them out like a dishrag, and here I see this horse shit about reward money—"

"It's shocking, that you'd ever use such language—"

"Be shocked," I said. "I don't care."

"It's plain that you've worked yourself into a nervous state."

"A nervous state! My nerves have never been better, Irving Wensley, but thank you for your concern."

"When you come back—"

Something slick and venomous reared up inside me, something angry and ready to strike. "I don't *want* to come back, you rat bastard. Speaking of nerves, you've got some, thinking this is water under the bridge, thinking *I've* forgiven *you*. Now you're going to give me a nice, quiet divorce and we'll go our separate ways, and I'll never have to see your cheating face again. That's what I want. That's *all* I want from you."

He chuckled, a sly, oily sound. "Oh, Adella. Divorce is out of the question. You know I'd lose face with my congregation. My revivals would dry up in an instant, if word got around that my wife had divorced me. But most of all, there's Senator Logan to think of."

"The senator can fly a kite to Hell."

"Logan will be my passage into politics, and you will speak of him with the respect he deserves."

"Make me!" I laughed.

Irving paid no mind to my insolence. He went on in that same austere calm that flicked on the raw. "The senator has been kind enough to put up the reward money, and once he'd committed to the cause, the papers showed natural interest. I've no doubt that with the senator's kind assistance, you'll soon be back home where you belong, and in a couple more years this spectacle will be forgotten. So no, my darling, I'm afraid there will be no divorce. Can you imagine a divorced man winning an election? Maybe in some northern state, but it will never happen in Kentucky. You took a holy vow to stick by me through thick and thin, through good times and bad, and now that I've got a real hope of a career in politics, I'm not about to part with what's mine. I don't see what you've got to complain about, anyway. Hasn't life as a preacher's wife given you everything you could have asked for?"

"Everything," I agreed, "except a husband I can trust. Or respect."

His patronizing sigh sent a bolt of rage right through me. "When can I expect you home?"

"You'd like to know, wouldn't you? Give you time to shoo all your floozies out the door? I'm not coming back—not ever—not if Senator Logan offers ten thousand dollars as a reward. I'll see to it that no one ever finds me, and you can chase me all the rest of your life, but you'll never catch me. How do you like them apples?"

"You'll be back," Irving said, cool with assurance. "A thousand dollars is a lot of money, and the article will continue to run in every major paper in the country till you're home safe again. You mark my words, Adella: I'll have what's mine, in the end."

The line clicked, then hummed faintly.

"I'm sorry," came the operator's tinny voice. "It seems the call was dropped. Would you like—"

Without a word, I replaced the receiver on its hook. I left the booth, left the store. The clang of the shop's bell was like a knife in my skull. Right as I'd been about Irving's sins, he was just as right about the power of the senator's money. With a bounty tacked above my head, it was even odds whether I made it to Wenatchee a free woman, or found myself the captive of some desperate character. After all, whose life wouldn't be changed for the better with a thousand bucks in his pocket?

Returning across the town with my cap pulled low, I could feel the force of panic pressing against my throat. It stayed there, urgent and thick, all the way back to the alley.

18

Louisa and I left Omaha late the next morning, flattened into the space between two fruit cars so as to evade the notice of the bulls. As the train began rolling west, we climbed up to the roof of a car and perched there, side by side, watching the morose earth expand below.

The land was drier there than any place I'd seen that hardscrabble summer. It rose and fell in shallow brown waves from horizon to horizon, the unvaried bleakness broken by stands of trees whose leaves were already bronzing around the edges, or a distant purple fadedness of buttes and hills. The sight of so much ruin wracked me with a sharp and peculiar worry. The forlorn land seemed a harbinger or prophet, warning me of the stumble and fall to come—the imminent loss to follow. It seemed foreordained that Louisa would learn, sooner or later, of the bounty on my head. And turning away from the blighted prairie, watching Louisa's sharp features in profile—her long-suffering, infinitely patient eyes—I was forced to admit that I really didn't know what she would do once she found out I was worth a thousand dollars, cash in hand.

That fear wasn't the worst, however. Bleaker still was knowing that I had no intention of revealing my secret. I could have helped Louisa return all the sooner to her child, but I prized my freedom above all else, even above Louisa's need.

Does that make me wicked? I asked myself endlessly as we rode out of Omaha. I still ask the question, to this day. Does it make me wicked, or does it make me human? And can either failing be forgiven?

At least one thing was clear: my silence in the face of Louisa's pain certainly made me selfish. I'd never thought myself a stingy person before.

We rode atop that fruit car for hours. Eventually I understood that I'd solve none of my spiritual quandaries that morning. The most important thing was to move on, get a little closer to Wenatchee, survive another day. So I stretched out on my belly in a bid for some sleep. Despite the vicious sun climbing higher by the minute, we stayed cooler in the breeze of motion than we would have in the confines of a car. And after days spent tramping around Omaha, I counted it a simple pleasure to cover the miles without any effort.

When the steady vibration of the train lulled me into a stupor, I allowed my eyes to slide shut so I could forget, for a time, the stark and unvaried suffering of the land, and I dozed and drifted somewhere between sleep and waking, one foot in the present problems of survival that never left me, the other in a hazy half dream of the clearing behind my childhood home, where I would lie for hours under a bower of prairie roses, watching a gentler sun glow pink and sweet around the edges of the petals.

A familiar bang and buck jarred me out of that dream—the violent transfer of energy as the train slowed.

I scrambled up quickly to seize hold of my rucksack, which I'd laid out between Louisa and myself. The last thing I wanted was for that old pack to go flying off the side of the train with all my goods inside. As I bolted up, I saw that Louisa had already pushed herself upright, or perhaps she'd been riding sitting up and wide awake for some time while I'd been locked in my lazy slumber.

"What in heck," I blurted. "Why are we slowing?"

The very next thing I noted was that we were not approaching any town or yard. In fact, the train was slowing in a great tract of unrelieved, sunbaked brown—acres of dead corn flattened by the wind, and beyond the defeated cornfields, a long, grassless range devoid of sheep or cattle. That emptiness extended all the way up a shallow slope to where the land folded in upon itself, ancient hills abutting the northern sky. Aside from the Platte River, docile and gray to my left, there was nothing else to be seen but a lone farmhouse some quarter mile from the tracks.

"Louisa," I said, "what's going on?"

She made no answer, and only very slowly did I realize she was staring straight ahead, due west, where the rail line vanished. There, a great, pale mass had gathered, shadowed near the earth, so brightly illuminated in its upper reaches that I could scarcely stand to look at it. I shielded my eyes with my hand, trying to discern the place where the towering wall ended and the hot, glaring sky began. The two became one in a violent flare of sunlight. The cloud stretched from north to south, sweeping in absolute mastery over the barren range and the devastated corn, swallowing the river.

"A storm," I said hopefully. "Thunderheads. We'll have rain, thank God."

"Those are no rainclouds," Louisa answered. "Not like any I've ever seen."

The crawling train shuddered to a halt. Far up the line of cars, the engine puffed out smoke like an anxious breath, and soon the only sound was the wind moaning along the bend of the river, rattling the desiccated corn.

For several moments we sat there, stunned and motionless, watching the strange wall ahead. I blinked and squinted under the sunshade of my hand, eyes running with tears in protest of the too-bright glow. With a cold dawn of horror, I realized the cloud was moving—rippling—great billows of its body pouring and tumbling down upon itself as it sped closer to where our train was stalled helplessly on the tracks.

Louisa lurched to her feet. "Good God, Del, it's a dust storm! We've got to get down from here."

"Into the car!" I knew that idea was hopeless even as I said it, for the slatted wood of the fruit car would do nothing to keep out the suffocating dust. The whole train was made up of such cars—or open-topped coal carriages, which would offer even less protection.

Louisa edged past me, making for the ladder. "The caboose—it'll be solid."

"The crew will take shelter there!"

"They'll let us in. They won't turn ladies out into a dust storm."

"They might not have the room, Louisa!"

We both scrambled down the ladder, and I had to restrain myself from going too fast. I didn't want to step on her hands in my haste.

She leaped from the final rung, landing beside the track. "There," she cried, and took off running into the field of flattened corn before I'd even reached solid ground myself.

Down the long, rust-red line of the cars, I could see the locomotive's crew climbing from their hatch, leaping to the ground, running along the tracks for the safety of the caboose. Their thin shouts came to me over a rising hiss of wind.

"Louisa, wait!" I stumbled after her, feet tangling among fallen cornstalks, the rucksack bouncing on my spine. At the edge of my vision, reality blurred into the onrushing dust. The storm was gaining on us, and Louisa seemed to be running out into the open field, where she would be vulnerable, exposed—where the blast of wind and blowing sand might scour her very flesh away before my eyes, reduce her to a sudden and final nonexistence.

I glanced beyond my friend just once and saw the farmhouse standing among the flattened crop, its roof sharp and black against the rush of gray. Willing a fresh burst of speed, I caught up with Louisa, and side by side we broke from the corn into the trampled remains of a yard. The skeleton of a chicken coop flashed past, all its boards torn away, and I swerved just in time to avoid tripping over the base of a well pump. The pump itself was gone, looted by passersby.

"The house is empty," I shouted.

We thundered up the porch steps together. Louisa threw herself against the door. Thank God, it opened. Desperate, panting, we spilled inside; I slammed the door shut, then made a quick circuit of the house. The windows were all intact, save for the one in the bedroom, where a single pane had been smashed. A tattered quilt lay across the bed. I snatched the blanket, shut the door, and stuffed the quilt into the crack underneath, praying it would be sufficient to block the worst of the dust.

"Into the kitchen," I said.

The wind's moan had risen to a howl. It picked at the shingles of the roof, beat the shutters around the windows in a furious tattoo. The light in the kitchen dimmed rapidly, taking on an eerie reddish hue. Commanding myself not to lose my head, I peered into cupboards and corners, searching for anything we might use to survive the next few hours—or days. Whoever had abandoned that house had left little behind, only a few old jars of pears in one cupboard, and in another, a heavy blue squash that had begun to rot at one end. Two pails stood beside the stove, both covered by wooden planks. When I tipped back the planks to peer inside, I found the buckets full of water. That was a bit of luck, at least, given the state of the well pump outside. I thought the buckets might hold enough water to sustain us for three days—four at the most.

The windows began to ping and tick. The wall of dust had reached us. The sound increased to a steady rattle, then a roar. The abandoned house groaned; the kitchen window wobbled in its frame. I dragged Louisa into the corner farthest from the glass while the dim light snuffed itself with a relentless hand, and just before a dense, black nullity consumed us, I wrapped my arms around my friend. The sun died. Night descended, heavy and absolute.

I can't say how much time passed. Gradually our breathing slowed, Louisa's and mine. I could no longer feel my heart pounding against her cheek, and she turned her head and rested against me more easily, with a calm surrender that said we had both survived, and knew it— or at least, if we'd been taken by the storm and had crossed over into paradise beyond, we were still together. That was enough. We went on holding each other because there was nothing else to feel. The world had collapsed upon itself. Whatever existed now dwelled only in the space between our two still-beating hearts.

Bit by bit, that unsettling reddish glow returned to peer in at the kitchen window. When I could make out the rough shapes of table and iron stove and the drain board across the room, I loosed my hold on Louisa, gave her shoulders a bracing shake.

"You all right?"

"I think so," she said.

I groped my way to the water pails. Reaching back with an automatic gesture, I found the tin cup that hung from a hook on my rucksack and dipped the cup full. Before I slaked my own thirst, I brought the water to Louisa. When she'd drunk down her share, she made her way across the umber void and filled the cup for me, and I took it from her hands with a sacramental reverence. The water tasted of earth and age, of something long enduring. I wiped my mouth on my sleeve and breathed in so deeply that my chest ached, and when the water hit my stomach, I was satisfied at last that Louisa and I were both still among the living.

"What do we do now?" Her voice sounded so small in the muffled quiet.

Go on living, I thought, but didn't say.

I felt my way across the kitchen to the cupboard, where one of the jars of pears appeared, smooth and matter-of-fact, below my groping hand.

"Hold on to me," I said.

Both of her hands slipped around my arm. I couldn't see her face but only a suggestion of deeper black in a shape I knew to be Louisa— the height I had memorized, the familiar tension of her shoulders, the curve of her curls that lifted, never tame, above her ears.

I led her through the darkness in what I hoped was the direction of the parlor. My feet slid along the floorboards, which seemed to bend and sink as I moved as if I were walking on water. The only thing of any substance left in that world, the only reality, was Louisa. Her hands on my arm. Her hands that held me together.

My knees bumped into the back of the sofa. Guiding Louisa side- ways, I skirted the couch and shuffled to the front of it. Then we sat, facing the two windows that flanked the front door, close enough that our shoulders and knees pressed into one another, a necessary reassur- ance. I found my new fork in the rucksack and pried open the jar of pears, and we speared up chunks of soft, sweet fruit and ate them in turns, watching the windows brighten to a ruddy hellfire glow.

"How can anything be so quiet?" Louisa said. "It's like everything has disappeared, except what I can feel—this sofa, and my heartbeat. And you."

"My husband always said the end was nigh. I guess maybe he was right."

"You never told me what happened," she said. "Just that he was no good to you."

She waited in the stillness. Her patient curiosity drew the story from me; I could feel the pull of her wanting to know, and the immi- nent relief of telling. For the fiftieth time that day, I weighed how much I ought to confess.

"You see, my husband is a preacher."

Louisa burst out with a laugh. "You? A preacher's wife?"

"He's *the* preacher of our town—of our whole valley, in fact. And you wouldn't be surprised if you'd seen me back home. I was a real, proper lady once, wearing nice, little dresses and keeping house and—oh—doing everything a preacher's wife is supposed to do. I did everything except keep my head down and my mouth shut when I caught him fooling around with another girl."

A silence fell between us. I fished for another piece of pear, but we'd eaten the whole jar, so I tipped it to my lips and drank the sweet juice till it ran down my chin.

"You know, I still envy you," Louisa said at length. "Isn't that terrible? Knowing how bad you had it—and that is pretty bad, Del—I'd still go back to him. It'd be worth putting up with a no-good two-timer if I got to have a nice, pretty life. That's all I've ever wanted, but it's never been mine, not even for a day."

Before I could frame an answer to that nonsense, Louisa sniffed. Her shoulder jumped against mine, and I realized with growing astonishment that she was crying.

"I just don't understand," she said, choked up by a vast, terrible, lifelong yearning, "I don't understand why I don't deserve it."

"My God, Louisa, you do. You do deserve it all." Hastily, I set the jar on the floor, and I threw my arms around her again, murmuring into her hair. "You'll have it all someday."

Her answer was so small and frail, I couldn't quite believe the words came from her. "I don't know. I've been thinking . . . I'm afraid . . . that even once I'm back home for good, if any man ever found out I'd gone out on the rails—if any man knew I'd ever been a hobo—he wouldn't want me."

It was on the tip of my tongue to say, *To hell with men. You don't need one, Louisa, no one does,* but I didn't know what she would think of such a speech, and I didn't want to talk, anyway, with my arms around her, my cheek resting against her warm crown. She smelled of sunlight—which, for all I could say, we might never see again—and dry sage, the open land, the wind moving and moving.

The oppressive flush remained in the sky all that day, and when my confused senses at last decided that evening had come, the meager light faded all too quickly, giving way once more to a night black as pitch and still as the grave.

I made Louisa sleep on the sofa, with an old velvet cushion for her pillow, while I rolled out my mat along the floor, close beside her.

"I feel like you're a hundred miles away," she said quietly.

Without a word I raised my hand from the mat, reaching through the darkness. I found her at once, for she had reached for me, too. Our fingers laced together.

Our talk drifted this way and that, losing itself in the lanes and alleys of half slumber, till finally we both surrendered to exhaustion and our separate dreams overtook us.

When I woke to a feeble sunrise, I found that my hand had fallen back against my mat sometime in the night. But I could still feel Louisa's fingers twined with my own, and I thought the feel of her might remain pressed into my memory forever.

19

We sheltered four days in that abandoned farmhouse. A pall of dust hung over the land; each day was scarcely any lighter than the one that had come before. But the farmhouse gave us good rest, and we found a few items to take with us on our journey—a small aspirin tin that contained a pair of fishhooks and some line, the old blanket I'd stuffed under the bedroom door, and in the dark corner of a closet, inside a forgotten box of letters, a few shell buttons which we hoped we might trade for something to eat.

We would have stayed longer, till the dust settled and the sky returned to its accustomed blue, but we'd eaten through almost all the food in our packs and everything we'd found in the kitchen—even the squash, from which I'd pared away the rotting parts, roasting the remainder on a fire I built out of dried-up cornstalks in the yard. When we drank the last of the water from the buckets, we knew it was time to move on.

With lengths of old kitchen towel tied around our faces to keep the worst of the dust from our lungs, we continued our journey. I hoisted my rucksack, to which I'd strapped the folded quilt, and Louisa slung her bindle on her shoulder. In a sober silence, we descended the porch steps and pushed out into the dim, red glow of day.

The sun, like a portent of some relentless cataclysm, stared from a brown sky. I could look right into its pitiless face without my eyes so much as watering. Below its fat gloating body, I could make out the straight line of the iron rail—the only singular and distinct object in an endless blur of drab haze. The train we'd ridden had vanished, though I couldn't have guessed when it had pulled away. We never heard its going, not with the air muted and enclosed by the remnants of that storm.

"Guess we should go back to the rails," I said, "and hope another train comes along. Think we'll be able to catch it at a run?"

"It'll slow to come through this mess, I believe," Louisa said thoughtfully. "We might as well try."

But no train headed west that day. We followed the tracks as they bent along a subtle curve of the river. The red sun climbed behind our backs, and we went on walking the rails, placing our feet with care on sleepers half-buried by the sifting powder. The trail of our footprints reached back into an otherwise featureless distance.

By midday, I'd fallen into a stupor from hours of walking, but little by little, a miraculous new awareness of color lifted me from my apathy. The haze that had choked out everything—save for the hard, sharp line of the tracks and a suggestion of the Platte River somewhere to my left—was grading subtly from red to yellow. I blinked at the expanding world. Surely a little more of the land was visible now, still the same beaten and suffering land, but the subtle undulations of far-off hills proffered themselves through a gust of powder. A sheet of golden sunlight flowed along the contours of a distant formation, some long-eroded plateau with rickrack scars up its sides, where once, in better times, rivulets of water had run.

"Do you see that?" Louisa asked suddenly. She pointed ahead.

At first, I noticed nothing but the same drear through which we had trekked all day. But I could hear the river now—yes, the dust really was dissipating—and then I caught the faint outline of a house up ahead, revealed and hidden again between clouds of mobile dust. There was no telling how far away the house was—one mile or two—but the mere sight was enough to restore my vim.

"It's blowing over," Louisa said. "I think the sky will be clear by evening."

"God willing and amen."

The sky cleared much faster than Louisa had predicted. A fresh wind came up off the river and a burst of startling blue spread its wings overhead. That glimpse of clear sky disappeared in a moment, but it lent us yet more hope; we whooped and danced along the iron trail. By the time we reached the small house beside the tracks, we could see for miles into the prairie. The air had cleared enough that we both removed the towels from our faces and sucked in the rich, wet smell of the river with greedy satisfaction.

The building we'd spotted some ways back proved to be no proper house, but rather a shack, set off the rails amid a stand of scrawny trees. It was little bigger than a woodshed, its walls made from sun-beaten planks, its roof a hodgepodge of corroded tin. The trees cast a feeble shade from a canopy of leaves that had obviously been limp and brown before the dust storm had come. Now the leaves looked like nothing so much as cobwebs hanging with the weight of age and melancholy. A fence made from willow saplings surrounded the lot, and through gaps in the wattle, I could see a few hens pecking in the deep powder. A yearning for eggs overtook me, so strong it would have brought tears to my eyes, but they were much too dry for weeping.

I was about to make some remark to Louisa—ask whether she thought it would be worth the effort to knock on the door and inquire after jobs—when, with a bursting sensation and a coppery smell, a hot trail of blood poured from my nose, over my lip, into my parched mouth. I cussed and stopped in my tracks, pinching my nose, tipping back my head to avoid spattering the front of my shirt. Blood-stained clothing wouldn't help me find a day's work.

Louisa noticed my sorry state. "Good God, Del. Hold on."

We both groped for the towels we'd worn over our faces, but I'd stuffed mine up into the space between my rucksack and my back and couldn't lay hold of it. Louisa pawed through her pockets, then pulled a surprisingly large collection of folded rags from one. She offered me a square of cloth. It was already stained with rusty brown, though the rag had clearly been washed many times. I understood at once that this was her means of coping with her monthly indisposition out here on the rails. There was nothing for it. I overcame my squeamishness and stuffed the rag up my bleeding nose.

Just as I turned to Louisa with a sheepish grin, she gave a little jump, gazing past me at the rustic shack. I was expecting to find something startling, but when I followed the direction of Louisa's gaze, I saw only the hut with its meager contingent of chickens. The shade trees rattled their wasted leaves, and a dust devil went spiraling across the yard, past the uncovered stoop before it attenuated itself and vanished into the glare.

It was there, where the dust devil crossed the shack, that I saw the woman. She was thin and gray as everything was thin and gray, and she sat on the steps of her small, huddled house, unmoving, unblinking. She didn't even seem to realize that Louisa and I were there.

We shared a questioning glance. Ought we to call out to her? Poor as she looked, it seemed unlikely the woman would have a day's work for us—or if she had any work, certainly she couldn't pay. But I was a Southern girl, and to pass her by without some greeting would have been powerfully rude.

As we loitered on the tracks, the woman's face lifted as if some nightmare voice had commanded her to look up and see. She stared at us for a long time, slack-faced. Then she rose from the stoop with the stiffness of an old grandmother, though she couldn't have been far north of forty.

"You're bleeding." Her voice was so quiet, so dry, I could scarcely hear her over the desultory clucking of the chickens. "Come in."

She didn't wait for any answer but walked up the steps and disappeared into the shack. Louisa and I stared at one another again, till
finally, with a shrug, Louisa led the way through the gate, into the
woman's yard. The chickens flapped and scattered from our path as
we crossed a struggling garden—pole beans, a few weak melon vines
fainting along the ground, some exhausted potato plants and stunted
carrots poking up through loose dust. I could make out no sign of any
road beyond the fence, nor any lane. There was only the rail and the
same uniform waste that had swallowed up the summertime, clear out
to the horizon.

The woman had left the front door hanging open. We stepped
inside. The shack's interior consisted of two rooms, and the one in
which we stood was not spacious. It was dominated by two iron-framed
beds pushed against opposite walls—one large enough for an adult, the
other so small it could only belong to a child. A narrow doorway led
to the other room. A threadbare length of flowered cotton hung from
the lintel in lieu of a proper door, and the curtain was pulled aside,
held back by a large, rusty nail. The second room was little more than a
pantry, narrow and dim. It contained a cupboard of brilliant blue, the
milk paint cracked and flaking. Red flowers and curling vines ran up the
cupboard's sides. Despite its shabby state, the colors were the brightest
I'd seen for days, and I stared at the blue and the red as the quiet woman
rummaged in that cupboard, her eyes vacant.

"Set yourselves down right there on my bed," she said over her
shoulder. "I don't mind."

Wary in the stillness, Louisa and I perched side by side at the edge
of the larger mattress. Our clothes, of course, were covered in dust
and I had no wish to mar the quilt on which we sat. It was faded and
much repaired, but someone had put a good deal of care into its creation; every colorful hexagon had been stitched with a precise hand.
The bed across the room—the child's bed—held nothing but a bare
mattress with a rumpled blanket at its foot. A stained pillow lay on

the floor nearby. It gave the impression that some imp of a boy or girl had recently been playing there, and had run off to a new adventure, leaving the bed a mess for Mother to handle. But where was the child, I wondered, and why was the place so insistently quiet?

At this moment, the woman returned from the second room. She held a small earthen pot and dipped her finger into the salve it contained.

"Take that rag away," she said to me.

I did. Before I could so much as flinch, the woman had stuffed her finger right up my nose with as little hesitation as gutting a fowl. I let out a yelp, for the salve stung and made me squeeze my eyes shut, but I could already feel that the bleeding had stopped. One good sniff nearly caused me to choke on the medicinal reek. To preserve the last shred of my dignity, I wiped my face with the rag and stammered out my thanks.

She made no answer, only took herself to the front door and stepped back into the day's glare. The woman sank on the stoop once more as if Louisa and I weren't there.

"We ought to do something for her," Louisa whispered, "seeing as how she was so kind to us. But I don't think there's much point in asking her what needs doing."

I nodded. Our hostess carried an undeniable air of ruination. Had it only been the dust storm that had devastated her so? Terrible as that storm had been, I felt instinctively that something else gnawed at her heart—a greater loss than I could comprehend.

"You go out and talk to her," I said to Louisa, "or try to talk. She might tell you what's eating her. I'll take a look around the place and see if I can't find some chore that needs doing. We can't just leave without any payment."

Louisa crossed to the open door and settled on the stoop, close beside our silent hostess. I entered the second room to inspect the cupboard—perhaps, I thought, it might contain a few smoked ham hocks and onions, something I could use to cook up a meal for the woman. The second room revealed another door which could only lead to the back of the shack.

Perfect, I thought. *I'll search the house for storm damage.* Maybe we could repair shingles or clapboards before we took our leave. That would be a suitable trade for the medicine the woman had given me.

When I opened that door, however, all thought of work fled from me in a great, white crash of dismay. On the shack's narrow porch, immediately at my feet, lay the body of a little dark-haired boy. He couldn't have been older than six or seven years. He was thin—so terribly thin, with his cheekbones sharp below his waxen eyelids, the joints of his limbs knobby and stark. I swallowed hard, and stared at the bluish cast to his skin, the sure sign of death. There was no coming home again for the little mite. He'd been gone too long for any hope of revival.

A red dog, just as skinny as the boy, lay curled up beside him. The dog watched me with sorrowful eyes and whined once, but never lifted its head.

Now I understood the mess of the child's bed. The rumpled blanket, the pillow cast aside—not in sprightly play but in sudden desperation, a mother's haste to save her baby, to pull him back from the far, impossible side of the grave.

The weight of it all—the loss, the injustice. This emergency, as Skipjack had called it, which never let up and never varied unless it was to get crueler and harder—the weight of it buckled me. I fell to my knees beside the child. With my palms on his head, with the coldness of death under my hands, I prayed. I commanded the boy to rise, to live, to be anything but a wasted life, an innocent thing so callously used and thrown away.

But he didn't rise, of course. I am no miracle worker, and anyway, miracles only proceed from a God whose eyes are open.

After some time, I composed myself, wiping my tears away. I stroked the dog's smooth head, and it licked my hand, then curled itself tighter beside its little master. When I climbed back to my feet, a wave of dizziness and grief overtook me, but I pushed all that aside and set off through the whispering trees to the front of the shack. I knew now what work Louisa and I must do.

They were still sitting on the front stoop, Louisa and the bereaved mother. Pausing, gathering my wits and my will for the task ahead, I watched Louisa rub the woman's back and murmur to her. The woman shook her head now and then or nodded, but said nothing.

Louisa noticed me there among the gray trunks of the trees. She stood with an easy grace and crossed the yard, puffs of dust rising from every step.

"I haven't learned much," she told me. "Only that she's a widow, and . . . My God, Del, the look on your face. What's the matter?"

I took Louisa by the shoulders, held her steady while I explained. Knowing that Louisa was a mother herself—that she, too, had a little boy—I half expected her to break down in a fit of sorrow, to be felled by the blow of loss as I'd been felled back there on the porch.

But her eyes only lowered, and she pressed her lips together in that thoughtful way, and finally she said with more acceptance and control than I could credit, "Now I understand. Yes, of course. Let me talk to her again, the poor thing. Then you and I will go and dig the grave."

I remained there among the whispering trees while Louisa returned to the stoop. She took the woman in her arms, leaning close to whisper in her ear. Like the surge of some inevitable flood, the mother's grief broke at last, spilling across the dry world in a terrible wail. Louisa rocked her, and spoke to her, and went on holding her for as long as her cries lasted. And when in time the mother stilled herself, I crept forward and laid my hand on her bowed head, and let my tears fall with hers into the dust.

"I haven't been able to bury him," the woman sobbed. "There's nothing to wrap him in but his blanket, and if I do, I'll have nothing to keep, nothing to remember him by. But I can't put him in the ground. I can't throw dirt on his little body—oh God, oh God!"

Carefully, I maneuvered up the steps and found my rucksack, which I'd dropped on the floor of the shack. I unstrapped the old quilt I'd taken from the abandoned farmhouse, carried it outside, and stretched it between my arms so the mother could see the bright diamonds of color—red and blue, green and purple, sunny yellow-gold—all the colors a little boy would like.

"Look here," I said gently. "We'll wrap him in this. And he'll sleep well in such a fine bed. It's a good, sweet shroud for a good, sweet boy."

The woman nodded, then buried her face in her hands. I folded the quilt and placed it reverently on her lap, then I went to find a spade and a place to lay her dear little child to rest.

20

We stayed the night in the home of the grieving mother, for Louisa feared leaving her alone through the long hours of darkness, in the emptiness of the shack that had, only days before, rung with the laughter of her boy. Neither of us would have dared to desecrate the child's bed. I rolled my mat out on the floor, and Louisa got into bed with the weeping, shuddering woman, and held her till her breath grew steady and even. Listening to the wind sigh among the failing trees, and over the fresh new grave I'd dug among their roots, I prayed that the mother's dreams would be merciful.

At dawn's light, we took our leave. Louisa embraced the woman, whose name we'd never asked—nor had she asked ours. I patted the skinny red dog, who kept his vigil at the head of the grave. The dog whined at me, wagging its tail. And then we walked on, Louisa and I, into the west, following the long, black thread of the rail.

Neither of us spoke much. Louisa was sunk, as I was, in private thoughts. No doubt she was preoccupied with memories of her own boy—fear for his safety. For my part, I was haunted by the thought of every mother and child I'd left behind in Harlan County. I hadn't learned what had claimed the life of the boy we'd buried; it had seemed too great a cruelty to ask. Disease, or starvation, or any other kind of want, or the smothering effect of that hellish dust—anything could have done it, anything at all in this new and hostile world, this ended world in which we were yet obliged to go on living. The miners' strike, on top of everything else—had it ended, or did the conflict rage still, worse than when I'd left? Surely in the weeks since my departure, some of the mothers of the valley had laid their precious little ones to a final rest. And where was I, who could have aided them in their time of need, who might have offered some comfort? Nowhere, as far as they were concerned. The preacher's wife had abandoned them in their hour of greatest need.

Oh, I felt rotten that morning. I knew myself to be a selfish and miserable sinner, right to the pit of my soul.

After some ten miles of walking, just before the sun reached its zenith, we came upon the town of Cozad, tucked in tidily between the tracks and the Platte River. It was a Sunday, which I only discerned by the ringing of a church bell across the rolling brown hills. We entered the town as the last of the congregation was filing into a picturesque meetinghouse of brick with a whitewashed steeple. As we trudged a rutted road past the church, my attention was drawn by a mild commotion just outside the chapel door.

"Go on, get out of here. We don't want your nonsense this morning. Take it somewhere else, Bill."

That was the pastor, judging by his fine suit and his air of authority—a tall man waving his hand at a hunched and hairy figure who gesticulated and cussed.

The pastor's words sounded so like Irving's that day when he'd chased the two hobos from our picnic. That day when I'd found him with another woman in his arms. I stood staring at the scene while Louisa walked on a few paces, unaware of my turmoil.

Bill was a bent and scraggly man dressed in a scarecrow's patchwork. He made a guttural growl and lunged at one of the ladies who'd been tripping up the pathway to the door. The woman shrieked and hustled inside while the pastor laid hold of Bill's shirt collar and spun him around.

"I said get on with you," the pastor shouted. "I've got a service to run, Bill, and I won't have you disrupting it."

Louisa had returned to my side. She gazed at the scene with that quietly thoughtful expression I'd come to know so well. "The state of him," she said. "So dirty and ragged—it's enough to make you believe you can smell him from here."

"I think maybe I *can* smell him. Poor fellow; must have lost his mind."

Louisa watched the pastor shepherd the last of his flock into the meetinghouse. Then he shut the door firmly in old Bill's face.

"That does it." Louisa left the road. She began marching up the path toward the church.

"Hold on!"

I scuttled after her, dead certain she intended to pound on that door and give the whole congregation a piece of her mind. But she approached the shambling figure of the outcast man, then slowed and held out a hand as if to shake. Bill stared at Louisa in her trousers and man's shirt like he'd never seen such a mystery in all his days.

I caught up to her then. A whiff off old Bill hit me like a fist. The man reeked of sweat and urine, and fouler things. He hadn't shaved or cut his hair in years; he seemed more bear than man, and the wild light in his eyes frightened me. A frantic urge to pull Louisa away from him overwhelmed me, yet I didn't dare move too quickly around that strange specimen of humanity.

"Hello, Bill," Louisa said. "I don't guess you remember me. It's been an awful long time since I was in town last, but you and I were real good friends back then. What do you say, old pal? Isn't it something to see little Louisa all grown up? Put her there, for old time's sake."

Now, this was pure fabrication. Louisa had never set foot in Cozad before. But her brightly familiar tone had the intended effect. Some of the wariness left Bill's narrow eyes. He licked his lips, eyeing Louisa's hand, and finally extended his own. Louisa shook it gravely.

"My friend Del and I were just heading to the old swimming hole," Louisa went on sunnily. "It's going to be another walloper of a hot one. Why don't you come along and take a dip, Bill? We'll have an awful good time."

Bill cast about for a moment, uncertain, even shaken. I could almost read the tumble of his thoughts—he hadn't the least idea who this odd slip of a girl might be, but Louisa had clearly shown him more kindness than anyone else had that day, perhaps more kindness than anyone had shown him for years.

"Yeah," he finally rumbled, "why the hell not?"

Briskly, Louisa led the way across the road and over the empty railroad tracks, toward a bend in the river. I stepped along at her side, glancing back now and then at the great, dirty hulk who followed tamely behind.

"What on earth are you thinking?" I muttered.

"He's clearly lost his wits," she answered quietly, "and has no one to look after him. He might find more charity at that *church*"—she all but spat the word—"if he didn't smell like a pigsty. If we can coax him out of his clothes and into the water, we can clean him up some. Then he might have a little more luck getting the help he needs."

"Do you really think this will work?"

For an answer, Louisa shrugged. She gave me a frank little smile. "We can't just leave him to suffer, can we?"

Across the railroad, we made our way down into a shallow wash at the river's edge. It was a proper swimming hole—Louisa must have spied it from the road—for the comings and goings of generations of children had beaten a trail into the thicket. We followed that trail to a sandy clearing surrounded by a perfect ring of trees, save for the place where the river cut in to whisper against the bank. The current was slow and easy there, the river breaking itself into several streams punctuated by small, sandy islands furred with brush.

Bill came blundering down the trail behind us, muttering and grunting, breaking branches as he went. I drew a deep breath, preparing to think up some clever means of getting that man out of his grimy clothes without stripping off my own—but I needn't have taxed myself. The moment Bill saw the water, he let out a whoop like a boy who'd just been turned loose from the schoolhouse. He shambled right past Louisa and me, stripping off his shirt and tossing it aside, hopping on one leg, then the other, as he shucked off his trousers and left them lying on the sand. At the water's edge, he shimmied down his shorts and kicked off his shoes—both of their soles thin and peeling away from the leather uppers—and with a great shout, he went stampeding joyfully into the river.

"Well, that was easy," Louisa said. "Come on; help me gather up his things, and then you can find that bar of soap in your pack. Guess we've got some laundry to do."

While Bill swam contentedly in the cool water, Louisa and I crouched beside a flat stone, soaping his dirt-stiffened clothes and beating them against the rock, and rising and soaping again. It was tiring work. I don't believe Bill had so much as removed his duds for years, let alone washed them, and we labored for more than an hour till we'd beaten the last of the grime from the cloth.

Yet despite the weariness of my arms and back and the force of the midday sun, I don't think I'd ever enjoyed a job so well. Bill was a remarkably smart swimmer. Whatever he'd forgotten of his life, his family, his very self, he'd retained his instinct for water, and he splashed and played in the shallows with a childlike abandon, animated by so pure an innocence that I couldn't help grinning. He ventured deeper into the river, took a breath, and arched into the water. His wrinkled, old behind breached the surface. Then his skinny legs kicked up in a white splash, and he dove down and vanished for a spell, only to burst up in some unexpected place with a sputter and a laugh and wave at us on the shore, his new and dearest friends.

After we'd finished the washing, we carried Bill's clothes to the branches of a willow tree and strung them out in the sunshine to dry. Bill was tuckered out by then. He hauled his naked bulk from the river and flopped down on the sandy shore. Sprawled in the lazy heat, he drifted into a contented sleep while Louisa and I propped ourselves against the willow, dozing likewise in a pleasant warmth.

When I woke, Louisa was no longer beside me and the clothes were gone from the branch overhead. I found her a little downstream, coaxing Bill into his slightly damp trousers and shirt.

"They'll be letting out of church about now," she was saying to Bill. "You head back up there and talk nicely to the preacher. I bet he'll give you some supper, if you ask."

"Okay," Bill mumbled.

"But you have to be nice, remember. No yelling and no cussing. Just be sweet as honey and say, 'Please may I have a bite to eat,' and he won't be able to resist you, looking as clean and fine as you do now."

"You're a good girl," Bill said gruffly.

Louisa stepped back and looked up at him with an expression of delighted surprise. "Why, Bill, thank you. You aren't such a bad fellow, yourself."

Before she could say another word, he swept her into a bear's hug. The suddenness with which he grabbed Louisa sent my heart to racing, but she only laughed and held him in return, then planted a peck on his wrinkled cheek and pointed up the trail. Bill hurried back toward the town. He paused at the lip of the wash, calling a goodbye, and then he was gone.

We camped that night right there among the willows, sharing a supper of canned beans and some dried plums Louisa had picked up back in Omaha. We heated the beans right in the can, in the coals of our fire, till the label charred and flaked away. We took turns with the spoon—a mouthful for me, then one for Louisa, and me, and her, till the can was empty and the sun had sunk below the land, and only a secretive blush of pink remained in the broad night sky.

Louisa got up and crossed the clearing, wandering out to the edge of the river. There she stood with the toes of her boots just touching the water, looking up into the curve of the sky. The stars were emerging in majestic procession, innumerable, a bower overhead, sheltering the world under a subtle and transformative light. Beyond the opposite bank with its cadre of willows and cottonwoods, the land sloped up almost imperceptibly, rising from the river to the starred and singing hem of night, and the earth that seemed so hostile by day was revealed to me as an expanse of restful shadow and rippling light. I saw that for every low place, there was a rise, and a cresting—that hill followed valley and valley followed hill from one endless end of that great unfolding to another.

"Come here," Louisa said to me.

I went to her. Of course I did. The water moved past us, mingling its low, soothing voice with the chanting of night insects. The air was sweet with the mercy of flowing water.

"Let's go for a swim," she said.

"Now?"

"Why not? It's still warm enough that we won't freeze when we come out."

She stripped off her clothes, so I did the same, and followed her into the shallows. The water bit into my body and sped my heart. Louisa joined her hands together and her marble whiteness arched against the violet sky; she dove under the surface with a gentle splash, while I stood bare and aching from the cold, staring at the place where she'd disappeared.

As the last light vanished and a chill set in, I left the river and stirred our fire, and I lay on my mat in the halo of its heat without a stitch on my body, letting the last drops of water evaporate from my skin. The leaves of the willow thicket carried on a quiet dialogue with the river.

A whip-poor-will called overhead. And I watched Louisa, submerged to her neck in the water, tipping her head back to rinse the soap from her hair. In the delicacy of twilight, in its rapid fade into full night, I understood the impermanence of youth and happiness, of life itself, and every moment that passed was a treasure I possessed, and each moment was of greater worth than all the fine things Irving had filled our home with—the flowered wallpaper and electric lights, the telephone, the velvet sofa and chairs. What was any of that worth, compared to this? This treasure buried under the grim, brown surface of that year.

Louisa emerged and stood among the willows, her back turned to me as she watched the river slide past. Water ran in golden beads from her skin.

By and by, she returned to the fire and dressed in her oversize shirt, which covered her almost as much as a nightgown would. She'd restrung the locket on a new piece of string, and now it hung from a broken branch. She retrieved it, clicked the golden disk open to gaze for a while at Eddie's picture. Then she slipped the loop over her head, tucking the pendant inside her collar the way she always did. I sat up to make room for her at the end of my mat. The night was still warm, and I had no inclination for clothes just yet—I wouldn't, till the mosquitoes rose to their busy work.

Louisa sat on my mat, drawing her knees up under her shirt, folding her arms around herself. The firelight touched her, here and there, with fragments of gold.

"You're awful comfortable in the ivory these days," she remarked.

"Sorry," I said. "Do you want me to put something on?"

She laughed. "Heavens, Del, I don't care. Only it's funny, the way you were so concerned that first night. You remember, down in Arkansas. The hot spring."

I surely did remember. "Guess I'm not so much of a proper lady anymore."

"The rails will do that to you."

With a contented stretch, I asked, "Do you think it's permanent?"

I'd been joking, of course, but Louisa gave me a pinched and sober look. "I hope not."

I recalled the gentle way she'd handled Bill, and the comfort she'd given to the grieving mother the day before. She was good—good right through to the heart, not because she saw some advantage to herself in kindness, but merely because kindness was her natural state.

In a turmoil, I stood and retrieved my clothing, dressing quickly in the darkness beyond the fire.

What right did I have to keep my secret from Louisa? She deserved to be home with her son. She deserved to be in the arms of a man who would love her, and treat her gently, and give her the pretty life she longed for. It was my own selfish desire for freedom that kept her imprisoned by the rails. *I should tell her now,* I thought. *Send her to the nearest telegram office first thing in the morning, sacrifice for her the way she has sacrificed for so many.*

And yet I couldn't make myself speak, for to go on back to Irving would be to part with Louisa, and my heart could never withstand the blow.

When I returned to the mat, Louisa said quietly, "It's so dry out there past the river."

I made some small reply, a hum of agreement.

"Even last year, it wasn't like this."

"Last summer was hot," I said. "At least it was in Kentucky."

"But not like this. It's different. Settled in, like the dryness is here to stay."

I thought of how quickly the dusk had melted and deepened out there on the water, while Louisa had tipped her brown throat to the sky, letting the current carry the soap away. I said, "Nothing stays forever. There's no such thing as forever."

"I know," Louisa said, calm now and sober. "This can't possibly last."

21

In Cozad our luck turned around. Two days after we arrived, a freighter bearing the Union Pacific badge paused for the night in the railyard and noisily coupled a half-dozen gondolas. The cars carried far less grain than they ought to have done, that time of year. Louisa and I agreed that we would be on that freighter before it rolled out of Cozad next morning. July was halfway gone by then. Our destination still lay far to the west.

That train saw us only as far as the village of Bayard, spitting distance from the Wyoming border. There it stopped, early in the afternoon, and the locomotive left the cars behind, carrying on alone into the distance for reasons I could only guess at.

We climbed down from our boxcar and stood in the stillness and the heat, watching the locomotive shrink to nothing along the westward track. A squat brick depot dozed in the sun. Beyond the depot, a few houses and a general store looked small and stricken in the yellow light, and beyond those, a spire of pure, pale stone needled into the air. An old Model T went chugging by on a road whose pavement was the color of the day's glare. Wind threw miniature pebbles and fragments of straw against my legs.

"Well," I said to Louisa, "now what?"

"We look for work, I suppose, till another train comes through. Same as always."

"It's afternoon already. No one'll have work at this hour—not that's worth doing. Not that'll pay a hill of beans."

My mood was sour, for I'd spent the whole morning dwelling on the question of Irving's thousand dollars. More to the point, I'd spent the morning wrapped in a kind of inner inquisition, demanding to know why I balked at this chance to help my friend. If I were a good person, as I'd heretofore believed myself to be, then shouldn't my decision be an easy one?

"Guess you're right about the work." Louisa cast around for a moment, taking in the smallness of the town, the empty sweep of prairie that surrounded us. Her eyes landed on the spire of stone and she brightened. "Then we'll have a little vacation."

"A vacation?" I said. "Have you gone crazy?"

"We can't work every day, Del. And when will you get a chance to do this again?"

"Do what?"

"Climb Chimney Rock, of course."

Before I could object, Louisa set off across the railyard, swinging her bindle with a jolly air.

I had little choice but to follow. We traversed the town of Bayard in a few minutes' time, then set off across an expanse of dead grass and sage. The spire of Chimney Rock dominated the prairie, a great mass of stone jutting up from a conical brown hill, which flared evenly to the ground like a woman's skirt. The tower of stone was taller than anything I'd seen before, taller than the skyscrapers in St. Louis, tall enough to touch the small, white moon that drifted in the pale heat of a midsummer sky.

That heat had gathered itself with an accustomed brutality. Sweat ran down my neck, soaking through my shirt, rousing horseflies from the tall grass. I was hard-pressed to slap the flies away from my face and forearms before they sunk their vicious jaws into my skin.

After more than an hour of trudging through the unvaried buff of the landscape, I looked up to find that Chimney Rock was almost close enough to touch. Its base carried a suggestion of color in the stone—rosy-pink and yellowish-gray, with crags running down its steep slope in thin veins of purple. At least the color was something novel. If I'd been forced to stare into the anemic tones of the suffering prairie for one more minute, I was sure I'd scream just to break the damnable monotony.

Louisa reached the base of the hill first. She began to climb with an energy that astonished me. I pursued her in silent concentration, scrabbling with my hands among tufts of sage and loose chips of sandstone. Whenever I began to flag under the heat and the weight of my pack, Louisa looked back at just the right moment, as if she could sense my weariness and frustration, and she laughed good-naturedly, or barked out encouragement, or made a little joke to chivy me along.

By the time we reached the peak of the hill—and the base of the massive stone spire that crowned it—my head pounded from the effort. I stood at Louisa's side, and together, both of us panting and wiping the sweat from our brows, we looked down on the great dun-colored sweep of grassland. Streams and rivers glimmered in the late afternoon sun. Pale threads of unpaved roads spooled out and lost themselves in the impossible vastness of the prairie. The train we'd ridden that morning looked small as a child's toy far below.

"Now that is something." With hands on her hips, Louisa turned slowly, taking in the grandeur of the view.

I groaned and sank into a squat, pressing both palms to my aching eyes.

"You all right?" she asked.

"Headache."

"You've sweated too much. Lost your salt. Here; get that pack off. Let me help."

When she freed me from the rucksack, Louisa untied its strings and began rummaging inside.

"What are you after?" I said, rather snappishly.

"Ah—here it is."

Louisa produced a small, red-and-yellow tin marked *McKesson's Talkies Throat Pastilles*. I recognized the box, of course. We kept our supply of salt inside, due to its reliably tight-fitting lid.

She flipped the tin open. "Hold out your hand."

Louisa deposited several pinches of salt on my palm till she'd heaped at least half a teaspoon there.

"Now eat it," she said.

"You're crazy."

"You need to replace the salt you've sweated away, Del. Otherwise your head will go on hurting."

She was right, and I knew it. Grimacing, I brought my hand to my lips, extending my reluctant tongue. The potent taste contorted my mouth and wrung from me an involuntary "Ugh!" but Louisa commanded me to keep going till I'd taken the whole dose. Saliva flooded my mouth; I choked and writhed, but soon my palm was empty, except for the sheen of my final lick.

"Now drink." She passed me the canteen.

Gratefully, I swallowed mouthful after mouthful of flat, tepid water till the noxious bite of too much salt had faded.

Then I rocked back onto my bottom, gripped my knees, and burst into tears.

Louisa had cared for me so tenderly—not only now, but since the day we'd met. Even when she had insisted that we must part, that we couldn't travel together—even then, she'd looked after me, guided me, taught me how to survive. Not because I'd occupied any special place in her heart. Merely because kindness was her truest nature. How many times had I watched her minister to others? How often had I seen

Louisa look through people's misery, through their oblivion and their pain, to find exactly what they needed?

And when she saw what another soul needed, she gave to them freely, if it was in her power to give.

In the revealing brightness of that day, with the savor of salt still on my tongue, I knew I could no longer keep my secret, not if I hoped to have a soul worth saving.

"Louisa," I said through my tears, "I've got to tell you something."

She sat beside me, waiting as patiently as ever while I gulped and shuddered and marshaled some semblance of control.

"I told you my husband's the preacher of my town," I finally managed. "What I didn't tell you is that he's got a lot of money. I mean—he's taken money. From his flock. From the church. From the senator."

"The senator? Which one?"

"Logan," I said.

"Who?"

"Just listen, please. Back in Omaha I saw a newspaper with my face printed right there on the front page."

"You *what*?" She sounded almost amused.

"Listen; it's serious. Irving—my husband—or maybe his friend Senator Logan . . . Someone has been running articles in papers all across the country to tell everyone I've up and left him."

"The nerve of the guy."

"That's not all. Irving is offering a reward for whoever nabs me and returns me to Harlan County. It's a thousand dollars, Louisa. A thousand-dollar reward."

A sudden wind moaned around the base of Chimney Rock, riffling my hair and tugging at my clothes. The sweat cooled on my skin, almost to the point of chilling me. I couldn't look at Louisa.

After a minute, I said, "I think you should send a telegram to Irving. Or phone him; I'll give you the number. Tell him you've got me. Claim the reward. If anyone deserves that money, it's you."

"Fat chance," she answered at once. "What kind of a drip do you take me for, Del?"

"You were right, when you said I was a fool to leave my nice, easy life behind. You were right. I'm going back."

"Like hell you are."

"But Louisa—"

"Go back to a man who broke your heart, a man who doesn't respect you? Why, he's a hypocrite—telling others how to live their lives while he's carrying on with other women and robbing his followers blind. I'd like to see you try and go back to that snake."

"The money will get you back to Eddie. You won't even need to pick apples. A thousand dollars will set you up for years—"

"And where will you be?" She rounded on me, speaking with such vehemence that I had no choice but to look at her. Those penetrative eyes pinned me like a butterfly to a collector's card. I couldn't move, couldn't breathe in the face of her lioness strength. "You'll be trapped in a life that doesn't suit you—a life you risked everything to leave. Do you think I could rest easy at night, knowing I'd sold my best friend into misery? I don't need a thousand bucks from your rat-bastard husband. September isn't so far off, and neither is Wenatchee. I'll earn my pay the honorable way, by working for it—not by turning you over to a lying, cheating thief."

Such a wave of relief crashed over me, I felt as if I'd been flipped end over end. Fresh tears burned in my eyes, but they were joyful now. Without another word, I threw my arms around Louisa's neck. For a long while we stayed that way, laughing while the wind buffeted us and the tears dried on my cheeks.

Later, after my weeping was long finished, we hunted among the boulders and outcroppings at the base of the sandstone spire, searching for the names of travelers carved into the rocks. Dozens of men and women had left their mark, scratching away the dark varnish on the faces of the stones, proclaiming to a hard world that they'd made it this far, that they were still alive. My heart ached, for all those pioneers had long since passed away. The most recent date I could find was almost a hundred years in the past. I ran my fingers over one name, then another, feeling the permanence of all those declarations, till Louisa beckoned to me across a stretch of open ground.

She'd found a patch of unmarked varnish on the flank of an upright boulder.

I knelt in the dust and drew my pocketknife. In moments, I'd scratched Louisa's name into the rough surface, then my own.

"That's right," she said. "You and me."

22

July blazed into August. The fields and prairies withered still more under the persistent heat, and the foothills of the great, blue mountains wore a pallor like sun-bleached bone. The trains carried us aimlessly northward and south again, through Wyoming, Colorado, the eastern ranges of Montana, from one small town to another while we searched for work with less success than we'd enjoyed earlier in the summer.

If we'd dared to venture into any of the few cities that dotted the rangelands, we might have had an easier time. Folks were more prosperous in larger towns, and industry more common. Plus, we might have lucked into a jungle or two, where the hobos' rule of "share and share alike" would have made our meager supplies stretch much farther. Cities, however, were a gamble we couldn't afford. There was no telling how far Irving's dastardly campaign of news articles might have reached, and I already felt wary enough in the tiny, nowhere hamlets that strung themselves like rustic beads along the rails.

At least September still lay ahead with its sweet promise. By night I dreamed of ripe, red apples filling my arms. By day I spoke languidly to Louisa of the plans I was making for that Wenatchee money. What did it matter if times were harder now than ever before, if we went days without work, without pay? What did it matter that all my money was gone, that I had only a few pieces of jewelry left to my name? The apple harvest was but a few weeks off, the vast rolling orchards of eastern

Washington nearly within our reach. We would be in Wenatchee soon, and then all our troubles would fall behind us.

"I'm going to open a hat shop," I declared one afternoon, "with my share of the apple money."

We were lying on our backs atop a slow-moving boxcar, somewhere between Casper and Buffalo, rolling through a long stretch of anonymous brown hills.

"It's hard to imagine you selling hats," she told me, "scruffy thing that you are."

"But I was real stylish in my last life." I amended with a sheepish laugh, "Well . . . stylish by Cumberland standards."

"You'll have to go to a proper city if you want to sell hats," Louisa teased. "Do you dare?"

"Nonsense. I'll be the last word. All the fanciest ladies will come a-running to wherever I hang out my shingle. After all"—lifting my arms to the sky, then my legs, I displayed my wool trousers and man's shirt; the cuffs of my trousers slipped down to reveal the dark hair bristling on my shins—"just look what a fashion plate I am."

Louisa giggled. I wanted to tell her, *I'll set up my shop wherever you are. I don't care if it's not in a city. I don't care if no one comes running. Just let me stay wherever you land. Let me be close to you; that's all I ask.*

Instead, I laughed again and threw one arm across my eyes to shut out the glare of the sun. "You know what my hats will have—every one? Silk flowers. It doesn't matter if they aren't the mode anymore. I like them, so silk flowers it is."

"Disgusting pink ones," Louisa said, "the size of your head. And peacock feathers stuck in the band."

"Entire peacocks perched on the crown."

We fell silent. The train groaned and rattled below us. The world groaned in its long agony, rattling its dust and its bones.

As August aged and work remained as scarce as ever, I convinced Louisa to take my gold chain to a pawn shop in Rapid City, which I dared not enter. We were camped a few miles from the fringes of town, among the cottonwoods where the railroad spanned itself in rust and black across the muddy thread of Boxelder Crick.

"Are you sure?" she asked, holding the chain up to examine its delicate glint.

"It's only a trinket Irving gave me. I'd rather have the money."

After she climbed the steep slope of our gully and vanished over its lip, I sat in pensive silence trying not to fret over the fact that the money was gone. Work was perilously scarce in the fields and rail towns, a sign of how bad things had gotten everywhere, how grim the future was. But Wenatchee waited, that land of milk and honey. The bright promise of abundant orchards remained, and Louisa trusted in the apple harvest so wholeheartedly that I couldn't help but do the same.

I quieted my fears with a half-remembered verse of scripture. It passed through my mind lightly, like a song heard across a great distance. *Tell the righteous it shall be well, for they will eat the fruit of their doings.*

Several days later, in the middle of August, we reached Billings, Montana—or the farm country outside it, for I, of course, refused to venture too near its busy roads and tall buildings. Louisa declared that just fine and dandy, for she'd spotted acres of raspberry cane as our train had approached the yard.

"With a little luck," she said, "we can hire on to pick the berries."

We left our train in an optimistic mood, evading a lone and rather indifferent bull in the railyard. With Billings at our back, we hiked down a dirt road in the direction of the berry farm. The walk was pleasant even in the late-summer heat, for an irrigation canal ran swift and green beside us, filling the afternoon with a rich, spicy fragrance, and the cottonwoods that drank deep of the canal offered the windy mercy of their shade.

Some half mile into our walk, we passed an old log cabin that had evidently been repurposed in the aftermath of the Great Crash. A large sign stood close beside the road, reading *Women's Charitable Society of Billings*, complete with a cherry-red arrow that pointed the way up a narrow lane to the cabin's front door. Below the arrow, words had been stenciled with meticulous care: *HOT MEALS—MEDICINE—RELIGION for all in need of aid.*

I must have made some noise to betray my disapproval, for Louisa looked at me with a light of amusement in her eyes.

"These charity clubs," I said, "are nothing but a bunch of well-off women, the bored wives of businessmen, trying to make themselves feel better about living off the backs of the poor by doing a few good deeds here and there."

Louisa burst out laughing.

"I'm serious," I said. "You think I didn't see my fair share of these clubs while I was back in Harlan County? I know the type." I'd been the type, myself, till recent days.

"They can't be so terrible," Louisa said. "Anyhow, don't you think charitable works ought to be encouraged, no matter what one's reason or motive might be?"

Tired and hungry, and no doubt still a little haunted by my worries over money, I responded with a haughty coolness. "No, I don't. If a person wants to do good in this world, he should do *real* good—not force a fellow who's down on his luck to sit and swallow a load of preaching before he can swallow a bite of food. Either you want to feed the hungry or you don't. And I don't believe folks who live off the labor of the poor ought to skate by feeling smug and comfortable about themselves just because they've given a hobo a slice of bread or a spoonful of cough syrup. That doesn't outweigh the damage these rich folks have done— *are* doing, every day."

"What," Louisa said dryly, "do you think no one should even *try* to do better? We should all just go on as we have, blundering through life, hurting one another, never paying enough attention to beg pardon for our mistakes?"

"Oh, let's not argue," I said. "You won't change my mind and I won't change yours. Let's not spoil a nice day. Let's just get whatever money we can—or I'd settle for something decent to eat, for a change. I'm tired of dried meat and prunes."

When we reached the raspberry farm, we found our timing was good. The farmer was willing to hire one of us on for a few days of picking, rounding out the crew he'd already employed.

"Not sure I need two more pickers, though." He eyed Louisa's slight frame, then nodded to me. "You look sturdier. You can do the work."

"Louisa's every bit as sturdy as I am," I said, "even if she is a little small."

The farmer hummed skeptically. His eyes slid away from us, toward the rows of berry canes where the other workers were already belting the wide, flat pickers' boxes to their waists, preparing to venture into the dense plantation.

At that moment, a donkey brayed, drawing the attention of all three of us. The shaggy beast trotted in our direction, trailing a broken rope from its head collar.

"Dad blast it," the farmer blurted. "Jim's out again. The critter's too smart for his own good."

Eagerly, Louisa said, "Has he been breaking free? I'm good at repairing fences. Did it plenty down in Nebraska."

"And in Illinois," I added. "She put up a whole row of posts herself and nailed the boards. Honest Abe; I saw it with my own two eyes."

Louisa was never one to let an opportunity pass her by. She caught the end of the donkey's rope as he tossed his head and tried to swerve around her. Talking sweet and moving slow, she soon had the beast standing placidly at her side, allowing her to scratch between his ears. The donkey blew a rough salute through his nostrils, tame now and content.

"I'll make you a deal," Louisa said. "Give me a day to work on your fence, and if Jim here can find a way out by sunrise tomorrow, you won't have to pay me a thing. I'll only collect if your donkey stays put till morning."

The farmer shrugged. "Seems fair enough. If you can keep that ornery animal inside his corral, it'll be worth the cost."

I shared a grin with Louisa, then we parted ways. She led the donkey toward a small collection of pens and outbuildings nearby. I rushed to stow my rucksack at the foot of a willow tree, in a haste to join the other harvesters.

Picking raspberries wasn't especially difficult work. Each harvester, with a lightweight basket strapped to their body, moved down a row of tall canes, plucking ripe berries from the plants. When we'd filled our baskets, we returned to the edge of the field and deposited the berries in one of the long, wire hods that stood waiting on the grass. Every hour or so, the farmer's son would come rumbling past in his rust-bodied truck to collect the hods, replacing them with empty wire crates.

My row was the last in the field, separated from the rest of the farm by the track on which the farmer's son drove. Across the track stood the animal pens, and as I worked, I watched through a screen of thorny canes as Louisa inspected the boards of the donkey's corral, leaning against them to test their resistance, prodding at the wood with an awl to find the rotted places. The donkey seemed to like her. He pestered her while she worked, turning his head sideways to slip his muzzle between the boards, lipping at the loose fabric of her sleeve. Now and then the donkey shoved her with his head, demanding that she scratch between his ears, and whenever he did, Louisa cussed and swatted the animal away, which only seemed to make him more determined in his affection.

Despite the simplicity of my work—or perhaps because of it—I felt an urgency to prove my mettle. The fifteen dollars were gone. The rest of my jewelry would soon follow unless I could earn a substantial wage. Wenatchee might not be so terribly far off, but we hadn't reached it yet, and I was grimly determined that Louisa should make it to her destination in fine fettle. Nothing must interfere with her plans for the apples and the money she would earn. Nothing would hamper Louisa, if I had any say in it—certainly not a shortfall in our wages.

I guess I pushed myself harder than I ought to have done, for by midday my head was pounding, and the great jungle of canes seemed to tilt around me with every step. Sweat ran down my neck and back, chafing where the harvesting belt cut into my skin. I could feel myself slowing, my steps dragging, my fingers growing clumsy among the small, black thorns.

I don't remember falling. I only remember landing on the ground with the harvesting basket crumpled under me, the smell of crushed raspberries overwhelming in the swimming heat. I felt a terrible, searing pain in my right foot. Its flash and burn seemed brighter than the sun. Louisa shouted my name, and the thud of her boots as she ran toward me vibrated through the ground up into my sprawled body. I croaked at her, "I'm sorry. I went and ruined a whole damn box of berries."

Louisa dropped to her knees beside me. "My God, Del, what happened? You're red as a beet."

She laid a hand on my forehead. The world seemed to contract around her touch—the heat and the pain and the gray, dragging weight of my worries dissipating into a vapor, blowing away. For a moment the only reality was the coolness of her palm and the comfort of her presence.

"I think you've given yourself heat stroke," she said. "Come on; try to get up. You need water and shade."

I did my best to rise, but the moment I moved my right leg, the pain flared up, white-hot. My whimper turned, of its own volition, to an outright howl, and after the first wild cry left me, I mustered my words and shouted every foul-mouthed cuss I'd ever heard into the swimming sky.

"I've got to get your boot off, Del. You might have broken something." The clink of a belt buckle followed. Then Louisa thrust her hands before my face. She held her belt, doubled over. "Bite down on this."

Louisa placed the leather gently on my tongue. It tasted of salt—of sweat, I realized with a surge of nausea—and accumulated grime. Louisa crouched in the dust and lifted my right foot with care, but even that light touch sent a fresh stab of agony up my leg. Clenching my jaw, I sank my teeth into the leather. In the moments after, I knew nothing but a wave of agony so intense it sent a shower of bright sparks flying where my vision ought to be. Vaguely, I was aware of fingers laced with my own, squeezing my hand. When I could breathe again, I opened my eyes and found Louisa peering anxiously into my face. I tried to keep her hand in mine, but my grip was weak. She took the belt from my mouth.

"No bones sticking through," she said. "That's good. But your foot might still be broken. You need a doctor."

"We can't pay a doctor."

Louisa ignored my protest. She stood and gazed around the farm in that pensive, searching way she had, unhurried despite the emergency, determined to think it all through.

"The farmer's boy just came through with this truck," she said. "He won't return for another hour. I might run to the farmhouse, but there's no telling if anyone is there. Aha." Her eyes lit on the donkey's pen.

"Oh, no," I said. "You're crazy if you think I can ride in this state."

"I can't carry you on my own, and God knows where the rest of the workers are by now. They might be acres into the berry field. Heat stroke is serious, Del. It worries me more than your foot does."

Before I could raise another feeble protest, Louisa took off across the dusty lane. In moments, she'd slipped into the donkey's pen, fixed a lead rope to his head collar, and walked the animal out through the gate. I writhed on the ground, spitting more bitter words into the dust—for by that time I'd realized where Louisa intended to take me. But there was nothing I could do. She was right; I needed help, and for all I knew at that moment, I needed it urgently.

All too soon, Louisa and the donkey stood over me. The animal lowered his head to sniff at me, his sweet, warm breath puffing across my cheek.

"Get back, you damned beast!"

"Don't talk that way to Jim," Louisa said calmly. "He's a perfectly nice fellow, once you get to know him. I only hope he'll stand still while I figure out how to get you onto his back."

Jim obliged placidly enough. Louisa pulled me up to stand rather precariously on my one good foot, then she instructed me to lean over the donkey's back while she braced a shoulder against my bottom and heaved. Scrambling, grunting, and clinging desperately to the donkey's mane, I managed to swing my injured leg over his back and sit more or less upright. Louisa dragged the animal behind her, with me on his back, while she darted about gathering my rucksack and my discarded boot. Then we set off down the farm's long drive to the unpaved road beyond. I kept my jaw clenched tight to prevent myself from further deriding the flock of hoity-toity busybodies who surely waited for me.

My head was still pounding and spinning by the time we reached the aid society's log cabin, and a dreadful wobbling sickness to my stomach seemed to meld with the noisy drone of the cicadas till I couldn't tell if the relentless buzz emanated from inside me or from somewhere out there in the brush and the hills.

"Hello," Louisa hollered as she led the plodding donkey up the lane. "Anybody in? We need help!"

Through the yellow heat, I could just make out two women in tidy, stylish dresses stepping from the cabin door. One of them shrieked at the sight of me, throwing up her hands to cup her own face. The other ran toward us.

"Goodness gracious," the woman said to Louisa, "what on earth has happened?"

Only then did I recall the red mess of crushed berries all down the front of my shirt. "Not blood," I managed weakly.

"My friend might have broken her foot," Louisa said, "and I think she's got heat sickness. Is a doctor handy?"

In short order, a half-dozen ladies emerged from the cabin to lift me from the donkey's back. They were kindly, all of them—I will say that. But as they carried me, slung between them like a sack of potatoes, I looked on their fine clothes with sour suspicion. The soft, white hands that bore me were unmarred by labor, adorned with fine rings and delicate bracelets. Pearls encircled their necks and clustered at their ears. I'd been right about the Women's Charitable Society of Billings. It was a sorority of well-off ladies—the sort who couldn't possibly understand what life was like for Louisa and me. What life was like for all those who toiled and suffered and died in the gutters of this ruined world.

If I'm perfectly honest, I think what I disliked most about those women was the reflection of my own former life. I'd lived much as they had in my eight years with Irving. I'd learned to blind myself to the poverty around me. I'd convinced myself that no one in the valley was as badly off as they seemed. For if I'd looked too directly at what had been right there before my face, I would have seen the injustice all too clearly—the injustice I'd helped perpetrate.

Luckily for me that day, one of those ladies was a nurse with proper medical training—the oldest of the bunch, a woman with wire spectacles perched on her nose and salt-and-pepper hair pulled back in an old-fashioned bun. Her name was Bethany, and the others deferred to her with a smooth complacency.

"Get her up on the table here, girls," Nurse Bethany said. "Then Jessie must go and fetch some ice. Ann, bring that cool jug of water from the kitchen—and a cup with a good, sturdy handle. Madoline, you can fetch those clean rags from the back room. Stand back, the rest of you. Give me some light to see by."

I was deposited like a parcel on a long, smooth-topped table beside the cabin's largest window. The women melted back—all except Louisa, who remained stubbornly at my side. The aid society's cabin was well-appointed on the inside. A half circle of plush, upholstered chairs was arrayed around a tea table, on which sat a silver tray and service. Scattered haphazardly about the cabin were cups of coffee and small porcelain plates bearing half-eaten finger sandwiches; evidently Louisa and I had interrupted the ladies' afternoon social. Two tables, large enough to accommodate a whole jungle of hobos, stood before a river-stone hearth. Each table was covered in spotless white linen. And there before the hearth, watched over by a mournful Savior suffering on his cross, stood the expected lectern from which these do-gooders no doubt preached at a captive audience before the latter would be allowed to partake of the promised hot meal.

Bethany looked down at my ankle. It was already swollen and dark. "What's your name, dear?"

Befuddled by the heat sickness, I opened my mouth to tell the truth.

Louisa spoke before I could. "Shirley. Her name is Shirley Johnson."

"And you've been . . . traveling together?" the nurse asked delicately.

"We're hobos," I answered. "There's no point beating around the bush."

"Well, Shirley," the nurse said, "you don't seem to be suffering from shock. That's an encouraging sign. But I must examine your foot and I'm afraid it will hurt."

Louisa reached for the buckle of her belt again.

"No," I said quickly. "I can bear it."

Bethany adjusted her spectacles and touched my ankle lightly. "There is some bruising already—probably more to come. There's not as much edema as one would expect with a fracture. Of course, that depends on where the fracture lies."

She prodded lightly at the arch of my foot, then bent each of my toes. Suddenly the nurse's touch shifted from gentle to probing. I winced as the practiced fingers bore down more firmly on tissue and bone. When she rotated my foot, testing the integrity of my ankle, I cried out in helpless pain.

"The worst is over." Bethany looked up with a smile. "You're lucky. There's no break—or at worst, there might be a hairline fracture. I'm fairly confident you've only sprained your ankle, but I'm afraid you must stay off your feet as much as possible for a week at least—maybe more."

"A week," I cried. "We can't stay put for a whole week! We've got to be in Wenatchee soon."

"Hush." Louisa's hand came down gently on my shoulder. "The most important thing is that you're not badly hurt. We can deal with the rest."

I clutched her wrist in silent apology.

Nurse Bethany wrapped my ankle in a stiff linen bandage, and as she worked, she directed her cadre of fine ladies with smooth, confident commands. They trickled cup after cup of water into my throat, one sip at a time, till I was steady enough to hold the cup in my own two hands. The ladies wrapped chips of ice in white cloth and stuffed them under my armpits, piled them on my groin, even wrapped a cold cloth around my head. I was made to stay put on the tabletop, recuperating slowly from my heat sickness while the aid society resumed their luncheon and fixed a plate of sandwiches for Louisa. They would feed me, they promised, once they were sure I could keep a meal down.

Louisa perched on one of the overstuffed chairs, talking with the women earnestly while I sulked from the other side of the room. The sight of her struck me with a bleak, hopeless pang—Louisa in worn-out trousers and a dirty, old shirt, sitting with her ankles properly crossed, holding the fine porcelain plate in one hand, nibbling delicately with

the other. These women with their lovely clothes and their easy lives—
they were everything Louisa longed to be.

She regaled the society with stories of our travels, and they listened in rapt silence. I sipped the water slowly, as Nurse Bethany had
instructed, while Louisa recounted the day of our first meeting, the
places we'd traveled to, the jobs we'd done—more jobs, I realized now,
than most men ever worked in a lifetime. Surely, we'd done more work
than these women would ever do, with their wealthy husbands to care
for them, with the shield of their money to keep them safe against the
slings and arrows that battered the rest of us, that stuck in our flesh,
that drained the hope from us a little more each day.

Louisa reached the part of our story I most dreaded to hear—the
grieving mother we'd found somewhere in Nebraska. The ladies began
to sniffle. They pulled their dainty kerchiefs from sleeves and handbags,
dabbing at their eyes.

"Don't you cry about it," I snapped, propping myself up on an
elbow. "Don't you dare cry for us. It's yourselves you should be crying
for—and your children."

Louisa stared at me, her brows pinched in disapproval.

"It's only getting worse," I said to them all, "this emergency. This
bleakness. It's only the poor who've had it hard, so far, but you mark
my words—this is a hungry beast, and once it's eaten the poor alive,
it'll turn on you next. Your husbands' money will run out—you'll see,
soon enough. And then it'll be you and your children who are in the
monster's gullet."

"Shirley!" Louisa exclaimed. "Get control of yourself, for goodness' sake."

"I'm sorry," I said, more because I couldn't bear the stricken look
in Louisa's eyes than because I cared for the feelings of the aid society.
"I'm sorry. It's only the heat sickness. And after you've all been so kind
to me . . ."

"Think nothing of it," Bethany said. "These are hard times for everyone. We're none of us quite ourselves, lately."

I groaned and sagged back on the table. The ice was melting in the heat of my fury, saturating my clothes with cold water and beading in my hair. I didn't know whether I despised those ladies more—with their unthinking ease and their unearned wealth—or myself, for hadn't I once been among their number, just as blind and contented as they?

23

We had no choice but to stay put on the bank of the Yellowstone River, waiting for my ankle to steady up enough that I could hop a train. Day after day, Louisa ventured into Billings in search of pay. Sometimes she found it, and some days she wandered the streets for hours only to return with empty hands and a distant dread in her eyes. The summer was unraveling faster than either of us could credit. Leaves hung limp and yellow from the sparse trees, and the light no longer dallied at the end of the day. September loomed all too near, but Wenatchee seemed as far beyond our reach as it had ever been.

When Louisa left each morning, I sat on the bare, sandy earth under the timid willows, my bootless foot stretched out before me, and I would stare at the wrapping around my ankle as if I could work a miracle by sheer force of my will. If need and desire and the cold pressure of desperation could have healed me, I would have jumped up and danced, singing "Hallelujah!" like the sick who'd thought themselves cured at Irving's revivals. But my ankle remained weak and painful. I could do nothing but wallow in my uselessness, staring over the turquoise plane of the river and its bar of naked gravel to the bluffs and white-faced cliffs beyond.

Each day I convinced myself that I must send Louisa on alone. For her good, I must tell her to get to Wenatchee without me. I worked myself up into a state of such resolve that I even laid plans for supporting myself in Billings once Louisa and I parted. *Hold your nose and go back to the ladies' society,* I told myself. *Ask them for work, for shelter—commit to join their church, if that's what it takes, for surely Del Wensley, of all people, can put on a display of godliness to rival the piety of any Catholic nun.* But then Louisa would come back to me—sometimes with a bit of bread or a jar full of honey, sometimes with a few coins, more often with a hangdog expression—and my resolve would wither, and I couldn't force myself to say the words I knew she needed to hear.

Why did Louisa never decide for herself that she must go on alone? That was a question to which I never found a satisfactory answer. Not for lack of trying, either—the mystery of Louisa's steadfast companionship preoccupied me through the long, hot hours I spent on that riverbank. Truth to tell, the question haunted me long after, through all the dismal years that went on turning even though the summer of '31 had fallen into memory.

What was I to her? Companion or comfort, a bulwark against the lonesomeness of the rails? Or simply a means to an end? At times I foolishly dared to hope that I was as precious to her as she was to me. Those days beside the river, I'd come to understand that Louisa was the very sun of my life, the fire and the hours around which all my seasons turned. To contemplate our separation was to look upon a bleakness worse than any my tarnished faith had imagined. For I had never seen the face of God, nor heard His voice. But I had held Louisa's hand. I'd given her my shoulder as a pillow in her sleep.

Some days, I wished with a reckless fury that Louisa would speak— that she would tell me just what I was to her, so that I could know in turn exactly what she was to me. But she never raised the subject, only went on working, or not working, and returning to my side as mellow evening fell, and together we would sit on the gray ground, not quite close enough to touch, listening to the river as it chattered over the stones, listening to the mourning doves that called to one another, and answered.

At least I can say that I wasn't entirely useless, despite my bum ankle and my tattered, distracted heart. The Yellowstone River teemed with fish that year. My first day on my own, I dug the small aspirin tin from my pack—the one I'd found in the abandoned farmhouse back in Nebraska—and untangled the fishing lines. I sharpened the hooks, patiently scraping their points against a smooth stone, and then, hobbling and wincing from the effort, I tied the lines to the branches of the tree that stood nearest the water's edge.

The first day I caught nothing, for I hadn't yet discovered the red wigglers deep in the leaf litter below the willows. Once I chanced upon those worms, however, I pulled in two or three good-sized salmon a day. Cleaning the fish and salting them kept me busy for a few hours, here and there. But after a time, when my hooks had been baited again and cast back into the water, and I'd laid the strips of red meat to dry on a flat, sunny stone, I would fall back into my despondent musing about Louisa and the apple harvest—Louisa and me.

Four days into my convalescence, I remembered that idle hands are the Devil's playthings, and determined that I needed more busywork to keep my mind off my troubles. Therefore, I set to fashioning a cold-smoking house out of downed willow branches and the little bits of twine I'd gathered here and there along my journeys. My mother had been a great smoker of all kinds of meat; as a girl, I'd often helped her with the work. It came back to me easily now, and soon I had a sturdy rack of twigs standing on the shore, surrounded by a tepee of leafy branches that kept the smoke more or less inside.

Louisa, when she returned from Billings that evening, declared the smoked salmon the tastiest thing she'd eaten in ages, even better than those fancy sandwiches the aid-society ladies had given us—though I thought willow made for a very poor-flavored smoke. It didn't have a patch on the hickory we used back in the Cumberland. Nevertheless, we were well fed on the banks of the Yellowstone, so at least our suffering was confined to the endless fretting inside our heads. In the balance, I do believe I'd rather be worried than hungry—though neither is especially easy to bear.

Six or seven days into our forced intermission, I'd smoked so much fish that the stuff was just about coming out my ears. I untied the lines from the willow tree and packed them away in the aspirin tin, and settled near my tepee of branches, which still leaked a little smoke from its final fire. Evening was descending in a rosy flush over the peaks of the nearby mountains. Louisa would be back soon—any minute, in fact. This time I was dead set to steel myself and take her hand, give my blessing to do what she was dying to do: get on for Wenatchee, leaving my useless hide behind. For her sake, I would do it. It would be an act of . . . what, exactly? Sacrifice or love. Maybe there was little difference between the two.

As I sat watching the water and the light—same as I'd sat for days on end—I heard the click of stone against stone and turned, expecting to see my friend picking her way across the broad wash of the riverbank. What I found instead startled me so much that I froze in place, staring like some critter surprised by a hound.

An entire mob of people had appeared on the bank—seven, eight of them, maybe more. My heart sped so madly that for one frantic moment I was sure I was about to keel over dead. *A whole gang of folks who've found me out,* I thought. *They've come to nab me so they can collect the reward.* Apparently the newspaper articles had reached all the way to Billings. Maybe the women at the aid society had recognized me, despite the false name. It was just like the rich to want more and more, to convince themselves that enough was never enough.

Then my better sense caught up to my racing heart. This was no city mob. They were ragged and weary, with rent clothing that gaped here and there to reveal thin bodies underneath. Most carried bundles on their backs. One, a woman with a quietly devastated face, held a baby in her arms. As the group approached, I saw that four of them were young—children.

A man in his forties seemed to be their leader. He ranged ahead of the others and lifted a hand in greeting. "Hello, friend. We don't mean to intrude. We smelled your smoke and thought there might be a camp nearby. A jungle."

"You're hobos," I said, more relieved now than frightened, but still plenty wary. "I'd stand to say hello if I could, but I'm afraid I'm useless these days." With a brusque gesture, I indicated the wrapped foot that was the devil of my very existence. "Where have you folks come from? You're welcome to share the riverbank; there's plenty of it to go around."

The man introduced himself—Al Werther—and his family, for they were a family, all of them, cast out from their farm in the panhandle of Oklahoma.

"Tenants," I said, sober with understanding.

"I'm afraid so." Al offered a sheepish smile that did little to hide the shame in his eyes. "My brother, Frank, here—he and I worked our daddy's farm from the time we were boys."

"And the bank took the farm," I said. It wasn't a question.

"We might have held on to it," Al said, "even with the drought and the dollar going so soft these late years. We had a good operation on that land. It was plenty fertile, and Frank and me, we're damn good farmers, if I do say it myself. But Mary and me—well, our first child was awful sickly. The doctor's bills piled up so high we had no choice but to mortgage the place."

Frank looked a few years younger than his brother with a livelier spark in his eye. "I made Al do it," he said. "Mortgaging the farm was the only way to pay Junior's doctor."

I smiled at the eldest of the children, a dark-haired boy with a thin, sober face. "I guess you were worth it."

At once, I knew I'd made a dire mistake. The woman who held the baby turned her face away, but I caught the grief in her eyes, as fresh as the day she'd laid her child in his grave.

"Oh," I said. "I didn't understand. Please forgive me, Mrs. Werther. I didn't mean to—"

"It's all right," Al said quietly. "You weren't to know, ma'am. In the end, our boy died anyhow. You'd think the bank would have more mercy on a family suffering as we were, with a child just newly laid to rest."

"When have the banks had mercy on anyone?" Mary said quietly. "Mercy won't turn a profit."

"I don't regret it," Frank declared. "I would have cut off my own right arm if it had kept Junior alive."

"You took to the rails, then," I said, grasping desperately for a change of subject.

Al nodded. "Yes, ma'am. We've been riding trains for weeks now, looking for good work that'll let us put down new roots. What's the situation like in Billings?"

"Not so good," I admitted. "The soil's awfully dry here for putting down roots. Nothing steady enough for newcomers."

At those words, despair crossed the faces of everyone in that ragged group, including the little children. I cursed myself for speaking, even if it was the truth.

"But there's plenty to eat," I said quickly. "Look—you see that bundle on the big rock there? Go on over and fetch it, you kids. See what's inside."

The four children, thin and dirty as scarecrows, brightened a little at the promise of a surprise. They scampered across the rocks to the flat boulder where I'd stored several pounds of smoked fish, wrapped and tied in my old raspberry-stained shirt. Giggling, they picked at the twine and peeled away the layers of cloth like it was Christmas Day, and when they saw the great pile of sweet-and-smoky fish, they let out one collective whoop fit to wake the dead.

"Eat as much as you want," I called to the children. "All of you. Dig in."

The Werther family tucked into that smoked fish like a pack of starving dogs while I looked on, warmed by the fact that I could bring them some comfort in the midst of so much sorrow.

"Del, who the heck are these people?"

I looked up to find Louisa standing over me. I hadn't heard her approach. In the fading pink light, she watched a week's worth of provisions disappear into the mouths of perfect strangers, but she didn't seem angry—only mystified.

Quietly, I explained, and she sank onto her heels beside me.

"That woman has a baby young enough for nursing," Louisa said. "They need more food if that little mite's going to survive."

"I can give them the fishhooks," I offered.

"That's a start, but it won't go far enough. We'll tell them about the ladies' aid. Maybe Bethany and her friends can help."

"For a day or two, sure. But these folks can't set down here in Billings. You know better than anyone else—there isn't enough work. What they need is food enough to keep on going. If they can make it all the way to the West Coast, they might have a chance."

"Or if they can reach Wenatchee. The men can find steady work there."

At the mention of our destination—Louisa's destination—my throat tightened. I was still resolved to tell her the way it must be. We would part that night, or the next morning, forever.

"There's something we can do for them now, though," I said. "Go and get my rucksack. It's there under the tree."

Louisa fetched my pack while the Werthers ate and chattered among themselves, and a fine, white sliver of moon came up over the mountains to hang in the soft blue of night. I reached into the secret pocket where I stowed my dwindling supply of jewelry. By feel, I located my wedding band. When I held it up between my fingers, it glinted in the tentative moonlight.

"Take this," I said to Louisa. "Hurry back into town before the shops close. Get as many pounds of flour as you can."

She stared at the ring as if in doubt. I guess she was weighing the use of feeding so many strangers—and wondering whether that ring might be the last bit of fortune she could count on to see her to her own destination. The children's laughter mingled with the sound of the river, and the baby gave a mewling cry.

The sound of the infant's fussing seemed to decide Louisa. She took the ring without a word, closing it in her fist. Then she left me, headed for Billings.

You'd better get used to that, I told myself, *the feel of her walking away.*

Louisa returned well after dark. The Werthers had built a little fire by then, back among the willows, and Uncle Frank was telling the children a story. His voice and the cadence of his tale carried to me now and again. Sometimes the children laughed or called out an answer to one of his questions. I knew the moment Louisa returned from town, for the story broke off and Al exclaimed, "It's too much, we can't be such a burden to you," while Mary said tearfully, "God bless you, both of you. You ladies have plumb saved our lives."

I remained there on the river stones, my bad foot stretched out before me and my other leg folded up where I could wrap my arms around it, just for the sake of having something to hold on to. The river flowed past, unconcerned, and the stars moved above me in their ancient courses.

By and by, Louisa returned to my side, but she said nothing, only stood with her hands in her pockets, gazing at the dark bluffs across the water.

"That ring," I said. "It was just about the last bit of anything I have. The money's all gone now. But I've got a set of pearl earrings left, and my silver bracelet. You're going to take them, Louisa, and get on to Wenatchee. Without me."

She made no answer. The children laughed again, and the fire crackled bright and jolly among the willows.

"You hear me?" I looked up at her, though it cut me deep to do it. "I'm no good anymore, and I can't stand to hold you back. September's almost here—"

"Shut up," Louisa said.

I did.

She extended a hand. I took it, and the light of the moon was inside me, running all through me as she pulled me up to my good foot. She captured my arm across her shoulders and helped me hobble down to the dark line of the water.

"You stand there," she said, "and don't give me any trouble."

She knelt on the damp stones, began unpicking my bandage. With a delicate grace, she removed the linen to expose my swollen ankle. Night air brushed cold against my skin.

"You spent practically your last penny," Louisa said, "to feed that family. And you think I'd leave you behind?"

"Louisa—"

"Be quiet, Del." She splashed a little water up onto my foot, and her hands with all their calluses and scars moved so gently over my skin. "Let's hear no more about this crazy idea."

I couldn't have spoken another word if I'd wanted to. Tears choked me, and the guilt in my chest was pretty near enough to crush my heart. I would be the reason why Louisa missed the apple harvest. I should have been stronger, I knew. I should have insisted, reminded her of Eddie, pushed her away from me with all the force of the love I bore for her. But I could no more force her from my side than speak God's true name. The words just wouldn't come.

257

24

Three days later, the Werthers had moved on from our riverside encampment and my ankle was sturdy enough to walk without too much pain.

"I'm going into Billings for a day of work," I said to Louisa that morning. "We need the money worse than ever. Goodness knows if we'll even be able to reach Wenatchee on what we've got left."

"But if you're spotted—"

"I'll deny everything," I said, "claim they're mistaken. Tell them I've never heard of Irving Wensley in all my life. Surely if I never admit to my real identity, no one can claim that man's damn fool reward."

Louisa paced along the edge of the river, hands clasped behind her back. "I don't like this, Del," she finally said. "I don't think you should risk it. I'll go and work; you stay here, out of trouble."

Resolute, I shook my head. I'd lost track of the days, but it seemed likely that September was upon us already. The great castellated expanse of the Rocky Mountains still loomed between our present location and Wenatchee. If we hoped to make it to the orchards with enough strength to work the harvest, then I must find a day's pay or sprout the wings to fly.

Louisa took me by my shoulders, as I'd so often done to her. I couldn't look away.

"Are you sure I can't change your mind?" she asked quietly.

"Nothing in the world can change my mind. It's do or die, Louisa. And I'll be damned if I don't see you to Wenatchee on time. If you won't take Irving's money, then I'm determined to see you back home with your little boy some other way. It's what you deserve."

She leaned close to me. I thought she would embrace me, as we'd done countless times before in moments of joy or sorrow. Instead, her lips brushed against mine—light as the touch of starlight, and so briefly I was half-convinced it hadn't happened at all. Then she turned from me abruptly and stalked up the rocky strand toward the willow grove.

Neither of us spoke as we disassembled our camp and left the riverside. I kept asking myself what had just happened, whether Louisa had truly kissed me or whether I'd only imagined it. Was the wild leap of my heart due to embarrassment or longing—and did I dare to speak of it? Did I dare to admit it had happened, even to myself?

No answers came to me as we crossed the tracks into Billings. We took it slow, coddling my ankle. The feel of Louisa's kiss remained on my lips like the burn of salt, yet I could make no sense of it, and as we entered the town, I had the misty, gray impression that we moved through the middle act of a dream. Louisa walked a little ahead, swinging her bindle from one hand. The road sent up a red-gold dust to catch the morning sun, the light hanging around Louisa in brushstrokes of fire.

We struck a vein of luck that morning. Louisa stepped into a bakery to spend a few of our dwindling pennies on a loaf of bread. She came out of that shop with a warm round of rye tucked under one arm and a beaming smile.

"There's a whole family uptown that's been hit by typhoid. The baker just told me."

"How awful," I said.

"The town doctor expects they'll all recover, thank goodness, but meanwhile they're hurting for someone to do the washing up. The family is hiring, the baker said—today and tomorrow."

We ate our bread as we walked across town, searching for the address the baker had given Louisa. Many of the storefronts we passed had the flavor of the Old West—flat-topped brick constructions two stories tall, board-sided mercantiles with their painted signs fading away to a whisper. Despite the sense of having wandered decades into the past, I kept my wits about me and my eyes sharp. Billings was a big enough town that I was more likely to find another treacherous newsstand displaying my picture than not.

Before long, we found the address in question—a big, Victorian home, painted forget-me-not blue, across the street from a brick church with a steepled bell tower, and a little park that still managed to look inviting despite the summer dryness. A crowd of some eight or ten women had gathered in the front yard, and a white-haired matron was addressing the group from the porch of the blue house. Louisa and I slipped in among the others.

"I've just spoken with Dr. Thomson," the white-haired lady said, "and he assures me my son and his wife, and all six children, have turned the corner and will recover their full health. Praise God for His mercy. But the washing has piled up so badly, my daughter and I simply can't keep up. We've borrowed some good kettles and are heating them now in the backyard. Anyone who's willing to spend the day washing, I'll pay a full dollar each. And there'll be baked beans and corn bread for lunch and supper—all you can eat."

Such an opportunity wasn't to be missed. Louisa and I were among the first to step forward, and soon we were installed in the yard behind the stately blue home, stirring borax into steaming kettles and stoking the fires.

The poor family inside the house must have had a devil of a time. I'd never seen so many sheets and towels and nightshirts as were heaped on the back porch, all of them stained with every conceivable foulness. The girls who'd agreed to take on the work hoed in with a grim energy, a determination to get through the worst of it as quickly as possible so we could move on to the clean rinse water and the drying. We all tied strips of cloth around our faces to protect ourselves from infection, and away we set with a collective will, dunking and pounding and scrubbing the sick-stained linens.

Louisa hovered near me all through the morning, watching me with a sharp eye. The work was every bit as hot as raspberry picking had been, and I could tell she was afraid I might take sick from the strain, maybe bust my other ankle and doom the final lap of our journey altogether. But aside from the occasional twinge in my foot, I felt as sturdy as ever. Better yet, the cloth mask left only my eyes exposed, which went a long way toward restoring my confidence.

I even began to take a little fun in the work. The whole gang was pleasant and friendly, each woman sharing gossip and jokes and recounting the stories of the talkies they'd seen at the new cinema downtown.

At midday we had our promised feeding up. My hands and forearms were red raw from hot water and harsh soap, but my stomach was fuller than it had been for weeks, so I returned to work eager and energetic. My spirits picked up still more when the white-haired old gal—the grandmother of the family—pushed open the screen door and came out, ample rump first, dragging a wheeled bar cart bearing a tabletop radio, its rounded corners gleaming in polished mahogany.

"You girls have been working so hard," the grandmother said, "I thought you'd like a little entertainment."

One of the workers called up to her: "The station out of Missoula reruns *Easy Aces* this time of day. How good is your tuner?"

The tuner worked passably well. Through the crackle and hiss of radio static, we listened in on the comic banter of the bridge-playing couple, and the laughter did make the task of wringing and hanging all those linens a little less onerous.

I enjoyed myself tremendously till the announcer cut in with the top-of-the-hour news. "The nation is still gripped by one question: Where is the runaway preacher's wife?"

I guess I don't need to tell you that the blood froze in my veins. Louisa looked at me, eyes wide above her cloth mask. All I could do was stare back at her in helpless astonishment. The newspaper articles were bad enough. Never had I imagined the story had spread so far or gained such attention. Whether it was the ample bounty tacked above my head or the involvement—however peripheral—of a senator, I couldn't have said. Maybe it was only because there was precious little to capture the imagination in those gray times, and folks hungered for any distraction from their troubles. One way or another, while I'd languished on that riverbank, my infamy had grown to legendary proportions.

"Oh, turn it up, will you," one of the girls asked. "I want to hear about this."

"Yes," another said. "I've been reading the articles in the paper. They say there's a big reward if she's found!"

The heat of the kettles pounded against my cheeks. I turned the crank of the laundry mangle with fresh vigor, hoping the sound of it would drown out the radio, but no such luck. All I got for my efforts was a greater quantity of water splashed across my trouser legs.

The announcer's voice seemed to fill the yard—the whole town— with his brisk, accusatory words. "Despite the generous reward of two thousand dollars, offered by Mr. Irving Wensley of Harlan County, Kentucky, the whereabouts of Adella Wensley remain unknown."

Two thousand! I sucked in a great gasp of shock and immediately inhaled a mouthful of spit. A coughing spell overtook me, and desperate tears sprang to my eyes. Louisa had been working the other end of the mangle, gathering up the wrung-out sheet as it fed through the rollers. She paused with the damp sheet wadded in her arms, watching me choke and sputter. With that cloth tied around her face, I couldn't read her expression. Was she worried for me, or . . . speculating?

The announcer was still rattling off his story. "Mr. Wensley and Senator Logan have been working together to find Mrs. Adella Wensley. The minister's wife is not believed to be the victim of a kidnapping, despite recent rumors to the contrary. Mr. Wensley reports that although he has received several leads on his wife's possible location, she remains at large. However, she is believed to be somewhere west of Omaha, Nebraska, and is almost certainly traveling by rail. Adella Wensley's whereabouts may still be a mystery, but one thing is certain: with two thousand dollars and a senator's reputation on the line, whoever finds the runaway wife and returns her safely to her husband will be a happy fellow indeed."

The girls burst into chatter over the story—*my* story.

"Can you believe it? That preacher's wife is still on the lam! It's been weeks now—months!"

"Good for her. I'll just bet she had her reasons for going."

"They say she's been riding the rails, took up as a hobo."

"That's ridiculous. Ladies don't ride freight trains."

"Maybe she's not a lady. Not anymore."

Surrounded by those chattering, keen-eyed girls, I didn't dare raise my face from my work, dead certain the stricken horror in my eyes would give me away. All I could do was keep my head down and work on till sunset came and we were paid our wage. Once I had that dollar in my pocket, nothing else would matter. We'd be on the next train out of Billings, and God willing, I'd manage to keep one jump ahead of Irving's scheme.

When evening fell, we collected our pay and set off across town, headed for a certain alley near the railyard where we'd decided to spend the night. Louisa and I had already stowed my rucksack at the back of the alley, under a pile of old pallet wood, for the pack would have been too great a burden to bear as I'd limped about looking for work. After a day of laundering, my hands felt as if they'd been sliced by razors. The skin had split along all my knuckles and in the tender places between my fingers. Bad as my hands were, the discomfort couldn't compare to the anxiety that gnawed at my stomach.

I kept hearing that radio announcer's voice repeating inside my head. The nation was gripped by the question of my whereabouts. Irving's stunt had bled from the papers into radioland. What hope did I have of remaining a free woman? The breeze tumbling through the city struck me on the back of the neck. It didn't cool me down. It felt like the hot breath of all those who pursued me.

"Well," Louisa said when we'd separated from the rest of the work gang and found ourselves alone on a peaceful stretch of sidewalk. "Seems that man of yours is more determined than ever to have you back."

"Two thousand," I answered faintly. "That's a lot of money, Louisa."

"I know it is."

No reading her mood, her thoughts. She spoke so neutrally she might as well have said the grass is green and the sky is blue.

We crossed a road that seemed far too wide; I was itching with the urge to get back to our alley and hole up out of sight. I didn't want to think about the money, the radio, or the papers. All that mattered to me was the road ahead. We weren't far from Wenatchee now. Two more days on the rails, maybe three, and we'd be there. And once Louisa'd been paid for the harvest, I'd no longer have to wonder whether she might turn me in—whether I might mean nothing more to her, in the end, than an easy source of cash.

"Damn it," she said suddenly, "I left my bindle back at that house. How could I be such a dummy?"

Startled, I glanced at her and saw that it was true. Her hands were empty.

"I've got to go back and get it," she said. "I won't be long. You keep going—head for that alley, like we agreed."

"Wait—I'll come with you."

"There's no need. I'm faster on my own. In fact, I bet I'll catch up to you before you've made it back to the alley." She turned on her heel. "Back in two shakes of a lamb's tail."

Then she hurried back across the road, not glancing at me once. "Damn it," I muttered.

Nothing about this development sat easy with me. Louisa wasn't the forgetful type, even when she was worn out. She was the last hobo I would expect to leave a bindle lying around.

But the sooner I made it to the seclusion of the alley, the sooner I could rest away from the threat of prying eyes. I headed for the heart of town, hobbling double-time along the sidewalk, pursued by a prickle of dread up my spine.

I hadn't gone more than a block when all my instincts snapped to sudden alertness, every hair standing on end. In those first frantic heartbeats of alarm, I didn't know what had roused me. I had a vague awareness of something large to my left, something that shouldn't be there, or shouldn't be so close to the sidewalk.

Then my mind caught up to my reeling senses with a flash of rapid awareness: a yellow motorcar slowing immediately to my left, the door flying open.

"Louisa!" I cried, just as a hard hand darted out, quicker than I could bolt away. That hand clamped around my wrist, jerking me toward the car with such force that my vision departed in a flare of white. I collided with something rough and rigid. The breath left my body.

"We got her," a man barked. "Drive, Billy, drive!"

I blinked, kicked, clawed at the unknown confines around me as an engine roared and the momentum of acceleration knocked me sideways. I could see again. I was in the dark footwell of a car—the floor of the back seat—with a man's legs before me.

I clawed at his knees, scrambling to pull myself up to the seat, desperate to reach the windows, to yell for help if I could.

"Easy, missus," the man said. "We ain't gonna hurt you. We just want the money, so come along peaceful and everything will be all right."

Crouched on the seat, clutched in a tight fist of horror, I pressed my hands against the rear window as if I could push the glass out and break free, as if I could spring from that car and run back to Louisa—who was nowhere to be seen, vanished into the sleepy blur of the town.

25

The car took a sharp left turn, throwing me against the door. Briefly, I considered pulling the handle and throwing myself from the vehicle, but I'd been a hobo long enough to know the dangers of jumping from a speeding vehicle. The driver was going much too fast; I couldn't risk it.

"Where are you taking me?" I demanded.

"Now, now," the driver said, "there's no cause for alarm."

"No cause for alarm!" I hollered. "You scoop a woman right off the street and then you try to tell her there's no cause for alarm!"

The man who sat with me in the back seat held his hands up in a gesture meant to calm me, as if I were the dangerous animal that had cornered him. If I'd had the claws of a wild beast, I would have taught him a thing or two, and he wouldn't have forgotten the lesson in a hurry.

He said, "You'll be kept properly, and safe, in a good house with a good bed. Got plenty of food. Bet you haven't had enough to eat in a while, right? Riding the rails all this time."

"Hold on," the driver said, "turning again."

Soon the man had pulled off the road, close beside another house— finely built and two stories tall, like the house I'd worked at that day.

The driver cut the engine. I saw my chance and took it, wrenching the handle of the door, but the driver had parked his car so close to the house that the door only thudded into the clapboard, leaving a gap of a hand's breadth for me to try and wiggle through. I cussed.

"All right," the one in the back said. "Take it easy, now."

I eyed him carefully. He was somewhere in his midthirties, his face sun-browned and heavily lined. His hair and mustache were of a bronzy color, almost blond, and his eyes were quick and darting. He seemed to note my every move, the slightest flick of my finger, the jump of the pulse in my neck.

He said, "Just come along nice and easy. We ain't gonna hurt you. You'll see we're proper, nice fellows if you give us a chance, Mrs. Wensley."

"I don't know who that is," I said.

The driver laughed. There was a rattle in it; I guessed him to be a smoker. Or a miner. "Bullshit, you don't know who that is."

The man in the back said, "Watch your language, Billy. She's a lady, after all."

"Like hell, she is," Billy countered. "Riding the rails, and dressed that way? Covered in dirt? A lady, my ass. Enough messing around. Get her upstairs where we can keep an eye on her. Then you're going into town, Dan, to send that telegram. The sooner we've got her out of our hair and the money in our pockets, the better."

Dan opened his door and slid out slowly, never taking his eyes off me. I remained in the back seat, eyeing both men. Before they reached for me, they glanced around the street to see who might be watching.

"I'll scream," I said. "I'll scream so loud I bring the whole city here to witness. You've kidnapped me—that's the plain truth. It's a crime, and you'll pay the price like any criminal."

They shared a look. Dan seemed to accuse Billy with his eyes, with the set of his mouth, till Billy muttered, "Fuck it," and reached into his pocket.

He drew a derringer, pointing it straight at me. I could do nothing but stare at the gun; I couldn't even breathe. Small though the derringer was, the black hole of its muzzle seemed to yawn wide enough to swallow the world.

"Get out," Billy said, "and don't make a peep unless you want me to splatter your brains all over the side of this house. You understand?"

I nodded. What else could I do?

The men stepped back, and somehow I convinced my limbs to stop shaking long enough that I could slide along the car seat and extract myself. I stood shivering between them, my eyes blurring with tears.

"Inside," Billy said. "Move it."

With Dan leading the way and Billy's gun behind, I was marched around the corner of the house, up the porch steps to the front door. We moved so quickly that I hadn't much time to guess my whereabouts—not that I could have identified much, being a newcomer to this city. I noted that we were in a neighborhood, however, not some business district or warehouse row. The street was lined with impressive homes, as prosperous a neighborhood as Billings could boast.

The men bundled me into the house before I could observe much more of my whereabouts. They even hustled me through the parlor and dining room, so I had little opportunity to register the details of the home, no chance to gather any information I might have used against my captors. It was a perfectly ordinary house, about as well-appointed as the one I'd shared with Irving.

The men led me up a staircase to a short hall. There was only a single door in that hallway—closed. Dan fished in his pocket, withdrew a ring of keys. He fussed with them for a moment till he found the right one and unlocked the door. Both men accompanied me into the room—a garret with a low, sloping ceiling. A bed with an iron frame took up most of the space, but there was also a small dresser and a washstand. An oval mirror with a gilded frame hung beside the door. Two narrow windows looked out over Billings, letting in the deep, warm glow of sunset. In one corner, a second door stood open, revealing a tiny bathroom with a claw-foot tub.

"Sit down," Billy said.

My heart hammered in my throat. Sweat dampened my underarms. Slowly, I sank onto the edge of the bed.

"Here's the way it's gonna be." Billy slid the derringer back into his pocket. "My brother here is gonna drive downtown and send that telegram to your husband. I'll be downstairs keeping an eye on things. If you get up to any funny business, I'll make you wish you hadn't, so keep your head on straight. You get me?"

I nodded. The tears coursed down my cheeks, but I didn't dare lift a hand to wipe them away. It seemed the slightest move might provoke Billy to violence.

"I'll give you an hour to get cleaned up," Billy said. "Then I'll bring you up something to eat. But you'll keep your mouth shut and do as I say till we've got the money and your husband has come to collect you, won't you, Mrs. Wensley?"

Briefly, I considered denying my identity one last time. But the jig was already up. I nodded again.

"Good girl," Billy said. He and Dan both backed away.

"I'm sorry," Dan said to me as his brother slammed the door shut.

I was on my feet in an instant, but I had no real hope of escape. The key clicked in the lock, just as I'd known it would.

The brothers' footsteps descended the staircase. I was left alone in a dense, accusatory silence. I did my best to breathe slowly so I wouldn't go dizzy in the head. No matter how hard I pressed the heels of my hands against my eyes, I couldn't hold back the tears.

Louisa was the only thing I could think of. The kiss that morning, beside the river. Now I understood its meaning. It was the kiss of Judas. Surely Louisa had played some part in this turning of my fate. Maybe she'd finally decided to take the money—conspired with these brothers to deceive and imprison me. Who could say what she'd gotten up to, who she'd met, who had poisoned her against me all those hours she spent without me in Billings while my ankle healed up? How had the men recognized me, after all? They sure hadn't been in the wash gang. Maybe Louisa's going back for her bindle had been some kind of signal, a device the three conspirators had cooked up among them.

There was no need to do it this way! My heart cried out as if Louisa might hear. *I would have gone back to Irving willingly, for you.*

The more my tormented thoughts chased themselves around and around my head, the likelier it seemed that Louisa was involved somehow. But even in the depths of that misery, it mattered less that Louisa had betrayed me than that we should be separated now. In the darkness of my thoughts, her face, her presence at my side, eclipsed everything else. In a great rush of panic and pain, I felt that if I must be parted from Louisa, then nothing was real, nothing mattered. The last color and sweetness had drained at last from the slow-dying world.

I staggered to one of the windows in my garret prison, my chest aching with a futile wish to see Louisa below, to lay eyes on my friend one last time. The street was empty, of course, save for a few neighbors going about their mundane business and a blue car making its way lazily across town. I did find the redbrick steeple of the church, however, and as I stared at it in dumb recognition, its bell began to toll the hour. This house wasn't far, then, from the one where I'd worked throughout the day.

Maybe Louisa isn't to blame, I told myself, fanning the feeble spark of hope. *Maybe she had nothing to do with it. These men spotted me as we walked to the blue house for work this morning. Louisa will find me once she realizes I've gone missing. She hasn't sold me out—not like this.*

I thought of Billy with his damned gun, his hot temper, his dagger eyes. A new fear seized me—one far worse than my dread at being shuttled back into Irving's hands.

Safer for Louisa if she doesn't come looking. And then—*Oh, God, what if she does come for me? What if that bastard pulls his gun and*—

I couldn't go further, even in thought; the possibility was too horrible. Being separated from my friend was a sad enough fate. The

273

emptiness of a world entirely devoid of Louisa was too immense to comprehend.

If I could only know that she'd played some part in my abduction—that she would get a fair cut of the two thousand dollars—I could just about accept my fate, and swallow down the bitterness of life as Irving's meek, simpering wife. If only I could be assured that Louisa had gained from my loss.

Half-heartedly, I pried at the window, but the sash had been painted shut long ago and I couldn't make it budge without some sort of tool. My bone-handled knife did no good; I could only run it around the inner frame of the window, not the outer. I tried the other window, only to be met with the same problem. The roof was far too steep, anyway; even if I could get out, I'd more likely fall two stories to the hard earth than climb to safety.

My goose was cooked, and I knew it. There was nothing to do but surrender to this cruel twist of fate and wait for my damned husband to appear.

Since there was nothing else to be done, I availed myself of the bathroom. I hadn't soaked in hot water since that dip in Arkansas, but I took no pleasure in washing myself in the claw-foot tub. Submerged to my chin, the water going cloudy with my grime, I stared at the flowered wallpaper and allowed my dark thoughts to wander where they would.

Soon I would be back in Irving's clutches, forced to play the role of the forbearing wife who blinded herself to her husband's infidelity. And that was to say nothing of Irving's hypocrisy, his preaching about wickedness while he wallowed in the blackest sins. Irving had nothing to give—nothing of real substance. He only knew how to take and take, even from those whose hands were empty.

And I would be made to pretend—maybe even confess before the whole church—that these months on the rails had been a mistake, the impulsive devilry of a sinful heart. How could I do it, how could I betray Louisa's memory by claiming this had all been some iniquitous folly?

By the time I washed my hair and rinsed it as best I could in the dirty water, I'd made up my mind that some good must come of this forcible separation. One way or another, I must convince Irving to give the money not to Dan and Billy—who, after all, had committed the crime of kidnapping—but to Louisa alone. She, after all, had kept me safe and whole. If it took every spark of my intelligence, every ounce of my charm, I'd see to it that Louisa was the sole beneficiary of this tragic turning of fate's wheel. Just *how* I'd convince my husband to reward my traveling companion instead of the two toads who'd nabbed me was a problem for another day. Anyway, I figured I'd have plenty of time to work it all out while I waited in the garret.

Thus satisfied—or as close to satisfied as I could get, given my circumstances—I pulled the stopper from the tub and watched the water drain away. Then I climbed out, feeling somehow dirtier than when I'd climbed in, and dried myself with an old, pink towel, resigned to my fate yet resolved to make the best of it.

I was halfway dressed when I heard an engine sputter and cut outside the house. Quickly, I pulled on my sweat-stiffened shirt and crossed the attic room to peek out the window. The yellow Pontiac had returned. Dan was better at parking cars than his brother. He'd left the Pontiac on the street this time, rather than butting it up against the house, as Billy had done. He got out of the driver's seat and closed the door with more vigor than was necessary. His obvious frustration piqued my interest. Had something gone wrong with the telegram?

In moments, the front door opened downstairs. I pressed my ear against the keyhole of my own door, holding my breath, straining to catch whatever I could of the brothers' conversation.

". . . office is closed for the night." That was Dan.

Billy gave some answer, but I couldn't make out his words.

"Shit, Billy, it ain't my fault! We'll have to send the telegram tomorrow."

"First thing." Even with the whole house between us, I could feel the rage in Billy's voice. That man frightened me. "At crack of dawn, you get that telegram sent, you hear me?"

So Irving hadn't been notified—not yet. My mind tumbled with new possibilities. If I could convince my captors to let me out of the room, I might break free of the house altogether. My ankle was still weak, and no good for running, but if I stuck carefully to the deepest shadows of night, I could work my way slowly to the railyard, catch a freighter before the brothers could lay hold of me . . .

Footsteps on the stairs. I jumped back from the door, dropping onto the edge of the bed, and I folded my hands meekly in my lap, praying I looked like the picture of complacency. The key clicked in the lock; the door squealed on its hinges to reveal Billy with a wooden tray balanced on one hand. The other hand was busy stuffing the key ring back into his pocket. The tray bore a plate with a ham sandwich and a heap of potato salad, along with a green soda bottle.

Billy narrowed his eyes at me, kicked the door shut behind him, and set the tray on the nightstand beside the bed. "Eat up."

"When are you going to let me out of here? And who tipped you off, anyway? How did you know it was me?"

"None of your damned lip. We'll keep you safe till we've got our money, and then you can go wherever your husband says you can go. You'll be none of my concern then. But till we get paid, you'd be smart to keep your mouth shut and stay on your best behavior. It won't be no trouble to do away with you and tell your husband you ran off. You get me?"

I swallowed hard. "Yes, sir, I get you, all right."

He took the key ring from his pocket again. A small, metal bottle opener hung among the keys. Billy pried the cap from the 7UP bottle.

"Drink up, too. Drink it all. I'll be back in half an hour to get the tray."

Billy vacated the room and promptly locked the door. As soon as he left, I took the bottle to the bathroom and dumped its contents down the sink. Everyone knew 7UP was lithiated—a sedative, however mild—and I had no intention of letting my wits be slowed. I was thirsty, however. I filled the bottle with water from the tap and drank till my head cleared a little and my heart beat steadily once more.

The sandwich was ham and cheese, the potato salad surprisingly tasty, though Billy had neglected to provide a fork. That didn't bother me any. I'd been hoboing long enough to feel no shame about eating with my fingers, and when I finished my supper, I returned to the window that faced the old church steeple, licking my fingers clean, watching night descend over Billings.

The warm tones of sunset had all but faded from the western sky, obscuring the high ramparts of the Rockies, flattening the foothills so they seemed to draw in closer, like the walls of a butchering chute. The stars emerged rapidly, and the moon, a pale sliver, cast its feeble light along the rooftops and the church spire. Muffled sounds came to me through the glass—a man calling to a dog or a child, a woman's laughter, the coughing of a motorcar on an unseen street. I could just make out a few notes of piano music drifting from somewhere farther up the block, and the music pulled at my overburdened heart with a melancholic grace.

From somewhere closer, below my window, I heard the light clink of glass bottles. Billy or Dan must be setting their empties out on the back porch, I figured. How those two men could go on about their daily lives was beyond me—as if they hadn't just kidnapped a woman off the street! Viciously, but not without reason, I prayed they would reap what they'd sown, especially Billy, who was far too quick with a threat for my liking.

A shadow darted below, down at the edge of the street near Billy's Pontiac. I leaned closer to the glass, squinting into the darkness, trying to discern what had moved there—some critter, or a person? Gradually my eyes adjusted, and I made out a small, slender figure in a white shirt, crouched a little way up the street and busy with some object on the ground.

The hunched figure moved its hands energetically. Mystified, I watched orange sparks flare and vanish, flare and vanish. The sparks appeared a third time, and a blossom of fire opened suddenly in the darkness. Only then did I realize what I was seeing—who I was seeing.

Louisa scooped that fire up in her hands. For one wild moment I didn't understand how she did it, and I almost cried out in alarm. Then, as she whipped back her arm to throw, I saw the soda bottle in her hand, the burning rag stuffed in its neck.

I could do nothing but stand there, gaping like a catfish, as Louisa hurled the burning bottle directly into the Pontiac's grill. The fireball burst so brightly, I had to throw up an arm to shield my eyes. When I looked again, vigorous flames engulfed the hood of Billy's car. Louisa was nowhere to be seen.

Well, you can imagine the caterwauling that followed! Billy and Dan ran to the street quick as scorched cats, and the neighbors came running, too, all of them shouting and scampering and hollering for someone to phone for the fire volunteers. I gawked at the scene, swimming in a thick, dreamlike haze, while the men formed a bucket brigade, transporting water in pails from God knew where to dump it on the burning Pontiac. Their efforts seemed to make little headway, and soon some of the men began shepherding women and children farther back from the spectacle, clearly afraid the whole engine might blow.

Fear finally worked its way past my dull surprise. What if the house should catch fire? I was stuck up in that garret. Neither Billy nor Dan seemed much inclined to remember me as they ran circles around their car, cussing and wringing their hands.

Again, I heard the hollow thump of feet pounding up the stairs—quickly this time. Someone was running to my room. I spun away from the window to face the door. Dan must have come, I thought, to pull me out before the situation grew even more dire. But there was no efficient click of a key in the lock. Instead, something scraped and prodded and jiggled on the other side of the garret door, and I heard her voice muttering, "Come on, damn you, give!"

"Louisa!"

She growled out the dirtiest cuss of all. The latch gave way with a metallic ping, and the door swung open to reveal my friend. The thick piece of wire she'd used to pick the lock lay between her feet where she'd dropped it.

"Come on," she said.

I didn't hesitate. We thundered down the stairs together.

Louisa caught my arm at the foot of the staircase, for I'd turned toward the front door.

"Not that way," she said. "Everyone's out front trying to put out the fire. The kitchen—follow me."

We flew through the kitchen door to the back porch, then down the steps to the flat, dark yard. The stink of burning kerosene slapped me in the face. Louisa led the way to a picket fence where some of the paling hung askew. She squeezed through and I followed, splintered wood grazing my face and arms. We crossed two more yards, my ankle burning and wobbling as I struggled to keep up with Louisa. But no one shouted in alarm. No one saw us at all; the whole neighborhood was occupied with the fire.

When we emerged back onto the street, we found ourselves in a quieter part of town. Glancing over my shoulder, I could see the glow of the fire where it limned the rooftops, and picked out the slope of the church steeple. Otherwise, the night was still, and we carried on across Billings at an unhurried pace till we both caught our breath and even the light of the fire had dimmed to nothing.

26

We couldn't remain in that town, not even till morning. We visited our chosen alley only long enough to retrieve my rucksack from behind the heap of pallet wood. Then we concealed ourselves in the shadows at the edge of the railyard, hoping for an opportunity to break across the ground and slink inside a boxcar. But half a dozen bulls patrolled the tracks—maybe looking for the arsonist, for all I could tell—and at last Louisa shook her head, tugging at my sleeve. We slipped away from the yard, heading for the water tower a mile or so outside of town.

When Billings was far enough behind that I no longer feared to speak, I tried to work up the nerve, but a great ball of guilt had settled in my throat. I couldn't swallow it down or cough it away; it choked off the words I knew Louisa deserved to hear from me. She'd just risked life and limb to set me free. If I confessed that I'd suspected her of playing some part in my kidnapping, I could never look her in the eye again.

"You came back for me," I finally managed. Inadequate, weak—a poor substitute for all the things I wanted to say.

"Of course. You did the same for me." She lifted the locket from her collar, let it hang against her shirt where I could see. "Remember?"

"When I was up there in that room—locked up in that house—I made up my mind that I'd go back to my husband, but I'd get the money out of him myself rather than let those two shits of brothers claim it."

She laughed softly. "You really think your husband would have allowed you to keep all that money?"

"I never meant to keep it for myself. You should take it. I've told you before. I'll do it—and gladly, Louisa. I'll go back to Irving if I can get the money for you. You deserve it, if anyone does. It's yours."

Through the blue of night and the flattening shadows, she cut me a sharp look. "You left that man for good reason, Del."

"You could get off the rails for good, start building that life you want—"

"I won't hear of it." She sounded angry now. "Not one more word. I've told you already; there's money enough in Wenatchee, and I mean to earn it the respectable way. I could never sell you out, Del. You mean too much to me."

Such a wave of feeling rose in me that I could scarcely breathe—a longing and a triumph, a great, hot knife's blade shivering in my heart. It was the sweetest pain I'd ever known.

"But I suspected you," I said. "I thought you were working with those brothers—"

She laughed. "What, me?"

"It wasn't right of me. I should have known better, after you stayed with me all that time at the river, waiting for my ankle to heal. It was downright rotten of me to think you'd done it."

"I hope I've convinced you now," she said. "That stunt with the fire—I've gone and busted the hobos' code worse than anyone ever did."

A fresh peal of remorse rang in my head. My stomach went sick. I hadn't considered the code till now.

"We've gone and messed Billings up for good," I said, "between the two of us."

"I'm just thankful that poor family got out when they did—the Werthers. The whole city will turn on hobos something terrible. I might regret it, someday"—she slipped her hand into the crook of my elbow—"but I think that day's a long while off. Right now, all I care about is that you're free, Del."

"We won't be welcome in many jungles when word gets around."

She gave another laugh—a harsh one. "You said it. The story will be clear to the Mississippi in a few more days. What does it matter, though? We're almost to Wenatchee. We'll stick together, for our own sakes. We're all we've got now, you and me. Maybe we're all we need."

The water tower rose from the darkness, a great cylindrical hulk supported on four spindly legs. I could just make out the long pipe of its spigot, raised to the sky, almost touching the stars.

We climbed the ladder that ran up one of the tower's supports, then set ourselves at the edge of its narrow platform, far above the tracks, awaiting the next train. I let my legs swing easily in the new coolness, feeling the promise of autumn in the air.

Louisa told me then how she'd come to rescue me. "Almost as soon as I left to get my bindle," she said, "I was hit by a terrible, dark feeling, like something bad was about to happen. I turned right around and started back the way I'd come—back to you, Del—but the feeling got worse with every step I took. I was as close to panic as I've ever been. And just as I rounded the corner and had you in my sights, that yellow car went flying past. I saw it all—the way it slowed down as it came up beside you. I knew you were as good as caught then. I couldn't do anything about it, not even yell to warn you, it all happened so fast."

"It surely did," I said.

"Well," she went on, "I realized pretty quickly that I wouldn't catch the car by running. I made up my mind right then and there to remember everything about the way that car looked. I started to head back into town, asking myself whether I should alert the cops that there'd been a kidnapping or whether that'd make the whole situation worse. The cops, you know, might have decided to claim the reward money for themselves. But before I reached Main Street, I saw the same yellow car headed up from that direction. I was dead sure it was the same. How many yellow Pontiacs could there be in that bum town?"

"One of those rats tried to send a telegram," I said. "The office was closed; he had to come back home again almost as soon as he'd left."

"I made note of where the car turned, and then I hunted up and down that whole street till well after dark. Finally I found the car parked outside that house, and when I chanced to look up to the highest window, there you were licking your fingers like you'd just had a real feast."

I chuckled. "Only a ham sandwich and potatoes. The jerks tried to get some 7UP into me—drug me up a little. Did you ever hear of such a thing?"

"Right then—when I saw you in the window—I knew what I had to do. I figured you'd been locked in that house somehow, or you would have made a run for it. So I rummaged around the back porch till I found something to pick a lock with, and there was a little can of kerosene out back of the kitchen door, and pop bottles all over the place. I guess you saw the rest of it."

"Guess I did. You made some spectacle."

"Billings will never forget," Louisa said.

"Neither will I."

The whistle of an approaching train silenced us. To the east, the engine's lone eye blazed white against the darkness. We drew in our legs and scuttled around the curve of the water tower while the engine approached and slowed, pretty near deafening us with the hiss of its steam. I pressed close beside Louisa, every nerve of my body alight while the crew shouted to one another and the tower's mechanism clanked and shivered. The pipe lowered to gush a supply of water into the engine's holding tank.

When the operation was finished and the engine began whining back into gear, Louisa took my hand to lead me around the belly of the tower. The engine crawled away, cars passing slowly just a few feet below us. She tugged me to the place where the platform and its railing gave way to the great bent neck of the water pipe. There was just enough of a gap there that we could jump down, one at a time.

Louisa considered the cars rolling toward us, their increasing speed. She pointed to one—an open-topped gondola filled to its brim with hundred-pound sacks of flour.

"I'll go first," she said.

She dropped into the gap just as the flour car reached us. I followed quickly, trying to land on my side rather than my legs. I didn't know whether my weak ankle could withstand such a drop. I hit the compacted sacks with more force than I was prepared for; the impact shocked the breath from me, but I recovered quickly and crawled across the flat sacks to where Louisa had landed.

She was all right—I saw that much when I reached her, for she was grinning and making herself comfortable, lying back to gaze up at the stars.

"God Almighty," she said, "just look at that, would you, Del?"

I pulled myself free of the rucksack and settled beside her. A black density of stone rose up to one side—the flank of the Rockies—and over that bastion a cascade of light spilled like a waterfall. It was the Milky Way, the stars in all their bright infinity. It was a road I swore I could follow from my heart to the fullness of Heaven.

Louisa laughed again, that musical note that said there was beauty to be found everywhere, and she was as unsurprised as ever to have found it.

I turned my head on the flour sack, watching her—only her, the starlight picking out her face in profile so she was the only sharp and true thing in all the fast-moving world.

There was still something inside of me—words, inadequate words. I could never speak; mere words would never be enough. This thing we held between us, this delicate friendship—it might break if I said anything. Everything might shatter, then, and leave me empty. It was enough for me to hold what I could hold, and cherish it in silence.

The rest, I could leave unspoken. And anyway, how could I speak the unspeakable? Like the name of God, it was a truth too perfect for my tongue to shape, too enigmatic for my heart to understand.

We rode on all through the night, watching the stars, saying nothing. We were all we had now, Louisa and me. And that was enough to content me.

27

For a night and half a day, the train followed the sweeping curves of the Yellowstone River into stone shadow and out again, through pass after pass of narrow granite where the air was thin and cold, and our ears protested the elevation and subsequent plunge into deep valleys of solemn black pine. At midday we left the cool, blue steeps of the Rockies behind us. The train rolled out across the breast of a golden plain. The treeless expanse was more desert than farmland. Here and there, jagged stone broke through the pale monotony of sage like dark slashes in a tanned hide. Far beyond the plain, against the glare of the northern sky, the earth folded into smooth, even hills that overlapped one another like the waves of a peaceful sea. I sat atop the flour sacks, arms folded on the edge of the gondola, watching sunlight chase shadows along the crests and flanks of countless hills, while far to the west another mountain range beckoned. We had reached Washington at last. It was the first or second of September, maybe a little later. The long road Louisa and I traveled together had all but reached its end.

She was as melancholy, as quiet as I. Sometimes I tore my gaze from the rolling light to look at her, bundled around herself, hugging her knees while she watched the mobile, indifferent land. Sometimes I would find her with one hand clutching the gold locket, and I knew she was grateful to find this season drawing to its long-awaited end.

Don't think I wasn't glad for her. Nothing in the world could please me more than Louisa's happiness. But the millstone of Irving's reward money still hung around my neck. What hope did I have of remaining close to Louisa once the apple harvest was finished?

Hour by hour, the western range grew a little taller, its abrupt brown wall of foothills rising and fattening over the plain. The air smelled of juniper, of heat, and the sky took on a water-like transparency, the sunlight high and glaring, so white I had to hide my face between my knees. Comforted by the darkness, I convinced myself for a while that I could ignore the swift passage of time. We wouldn't say goodbye after all; the lazy summer would go on forever and so would we, in our quiet campsites with only the crackle of firewood and the coo of the brown doves, and Louisa's laugh, or her voice when she sang, as she sometimes did, out of nowhere, purely because her heart longed for music.

But soon an undeniable sweetness filled the air, pushing back the smell of the sage flats and the black-stone wilderness. It was the scent of ripe orchards, and no mistake.

"Look, Del!" Louisa cried. "There it is—Wenatchee!"

Reluctantly, I raised my head, blinking into the glare. We'd come to another river, wide and fiercely blue. On its opposite bank, the dry ridges of the foothills reached for us with greedy arms, their slopes greened by a carpet of heat-stunted trees. Once we'd crossed the river on a long iron bridge, the geometry of the orchards' rows flashed and expanded in dizzy patterns around me, then collapsed again as the train moved past. Near the track, I could see apples clinging to boughs like gems—red and topaz yellow, the soft greens of jasper and jade. The sight should have filled me with hope and energy—so many acres of fruit to pick, money growing from the trees. But the only smile I managed was a false one, manufactured for Louisa's benefit.

"Look at all that fruit," she said. "By God, it's been a long journey—and a hard one. But we're here. We made it."

"We made it," I said.

"Just in time, I guess," she added with a laugh. "There's no way I'll be welcomed in a jungle again, once the story gets out—the car, I mean."

"You'll be a legend."

"Not the good kind. Well—what does it matter now? Soon this will all be behind me."

I almost asked, *All of it? Do you want to forget it all, or is anything worth remembering?* But I was afraid of how she might answer, so I held my tongue. The engine cried. The boxcars jarred against one another as the train began to slow. I hid my face in my arms again, and made a determined peace with the not knowing.

Our train came to rest in a yard between two great walls of fruit-shipping crates, stacked higher than the boxcars. The crates stood empty, awaiting their cargo. Nevertheless, a sticky-sweet odor of fermenting fruit hung over the yard, and flies buzzed in maddening circles around the crates and the trucks parked nearby.

There were no bulls to harass us as we descended from the gondola. In fact, the whole yard was strangely quiet. I'd seen the town of Wenatchee on our approach across the river, spread like a faded blanket between the water and the sheer face of the hills. It wasn't the biggest city I'd laid eyes on, but it sure wasn't small. The stillness of the railyard in such a sizable town struck a spark of caution inside me. Where was the bustle, the industry? Where were the linemen and the farmhands ready to load crates onto fruit cars? Come to that, where were the apples? As Louisa and I passed the impossible stacks of crates—hundreds of feet long, twenty feet high—daylight showed through their slats.

Maybe we're early, I told myself. *September is young yet. Maybe the harvest has only just begun.*

Louisa was so eager for work, she all but trotted down the long line of crates, and I was hard-pressed to keep up. She led me to a stretch of hot pavement well beyond the tracks, between the last of the crates and a collection of sturdy warehouses built from pale yellow brick.

There a handful of flatbed trucks stood idle in the sun, narrow-faced and beetle-browed, dulled by the summer dust.

A driver—the only figure to be seen across the whole expanse of the yard—leaned against the green door of his truck. With one boot braced on the running board and his cap pulled low across his eyes, he pulled on a cigarette, paused, and exhaled a cloud of smoke.

Louisa called to him. "Excuse me, sir."

The driver lowered his cigarette a little.

"We've only just arrived," she said, closing the last few feet of blacktop. "We've come to work as apple pickers." She stood grinning at the man.

"Oh, have you," was his laconic reply.

"I hoped," Louisa said, "you might know which orchard is best for traveling pickers."

The man shrugged. He flicked the ash from his cigarette. An air of despondency hung over the driver, over the whole yard—or maybe it was only the heat beating down on the pavement.

Louisa glanced in my direction. I caught the flicker of concern in her eyes, but it disappeared a moment later, replaced by her resolute smile.

"If you don't know which farm pays best," she said, "can we convince you to drive us to the biggest orchard in these parts? I'd be willing to bet the most sizable farm serves up the fattest wages."

The driver dropped the end of his cigarette on the pavement and crushed it beneath his bootheel. "I guess it won't hurt you ladies to give it a try."

The muted pulse of my anxiety flared up at those words. "Give what a try?" I cut in, but the driver only gestured to the back of his truck.

"Climb in, girls. I'll take you up to Henderson's place. Got damn near a thousand acres of trees. If anyone's hiring pickers, he is."

Louisa scrambled into the truck bed first, then reached down to take my hand. The rear portion of the green truck was as sticky and fragrant as the crates in the yard, so we remained on our feet as the engine turned over and the truck described a slow circle on the hot, dead pavement. Leaning on the slat rails of the bed, we watched the town of Wenatchee swell to consume us, then dwindle away as the truck turned up a dirt road that cut across acres of young orchard. Spindly saplings rose from the cracked, pale earth, their trunks no wider than two fingers held together. The truck threw up a cloud of dust, obscuring the city and the river in our wake, then climbed a long, shallow slope toward a crest teeming with mature trees. I could just make out a farmhouse deep in the orchard, a quaint white building with a peaked roof. Then a fold in the hillside lifted yet more orchard land into my line of sight, and the farmhouse vanished.

The green truck shuddered to a halt at the head of a long lane, below the crest of the ridge. The roadway meandered among the sweet green shadows of the trees. It looked no different from several other lanes we'd passed.

The driver leaned head and shoulder out his window. "Follow that road to the house," he called. "You can inquire there. Henderson'll be home, for sure—or his wife will."

Louisa jumped down from the truck bed, thanking our driver cheerfully. I descended with less energy. There was still something about the man's gloomy air that unsettled me.

"Good luck," the driver said without much conviction. He turned his truck in the middle of the road and headed back down the slope, trailing his banner of dust.

Louisa led the way up the lane, all bright eyes and bouncing step. As I followed her into the vast orchard, a dreadful awareness wrapped around me. Fallen apples lay on the ground beneath the trees, bright among the green shadows and the dappled light. The still air was thick with a too-sweet odor of rot, and the flies gave off a sustained, muffled moan. The orchard itself was perfectly still. No workers moved among the trees, no ladders leaned in the branches, no crates half-filled with fruit stood waiting in the shade. The place was abandoned.

I didn't want to draw Louisa's attention to that fatal stillness. I told myself I was only imagining the worst, that September was still fresh; we'd arrived before the usual contingent of pickers. All would be well. But as the lane bent around a curve of the hill and the white farmhouse came into view, I risked a glance at Louisa's face and found her stoic and pale. She, too, understood that something was wrong.

We ascended the final slope of the lane, and as we approached the farmhouse, a skinny red dog emerged from the coolness below the porch. The dog barked half-heartedly. The sight of that animal put me in mind of the little red terrier who'd curled beside the dead boy, somewhere back in Nebraska.

A man in denim coveralls stepped out onto the porch, cussing at the dog. The creature gave one last woof, then slunk back into the shade. Only then did the man notice Louisa and me—two forlorn and shabby ghosts wandering the orchard rows.

He puffed on a cigarette, watching us approach. He was clean-shaven with thin white hair, and his sun-browned face looked as wind-carved as the crags of the Rocky Mountains. The old farmer had seen more harvests than Louisa and I had seen years of life, put together. He nodded a cautious hello, but he never came down the steps to greet us.

"You must be Mr. Henderson," Louisa said.

The man nodded again. The cigarette went on burning between the fingers of his lowered hand. I kept my eyes on the curl of its smoke. I couldn't seem to meet old Henderson's gaze.

"We've come an awful long way to work the apple harvest," Louisa said. "We heard your farm is the biggest and the best. You'll find us good workers, too—just as good as any men you might hope to hire."

"I'm sure you probably are good," Henderson conceded. His voice was dry as the land, rasping like the orchard flies. "Wish there was something I could do for you."

For a moment, Louisa said nothing. The dog woofed into the silence.

"You mean," Louisa finally managed, "you aren't hiring pickers?"

"Not this year."

"But there are apples all over the trees," she exclaimed. "I saw them as we came up the lane. I saw apples falling to the ground! There's plenty of fruit. Can't we be of any use to you?"

"I wish you could, miss," Henderson said slowly. "Dearly, I wish it. But the sad truth is, no one in this valley's harvesting—not this year. Doesn't make any sense to do it."

Louisa drew a ragged breath. Then she merely stood there, staring at the farmer, without a word left to say.

"Why?" I asked. "What's the sense in leaving so much fruit unharvested?"

"Costs more to pay the workers than we can sell the crop for. Money's bad everywhere—money's just about useless, in fact, all across the country, so the papers and the radio say. If nobody can afford to buy apples, then why should I pay a mess of pickers to get them off the trees? Either way, I'll come out poorer. And the good Lord knows, things was already tight enough. No, girls—I wish I could say otherwise, but the whole damned year's worth of apples will have to rot back into the soil."

Henderson noted our devastation. His weather-lined face softened a little. "Listen, it's not so bad. I've got plenty of workers' cabins along the east side of the property. If you girls need a place to stay, you're welcome to put up here for a while. Wish I could do more for you—I don't like to turn away women in need—but a roof over your head and a cot to sleep in is something, at least. And you can have all the apples you want. Lord knows, I got nothing else to do with 'em. Take that lane there, and you'll find the cabins in about a quarter mile."

Louisa gave no indication that she'd heard—only stood there, motionless and staring.

"Thanks, mister," I said. "That's awfully generous of you."

Henderson lifted a hand in farewell, then returned to his house.

"Let's go," I said quietly. "There's no point in standing here."

Louisa never heard me, though I stood right beside her.

Timidly, I spoke her name, but she made no answer, and a colder fear wormed down into my gut. Not since the day her locket had been stolen had I seen my friend so despairing.

I put my arm around her shoulders and turned her away from the farmhouse, toward the lane that ran off between a neat symmetry of trees. Louisa moved automatically under my guidance. It was like handling a doll. I steered her to the lane, propelled her along it, through the shimmering haze of flies and the mocking smell of rotten fruit. Other than the droning of the insects, the only sound was an occasional hollow thud as another apple broke from its branch and struck the earth.

When we came within sight of a row of small, whitewashed cabins, Louisa froze at my side.

"Let's go," I told her gently. "We might as well get out of the heat."

She gave no sign that she'd heard.

"Louisa," I said, "please. Don't fall to pieces. Not you."

But my pleading came too late. I knew it when I took her by the shoulders, as I'd done so often before. She wouldn't look at me, didn't seem to feel the touch of my hands, and no matter how I held her and shook her and begged her to keep going, she never met my eye. She only stared up at the blank sky with empty, surrendering eyes.

"You have to keep going," I insisted. "For Eddie, Louisa. For him."

To this day, I don't know whether that was the right thing to say or the wrong thing. Those words broke something loose inside of her, something terrible and mighty which she'd worked all this time to contain, all the months of our acquaintance—and before that, too, I suppose. Now, though, with the hope that had sustained her blown away on the wind, Louisa no longer had the strength to keep despair at bay.

Her knees buckled. She fell to the earth, and I cried out and tried to catch her. But I was helpless to hold her up, and useless at holding her together.

She curled into a tight ball right there in the lifeless dust, wailing with a misery so pure and true I felt it as a hollow in my own heart. I couldn't stop her crying. Nor could I silence her. All I could do was stay by her side, weeping with a grief I would have gladly borne alone, if my pain could have spared her the suffering.

28

We lingered two days in one of the workers' cabins. The shack was equipped with a tiny potbellied stove, its top just large enough to hold our cook pot, and four iron-framed cots with mildewed mattresses and rusty springs. Rough as it was, the cabin was the finest accommodation we'd had in our months together on the rails. When I'd first stepped inside, throwing wide its door and opening its windows to clear out the musty smell, I'd hoped a proper rest in relative comfort would restore Louisa's vim. She, however, had sunk so deeply into despair that after two days I feared she might never fight her way back to the surface.

Most hours, she lay still as a corpse on her cot. Only her eyes moved, tracking the band of yellow sunlight that crept across the floor.

Far worse than her silence were the moments when she started up from her bed with an anguished cry—wordless, thin, like the last frantic call of some rare and magnificent bird when the hunter's shot picks it from the sky. Whenever she sprang up crying, I would rush to her side and fold her in my arms, and murmur comforts that did neither of us any good. To drive back her grief or reason it away was as far beyond my strength as to halt the stars in their courses and send them spinning in the opposite direction. I was useless to Louisa—useless to myself. And well did I know that she would have been better off, with a future as stable as anyone's could have been that terrible, long year, if she'd never met me at all.

The only time she spoke was our second night in the cabin. I'd coaxed her into sitting up and was trying to convince her to eat a little of the cornmeal porridge I'd heated on the stove. She held the tin plate of flavorless grits on her lap, staring down at her supper with indifference.

"I can't go on," she said weakly.

"Of course you can, and you will—for Eddie's sake."

Louisa shook her head slowly. "I mean I can't. There's nothing for me on the rails now. Billings . . . that car . . . Every hobo in the West will figure out it was me, sooner or later. I know how it works—how word travels. Someone will put two and two together, and then I'll find no welcome anywhere. No welcome, and after a while, no work."

I swallowed down my guilt, just enough to keep from bursting into remorseful tears. "You've got to take the money," I said. "For the love of Jesus, Louisa, send that telegram to Irving. Two thousand bucks will set you up for a good, long time."

"What would all that buy me, Del?" She rounded on me with such vigor that for a moment I thought she'd snapped out of her blue funk for good. "Oh, two thousand dollars would get me by for years, all right. And I'd spend those years knowing I'd sold you into wretchedness. Do you think I could live with myself, knowing that every day I lived easy, without a care in the world, you were crying your eyes out because your heart was breaking? Because you hadn't any love, and no hope to get free, and nothing to look forward to except bondage to a dreadful, lying man who probably treats his dog better than his wife?"

"Irving isn't so bad," I said weakly. "I can learn to live with him again. And you told me once—down in Arkansas, remember?—that I was a fool to leave such comfort and ease. I guess you were right. It was an easy life, and I'll go back now and live it without complaint. I swear I'll never complain, Louisa, nor shed a tear about it, as long as I know you're all right."

She sighed then and laid a hand on my cheek so gently I thought my heart would stop. "An easy life," she said, "but it isn't your life, Del. It isn't yours."

That night, I lay restless and scowling on my cot, which felt a thousand miles from Louisa's. My body was cramped from the effort of holding still. If I'd tossed and turned, the squeal of my springs would wake Louisa, and her misery had finally given way to exhaustion. I could see her face in the soft, blue moonlight that crept in through the cabin's small windows. She was at peace, finally, the despair of the past two days melted away into the mercy of her dreams. I watched the steady rise and fall of her breath, and pondered my few remaining choices.

Next morning, my mind was made up. Despite the stiffness of a sleepless night, I marched briskly up the winding track to the farmhouse, oblivious to the delicate, rose-petal beauty of the morning light as it hung and sweetened itself above the orchard.

I knocked on Henderson's door. The red dog whined and showed me its belly while I waited. When Henderson opened the door, still dressed in flannel pajamas, he raised his rough brows in a question.

"I don't suppose you'll be heading into town today," I said.

"Matter of fact, I am. Leaving in about an hour. You two gals looking for a ride back to the railyard?"

"No, sir," I said, "but I do have some business in Wenatchee, if you'll be so kind as to get me there."

Later that morning, I rode in the cab of Henderson's old Ford truck, my rucksack perched on the bench seat between myself and my silent, smoking driver. Henderson deposited me on the corner of Mission and First, in the heart of the shopping district, with a promise to return in an hour's time.

I thanked him and shouldered my pack, then wandered the streets in the still-crisp atmosphere of the early hours. Bakeries tempted me with the intoxicating smell of fresh-made bread, but I intended to pinch every penny I had now, even if my stomach suffered. The newsstand on one corner already riffled with the latest papers. I didn't bother to look for another article about my scandalous disappearance—Irving and his plans meant little to me now. I would resume my fretting over that husband of mine once I'd taken proper care of Louisa. She was my first and only concern that morning as I searched the streets of Wenatchee.

Finally, several streets away from where Henderson had dropped me, I located what I sought. The small wooden sign swung gently above the sidewalk, its faded paint proclaiming, "DeJoy & Smith, Pawnbrokers." A small board in the window read: "Welcome—We're Open."

The shop's bell seemed to clang in my very blood as I entered. The place was crowded with furniture, tools, a rack of fur coats, a shelf of newer-model radios. A dry, papery smell permeated the room, and below that note, the unmistakable bite of lubricating oil. Behind a great oakwood counter, a pair of slatted saloon doors tipped on their hinges, and a thin man whose balding head seemed too large for his body came forward to greet me with an affectedly casual air.

I set down my pack and reached into its hidden pocket, then laid my pearl earrings side by side on the counter. The silver bracelet joined the pearls a moment later.

"I see." The broker produced a jeweler's loupe from somewhere and held it, monocle-like, between cheek and brow. He made a great show of examining the pearls and the filigree braid of my tennis bracelet. "Decent quality, but not the finest I've ever seen."

"Cut the song and dance," I said. "How much will you give me?"

"I can't do better than fifteen."

"Fifteen!" The fact wasn't lost on me that I'd begun this whole mad adventure with that same amount of cash stolen from my husband's dresser. "All this is worth twice as much. Stop pulling my leg, mister."

He smiled a little too serenely for my liking and spread his hands. "You're welcome to take your . . . er . . . treasures elsewhere, miss, if you think you can do better."

The bastard had me where he wanted me. Both of us knew it.

I hesitated only a moment, then dug into the secret pocket again. It was empty now, save for my most cherished possession. Fist closed around my mother's wedding ring, I sent up a silent prayer for forgiveness. The ring was the last connection I still had to my home, my childhood—my family. But even as the loss sent an ache through my chest, a warm peace descended and settled on my brow. I would part with the ring for Louisa's sake. I would give anything for her.

The gold band made a small murmuring sound as I slid it across the counter. I watched impassively as the broker examined it through his loupe. He dampened a cotton ball with a vial of white vinegar, swabbed the ring, and gave a hum of approval.

"Forty-five for everything," he said, "take it or leave it."

"I'll take it. And if you'll be so kind, tell me how to find the bus station, will you?"

Louisa didn't seem to realize we were traveling again till our bus crawled to the summit of Snoqualmie Pass and the long black snake of Route 10 descended the western slope of the Cascades. I'd pleaded with her to rise from her cot, then commanded her to walk the quarter mile from the workers' cabin we'd shared to Henderson's waiting truck. She sat beside me on the bench seat, staring out the window in vacant silence as Henderson drove us back into town and wished us better luck on the road ahead.

Louisa had followed me obediently into the bus that idled at the sleepy station. She'd sat down promptly when and where I told her to, and maintained her composed silence while the bus carried us away from empty Wenatchee, up the hulking brown shoulders of the foothills.

Only now, as the deep blue-green of fir and cedar surrounded us, did Louisa truly stir.

She peered through the bus's window at the land through which we moved, and mile after mile her vim returned—or at least an awareness of something beyond her own misery. I believe those wet and ancient trees were the first things Louisa had truly *seen* for days. With a curious, thin ache of anticipated loss, I watched her watching the evergreens, the steep mountain terrain, the turquoise brooks that tumbled and laughed over slick stone. She raised a hand to the glass, pressing her palm against its coolness. This land that was home to her. She was going home.

I didn't need to tell her where we were, of course. Even after more than a year and a half on the rails, she recognized the road. She darted her head to take in the sight of the great craggy peaks, still white with snow at their tops, even after that long, miserable summer. Her eyes brimmed with renewed light. When her hands folded together in her lap, an attitude of placid acceptance fell upon her and filled my heart in kind.

Only an hour or so after we crossed the Cascade summit, the bus arrived in the little town of Carnation. My agony was at hand. I rose from my seat, and eagerly Louisa followed. The bus stop was nothing more than the corner of two anonymous streets—a flat-faced white apartment building on one side of the road, a post office and the afterthought of a train depot on the other. The bus roared, leaving us as well as a black cloud of exhaust in its wake. Once the bus retreated over a narrow bridge that spanned a whispering river, we were left in a perfect stillness that I was loath to break. A black Model A went chugging past. Cattle called and answered one another in a thin and dreamlike distance.

Louisa turned for the post office, narrowing her eyes. I realized she was reading the sign nailed to its side—proclaiming the name of the town. Then she looked at me for the first time since Wenatchee, since the cabin. I don't know what to call the light I saw, so bright and warm, in her eyes. I'm afraid to call it anything. Sometimes it's better not to speak of a hope or a longing, a need, because what if you're wrong? What if you shatter it all by giving it the wrong sort of name?

I asked, "Do you remember the way to your uncle's house?"

She nodded.

"Then go on," I said. "I'll follow you."

We walked some two or three miles along a straight, unpaved road, into a pastoral quiet, and here everything was green, even the fields where spotted cattle grazed. The afternoon was so serene, the sky so gentle, I might almost have convinced myself that the suffering I'd witnessed and endured those years since the Crash had been only a nightmare or a fantasy. The miniature town fell away behind a soft rustle of poplar trees, golden-leafed and swaying. Barn swallows darted over the fields, crossing our path as we traveled, and the iridescent flash of their wings made me feel as if I was walking on clouds or on some malleable, impermanent substance, one that might cause reality itself to come apart and bleed into this paradise of warm light and silence.

I thought, *The End is nigh. Irving, you were right after all.*

We'd already passed a number of small, poor houses set well back from the road, scarcely finer than the widow's shack where Louisa and I had dug that sad little grave. The rural homes looked much like those of the coal miners back in Harlan County, and I couldn't tell one from another—didn't know which held Louisa's heart. But when we came within sight of a small, peak-roofed cottage tucked among the spreading arms of an ancient apple tree, Louisa gave a sharp cry and set off running.

"Wait," I called, but of course it was hopeless. The weight of my pack and that weak ankle restrained me. I fell farther behind with every stride, and soon the gulf between Louisa and me was so wide I knew I would never cross it again.

In the sunglow and the distance, I made out the shape of a child playing below the apple tree. He turned his face to Louisa, and when he clambered to his feet and ran to her, she dropped to her knees in the lane, throwing her arms wide. The boy rushed to his mother, and Louisa folded and sheltered the child in her love.

As evening blushed over the valley, I found myself sitting alone below the huge and twisted apple tree, gazing up into the branches, following the paths of their dark convolutions against the mellow sky.

Louisa, of course, had insisted that I should come inside the house, but I refused—not out of any malice. But it had seemed wrong, somehow, to intrude upon the life Louisa had known before the rails. I'd been no part of the existence she'd led before her hoboing days, and something in me feared that if my awkward and burdensome presence intruded into her paradise, I would stain her world forever. She would never escape her history if I marked her too deeply. She would never rise above the hobo's life and find the pretty future she longed for.

"I'm more comfortable out here," I told her quietly. "And anyway, you need time to catch up with your boy and your uncle. You take all the time you need, Louisa. I'll be under the open sky. That's the hobo way."

She insisted on introducing me to her boy, however, and carried the small, bright-eyed child out to meet me, holding him against her heart.

"Eddie," she said in a tone so soft it seemed almost a prayer, "this is Del. She's . . . she's my friend."

The boy looked up at me in somber appraisal.

"Hello, Eddie. Pleased to meet you." How I ever managed to speak, only God can say.

Now, with evening closing in, Louisa was nowhere to be seen. No doubt she'd preoccupied herself with feeding and washing her son, tucking him into bed, as any mother would do.

The front door of the little gray house squealed, and I glanced over in hope, but it was an old man, stoop-shouldered and white-haired. He could only be Louisa's uncle Burke. I watched him make his cautious way down the steps of the porch. He carried a small, three-legged stool, the kind often used for milking cows, and once he'd navigated the steps without incident, he headed for my apple tree with a shuffling slowness and a sympathetic smile.

"You must be Burke Trout."

I started to rise so I could greet the man properly, but he made a restraining gesture with a hand as gnarled as the branches overhead. He positioned the stool close beside me and sank onto it with a little groan.

"Yes, ma'am," he said. "Pleased to meet you."

"Del. Pleased the same."

"Just Del? Haven't you got any other name?"

My smile felt a little fragile. "It's funny—Louisa once asked me much the same question. No, it's just Del, these days. Whatever other names I might once have had, I've got no use for them now."

"I wanted to thank you," he said, "for keeping Louisa together on the rails."

At that, I couldn't contain a genuine laugh. "No, sir—you've got it backwards. Louisa kept *me* together, all those months. And if you want to know the truth, I've been more hindrance to her than help. It's a wonder she didn't take off and leave me behind long ago. In fact," I added with a flush of shame, "she might be better off now if she'd done so."

Burke chuckled, reaching down to pat my shoulder. "I don't know about that. It's been an awful long time since I've seen that niece of mine. Many a night I sat up, after I got that little mite of hers to sleep, worrying that she'd be a changed person when we finally saw her again . . . if we saw her again. The rails can be dangerous, I hear."

"That they can."

"Times like these—the hardship, the doing what a fellow must to get by—it can change a person. But Louisa's still her old self. She wouldn't be herself, after all that time on the rails, if she hadn't had someone to love her. It's love that reminds us who we really are. It's love that holds the world together, even when everything tries its best to fall apart."

For a while I could say nothing. My throat was too tight, my insides too hollow, so I tipped back my head again and watched the pink fading to violet and gray among the branches and the turning leaves. I couldn't explain to Burke about my kidnapping, the car burned in Billings. If I'd been able to muster a single word, I would have confessed that I was the reason why Louisa could never take to the rails again. She must stay put now, where jobs were scarce—especially for a woman—and hope for the best in a world that made hope more foolish by the day.

All because of me. So much good my love did her.

After a spell, I found I could talk again, and I thanked Uncle Burke for his kind words. We swapped a few stories and had a few laughs, and though my heart was melancholy, it was also warm and full.

Twilight and the singing of the little tree frogs overhead brought a lull in our conversation. "Supper soon," Burke said. "Louisa got the little one fed early, but there's soup in the kettle now, and I made bread this morning. You'll come in for a bite, won't you?"

"Sure I will." But I didn't see how I could do it, how I could enter into Louisa's home and sit at her table as if I belonged. This new reality she was making, resurrecting . . . I could have no part in it. There was no more space for me in her life.

When a chill set in, Burke headed back inside, taking the milking stool with him. I rolled out my old army mat under the arching blackness of the apple tree and lay back, pillowing my head on clasped hands. I listened to the frogs' chorus and wondered what I ought to do next, where I ought to go. California, probably. Winter was around the corner, and Louisa had told me once that nights were so warm in the San Joaquin Valley, you could sleep with nothing but the stars to cover you.

The front door opened again. When I rolled to my side and lifted myself on one elbow, there Louisa stood in a frame of yellow light, backlit, so she was only a silhouette, but nevertheless I knew her. Not even the dress she wore now—like a proper lady with a pretty life—could disguise her from me.

Louisa came to me through the darkness. Her dress was a dropped-waist affair, made of simple white calico printed all over with tiny flowers. Tied collar, knee-length skirt—it had been out of fashion for years, but it transformed her, made her anew, and even by night she looked radiant. She had tamed her hair to lay more smoothly over her ears, and the boots were gone, replaced by a pair of black kid pumps with pointed toes. As I watched her drift through the dark like a visitation, the scrap of some Bible verse came to me. *I am crucified with Christ; nevertheless I live, yet not I. Not I.*

I sat up on the mat when she reached me. As I stared up at her, the motherly oval of her face seemed to eclipse the night and everything that had come before.

"Come inside, Del. You can stay, you know—stay here as long as you want."

"I wouldn't know what to do in there," I said.

Quietly, a whisper. "Please stay."

"Irving won't have given up yet. I've got to keep moving if I'll have any hope of being free."

She paused, and her eyes slid away from me, her mouth turning down as if in sorrow. She seemed on the brink of saying more, but she only sank onto the mat beside me. I watched her pull her knees up to her chest and hug them with those sun-browned arms—the familiar gesture, the way I'd seen her a hundred times before. But this was the last time.

"You can't keep moving," I said. "That's the point. That's the fork in the road we've come to. With everything that happened in Billings—"

She cut in fiercely. "I'd do it all again. For you."

"But you've got to stay put now. You've got to work out some way to earn money here. I know it'll be hard, but you're . . . smart." How clumsy I felt, how inadequate. "And you're a hard worker. And I'm glad for you. Because now you won't miss your little boy any longer. That's the most important thing."

She lowered her face, resting her forehead on her arms. The night was brimming, burdened by the words neither of us would speak.

"Anyhow," I said, reaching into my pack, "this will tide you over for a while, till you find a steady job."

I pulled out the money that remained to me—everything I got for my jewelry and my mother's wedding ring, minus the six dollars I'd spent on bus fare. I pressed the crumpled bills into her hand.

She looked at the dollars clenched in her fist as if I'd given her a bouquet of nettles. Her expression fell very slowly from disbelief into a mask of tragedy.

"Are you sure," I said, "you won't write to Irving—"

"Stop. Del. Don't say it to me again."

We both fell quiet. The frogs sang madly, livened by the autumnal damp of the air. Louisa smoothed the money, stacking the bills neatly, folding them over. Then she tucked the whole lot inside the collar of her dress, slipping the bundle of cash under the strap of her bra.

She said, "I don't want to lose you."

For a moment, the force of my pain left me mute, powerless to answer. With a will, I swallowed it down. "Don't worry," I said. "I'll come back for you, someday."

29

This story has a happy ending, if you can believe it.

Oh, I was bitter and brokenhearted when I said my last farewell to Louisa Trout the following morning, in the yard of her poor country home, under the rustle of the apple boughs. I wept as I walked those empty miles back to the town of Carnation, for the new world that shaped itself around me was nothing I could recognize.

In the town's meager railyard, I hopped a slow-moving freighter headed west to the metropolis of Seattle. I would have liked to stop there, find a jungle, and restore myself in the company of my own kind—but if I were recognized again, I'd have no friend to rescue me. I was on my own for good that fall, and sitting atop a boxcar, watching the emerald carpet of those fertile valleys unroll around me, I thought it likely I'd be on my own forever.

Town by town and railyard after railyard, I worked my way south as the summer of '31 faded into memory. A windy autumn took its place. Occupied as I was by the daily fight for a few pennies and a crust of bread, I found little time for looking back with regret on what I'd left behind. Even my nights were merciful. Whether I rested in some rough harvester's cabin at the edge of a field or in the loft of a barn, sweet with the odor of hay—or under a bare and lonesome sky somewhere outside of Chico, Sacramento, Merced—I was always weary enough to fall quickly into sleep, and I had no cause for nightmares. In fact, my dreams were often pleasant, graced by the calm radiance of a woman in a white calico dress, her half-seen face looking down on me with an expression I could never read, but which I nevertheless felt as a deep and eternal wholeness in my heart.

Winter passed swiftly in the San Joaquin Valley. I survived, one way or another. By spring, I landed in Oregon again, working the onions first, then cabbages and carrots. In the summer of '32, I got out east of the Cascades, but I never could bring myself to travel farther inland. I guess Irving's threat felt less imminent along the Pacific coast. Or maybe it was something else that tethered me to the west.

That year was bad—1932. The trains were packed with desperate, staring people of which I was only one. Most of them were headed for California, but plenty were headed from California back to wherever they'd originated, having found the Golden State rather tarnished and mean. That fall, Hoover was out, and Roosevelt was in—news which made its way down the rails along with all those hungry, helpless people. Word of Roosevelt's victory meant little to us then, for in our dust-smothered world, nothing ever changed except to get worse, day after day, town after town, railyard after railyard.

The End had come. The End kept coming. The End knew no ending. Yet as I rode the freighters from place to place, I would catch sight now and then of some small, insignificant view—a yellow cat on the roof of a house, its tail curled contentedly around its paws, or a lady's hand in the window of her white kitchen, drawing back a green curtain to see my train passing. Now and then, I would spot the bright dresses of a small child, hung out to dry below a gentle sun. Life soldiered on, despite what was lost—even if what was lost might never come again. And as my train passed, the comforting vision would fall behind, gone in a blink, the way things always go. In those moments, I would think of Louisa and wonder if she ever found reason to think of me.

The years tumbled like water over stone. Somewhere along the way, the new president did away with Prohibition and founded his corps and his acts and his administrations. Roosevelt's work didn't touch us much, out there on the rails, but in the cities, the folks had found renewed hope, and they praised the president's name.

By the summer of '33, I stopped hearing tell of the runaway preacher's wife. No one, in the jungles or workers' camps, still whispered of the famous Kentucky preacher or his reward money. I reckoned I was free and clear of Irving then. I guess I must have stepped a little lighter when I walked the long dirt roads from farm to farm in search of an honest day's work.

Thirty-six was hotter than any year I'd known. Thirty-seven, things got a little better, the freighters were less crowded, and whenever I found work, my pay was more generous than in any preceding year. We heard tell, us hobos, of something called "minimum wage," and then "public housing." Many of the friends I'd made on the rails became strangers after that year—absorbed, so I prayed, into the body of a society that seemed as if it might just recover and go on living, after all.

Now I've said already that I didn't look back with regret. That much is true. But not a day passed without my thinking of Louisa, in all those years of wandering. On the worst days, when the sky and the earth conspired to crush me between their hot and merciless fists, I remembered Louisa bathing in the calm waters of the Platte, tipping back her head, white throat exposed, and I told myself, *Nothing lasts forever*. And when the occasional joy came my way—for there's always some small goodness, even in the midst of ruination—I thought of the way she held me after I'd returned the stolen locket. How she said, *You came back,* and I answered, *Didn't I say I would?*

All those days. All those thoughts of her, though I hadn't seen her in years, hadn't spoken her name to a soul, hadn't heard her voice except in aching remembrance. Three thousand, two hundred and eighty-nine days—but who's counting—from the time I pulled Louisa aboard that freighter somewhere south of Kentucky to June of 1940. By then, the war was so foregone a conclusion that news of it reached even those of us who lived permanently on the rails. The war was a good thing, so we heard, for the country had thrown everything it had into making munitions and guns and fast planes and boats to carry America's allies ashore in far-off Europe, and that meant everyone who wanted a job would have one. No more straying up and down the tracks. The Great Depression was over.

In the nine years since I'd parted with Louisa, the hobo's life had come to suit me—or I'd come to suit the life. Whatever I'd been years before, in the far-off coal haze of the Cumberland, no longer mattered to me now. This was the life I'd made for myself, the life I'd chosen—the rumble of the trains, the shifting landscape, the world in ceaseless motion. But with the war effort and wages rising, with a respectable job for everyone who wanted one, would anyone still look with compassion or tolerance on the ragged souls who drifted from town to town? The End was nigh all over again. Maybe the world never stops ending.

Sensing another dissolution of another reality, knowing there was never any use in trying to stop the unstoppable, I became obsessed, in the fall of 1940, with a singular idea. At our last parting, under the branches of the apple tree, I'd promised Louisa that I would come back for her. Yet for almost a decade, I'd never even tried to find my old friend.

That was how I came to ride a freighter north out of cool, green Oregon, lying on my back atop a boxcar full of munitions casing, watching the sky lash swiftly overhead in bands of blue and mackerel cloud. When the sky dizzied me too much, I closed my eyes and tried to imagine what it would be like to see her again—what we would say to one another, what she would think of me, shabby and weather-beaten thing I still was, almost forty years old and looking every day of it. But whenever I tried to picture our reunion, the whole arrangement of hope and wistful longing receded to a blank, white distance. It was like watching a train roll away from you, so swiftly down the tracks that you've no hope at all of catching it, no matter how you run. There was only the long slow ache of distance and a vanishing point on the horizon.

The town of Carnation had grown a little bigger since I'd last seen it. The bell on the post office's door clanged when I entered, as bright and optimistic as everything had been in recent days. The postmaster took in my ragged appearance with a little frown of confusion, but he caught himself quickly and smiled.

"What can I do for you, ma'am?"

"I've come looking for . . ." My throat went unexpectedly tight. I hadn't said her name in so many years, and now I wondered if I even could. The summer of 1931 had receded to a place so far from where I now stood, it might as well have been a dream. Maybe it had been. Maybe waking from a dream is a kind of ending, too. "For Louisa Trout. She lives in this town—or she used to, anyway."

The postmaster smiled. "Oh, yes, I know the Trouts well. Old Burke died a few months back, sorry to say, and that red-headed niece of his moved to the city after he was buried. No Trouts left in Carnation, these days. Not that Louisa is a Trout any longer. She married Al Dimmick—oh, I suppose that was in '34."

A gray hollow opened inside, wide as the continent Louisa and I had crossed. Deliberately, I filled that void with a generous warmth. This was everything Louisa had wanted.

"Married," I said. "Well, isn't that something. Good for her."

"Anything else I can help you with?"

I hesitated. Not meeting the man's eyes, I said, "Don't suppose you have any forwarding address for the . . . the Dimmick family, do you?"

"I believe I do." The postmaster reached below his counter and produced a tin box full of address cards. His fingers walked through the cards as he spoke. "Al Dimmick's a fine fellow—do you know him? He was just offered a good job building airplanes at the Boeing factory out in Seattle. Didn't he jump at the chance, too, with those three kids to raise."

"Three?"

He pulled a card from his file box and slid it across the counter.

Sheepishly, I patted my trouser pockets. "I haven't got anything to write on."

The postmaster seemed to have an inexhaustible supply of tolerant smiles. "Hold on a minute."

He vanished below his counter. I heard the rustle of wastepaper in a basket. Then he popped up again with a plain, one-cent postcard in his hand.

"A lady was just here," the postmaster explained. "Started to fill out this card, but she made a mistake with the name. She paid for a fresh card rather than scratch out what she'd already written. I suppose she's particular that way. Since this card has already been paid for, you might as well take it."

He copied the address onto the card in his neat, upright hand, but he wrote no name.

"That's mighty charitable of you." I took the card when he proffered it and slid it at once into my pocket. I could scarcely stand to look at the thing, and it burned like a coal in my hand.

Later that day, I gathered a handful of roadside flowers and left them on Burke Trout's grave. Then I hopped another train bound for Seattle with Louisa's new address hard as a stone against my hip.

Seattle is no small town, and back then, it was bustling—booming, you might say, thanks to the fortunes of war. For three days, I searched the city, learning the lay of its streets and neighborhoods in the salt-scented mist of autumn. I would not ask the strangers I passed for directions. Somehow it seemed a thing I must do on my own, a question whose answer could only be found in the far-deep quiet of my soul.

On the evening of the third day, I found Louisa Dimmick's home—a sweet Queen Anne near the crest of one of Seattle's many steep hills. The house was freshly painted in soft, wistful shades, and all its windows sparkled in the fading October light. It was finer than any home I'd stepped inside for years.

Almost, I left the alley where I'd been lingering and crossed the street to knock on her door. Almost—but I never found the courage. You see, I'd never been able to say a useful word to Louisa in all the months of our friendship. And now, with years and countless miles of empty track between us, there was no hope that I could give voice to the unspeakable.

As I pressed myself against that alley wall in an agony of loss, I heard the laughter of children somewhere up the road. When I glanced in the direction of the noise, the breath stopped in my chest.

There she was. A woman in a smart green dress, carrying a bag of groceries in her arms. The old bob hairdo was gone, replaced by waves that tumbled to her shoulders, and the forelock above her pale brow swept up in a stylish pompadour. But despite the changes, I knew her. I would know her a hundred years from now.

A fine, strapping boy walked at her side, carrying another bag, talking to Louisa with an enthusiastic air. That could only be Eddie, twelve years old now, almost as tall and sturdy as a man. Two little girls followed on Louisa's heels. They were alike as two peas, dancing and jumping, giggling at their private game. The twins had their mother's copper hair.

The sight of that happy family made up my mind. Louisa's name was on my lips, as it ever had been, but I didn't call out to her. She'd told me once that all she wanted was to leave the hobo's life behind. So I remained in my alley, watching as Louisa and her children climbed the cement steps from the street to their pretty little home, their pretty little life. My heart was full, and her name turned to a prayer on my tongue. I think sometimes she had always been a prayer to me.

Warm with satisfaction, content with the knowledge that all was right in this world, I made my way back toward the railyard. As I neared the final street corner before pavement gave way to rails, the hunched blue body of a mailbox emerged from the dusk. There I paused and drew the postcard from my pocket. I delved into my old, tattered rucksack for the stub of a pencil. On the back of the card, I scratched out the line some other woman had begun, paused to think what I wanted to say.

How do you fit nine years of need and hope and knowing onto a scrap of paper? How do you form the letters of the One True Name? The message I settled on was inadequate, to be sure, and yet it said everything I could hope to say.

I came back for you.
-Del

In my unschooled hand, I wrote her name—Louisa Trout—above the neatly printed address. I let the postcard fall into the mailbox while my heart ached and seemed to grow beyond the borders of my weary, hard-used body. And as the mailbox's mouth snapped shut, I told myself that love is a thing that's given, not taken. If the love is real, then giving is enough.

As night closed in, I found a boxcar whose door had been removed or torn away, and I trotted alongside as the train began to roll. With the ease of long practice, I pulled myself into the train's dark belly and sat at the edge of my car, not caring which direction the train was headed or where the rails would take me. I watched Louisa's city diminish into a small, white circle of light, bright against the darkness.

The world was unmaking itself around me. The world would make itself anew. The engine sounded its long tin moan, and I kissed the tips of my fingers, raised my hand in farewell. Somewhere in a halo of light, Louisa was smiling while she tucked her children into bed. And maybe she heard that train crying in the old, half-remembered distance. Maybe she thought of me then, and smiled.

AUTHOR'S NOTE

Writing is a funny kind of magic. You can carry an idea around with you for months or years. You can nurture that idea, try to coax it to the surface, but it won't be rushed. Like apples ripening in an orchard, the fruit can only be harvested when the time is right.

I've been writing fiction full-time for many years now, and as any experienced writer will tell you, every book is different in character and process. Each novel comes about in its own way, in its own time. A new book is a roll of the dice, and sometimes books have their own ideas about what they should be and how their stories should be told.

The proposal for *October in the Earth*—the idea Lake Union Publishing bought from me—was about two women riding the rails during the Great Depression, one a doctor bent on reaching California by a specific date, for reasons she keeps secret from her traveling companion; the other the privileged young heiress of a wealthy family fleeing an arranged marriage to a man whom she despises. But no matter how I massaged that scenario and tinkered with the characters, the manuscript stubbornly refused to proceed beyond the first thirty thousand words.

Something about the story as I'd originally conceived it wasn't sitting right *with the story itself.* It was getting in its own way, tangling its feet in needless convolutions, and I started this book over again an astonishing (and infuriating) *six times* before I finally found the right characters, premise, and voice to tell the story the way it wanted to be told. *October in the Earth* is the shortest novel I've written as Olivia Hawker, and yet I spilled more ink on this one than I have on much longer works. The final manuscript came in at one hundred thousand words long, but I wrote at least two hundred fifty thousand words trying to fine-tune the concept and the characters, trying to get Del and Louisa just right.

My breakthrough came on the sixth attempt, when I finally looked at the characters themselves. The original concept was fun—two women from vastly different walks of life bond over a shared journey—but it would have been almost the same story if I'd taken it out of the 1930s and dropped it into any other setting. I realized that if I intended to write about the Great Depression, then I needed to tell a story that could only unfold among the specific challenges of the 1930s. The Del I'd originally conceived of—an earnest and kind young woman used to a lifestyle that had safely insulated her from the worst effects of the Depression—couldn't empathize strongly enough with the people who suffered through those grim years. She might genuinely *want* to empathize, but her history of extreme privilege would always make her the wrong voice to speak about the despair and deprivation of economic ruin and the yoke of the capitalist machine.

Once I understood who Del really was—once I was willing to put aside my preconceived notions about this book and listen to the story itself—I found that I'd actually begun writing *October in the Earth* more than a decade before. I still had the partial manuscript, in fact. It had been languishing on my backup drive for twelve years under the working title *Tin Moan*.

Set during the 2008 bank crash, the story followed the adventures of a young man who, after losing his job and seeing no plausible end to the economic crisis, decides to ride the rails like an old-time hobo, in search of a new reality. If I'd finished it, *Tin Moan* would have been my third novel. But I'd always found the manuscript painful to work on, since I'd begun writing the book mere moments after declaring on Facebook that I was never going to write again. You see, my first agent had just dropped me after failing to sell either of my first two manuscripts, and I felt sure my dream of being a full-time writer was over. It was better to end the whole farce now, I told myself (and my friends on social media); there was no future for me as a writer, and if I continued to try, I would only break my own heart more.

But as soon as I'd posted that dramatic declaration, a force seemed to take hold of me. I reopened the laptop I'd just closed, pulled up a fresh Word document, and began to type the opening to a new damned novel. It was as if some external power was telling me, "You're going to write *this* book, at least, whether you want to or not."

I genuinely desired to quit writing at that point, and the fact that I literally *couldn't* was agonizing. Afraid my husband, Paul, would catch me in the act and think I was a hypocrite, I took to hiding in our bedroom closet, hunched over the glow of my laptop while I pecked out the first half of *Tin Moan* with tears and snot running down my face. I felt like a fool for declaring I would never write again and then immediately returning to the source of my pain. I felt powerless in my own life, possessed by a force I couldn't understand. It felt like there was an invader inside my head.

Because *Tin Moan* always brought back memories of my ultimate despair (and the embarrassment of hiding in a closet), I rarely worked on the book, even after I regained my senses and carried on with building my career. But I never forgot about the book. The idea of a character riding the rails in search of a new life still intrigued me, and on the rare occasions when I dusted off *Tin Moan*, I still thought the prose was strong and promising. But the timing never felt right. The book just wasn't ready yet; it was still waiting for its moment.

I never understood the purpose of *Tin Moan*—or the force that made me continue writing, mere seconds after I'd publicly quit—until I surrendered to *October in the Earth* and agreed to write the book the way it wanted to be written. At last, I understood what the plan had been, all these many years, for the story of a desperate soul who takes to the rails in the midst of economic ruin. To my delight (and relief—Lake Union's deadline was just a few weeks away), the twelve-year-old partial manuscript lent itself remarkably well to Del's narration. It didn't take long to alter the original, changing the setting from 2008 to 1931, swapping the lead character from man to woman. Most of what I'd written in the seclusion of my bedroom closet, a desperate aspirant with a broken heart, made it into the novel you've just finished reading.

I'm still marveling at the curious magic of writing—the way some stories know how to wait until the time is right, the way you can carry an idea with you for years until suddenly it ripens and drops into your hands, when you'd all but forgotten it was there.

I included a little salute to the original—my sad closet manuscript— in the final lines of *October in the Earth*. It's funny, now, to look back on my tragic but very real emotions in those early stages of my career. I was so certain that my ambitions, my hard work, my passion for writing would get me nowhere, and I resented *Tin Moan* so furiously for forcing me to continue doing this thing that had, so far, brought me only misery. I never could have guessed, back then, what an affection I would develop for that partial manuscript—or how grateful I would be to *Tin Moan* for not allowing me to quit.

I'm glad the story stuck with me until the time was right. I hope I've done it justice. After all, I owe *Tin Moan* a debt of gratitude. It's the only reason I have my writing career today.

ACKNOWLEDGMENTS

My sincerest thanks to my editor at Lake Union Publishing, Danielle Marshall. Her enthusiasm for the original idea, and the early feedback she provided, helped me refine the concept for this story into the novel that exists today.

Jodi Warshaw, my developmental editor, did a phenomenal amount of work with the first draft of the manuscript. Her insightful perspective made the book into a much stronger novel. I'm delighted to have worked with her again after so many years; we make a great team.

I somehow managed to write this book while my husband, Paul, and I were actively immigrating from the United States to Canada. (Incidentally, writing a novel while you're also moving from one country to another is not an experience I would recommend to anyone.) Our new neighbo(u)rs were so welcoming and helpful while we settled in—and while I scrambled to complete this manuscript by my deadline. Thank you to Morgan, Dennis, Bridgitte, and her wonderful kids, and especially Bev, who stepped in as cat sitter on several occasions while we dealt with the various immigration-related tasks that took us out of town on numerous occasions, on very short notice. It's a real blessing to have great neighbors, and all the residents of the "Haunted Mansion" have proven that Canadians really are the nicest folks in the world. Paul and I are both so grateful that we get to be a part of this wonderful country, and the hospitality of our new friends eased our transition and made us feel truly at home.

My biggest thanks of all go out to my husband, Paul Harnden, who embarked on a lengthy road trip with me, covering most of the route Del and Louisa took—as closely as we were able to replicate that route using the highway system in 2022 rather than the freight-train network of the 1930s. I know what a rare gift it is to share your life with a partner who supports your passions, is always game for an adventure, and is still willing to stick by your side, even after eighteen days trapped in a car with you. I love you, Paul. I'll never forget that sunrise on an unpaved road somewhere in South Dakota, twenty miles from the nearest highway. I'm glad I got to see it with you.

ABOUT THE AUTHOR

Photo © 2018 Paul Harnden

Olivia Hawker is the *Washington Post* bestselling author of *The Fire and the Ore*; *The Rise of Light*; *One for the Blackbird, One for the Crow*, a finalist for the Washington State Book Award and the WILLA Literary Award; and *The Ragged Edge of Night*. Olivia resides in Victoria, British Columbia, with her husband and several naughty cats. For more information, visit www.hawkerbooks.com.